# ALPHA
# FEMALE

# ALPHA
# FEMALE

APRIL CHRISTOFFERSON

A TOM DOHERTY ASSOCIATES BOOK
NEW YORK

This is a work of fiction. All of the characters, organizations, and events portrayed in this novel are either products of the author's imagination or are used fictitiously.

ALPHA FEMALE

Copyright © 2009 by April Christofferson

All rights reserved.

A Tor Book
Published by Tom Doherty Associates, LLC
175 Fifth Avenue
New York, NY 10010

www.tor-forge.com

Tor® is a registered trademark of Tom Doherty Associates, LLC.

ISBN 978-0-7653-4420-5

First Edition: July 2009

Printed in the United States of America

0  9  8  7  6  5  4  3  2  1

*For Susan*

# ACKNOWLEDGMENTS

I've found time and again that my writing brings amazing people into my life. That's especially true with this book. After reading *Buffalo Medicine,* Dale McCormick, retired Forest Service special agent in charge of the Rocky Mountain region, wrote to encourage me to continue writing about important issues affecting the West. He offered to provide advice on future projects and, boy, did I take him up on that offer. I'll be forever grateful not only for the wealth of experience Dale shared to help me with technical matters, but also for his unflagging enthusiasm. Keith Young could not have been more generous or helpful in giving me an inside look at life as a law enforcement ranger in Yellowstone—and what a life it is! The same holds true for my son, Michael, who, as an interpretive and bear education ranger, gave me the greatest of gifts—my intense love of Yellowstone. I also turned to Randy Ingersoll, Mammoth Hotel pianist, who is a wealth of information on Yellowstone, and whose bloody encounter with a grizzly bear fourteen years ago only caused him to revere both the great bear and the park that is its home that much more. A huge thank you to biologist Amy Secrest for her tracking and telemetry expertise; and to Amy, Jane Aldrich (extraordinary friend and horsewoman), and Summer Shute for their keen eyes in reading my manuscript. I'm also happy to have the opportunity to thank Charlie Peterson, Steve Linville, Monte Ahlemeyer, Mike Montana, Dave Parry, and Dave Forsman for their many years of friendship and support.

In Natalia Aponte, I have been blessed with an editor whose instincts and friendship I rely upon and treasure.

I'm equally grateful to the rest of the talented gang at Tor/Forge: Tom Doherty, Linda Quinton, Paul Stevens, and Tom Espenchied. Special thanks to Ken Atchity of AEI, as well as to Mike Kuciak, Chi Li Wong, and Brenna Lui.

I'm proud to have a life populated with alpha females of many kinds. My mother and mother-in-law top the list of the two-legged kind. My daughters and sisters—by blood and by heart—are right up there with them.

My network of friends and colleagues—in particular, Kathleen Stachowski, Chris Barns, Jane Aldrich, Jeff Hull, and Jerry Black—fight the good fight for what remains wild and sacred on this planet. I'm honored to be part of that fight and inspired by their talents and commitment.

In loving memory of Barry Simon, Yellowstone Ranger Daniel Richards, Joan Ingersoll, Kevin Scharetg, and Murray Carroll, all of whom brightened this planet with their grace and spirit. Your light still shines strong.

To #253 and to Moxee.

To Tom Roy, for holding my feet to the fire.

Finally, to Steve, Ashley, Crystal, Mike, Ryan, and dear little Kamiah. Your decency, love, compassion, and sense of wonder not only inspire and delight me, they are my compass. My bedrock.

The writer Terry Tempest Williams said: "If you know wilderness in the way that you know love, you would be unwilling to let it go." I'm blessed to know both—and unwilling to let either go. I wish the same for you.

*In generations to come, this place will be a treasure of the people. They will be proud of it and of all the curious things in it. People will be proud of this spot. Springs will bubble up, and steam will shoot out. Hot water will fly into the air . . . No one knows how long this will continue. And voices will be heard here in different languages in generations to come.*

—Coyote's prophecy from Flathead legend

# ALPHA
# FEMALE

# PROLOGUE

Zach Knudtsen lied. A lot.

Only nine years old, Zach had already been caught
shoplifting twice, caused too many fights at school to keep
track of, and long ago been labeled "trouble" by his teach-
ers at his Canton, Ohio, elementary school. But the really
sad thing about Zach was that more and more, his parents
had taken to using that same term to describe him. It was
one of the reasons they decided to take this family vacation, to bring Zach to Yellowstone. They'd read about the
Junior Ranger Program in the Sunday travel section of the
Columbus *Gazette*, read the quote from a parent who said
that after exploring Yellowstone, completing his assign-
ments, and being awarded a Junior Ranger badge, her previously unruly child had somehow changed, proclaiming,
"I want to be a ranger when I grow up. I want to save the
wolves and bears."

And truth be told, so far this trip had given Amy and
Kevin Knudtsen, Zach's parents, renewed hope about Zach.
Before the trip, Zach's only interest, aside from getting in
trouble, revolved around eating and increasingly violent
video games, both of which had led to his being overweight,
which, in turn, had contributed to his low self-esteem and
lack of friends.

The Junior Ranger Program had instilled a sense of

purpose and, after easily fulfilling its first assignment—sighting five wild animals—the first day of his trip, a confidence in Zach that his world thus far had only succeeded in eroding. Perhaps this newly positive attitude would help Zach get off to a good start in the upcoming school year, which was only a month away.

Before the trip, Amy Knudtsen had made reservations at the Mammoth Hot Springs Hotel for a two-night stay. That decision turned out to be a godsend. For as much as Zach loved Yellowstone's animals, what had really fired his imagination and enthusiasm were the hot springs. After walking the Lower Terraces with his parents twice the day they arrived, they'd gone over the rules with him—"stay on the boardwalk and never, ever reach into the water"—and then given Zach permission to venture out alone. The boy spent hours each day wandering the boardwalks, staring into the steaming waters as they cascaded down scalloped terraces, looking for the filamentous-shaped bacteria that gave the waters their unique, almost iridescent colors. Attention Deficit Disorder had always made staying on task a terrible struggle for Zach, but something about the water's movement—its colors, the smells and sounds—calmed the boy's mind. And so his parents had extended their stay at Mammoth another two days. And those days had been some of the happiest the Knudtsen family ever experienced.

But now, on their last planned day in Mammoth, "trouble" had reared its ugly head again.

"See," Zach said excitedly, pointing down at the ground. "It's gone. The water. It used to come right up to that tree."

Kevin Knudtsen pretended to study where Zach pointed, when in fact he was debating how to handle the situation. It was only a little lie. Nothing to get upset about. Yet the therapist had told them they must confront Zach when he lied.

Kevin cleared his throat.

"That's impossible, son. Look there's no water within twenty yards of here. It stops there." He pointed toward Canary Springs. "You're just not remembering it correctly."

"Are you senile?" Zach said, his ADD kicking in. "The first day we were here there was water right there." His finger punched toward the ground.

"Zach, don't talk to your father that way," Amy said.

Zach glared at both Amy and Kevin, then took off at a run down the boardwalk, which climbed up and down and gyrated around the terraces of Mammoth's hot springs. When he rounded a bend up ahead, his parents lost sight of him.

They hurried to catch up with him. They'd decided to keep their clocks set at Central time, which meant it was still early—only 7:15 A.M. locally—and the day threatened rain. The usual crowds hadn't yet materialized, which might have made finding Zach difficult. Still, when they reached the bend where he'd disappeared from sight, at first the little boy was nowhere to be seen.

Then Kevin called out, pointing off to the side.

"There he is."

Zach had jumped down, off the boardwalk, onto ash-colored ground.

He'd run right past a sign that read: WARNING: THIN CRUST AREA. SCALDING WATER BENEATH SURFACE. LEAVING THE BOARDWALK IS UNLAWFUL AND POTENTIALLY FATAL. VIOLATORS WILL BE PROSECUTED.

Staring at it, horrified, his mother looked around to see if anyone was watching.

"Zach Knudtsen, you get back here," she called. "Now. You are in serious trouble."

Zach kept walking determinedly, his back to them.

"You have to go after him," Amy told Kevin.

The portion of the boardwalk they were on sat up high, above the parking lot and the two-lane road that led from Old Faithful to the park's headquarters, in Mammoth. A lone figure dressed in green and gray and wearing a felt hat strode across the road from the direction of the Visitor Center, toward the hot springs.

"There's a ranger," Kevin said. "We'll both get arrested."

"Kevin, you can't let him stay out there alone. He could

break through and get burned. I read a couple years ago about a girl dying from falling in a hot spring."

Furious, Kevin glanced around, then he too stepped off the boardwalk. By now, Zach had disappeared behind Orange Spring Mound—a large mounded shape that resulted from a very slow water flow, whose mineral deposits eventually created a feature that looked like the rounded shape of a cat curled tightly in a ball under a blanket. The area was strictly off limits—not only to tourists but to park personnel as well.

Kevin picked his way gingerly, finally catching up with Zach, who stared wide-eyed at the ground in front of him.

"You are in so much trouble, young man."

Zach pointed downward.

"Here. The water used to be here too."

"That's enough, Zach."

"Dad, I swear. I swear to God."

Kevin looked around. He'd walked over a hundred yards to catch up with Zach and had not seen so much as a drop of water along the way.

"What did we tell you? Not to step off the boardwalk. There are signs everywhere. Do you know what you've done? We could get arrested. So stop this nonsense about the water. You're in so much—"

"But I'm not making it up," Zach fumed. "That water, the orange-ish kind, there was a stream of it that came all the way here. Just yesterday."

"We'll talk about this later. Now, move. Hurry."

At ninety-eight pounds the boy was too heavy for Kevin to carry. He grabbed Zach by the shoulder and shoved him back in the direction of the boardwalk.

"I just hope no one's seen us," Kevin said. "Look," he pointed at the white travertine-covered earth beneath them, "footprints. They'll know someone was here. Why, Zach? Why? Why do you always have to ruin everything?"

Kevin slipped out of his rain slicker and began sweeping it across the ground, trying to erase the prints as he retreated.

Suddenly he realized Zach hadn't moved. He stopped, looked over his shoulder.

The boy's bulky shoulders had begun heaving in silent sobs. Zach's therapist said one of the problems with Zach was that he held all his emotions in. Kevin hadn't seen his son cry in years. As angry and panicked as Kevin felt, the sight broke his heart.

He stopped, straightened, and walked gingerly over to his son. When he tipped Zach's face up toward him, tears dripped down the round, sunburned cheeks.

"What is it?" Kevin said quietly.

"I did it."

"You did what, Zach?"

"I ruined the hot spring. I made it dry up."

"Son, that's impossible. There was no water up here. And if there had been, nothing you could do would make it dry up."

Zach's sobs were no longer silent.

Kevin looked around. They'd moved within sight of the boardwalk. An older couple stood there, staring at them. Amy had disappeared.

"The ranger," Zach wheezed between sobs. "During his talk, he said that just putting a finger in the water can change everything. I . . . I . . ."

"What, Zach? What did you do?"

"I put some stuff in it. Two days ago. Like Ole Anderson used to do."

"Who the hell is Ole Anderson?" Kevin said, glancing back again. The couple had disappeared now too. No doubt on their way to find the ranger. Soon Kevin and Zach would be sitting in a jail cell.

"The ranger talked about it. People who came here used to give Ole Anderson stuff, like coins, or jewelry, or pinecones. They'd pay him and Ole would put the stuff in the hot springs and it would get covered with limestone. Like a dip top, you know, a Tastee Freez."

Kevin grabbed Zach's arm.

"What did you put in the hot springs?"

Zach didn't answer.

Kevin squeezed.

"What, Zach?"

Zach started sobbing again.

"Just some coins. And that belt buckle Mom got me at the hotel . . . and . . ."

"What else?"

"My pen."

"You mean the pen we just gave you for your birthday? The one with your name on it?"

Tears streamed down Zach's face as he nodded.

"I ruined it. I made the water dry up. It might all dry up now, just because of me. We've gotta tell them I did it, Dad. It's all my fault."

Kevin pivoted back in the direction they'd just come from, yanking Zach with him.

"Hurry, we've got to find that pen before anyone else does."

Forty miles away, in the town of Pray, Montana, Heck Buckley held court at the local grill.

"There's only one solution to the wolf problem, and that's to kill every last one of the beasts. If the federal government won't do it, won't keep their promise to us law-abiding citizens, *we* will."

Buckley didn't flinch, never so much as blinked, while uttering those words to the *USA Today* reporter.

Corinne Rosales drew back, appraising him.

"Those are pretty strong words."

"Civil disobedience has been a foundation of this great nation since its beginning."

"Wiping out Montana's wolf population isn't exactly civil disobedience. It's criminal. You could face time in the penitentiary."

Buckley's laugh startled her. In her six years as a features reporter, she'd interviewed governors, Fortune 500

CEOs, movie stars, and never come across a specimen quite like this one. She found him almost as fascinating as she did repulsive.

"In this state? Girl, you haven't done your homework if you think the citizens of this state are gonna allow anyone to put me behind bars. 'Cept for Missoula—all those high-brow environmentalists—I'm a hero in this goddamn state. So is Chad Gleeson."

Any fascination Corinne entertained died with Buckley's use of the word "girl."

"You may be a hero in this state, Mr. Buckley, but to the rest of the world, you're treading on pretty sacred ground. The story about Chad Gleeson killing a Yellowstone wolf inside the park is making its way around the world, and the reaction isn't exactly warm and fuzzy. Most of the world seems to like the fact that Yellowstone reintroduced the gray wolf back in 1995. I just came from the park, where I interviewed the biologist responsible for the reintroduction. He says hundreds of thousands of visitors from across the globe have come to Yellowstone since 1995 just to see the wolves."

Buckley's fist slammed down on the table separating them. Coffee—the watered-down, cowboy kind—splattered the yellow Formica surface. Several nearby customers, tourists, looked their way. The locals—used to Buckley and his dramatics—at most grimaced, or shook their heads silently. But mostly they ignored him. A waitress appeared instantly to top off their cups.

"That's the problem," Buckley said. "Lies. They're feeding people like you lies. And you believe them, don't you? Every last one of 'em. Then you print them in your goddamn paper for the rest of the world to read. Hell, you media leeches are probably as much to blame as the fucking environmentalists."

"We media leeches report the facts," Corinne said calmly. "And the fact is that Chad Gleeson was carrying firearms inside a national park and that he shot and killed an animal on the endangered species list."

"Shot it in self-defense. It was him or that goddamn wolf."

"You think people buy that?"

"You wait and see. The judge is gonna buy it, 'cause it's true. Chad won't even stand trial."

"Can I quote you on that, Mr. Buckley?"

With a belly that took up all the space between his chair and the table, Buckley already looked like a walking heart attack. But now a web of veins popped up at each temple. They looked alive, like worms eating away at his skull under his dull, weathered skin.

"You can quote me on this," he said, leaning so close to her that she drew back at the spit tobacco on his breath. "You tell the world, we're tired of the lies. We're tired of letting a handful of the population rob us honest, hard-working outfitters of our hard-earned livelihoods. We've got the Lord behind us. And the Bible. We're not gonna let the goddamn wolves, or any of you goddamn wolf lovers— 'cause I can see you're one of 'em, I can practically smell it—put us out of business. You got that? You write all *that* down in that book of yours?"

Corinne made a show of closing the notebook she'd been jotting notes in, dabbing at a spot of coffee that hit the sleeve of her crisp white shirt, then pushing back from the table.

"I got it, Mr. Buckley," she said, standing, then sliding her tape recorder into the canvas bag, which she slung over her shoulder. "Every last word."

"Good. 'Cause we're tired of playing games. You tell them, the whole fucking world, that it'd be a mistake not to take us serious. My antiwolf coalition's growing by the day. Hell, our Web site had over three thousand hits yesterday. Got almost a hundred e-mails congratulating us about the dead wolf."

Corinne made a mental note to recheck the Yellowstone Anti-Wolf Coalition's Web page when she got back to her motel room. She didn't remember there being a counter that kept track of the number of visitors. Had the news about the wolf generated that much support for Buckley's cause?

"I'll do that, Mr. Buckley. I'll let the world know just how you feel. It will, in fact, be my pleasure to do so."

She turned and started to walk away, but suddenly stopped and pivoted.

"Oh, and Mr. Buckley?"

One of his bushy gray eyebrows shot up.

"What?"

"Don't ever make the mistake of calling me 'girl' again."

Buckley broke into a grin. A clump of chewing tobacco gleamed from the space between his molars and cheek.

"Ah, I see. You're one of them women's libber types. Or maybe a dyke. That's it, isn't it?"

Angry with herself for letting him get to her, Corinne Rosales stood there, staring him down. But Buckley'd had a lifetime of insulting people. A lifetime of stare-downs. He always won.

This time, he didn't even consider it a contest.

"Hell, I figured as much," he said, lifting the newspaper, then burying his face in it.

Corinne realized she'd just been dismissed.

# ONE

RESTORING OUR MOST PRECIOUS ASSET: WILDERNESS!

Annie Peacock's grip on the steering wheel loosened reflexively as she passed the newly erected billboard that hovered over the entrance to the tiny town of Gardiner, Montana. Below the billboard's motto (which Annie had heard no less than four times on the radio on her drive back from Livingston), a rotating globe featured bear and elk and moose, each safely perusing its own natural habitat. It radiated a warm and fuzzy feeling. The WERI—World Energy Resources, Inc.—logo proudly dominated the bottom right corner of the sign, which, by virtue of its size and grandeur, stuck out like a sore thumb next to the only other billboards in Gardiner: one for Holly's Drive-Thru and the other for a white-water expedition company called The Flying Pig.

Annie glanced across the Yellowstone River and the town, mostly sleeping now, and in the moonlight, saw the outline of the Roosevelt Arch stretching skyward, dusting the North Star.

Almost home. Strange how after only one year, the sight of the stone structure that had been welcoming visitors to Yellowstone's north entrance for over a hundred years—actually, the sight of the town in general—gave Annie a comfort that had eluded her after more than a decade in Seattle.

Tonight it damn near brought tears to her eyes.

She'd always hated driving the fifty-two miles between Livingston and Gardiner, especially after dark. Her headlights had caught too many deer, sometimes even elk or a moose, lying lifeless on the side of the road. Down the road, at the only body shop in town, she'd inevitably see the offending vehicle, its front grille smashed beyond recognition. But tonight those fifty-two miles had felt like three times the distance. She'd had to pull over twice to let the dizziness pass. Each time, as she lay across the front seat of her Subaru, the doctor's words came back to her, taunting her.

"It can't be the drug."

To which she'd finally, eloquently, blurted out, "Bullshit."

It hadn't been a particularly inspired, or articulate, response, but in her raw state, it had been the only one that came to Annie's mind.

At first, Dr. Rosenbaum looked like he'd just been slapped across the face, then indignation overcame his patrician features and he waited for an apology or, at the very least, an explanation. But Annie felt too damn sick, too drained, to try to educate another "healer" brainwashed by the pharmaceutical industry. Besides, she'd developed a built-in radar for detecting arrogance and Rosenbaum had set her meter off the moment he breezed into the exam room, clearly out of sorts about having to stay late in order to accommodate Annie's schedule—which he most likely would not have done had he not recently been designated a preferred MD for all of Yellowstone's 3,500 employees, and had Annie not held the position within the park that she did.

Trying to tell this one something he didn't want to hear would be a total waste of time, she'd surmised almost instantly. So she'd simply stood and walked out of the room.

Another doctor's appointment that had begun with hope—albeit a rapidly fading hope—and ended up a waste of time.

But she was almost home now. Only five more miles stretched between the arch and her house in Mammoth. Five miles of narrow, shoulderless, and winding road, with precipitous drop-offs to the Gardner River.

Annie tightened her grasp on the wheel, proceeded under the arch and then, a quarter mile farther down, passed through the unmanned entry gates, ignoring the sign to STOP BEFORE PROCEEDING.

Fifteen minutes later, close to elation, Annie pulled up to the stone house.

She stepped out of the car, taking immediate comfort in the night's warm embrace. Annie loved the night air in Yellowstone. It felt to her like worn velvet.

A coyote yipped twice, from over Bunsen Peak's way.

She quickly scanned the area surrounding the house.

The other thing Annie loved about nightfall was the sense of privacy it afforded her. How ironic that she'd moved to the West's wide open spaces only to find herself living in a fishbowl. The sign posted in her driveway: PRIVATE RESIDENCE/NO TRESPASSING might as well have said, FREAK SHOW, TAKE A PEEK. She sometimes arrived home from work to find tourists sitting on her front porch, or pressing their noses to the window—a sure sign her mother was either sleeping upstairs or engrossed in playing the piano in the back; for if Eleanor Malone became aware of intruders, she never failed to shoo them away, cane waving wildly in the air, Archie barking at her side.

In the year they'd all lived together in the stone house, Eleanor and Archie, Annie's twelve-year-old Labrador retriever, had become quite a team. Both were hard of hearing (or, as Annie saw it, increasingly selective in their hearing), both getting a little crotchety with age, and both touchingly devoted to the great love of their life: Annie. If that devotion meant ensuring Annie's privacy and the downtime she needed as she struggled with her health problems by chasing away trespassers, the two gamely—actually, Annie had observed, with some degree of glee—did so.

Thankfully at night, however, the tourists dispersed to places unknown, leaving Annie moments like this.

She took in the high-altitude air, breathed it deep into her lungs, and stood admiring the skyline, relishing more than ever the magical healing powers this new life—new world—had provided her.

Bunsen Peak stood tall, backlit by a half moon, and to the west, waiting for its turn to be bathed in the delicate glow, Electric. It looked less daunting than it had half an hour earlier, as Annie approached Gardiner. She often wondered whether the peak's name bore responsibility for the power it held over her every time she drove toward it, down Highway 89, returning from a trip to civilization—a force that pulled her back to a place, a life so unlike anything she'd ever expected.

A force that, she knew, would never allow her to leave.

Another coyote's wail—this one sounded like it came from up near the Hoodoos—transitioned to short, sharp barks. It turned Annie's thoughts to her devoted Lab.

She hurried to the front door, eager to see Archie. The silence indicated he hadn't heard her pull in. She put the key in the lock, turned it, and whistled for him as she opened the door.

"Arch?"

Annie slid inside.

The house felt strangely still. Archie must have followed her mother up to bed. More and more, if Annie wasn't home, he slept with Eleanor until she returned.

Something did not feel right.

If Annie was out late, Eleanor usually left a light on in the living room. Now the only illumination greeting Annie came from the kitchen.

"Mom?"

Hard of hearing or not, Archie should have bounded down the steps to greet Annie by now.

Several long-legged strides bore Annie across the narrow, spartanly furnished living room.

At the kitchen door, she stopped, dead in her tracks.

*"Oh my god."*

Shattered glass—jagged white pieces adorned with green shamrocks that looked cruelly, startlingly, out of place against the worn linoleum—crunched under Annie's feet as she stepped inside. The antique hutch Eleanor had brought with her from Seattle, in which she stored the precious china she'd inherited from her Irish mother-in-law, lay on its back, its door open and ripped half off its hinges.

"Mother?" Annie screamed.

At first she did not notice the bottle of wine perched precariously on its side, the top hanging over the edge of the counter—her eyes had instead been drawn to the deep red puddles splattering the aging beige linoleum.

Blood.

Annie dropped to her knees. Dipping a finger in one dark splash, she lifted her hand—it shook violently—and brought it even with her face. As she did so, she spotted the bottle. Relief flooded her. It had apparently toppled over during whatever awful event had transpired earlier in the kitchen, leaving its contents to drip onto the floor.

For the first time, Annie noticed the smell. Something burning. She looked up, at the stove. The stainless-steel pot Eleanor Malone used for her bedtime tea radiated waves of heat from its perch over a burner that glowed neon red. Annie reached for the pot, scalding her fingers on its stainless-steel surface. The water inside had long since evaporated.

Turning to dash for the stairs to the second floor, which she'd passed upon entering the house, Annie froze midstride.

A single piece of paper lay face up on the table where her mother took her tea, beneath the window that looked out on Liberty Cap.

Even from half a room away, something about the manner in which the letters had been scrawled across its face told Annie her life would never be the same.

She walked in measured steps toward it.

Instinctively, she knew better than to touch it; knew not to risk smudging a fingerprint or other DNA; evidence left behind.

For Annie Peacock knew—she had from the moment she first stared, jaw dropped, into the kitchen—that she was dealing with a crime scene.

Still, she reached for the note, stopping just short of touching it.

*And then God made man, to rule over the world and all its creatures.*

One sentence.

She gazed at it, trying to put out of mind thoughts of the scene that had to have unfolded—how long ago? minutes? hours?—in order for that sheet of paper to find its way there, in order for her kitchen to look as it did. Annie again screamed her mother's name.

She bolted for the phone on the wall, next to the back door, and punched a number on her speed dial.

"Yellowstone Law Enforcement."

A glint on the kitchen counter caught Annie's eye.

"Hello? Law enforcement," the voice repeated several times, its volume rising and falling with the swinging of the phone, which now dangled from its cord.

It felt like she was moving in slow motion as Annie walked to the counter, one hand stretched forward, groping; the other covering her mouth. Her eyes were glued to the source of the reflection that had drawn them: her mother's wedding ring. It had been pushed back, tucked between the cheesy set of canisters Annie teased Eleanor about buying at the gift shop, which featured the park's most well-known features—Old Faithful, Artist's Point, Minerva Terrace, and the Roosevelt Arch—and held either coffee, flour, bags of herbal tea, or dog biscuits.

A plain gold band on the outside, inscribed inside with the words *"From this day forward . . ."* along with the date *"6/29/45."*

Annie grabbed it, DNA evidence be damned; curled her

fingers around it. Clutching it to her chest, she closed her eyes and began to pray. She'd had trouble praying lately, actually for a couple years now, but now the words came in a flood.

*Please dear God, please, let her be okay.*

In bizarre fashion, the tinny, distant voice on the other end of the phone—now spinning, as the twisted cord unwound itself—harmonized with the one in Annie's head.

"Law Enforcement. Hello?"

Annie padded back to the phone, lifted it gingerly.

"This is Judge Peacock," she said, her voice assured, even measured. "Please send someone to my house."

The voice faltered upon hearing the identity of the caller.

"Your Honor . . . May I ask . . . what . . . what's the nature of the emergency?"

The sound clearly originated from behind Annie. There was no mistaking it. Archie's whimper. *It was coming from the cell.*

"Judge Peacock . . . ?"

All caution left Annie's voice as she shouted: "I need an ambulance, local police, all available resources," then slammed the phone into its cradle.

She reeled in the direction of the whimper, calling out to him.

"Archie?"

Throwing open the door at the far end of the kitchen, she crossed a short, unlit hallway, at the end of which another door—a heavier door, one made of sturdy, aged oak—stood closed.

The whimper again. Annie threw it open.

At first all she saw was the same eerily barren room that she'd tried to avoid ever since moving into the stone house.

Black wrought-iron bars adorned the only window. A piano sat dead center on the cement floor—it had been left there by Annie's predecessor, Judge Sherburne, whose wife, Rosemarie, was an accomplished pianist. Rosemarie had died suddenly, two months after Judge Sherburne had a stroke. When Annie moved in, Rosemarie had offered to

leave behind the black Wurlitzer. There would not be room
for it in the apartment she'd rented in Livingston to be
close to her husband. Annie had grown up listening to her
mother play and knew that Eleanor would be delighted not
to have to give up one of her greatest passions in order to
come live with Annie. She'd vowed to move the piano to
the living room for Eleanor, but hadn't yet followed through.
Therefore, each evening, Eleanor retreated to what had
once served as Yellowstone National Park's first jail cell,
Archie at her side.

Soon the house would fill with Chopin, Beethoven, or,
more recently, Eleanor's own compositions, inspired, as she
described it, by "the wonders of her new life." She'd entitled
her latest composition "Absaroka Symphony," in honor of
the majestic mountains lining the east side of the Paradise
Valley.

Annie had often been struck by the absurdity of the
sight—this fragile elderly woman sitting rigidly at the piano playing with a grace that frequently moved her daughter to tears, loyal dog lying at her feet—all framed by an
iron-barred door.

Now that door stood shut and locked.

On the other side, in a pool of blood, lay Archie.


*"Wake up, Will. Will!"*

Will McCarroll lifted his head no more than half an inch
off the bedsheet, then dropped it right back, pulling the pillow over it. He turned his face away from the two-way radio that vibrated noisily, practically walking itself across
the surface of the rickety nightstand that had the words *Government Issue, 1951* engraved on the side facing the equally
rickety bed where Will had just been sleeping like a baby.
Until the two-way sounded.

*"Will. We know you're in Mammoth for tomorrow's ar-
raignment. Janet saw you fishing up at Sheepeaters tonight.
This is an emergency. Pick up!"*

Wrestling his way into a sitting position, which meant

fighting the flannel blanket that had managed to encase him, Will groped in the dark for the radio.

"Goddammit, Mickey. This better be important. It's my first night in a goddamn bed in a month."

*"It's important all right,"* the voice replied. *"We just got a call from Annie Peacock. You've gotta head right over there."*

"Annie Peacock? You mean . . ."

*"Yes, Judge Peacock. Peter and Sheriff Holmberg will meet you there. And Livingston emergency teams."*

Getting awakened in the middle of the good night's sleep Will had been looking forward to for days now was bad enough. It having anything at all to do with Annie Peacock made it pretty much intolerable.

"Where the hell's Luke?" he growled into the radio. "Mammoth's his territory."

*"He's on his way to Bozeman with a suspected blood clot."*

"Bozeman? Livingston's half an hour closer."

*"Livingston's CT scan is down. Luke didn't know that though 'til he got the poor guy he was transporting from Roosevelt Lodge there. They're on their way to Bozeman General now. Hope he holds out. Luke said he's not looking good. Luke'll be tied up another couple hours, at least."*

"Well, shit. Wouldn't you know?" Will dropped back onto one elbow as he ran his free hand through a head of hair as thick—and unruly—at fifty as it had been at thirty. "If you've already sent for the sheriff and Livingston EMTs, why do you need me? What'd the judge do—choke on some of that self-righteousness she dishes out all the time?"

*"This isn't a medical emergency, Will. It's a crime scene. That calls for Park Service law enforcement. Right now that means you."*

"Crime?"

Will was nothing if not an inveterate professional when it came to his real job—which, as law enforcement for Yellowstone National Park, meant dealing with any crimes committed within its borders. That one word sent him flying to his feet. He held the two-way with one hand while he used the other to wrestle his way back into the green wool pants he'd tossed on the floor only an hour and a half earlier. They still reeked of horse sweat.

*"Just get over there, Will. They don't want me talking about it over the two-way. This is serious."*

Only one light in the four-hundred-square-foot metal trailer that housed backcountry rangers in their visits to Mammoth—the single forty-watt bulb above the front door—chased away the night's chill as well as its blackness. Will stumbled toward it. As he passed the bed poster, he reached for the Glock hanging on it.

Slinging the holster over his shoulder, he replied, "On my way."

# TWO

Lights flashing, Will raced north on the Grand Loop Road from the YCC village, which served as home to dozens of park employees, toward Mammoth. Wide awake now, adrenaline flowing, he wondered just what type of emergency could warrant Mickey's calling every authority from every jurisdiction within sixty miles.

Mammoth, which served as Yellowstone's administrative headquarters, consisted of a couple dozen park buildings—the Albright Visitor Center, administrative offices, the courthouse and jail, the residences of high-ranking park officials, as well as those of executives of Xanterra, the official park concessionaire company, and a hotel and gift shop—all of which converged at Mammoth Springs Junction, the intersection of the north route of the Grand Loop, which connected Mammoth to Tower Junction and then, farther east, the Lamar Valley, and the road leading south, toward Old Faithful.

Judge Peacock's residence—known by park employees as "the stone house"—sat like one of the area's exotic geothermal features, adjacent to the lower hot springs and their boardwalks, and a short distance south of Mammoth Springs Junction.

The stone house had originally served as the park's first courthouse and jail, but in the early 1900s, after construction of the Pagoda Building, which housed the current courthouse, and soon thereafter, the erection of a new jail, the structure became home to a series of resident magistrates. So close did it sit to the active geothermal springs that it was frequently enveloped in steam, giving it an eerie appearance. Liberty Cap, a copper-colored geothermal feature that reached thirty-seven feet into the air and reminded most first-time viewers of an erect penis, did little to correct that impression.

Speeding down the hill toward it now, Will caught glimpses of flashing lights approaching from the direction of Gardiner.

How the hell had everyone responded so quickly? At 70 mph—asking-for-trouble speed on the winding, shoulderless road from the YCC to Mammoth—it had taken Will less than three minutes to descend the hill.

The light show that greeted him once he'd rounded the bend near the horse stables and come within view of the stone house resembled the Las Vegas strip: ambulances, sheriff's cars, and local police lined the roadway and filled the parking areas surrounding the judge's residence. Several spotlights beamed skyward as workers—park rangers pulled from bed, like Will, as well as Xanterra hotel employees—struggled to set them up.

His SUV's lights swept across Liberty Cap as Will swung into the driveway.

Behind the judge's house, up along the boardwalk to Minerva, and on the trail leading to the Beaver Ponds, more lights flickered—beams sweeping back and forth, searching for something, no doubt something to do with the crime that had taken place, the nature of which Will still had not a clue about.

A sheriff's deputy nodded at Will as he jogged toward the back door of the house, where the activity seemed to be focused.

Will stepped inside. A string bean of a man with a shock of prematurely white hair stooped over the kitchen table, camera focused upon a piece of paper lying on its surface.

Les Bateman, the park photographer. Will's boss, Peter Shewmaker, stood hunched over beside him, examining the paper without touching it.

Peter glanced up. Forty-five and fit, like most of the park's law enforcement, Shewmaker prided himself in his athleticism and spent a good deal of time at the employee gym. Will knew it rankled his boss that during quarterly training and drills, Will—who never stepped foot in the gym—consistently outran and outmaneuvered him. While each man held the other in respect, Will's independent—bordering on maverick—ways had at times strained their relationship almost to the breaking point.

Shewmaker's features contorted into a scowl as he headed toward Will, clearly not happy to see him.

"Where's Luke?" he said.

"Transporting a tourist to the hospital in Bozeman."

"Judge Peacock isn't gonna like this." New concern deepened the spokelike lines that radiated from the corners of his eyes. He called to a sheriff's deputy to stand guard over the note.

With a sigh he motioned Will. "Follow me."

Shewmaker wove his way through the phalanx of emergency response personnel gathered in the small kitchen.

"What're we dealing with, Pete?" Will asked from close behind.

"Judge Peacock's mom's been kidnapped."

"The crazy lady with the cane?"

"Yep."

They pushed through a group of uniformed officers—two men from Park County and a woman from the Park Service—who were talking in low voices in the hallway beyond the kitchen. Will had been in this part of the house several times, as a guest at Judge Sherburne's infamous parties. He knew exactly where they were headed.

The cell.

"I need to talk to the judge," a deputy called out as they passed.

"She's already given Sheriff Holmberg and me a statement," Shewmaker replied. "Give her a minute alone now. Please."

"How'd the sheriff get here so fast?" Will asked. The sheriff's office was headquartered in Livingston.

"He was off duty," Shewmaker answered. "At a card game in Gardiner."

Shewmaker drew back to grab Will's elbow, shepherding him through the door at the end of the short hallway. It closed, shutting out one form of chaos behind them, but revealing another—more heart-wrenching and ugly—on the other side.

Will caught his breath.

Judge Peacock huddled on the floor, knees and hands covered in blood, stroking her yellow Labrador retriever's head and speaking to it soothingly.

The big dog's eyes were open, but glazed over. His tail flopped twice, however, when he saw Will. Judge Peacock looked up. Tears stained her face, but that didn't stop the expression on it from transitioning from one of shock and grief to a cold stare.

"You."

Shewmaker spoke before Will had a chance to.

"Luke's on another emergency," he said. "Up in Bozeman." He turned back to address Will. "Judge Peacock was going to ask Luke to take Archie in to Dr. Kennedy's. Sheriff doesn't want her to leave for a while. FBI's on the way and they'll want to talk to her right away."

"I'll take him," Will said.

Annie's reply came quickly, and sharply.

"Never."

Ignoring her, Will dropped to his knees besides the dog.

"What happened, big fella?" he said softly.

*Thump, thump.* Will's touch brought another wag of the tail.

"They shot him." The control Will was used to hearing in the judge's voice was absent. After a long pause, she continued. "Dr. Kennedy's setting up for surgery right now. I want to go with him, but I can't leave. Archie knows Luke.

He comes over and walks him when I have a long day. That's why I asked for him." Her voice cracked, threatened to give out on her. "I wanted him to be with someone he knows."

She looked at Will accusingly. The resentment she felt for him seemed to help her regain control.

"He's been through enough without being taken away by strangers," she said. "Or you."

Will stroked the dog's head again.

"It's you and me that have the problem," he said. "I don't see what that has to do with your dog. I'll take him for you."

Shewmaker chimed in. "I'd let him, Your Honor. Dog seems to like him."

Without waiting for Annie to respond, Will jumped to his feet.

"I'll borrow a transport board from one of the ambulances outside. We need to keep him immobilized."

He disappeared through the iron-barred door.


Out in the driveway, watching Will drive away with Archie, emergency lights flashing, Annie finally broke down. Shewmaker seemed not to know what to say so he just put an arm around her heaving shoulders and let her cry. They stood side by side like that, watching until the SUV's lights raced past the post office, then disappeared down the steep grade leading to Gardiner.

"Judge Peacock?"

Annie turned. Rod Holmberg, the imposing ex–Montana State linebacker and recently reelected Park County sheriff, towered over her. Annie had already given Holmberg and Shewmaker a statement when he first arrived, forty-five minutes earlier.

A stocky man wearing a denim shirt and jeans stood several yards behind him, watching hard-eyed.

"Have you found anything?" Annie asked.

Holmberg looked her straight in the eye.

"No," he replied. He'd handled half a dozen murders in his first four-year term, crimes of passion or drunken rage; but nothing like this. Still, his physical stature and earnest nature inspired confidence in Annie. "We've issued an alert in the three-state area. Every off-duty officer in Montana has been called on duty. But so far we have nothing."

"What about the park?" Annie said, turning to Peter Shewmaker. "They could still be inside it."

"I've called out every law enforcement ranger," Shewmaker answered. Even as he did, two more Park Service Law Enforcement vehicles pulled into Annie's driveway. "They've got orders to visit every campsite, every hotel and lodge. We've got patrols at every entrance. Not one vehicle will leave without being searched."

"Do you think they could have taken her into the backcountry?" Annie asked through tight lips. "She's not fit enough to walk far. She had a hip replacement a year ago."

Shewmaker reached out, placed a gentle hand on her shoulder.

"If they did, we'll find them. We've got trackers and dogs on the way. We'll begin an aerial search as soon as day breaks."

"Pete, Judge Peacock . . ." Holmberg said, breaking in.

"Call me Annie."

"Annie," Holmberg continued. "The FBI's here. We'd like to give Agent Richter a chance to ask a few questions, and go back over some of what you and I already talked about."

"Of course," Annie replied. "We can use my office."

With Shewmaker guiding Annie by the elbow, and the other two men following, they returned to the house, which had grown more chaotic by the minute, with arriving lab techs, search teams, and emergency response providers. But the noise level dropped to a whisper as the foursome walked through the kitchen, into the living room, and down a hall to Annie's office.

They entered the mahogany-paneled room. Annie's home

office in Seattle had been decorated with certificates, awards, diplomas, and framed newspaper articles about Annie and her record successes.

In marked contrast, nothing in this office spoke of her legal career. Instead, one wall sported a framed poster picturing the Grand Tetons, below which was inscribed the 1925, final entry in the diary of a fifteen-year-old Wyoming girl by the name of Helen Mether: *God bless Wyoming, and keep it wild.* Mimi Matsuda, an interpretive ranger Annie especially liked, had painted the two watercolors of Yellowstone trout—cutthroat and rainbow—displayed side by side on the wall behind Annie's desk.

Annie had placed her favorite piece on the wall facing her desk. It was a framed photograph Les Bateman had taken. He had come upon the female wolf above Slough Creek. She was a magnificent creature, thick, silvery-white coat, her lean, muscular body literally coiled for action as she crouched close to the earth. Les explained that she had seen him at the last minute. Just as he'd taken the shot, her eyes had turned to the camera, and it was that—her eyes— that spoke to, that haunted, Annie. A piercing green, with a keen intelligence. But it was the wildness they held that literally transfixed Annie. She often stared at that photograph, at those eyes, and believed she felt, for at least a fleeting moment, what it must be like to live wild, and with fear.

Annie would never have voiced the sentiment aloud to anyone, as she knew it was a grandiose comparison, but the wolf in that photo epitomized to Annie what she felt about her new life. Never had that been more true than at this moment.

On Annie's desk sat two other photographs: a five-by-seven of Archie and Annie, captured during their hike the previous summer along the Bechler Trail, and an eight-by-ten photograph of her mother and father.

The picture of her parents had been taken almost three years earlier, just days before the heart attack that killed her father and prompted Annie to invite Eleanor to move to

Seattle to live with Annie and Rob. In the picture, Eleanor stood behind Annie's father's wheelchair. Bending forward, she'd placed her right arm lovingly, cradlelike, around his frail shoulders. Her left arm stretched out along the top of his, which rested on the arm-support of his chair—Eleanor's frail but steady hand covering the hand that had once performed medical miracles at St. Luke's Presbyterian Hospital in Chicago.

Now, as Annie lowered herself into her chair, the picture drew her eyes to it. She closed them momentarily.

*I have to stay strong.*

She opened them, meeting the concerned gaze of the two men seated opposite her.

"How can I help?"

Agent Richter leaned forward in the leather chair that had once belonged to Annie's father. Despite his jeans and denim shirt, the close crop of his sandy hair and his rigid posture gave him away as an ex-marine.

"We need to know what cases you have on the docket."

"You think my mother's kidnapping stems from a case I'm hearing."

"Yes. Look at the Lefkow case. Or Brian Nichols in Atlanta. Judge Lefkow's mother and husband, killed by a plaintiff unhappy with the outcome of his lawsuit. Brian Nichols kills not only the judge who's trying his rape case—he takes out the court reporter and deputy too."

"I know that scene," Annie said. "I was a federal prosecutor in Seattle for ten years before I took this job." She did not miss the impact—which was considerable—these words had on Agent Richter. "The cases we deal with here, they just don't hold the same potential for that type of rage."

Peter Shewmaker looked over at Holmberg.

"She's handling the wolf case."

While Holmberg simply nodded, Richter leaned forward.

"Wolf case?"

Holmberg had removed his hat and placed it on his knee. He had a habit of running his fingers along its rim, which is what he did as he turned toward the FBI agent.

"Couple days ago," he said, "an alpha-male wolf was shot inside the park."

When he paused, Annie nodded toward the photograph on the wall.

"Actually," she started, but in her emotional state, looking into those green eyes made it hard for her to speak. She took a deep breath, however, and finished, "That's his mate, Number Twenty-two."

If the turmoil she felt, the connection with 22—deepened now by what had happened to both females over the past three days—caught any of the men's attention, they didn't show it.

Shewmaker took over again.

"Guy who killed him is named Chad Gleeson. He's a local outfitter, very popular. Lots of East Coast, big-money clients who want to come out West and bag a trophy animal. His dad's the mayor of Cooke City. Gleeson claimed it was self-defense. Wolf people aren't buying it. It's got everyone up in arms."

"Tomorrow morning's the arraignment," Annie added.

Holmberg and Richter exchanged looks.

"Gleason's got the support of Heck Buckley's Anti-Wolf Coalition," Holmberg offered to Richter, whose expression registered immediate recognition of the name and group. Then he turned back to Annie.

"Haven't they made some threats to you?"

"Nothing direct, or that I've taken seriously. They've been quoted in articles as saying they're ready to do what it takes to ensure what they see as their right to kill federally protected wildlife. They've stated I'm nothing but a puppet for the environmental groups, that I don't even exist in their eyes. That's their rhetoric—they don't buy into federal authority over wilderness areas or the wildlife living inside them. Especially when that authority comes in the form of a woman."

Agent Richter leaned forward.

"Sounds to me like we should take a closer look at that

antiwolf group." He studied Annie. "I want you to make a list of all the cases you prosecuted in Seattle."

"You're kidding."

Seattle seemed another world to Annie entirely, a lifetime so foreign it almost seemed not to have existed.

"I couldn't be more serious."

Annie fell silent. Thoughts of Stephen Kemberly suddenly entered her mind.

In 2004, Kemberly, a federal prosecutor, was shot, assassination style, while he sat working at his computer in the basement of his Capitol Hill home. The killer had never been found, but speculation pointed to a former biotech exec whom Kemberly prosecuted for fraud. Another avenue still being explored by investigators was Kemberly's very vocal and ardent gun-control advocacy. Annie had known Kemberly on a professional basis only, and had great respect for him, both as a prosecutor and a leader in the community. Annie's husband, Rob, had used the tragic event to try to persuade Annie to quit her job and have the baby they'd once planned. The events of the next year sometimes made Annie wish she'd listened to Rob. Instead, in part as a means of avoiding dealing with a marriage she was ambiguous about saving, she'd accepted a heavier load, dealing with increasingly violent crimes.

Annie had prosecuted dozens of fraud cases, and put away criminals for life.

"I suppose you're right," she finally said, emerging from the brief, disturbing trip into her past. "I'll get started on a list tomorrow."

"If you give me permission," Richter replied, "I'll also work directly with the King County court. I know a clerk there. She can start sending me records."

"Of course. But I'll make a list too—with a ranking of the cases I'd rate as higher in terms of this kind of danger. But that will have to wait until tomorrow night, after court."

Holmberg and Richter exchanged looks.

Holmberg spoke first.

"You're not planning to proceed with the cases you have set for tomorrow?"

"The only thing that would stop me," Annie said sharply, "would be the possibility I could go out there and find my mother myself. But I've been in this business long enough to know that's not going to happen. I'll leave your job to you, gentlemen. In the meantime, I'll go crazy if I don't continue with mine."

"Your cases can be continued," Holmberg said. "Or we can get Judge Marsano from Bozeman to come down."

"What are you suggesting?"

It seemed clear to Annie that Holmberg and Richter had already discussed this matter, but now Richter took over.

"Until we've done a thorough investigation, we want you to leave. We want to place you in protective custody."

Shewmaker's expression confirmed to Annie that he had not been in on this plan.

"You're not serious."

"Yes, Your Honor," Richter said, "we're serious. Dead serious."

"Leave?" A hint of hysteria entered Annie's voice for the first time. "And go where?"

She half stood, hands resting—fingers spread—on her desk's surface, her penetrating gaze moving from one man to the other.

"I have no one. My mother, my dog. They're all I have. And this park . . . do you have any idea what it means to me? What it means to other people like me? It's given me back my sanity. It's somehow allowed me to make sense of life again—what message would my leaving send?"

The suggestion to go into hiding had transformed Annie's grief, given it focus. She pointed toward Mammoth, toward the entry gate.

"Read the words over the Roosevelt Arch: FOR THE BENEFIT AND ENJOYMENT OF THE PEOPLE. I take that seriously, gentlemen. *Dead* seriously. I remind myself of those words every time I walk into that courtroom. I'm not about to give anyone the idea that they can affect that mission with threats, or even . . ."

"Judge Peacock," Agent Richter said. "Your mother's been kidnapped. And while finding her—alive—is our top priority, we also want to make certain nothing happens to you."

*Alive.*

The way he'd said it suggested there was another possibility, one that Annie could not bear to acknowledge.

Like a magnet, the larger photograph on her desk suddenly pulled her eyes back. This time, she let them linger. She reached for the photograph, held it at eye level.

On her mother's left hand, the hand resting so protectively, so intimately, on her father's, the gold wedding band jumped out at Annie. Annie hadn't realized, until that moment, that she'd slid the ring on her own finger.

At that same instant, Annie felt her mother's presence. So strong was the sense that Eleanor Malone was there that Annie turned, glancing wild-eyed around the room.

The three law enforcement officers looked on, concern reflected in their eyes.

And then Eleanor Malone's words, in her own voice— not Annie's recollection of it; it was, without doubt, Eleanor speaking to her—came to Annie.

Words she'd repeated dozens of times over the years. Words Annie had teased her about.

"This ring is my most cherished possession. *That's why I'll never take it off.*"

Annie removed the ring, stared at the inscription, old and faded.

"Judge Peacock . . . Are you okay?"

She recognized Peter Shewmaker's voice.

Annie looked up at him, met his gaze. She didn't know him well. As head of law enforcement, he had pretty much an office job. It was the law enforcement rangers who worked *for* Shewmaker that Annie had come to know. They were the ones who testified before her. But Shewmaker lived and worked in Yellowstone. That simple fact created a bond between them, and at that moment, made him feel like her closest ally.

"We'll find your mother," he said softly.

Agent Richter was clearly losing patience.

"These people aren't playing games," he said, his tone all business and no compassion. "We'll do everything in our power to get your mother back, but . . ."

He deliberately let the words dangle in front of Annie.

Annie straightened in her chair, brought herself as close to eye level with the men facing her as possible.

"I won't be canceling any hearings. Or going *anywhere*."

"Are you sure that's what you want?" Sheriff Holmberg said. "What happened tonight could be a warning. If you don't heed it, who knows what they may do to your mother?"

"If she left here alive," Agent Richter finished.

His words enraged Annie, gripped her in the gut.

Her eyes returned to the photo. To the ring on her mother's finger. Her mind returned to her mother's words. *That's why I'll never take it off*.

But she had taken it off. And Annie was convinced now that she knew why.

Holding the ring in her palm, she lifted her hand and met Richter's hard gaze.

"My mother left this behind for a reason," she said. "To tell me that she's still alive. Now it's up to you to find her. Before something horrible happens."

# THREE

WILL BARELY GLANCED AT THE LINE THAT HAD ALREADY formed at the counter in the visitor center—tourists waiting to ask the rangers the same questions they answered over and over again each day ("Where can we see a wolf?" "What roads are closed?" "When does Old Faithful go off again?"), get permits for backcountry camping or fishing, kids eager to be awarded their Junior Ranger badges. Will's uniform, as always, earned him worshipful glances from the little boys, and a glance of a different nature from many of their mothers.

Will did not notice.

He passed through the door marked EMPLOYEES ONLY and climbed the creaky wooden stairs—the originals, built by the military when they were called in to bring order to the park, back in 1909—to the second floor.

Two doors down the hall, he rapped on the frame of a door with a nameplate that read: *LES BATEMAN, PARK PHOTOGRAPHER.*

Les, his back to the door, stared out the window. At first he seemed not to hear, but then he turned slowly. With his tall, skinny build and a forward hunch to his shoulders, he had always reminded Will of Ichabod Crane.

"Came by to pick up those photos," Will said. "Of Twenty-one."

"For the Gleeson arraignment?" Les said. "Are you crazy? There won't be a hearing today, Will. Not after what happened last night."

"I just talked to Justine. The hearing's on."

Brow wrinkled, Les replied, "They must have called Judge Marsano down from Bozeman."

"Nope. Justine told me Judge Peacock's presiding."

"I can't believe she's going ahead with it."

"Surprised me too," Will said. "She's one tough lady."

"I hear you took her dog in to Dr. Kennedy last night."

"He was in bad shape. Hope he makes it."

"So do I. The judge is crazy about him. Now let's just pray her mother's found unharmed."

"You do the praying, Les. The rest of us will just do our best to help find her. Now, how about those photos?"

Les turned and shuffled to a tall black filing cabinet wedged between a door that said DARK ROOM and the corner. He rummaged through it—any true filing scheme apparently lacking—and finally emerged with a manila file, which he thrust Will's way.

Will shook the contents of the envelope out on to Les's desk.

A dead wolf, eyes wide open, stared back at them. A majestic creature—thick, black coat; eyes the color of golden wheat fields, even in death. Its chest, however, was not a thing of beauty. It had been blown away.

Will picked the picture up. Looked closer.

The only way to see the second wound, the clean shot to the animal's temple, was by knowing exactly where the bullet had entered. Will's eyes went right to it.

Seeing the photograph now gave rise to a rage almost as intense as the one Will experienced three days earlier, when he came upon the dying animal. Number 21. One of the first wolves to be reintroduced to the park in 1995. Twenty-one had survived the near extinction of the Druid pack and even, the previous spring—after a battle that left him hobbling along on three legs—a challenge from a younger male for the alpha male position in the pack.

Of all the wolves in the park, Will had the strongest attachment, the greatest admiration, for 21. And his mate, the alpha female, Number 22. The Druids were the closest pack to the backcountry cabin Will called home, above Slough Creek. His neighbors.

Will could hear Les talking, but it took a tremendous effort to emerge from the hellish state—a dementia, really, he'd often suspected that's what it amounted to—that took over his mind, his entire being, every time he was confronted with an image, real or captured on film, like the one he now held in his hands. The destruction and wanton killing inside what the world perceived as a safe haven—for animals and visitors. Yellowstone.

"Do you really think Annie needs to see that after what happened last night?" he said. "You saw what they did to her dog. You can admit the pictures later, if there's a trial."

Will's eyes shot up from the photo.

"That's the point. I want to make sure we get to trial. Listen, Les, I'm sorry about what happened to your friend, the judge, last night—to her mother. And to her dog. But that doesn't change what my job in this park is. And that's to stop sons of bitches like Chad Gleeson from coming in here and killing animals that are protected *by the law*." Will could see that the emphasis was not lost on Les. "There's been enough killing here this year. If Judge Peacock's not up to dealing with this case today, then she shouldn't have made the decision to go ahead with the arraignment."

Les gave Will an accusing look.

"You're still blaming her for what happened," he said. "Aren't you?"

Will locked steely eyes with Les, giving him his answer.

"Not just her," he said.

He paused.

"You're a religious man, Les. Let me ask you something. Does your religion tell you to go out and slaughter animals for no reason?"

"Come on, Will. You know that's not how it happened."

"Do I? No matter how you cut it, those bison would be

out there now, grazing in the sun, if it weren't for a church that decided raising a couple hundred head of cattle right next to Yellowstone was a good idea. And Judge Peacock's refusal to stop the slaughter."

Will turned away, closed his eyes, but he'd already learned that that didn't erase the memories from the previous winter. More than a thousand bison marching unknowingly to their deaths as they left the park in search of food.

"The Lord's highest priority is the protection of human beings, not animals."

Will turned wild eyes on the photographer.

"You're not one of them, are you, Les? Do you belong to that goddamn church?"

"What church I belong to isn't any of your business, Will, and you know it. Besides, do you know how hard last winter was on Annie?"

"Hard on *her*?" Will snorted, choking on a bitter laugh. "All I know is Judge Sherburne would've found a way to stop it."

"Annie's not Judge Sherburne," Les shot back. "Even if you two were friends, which we both know will never happen now, she wouldn't let that influence her decisions."

"Judge Sherburne took his job of protecting this park seriously."

"What is it with you, Will? Most people accuse Annie of leaning too heavily on the side of the environmentalists. Look at her record. She's every bit as passionate about fulfilling her responsibility to protect this park, and everything in it, as Judge Sherburne was. Or as you and I are."

"Sherburne would've found a way."

"Yeah, well, Sherburne's gone now, isn't he? And people like you should thank their lucky stars that Annie Peacock's the one who replaced him, and not some pawn of the current administration."

Will fell silent, studying Les. Les had been a fixture at Yellowstone for over twenty-five years—one of the mainstays at park headquarters in Mammoth. He and Will had worked together all that time. It was a good teaming of two individuals dedicated to their jobs, a teaming that didn't involve a lot of personal give and take. Could Will have misjudged the man so badly that he might actually belong to the Church Universal and Triumphant? He suddenly realized that maybe, for the sake of working together in the future, he didn't actually want to know the answer.

"You've really got it bad for the judge, don't you?" Will said, knowing the effect this would have on Bateman.

Face crimson, Les turned away and headed toward the open door.

As he did, Will turned the photo in his hand sideways.

"What's this?" he said, fingering its edges.

He was holding two photographs, not one. The second was stuck to the back of the picture of the dead wolf. Will pried the two apart with a fingernail that housed a thin line of dirt under it.

Les couldn't resist discussing the work that was his passion. He paused, returned to Will's side.

"That's another shot I took Friday," he said. "From a distance. You know I always try to shoot from a couple different perspectives."

Will studied it. When he looked up at Les again, his eyes held that gleam Les had seen many times over the years.

"Where were you when you took this?"

"I'd climbed on top of a rock . . . maybe two and a half, three feet high, from a distance of about ten yards."

"To the west," Will said. It was a statement and a question at the same time.

Les had to give this some thought.

"I think so. Yeah, it was to the west."

"I'll be damned."

Les bent closer.

"What?"

"Gleeson said he was hiking in the park. That he'd stopped for a break when Twenty-one attacked him."

"So?"

"Look here."

The dirt-lined fingernail pointed to a spot in the upper

left hand corner of the photo. It was faint, very faint—the trace of snow that fell the night before had all but melted, but at the tip of Will's index finger, an almost visible outline, in the shape of a near perfect rectangle, could be made out.

"I didn't see it Friday," Will said, angry with himself for being that sloppy, "when I was up there investigating."

Les reached for a magnifier sitting on the corner of his desk. Silently, falling into the pattern of teamwork that had most often characterized their relationship, Will handed Les the photo. Les bent low over it.

"I didn't see it either," he said through the collar of his uniform shirt, which he never succeeded in ironing flat. "Sometimes, depending on the lighting, the camera will pick up something the human eye doesn't."

Les handed the glass to Will, watched as Will examined the photo under its magnification. "What do you make of it?"

"Twenty-one was shot a mile above Trout Lake," Will recalled softly, almost as if talking to himself. "That's an elevation of over seventy-six hundred feet. It snowed up there the night before—just a trace. It had stopped by Friday morning, when I headed out, but I remember seeing snow on Thunderer.

"There was a tent," Will continued, eyes never leaving the picture. "Right there."

"It wasn't in your report."

Will shook his head.

"That's because it wasn't there when I arrived. And I didn't see this," he said, poking a finger at the picture. "They'd taken it down—probably after Gleeson shot the wolf, but before anyone got there. Which means Gleeson was lying. He camped there. He said he set out for his hike that morning, from outside the park, but he camped right there the night before. Everyone knows the Druid pack heads to Pebble Creek every morning at dawn. The son of a bitch was up there, waiting to ambush them." His fist struck out, denting the side of the metal filing cabinet. The sound reverberated across the room. "And he got Twenty-one."

Les let out a low whistle.

"Even if that's true, Will, it doesn't prove that Twenty-one didn't attack Gleeson, like he claims."

His square jaw set, Will laid the magnifier back on to Les's desk. He glanced at his watch. Nine ten.

He hurriedly gathered up both photos, slid them back into the manila envelope. Then he headed for the door.

"Maybe not," he said before disappearing into the poorly lit hallway. "But it proves one thing. That Gleeson lied about what he was up to. And when Judge Peacock hears that, it should be enough to make sure he stands trial."

# FOUR

GRIZZLIES AND WOLVES, BISON, ELK; MAGNIFICENT MOUN-
tain ranges with names like the Absarokas and the
Crazies—plus half the world's geysers—set Yellowstone
country apart from just about any other place on earth. But
there was another, little-known presence in Yellowstone
that made it unique. Only Yosemite, in fact, also laid claim
to this particular characteristic, for only Yellowstone and
Yosemite housed their own judicial systems—federal courthouses and magistrate judges who lived within the park,
handling all the crimes and misdemeanors that took place
within their protected boundaries.

Two years earlier, *Time* magazine's study of "dream ca-
reers" characterized these United States judge magistrate
positions as two of "the best jobs in the world."

Annie Peacock's dream job—*her entire life*—had, however, just turned nightmare.

*The only good wolf's a dead wolf.*

Annie turned away from the window, from the chaos just
beyond it. As she reached for the black robe hanging on the
back of her office door, the sight of her mother's wedding
ring, still on her finger, almost brought her to her knees.

She could not stop thinking about her mother.

About leaving the house the night before without telling
her she loved her. About the little tiff they'd had.

About the fact that normally, the commotion outside would mean that Annie could look out her office window and know—if she could not actually *see*—that one hundred or so yards away, Eleanor Malone's face would be pressed against the glass of the stone house's front window. Eleanor would have eaten this up. She made no bones about the fact that she missed the excitement of city living. A first-rate protest like the one going on now would have delighted her—were it not for the fact that her daughter was at the center of it.

Outside, no more than twenty yards separating it from Annie's chambers, the voice droned on through a megaphone.

*We're tired of the lies.*

In a day and age where entering courthouses across the country—federal in particular—entailed approximately the same degree of scrutiny as one might encounter trying to board an airplane with a seven-inch cheese knife in a carry-on, Congress had not allocated any money—not a single cent—to safeguarding the building where the judicial cases regarding the protection of one of this nation's most precious assets were heard. The Yellowstone National Park courthouse.

Protestors or not, had it not been for the fact that less than twelve hours earlier Annie's mother had been kidnapped, her house ransacked, and her dog shot, no officers would have been present this Monday morning while Annie prepared to walk into the courtroom. No one would have been there to monitor the rowdy crowd gathered outside as she donned her black robe in preparation for doing the job that had been assigned her—ensuring justice and order within Yellowstone's borders.

But a lot had changed over the course of the past few ugly hours, and now, as Annie readied herself to walk across the hallway and shakily pretend it was business as usual, six uniformed officers stood guard, one at the door to her chambers, reminding her of the end of life as she knew it. Reminding her that today her mother would not be eagerly awaiting Annie's lunch break, during which she loved to grill Annie for details of the morning's goings-on.

*Chad Gleeson's a hero, not a criminal,* a new voice, deeper and uglier than the first, declared from beneath the courtroom's windows.

Annie glanced across the hall, through the open double-doors to the courtroom in time to see her clerk, Justine Pearce, jump up from her desk in front of the bench, cross the room, and slam the glass-paned windows shut.

A *"testing, testing,"* was immediately followed by the screech of a microphone being adjusted.

*Are you listening America? Are you ready to hear the fucking truth?*

It took a single heartbeat for Annie to turn and call across the hall, where two Park Service Law Enforcement rangers stood. The expressions on their faces revealed the fact that nothing in their training had prepared them for this.

"Arrest him," Annie ordered.

"Which one?" the younger officer replied eagerly.

"The one with the microphone. They have the right to protest all they want, but I won't allow language like that in front of visitors, especially kids."

Relieved at having a more defined mission, the two uniformed men bounded out the door and down the steps to the Pagoda Building.

Annie moved to the window, parted its blinds, avoiding the thick, black hair she'd barely remembered to run a brush through that morning and the soulful, dark eyes reflected in its glass.

"Assholes," she heard a voice behind her say.

Justine's reflection joined Annie's in the window. Annie turned to face her.

Graying hair stacked lopsidedly on her head, face still glistening with her most recent age-defying discovery— emu oil, which she tended to overuse—Justine Pearce placed a gentle, protective arm around her boss, saying, "You okay?"

Annie simply nodded, then turned back to the window, Justine at her side.

Justine had served as court clerk for almost two decades, under Annie's predecessor, Judge Sherburne, which made for a bit of an adjustment period when Annie took over. Slowly but steadily, however, Annie had won Justine's respect and loyalty, and Annie had come to consider Justine indispensable, both in and out of the courtroom.

Now the two watched as the rangers walked determinedly up to the man holding the microphone.

"Good old Heck," Justine muttered under her breath.

Heck Buckley. Annie recognized him. Same hateful sneer on his unshaven face. Same camouflage pants and beer belly.

"He's something," she replied. "I saw him at a rally in Cooke City last fall. He had the crowd so worked up, I was glad no one recognized me."

Justine let out a *hrrmpph*.

"Good thing. They would've run you out of town. They're a mean bunch. And they haven't been too happy with some of the sentences you've handed down."

As Annie's eyes skimmed the crowd, she recognized others besides Buckley. Several had been in her courtroom before—one or two on multiple occasions, usually for carrying a firearm; sometimes, if law enforcement got all the breaks and was actually able to catch them in the act, for poaching. But with a park consisting of 2.2 million acres, most of it wild and difficult to access, and a backcountry ranger staff of only twenty-two to patrol its vast reaches, those occasions were rare. For Annie, the only thing that made up for the rarity of that occasion—rangers being able to produce hard physical evidence of poaching—was the immense satisfaction she experienced when it did finally occur. Annie had seen some of the lowest forms of humanity both as a federal prosecutor and in her year on the bench in Yellowstone, but her heart turned stone cold when she was dealing with poachers. In her year on the bench, she had often been criticized for the harsh sentences she'd handed down for poaching. Which is why Heck Buckley and his group had it out for her.

Suddenly, as she looked out her window, something did not feel right to Annie.

She turned to Justine.

"Notice anything strange about that crowd?"

Justine scowled as her eyes surveyed the scene outside.

"You know, I do," she said. "Where's Dayton and his group?"

"That's what I was just thinking."

Jeremiah Dayton was the head of the Church of White Hope. Annie would have expected Dayton and his followers to be right out there alongside Heck Buckley and the rest of the antiwolf protestors.

The Church of White Hope had moved into the area in the early 90s, on the heels of another, more famous, church—the Church Universal and Triumphant. Elizabeth Clare Prophet's group—often labeled a cult for its belief in communications from Ascended Masters, alchemy, the paranormal, and in particular that a nuclear-caused holocaust was coming—had purchased the Royal Teton Ranch, just northwest of Yellowstone and the town of Gardiner, in the late 1980s. Prophet was drawn to the area by the vast expanses of land, its energy and its remoteness, which afforded CUT some degree of freedom from prying eyes—until, that is, word got out that, almost overnight, the church had built a vast system of underground shelters to house seven hundred of its members for the seven years it would take for the fallout to clear after a nuclear attack. Locals and environmentalists became enraged at the reckless gouging of the once pristine landscape, especially after 32,500 gallons of fuel leaked from tanks at the shelter complex. Reporters flocked to the area as the world looked on in amazement at the spectacle of years' worth of food and supplies being stashed away.

Another charismatic religious figure—the self-proclaimed Reverend Jeremiah Dayton—was also watching. Dayton had been shepherding a nondenominational church in rural

Washington State. He preached an unyielding standard of Christianity, alternating brutal condemnation with promises of enlightenment and eternal life. Problem was that he'd made a mistake early on—basing his ministry on a simple, meager lifestyle, in which he lived in a trailer. Reading of Prophet's jet-setting, and the bizarre demands of the Church Universal and Triumphant on its members, which even the publicity did nothing to chill, he'd decided to follow suit, moving the Church of White Hope to the Jardine district—just up the hill from Gardiner.

Jardine and the entire area that looked out and down on the spectacular northwest corner of Yellowstone had once been a vibrant mining community. Dayton's message resonated with some of the locals, who joined the church. Unlike CUT, however, many of whose members actually moved onto the church property, living in rows of cookie-cutter cabins and long, motel-like structures—and at times even the offices in which they worked twelve- to sixteen-hour days—the Church of White Hope's members tended to live in the backcountry hills surrounding Jardine; while the Reverend Dayton and his family and a trusted ensemble of players moved into a grand mansion built on the church's well-secured, closely guarded property.

And while members of the Church Universal and Triumphant came from all walks of life—many of them successful professionals before abandoning their former lives—and, over the years, had assimilated themselves rather quietly and, and some believed, calculatedly, into the community—acquiring positions on councils and boards—the Church of White Hope consisted mainly of fringe members of the community. People who sustained themselves living off the land or doing odd jobs. People who avoided structure and community.

CUT had learned the value of keeping a low profile from the public relations nightmare of its early years. The Church of White Hope, however, had quickly aligned itself with several right-wing, controversial groups, including, when the gray wolf was reintroduced into the park in 1995,

Heck Buckley's Anti-Wolf Coalition—which is why Annie expected to see at least some of the CWH faces this day outside of the courthouse.

Annie had acquired a strong distaste for the church and its members, who were frequent defendants in her courtroom. She despised what they chose to call themselves. Judges were not supposed to hold such sentiments about parties that came before the court. If it threatened their judicial objectivity, they were duty-bound to recuse themselves.

In that one aspect—Annie being required to put aside her personal feelings when dealing with them from the bench—the two churches were not entirely dissimilar. During legal proceedings involving the Church Universal and Triumphant the winter before, it had taken all of Annie's willpower to remain objective about the church's role in what happened. Many a time since—every time she drove down the five-mile stretch of road from Mammoth to Gardiner, then up Highway 89 and on past the capture facility— she'd wondered if she'd remained *too* objective.

The possibility haunted her.

But as resentful as she felt toward CUT about its role in what had happened the previous winter, she would never have expected to see its members now, outside her window. It did surprise her, however, that the Church of White Hope appeared not to have a presence in the group that quickly engulfed the two officers she'd sent out there.

"Oh, oh," Justine cried. "This could be trouble."

Feeling trapped by the crowd, and its increasingly angry tenor, the younger of the two rangers drew his gun.

The protestors immediately became more agitated, shouting angrily, and for several seconds it appeared the ranger had only exacerbated the situation. But when the other ranger followed suit, and a jeep containing two U.S. deputy marshals screeched to a halt outside the courthouse, the group reluctantly backed off.

Annie and Justine watched as the rangers handcuffed Buckley and led him to the waiting jeep.

Several photographers gleefully snapped pictures of the incident.

Fortunately, the crowd of onlookers, almost all visitors to the park, had chosen to distance themselves by standing across the street. American, European, Indian, Asian, young and old, the group stood silent, still, against the backdrop— the solidity of the Albright building and the Yellowstone vistas extending endlessly east, toward Tower Junction and the Lamar Valley.

Annie was struck by the incongruity of it; the disappointment on the faces of those who'd come to Yellowstone for the peace and comfort it offered, an oasis in a world of chaos, only to find this, this . . .

Her thoughts were interrupted by the harsh ring of the telephone on her desk.

Justine hurried over to pick it up.

"Judge Peacock's chambers."

Annie could tell right away who was on the other end. She stepped eagerly toward Justine, hand outreached, but Justine was already saying, "Okay, we'll wait to hear."

She hung up and met Annie's anguished gaze head-on.

"That was Dr. Kennedy's assistant. She just wanted to let you know Archie's still in surgery. It's taking a little longer than they expected."

"Is he okay?"

"That's all she said," Justine replied, clearly wishing she had better news. "She promised to have Dr. Kennedy call as soon as he's finished."

Annie's heart sank. This didn't sound good. She wasn't sure how much more she could take.

Justine stepped toward Annie, placed a soft hand on her shoulder.

"Your Honor, are you sure you want to do this today?"

"Yes, Justine. It's what I want to do. It's what I have to do."

The concerned clerk hesitated a moment longer, hoping her boss would change her mind and call the hearing off. When Annie didn't reply, she finally said, with a sigh, "Okay then. I think they're ready for us."

All business now, she surveyed Annie, straightening the folds of her robe, then brushed a short yellow hair off one shoulder.

They both recognized it as Archie's.

Together, the two women marched across the hallway.


"Please rise."

The command proved unnecessary to all but a few of the onlookers—since the gallery of the courtroom only housed six chairs and the remainder had no choice but to stand. Today's crowd spilled out into the hallway.

"The Honorable Annie Peacock presiding."

Annie strode into the courtroom through the door behind the bench, scanning the faces staring back at her, which registered a vast array of emotions: hostility, concern, curiosity. As a prosecutor in Seattle, she'd been the center of attention in many a packed courtroom. She'd assumed this sight—reporters, protestors, armed law enforcement; the sheer number of spectators—to be a thing of her past.

But while she looked out at dozens of faces, the face that Annie could not get out of her mind was that of her mother. Images of Eleanor Malone came rushing at her. Images of her frightened, perhaps injured. Images of her hands bound, hair disheveled—Eleanor Malone couldn't bear to be seen in public with a single hair out of place.

Annie suddenly wondered if she'd made a terrible mistake in insisting on business as usual. What had she been thinking?

All these faces staring back at her, and then, as if trying to push Annie over the top, the waves of nausea began again.

Glancing around the high-ceilinged room, she realized one face was absent. Will McCarroll. Annie glanced toward Justine to see if she'd recognized the fact that the backcountry ranger, whose presence in Annie's courtroom—even on normal days—pretty much guaranteed an acrimonious hearing, was not present.

Justine had, indeed, noticed. She lifted her shoulder in a shrug, her eyes straying to the hallway outside.

Annie lowered herself to the bench.

"You may be seated."

At the defendant's table, a portly man in his fifties, wearing a sloppy black suit, and a cap of someone else's silver-streaked hair, whispered into the ear of an equally disheveled, bearded man in his thirties, this one in stained Carhartts and a red-and-blue flannel shirt.

Grant Owens had practiced law in Cody, Wyoming, for over three decades. His was a familiar face in Judge Peacock's courtroom. Licensed to practice in Montana as well as Wyoming, Owens advertised in all the local papers surrounding the park, and drummed up a good bit of business as a result. There was nothing quite like the desperation—and acute need for representation—families felt when one of their members was arrested during a vacation, facing the prospect of getting stuck in Yellowstone while the wheels of justice turned. Still, Owens hadn't managed to ring up a single case to distinguish his career until the year before, when two locals, both survivalists, were arrested for stockpiling what amounted to an illegal cache of hidden arms—enough for a small army to keep evildoers at bay—deep within the woods outside the tiny town of Emigrant. Owens's win in that case, based on a dubious and at best, shaky interpretation of Wyoming's code on such matters, skyrocketed him to popularity with local hunters and guides, despite the fact it was likely to be overturned in its upcoming appeal.

As the courtroom quieted and a wave of dizziness hit Annie, she pressed trembling fingers to her temples.

*Not now. Please not now.*

"The case before the court is Case Number 147282. State of Wyoming versus Chadwick Gaston Gleeson. Is the defendant present?"

Owens nudged the man at his side, sending him to his feet in a fashion that said he wasn't the least bit worried about the proceeding. Heavily hooded eyes met Annie's. They seemed to Annie to hold humor, and no hint of fear.

"It's Chad," he said matter-of-factly. "Not Chadwick."

Owens struggled impatiently to his feet beside him, giving Gleeson an elbow on his way.

"I'm sorry, Your Honor. Mr. Gleeson is—quite obviously—here."

Annie resisted studying Gleeson. She knew his type from her days as a prosecutor. The less she looked at him, the better. Two could play his game.

"I take it Mr. Gleeson has retained you, Mr. Owens?"

"Yes, Your Honor. He has."

"Mr. Gleeson," Annie said, having no choice but to address him directly. "The Lacey Act is the federal antipoaching statute that makes the killing, capturing, or wounding of any animal inside Yellowstone National Park a federal offense. It's illegal to hunt within the boundaries of Yellowstone National Park. It's also illegal to carry a loaded firearm. You've been charged with doing both. Do you understand the charges against you?"

Another wave of dizziness caused her to take a deep breath and close her eyes ever so briefly. When she did, she saw her mother, standing in the doorway to the kitchen, watching silently as Annie opened a bottle of wine.

"Are you supposed to mix alcohol with your prescription?" Eleanor had asked softly, after Annie ignored the silent stare.

Annie's eyes sprung open. A hardness slid down over them, like a curtain drawn at the end of a play.

Allowing herself to think about her mother now—entertaining the regret she had for the last words she'd ever exchanged with her—invited disaster. As long as the fate of the two beings she most loved—her mother and Archie—hung in the balance, Annie's only hope lay in going on with her life, her work. In going through the motions. She could fall apart later.

"Mr. Gleeson?"

Gleeson shifted from one foot to the other, his expression never losing its defiance.

"I know better than to carry a loaded firearm inside the park."

"Is that so? There seems little doubt, from the statement given the arresting law enforcement officer by a witness, that you were carrying one on Friday."

"I can explain why. I'd camped the night before outside the park's borders, to hunt. But when I decided to hike inside the park, I unloaded my gun. That morning, I stopped to rest, up above Trout Lake. While I was sitting there, minding my own business, I saw the wolf. It was circling me. I knew right then it was me or the wolf. That's when I loaded my gun. To protect myself."

Annie's gaze had been glued to Gleeson, but a sound from Justine—a clearing-of-her-throat that Annie recognized as a signal—drew her attention to the door of the courtroom.

Will McCarroll stood, manila envelope in hand. Staring at Gleeson with unabashed contempt, he looked astonishingly like one of the predators he so doggedly protected.

Annie stifled a sigh.

Will noticed Annie looking at him and nodded, but Annie did not respond. She turned her attention back to Gleeson.

"Are you asserting that you shot the wolf in self-defense, Mr. Gleeson?"

Owens jumped to his feet again.

"My client's life was endangered, Your Honor. If we were to go to trial, we're confident we'd be successful in establishing self-defense. However, we're also confident that, after hearing my client explain the course of events today, you'll drop all charges. There's no need to waste Your Honor's, and the government's, time and money on this matter."

"Very well, Mr. Owens. You may proceed."

Owens whispered in Gleeson's ear. The two exchanged a few brief words, then Gleeson began.

"As I said earlier, Your Honor, I started the morning out just outside the park's northern border, but then I decided I wanted to hike into the park."

"For what purpose, Mr. Gleeson?"

"Why does anyone hike in Yellowstone?" he replied sarcastically. "I'm a nature lover. Us hunters appreciate nature and wild animals more than these Easterners and foreigners who drive through expecting to see a wolf or a grizzly from the backseat of a fancy car. I'm willing to hike, and put work into seeing the wildlife this park has to offer."

Reporters in the gallery scribbled furiously in notepads as he continued. Recording devices were banned inside the courtroom.

"I'd camped outside the night before, then, like I said, I headed into the park for a hike. I'd been walking since before daylight, and I was tired, so I stopped, sat down on a log."

*"That's a lie."*

Will McCarroll jumped up from his seat at the prosecutor's table.

Annie turned on him sharply.

"Ranger McCarroll, you know better than to—"

"I can prove he's lying," Will went on, undaunted, waving the envelope in the air. "I have photographs. May I?"

Without waiting for a reply, he started toward the bench, envelope extended in the air.

Incensed, Owens jumped back to his feet.

"This is outrageous, Your Honor. My client was asked to testify and this man just interrupted him. And now he's approaching the bench without your permission!"

Annie glared at Will.

"Ranger McCarroll, sit back down."

"But Your Honor . . ."

"Now. Or I'll have you physically removed, and cited for contempt."

Will dropped like deadweight into his seat, but then turned determinedly to the man sitting beside him at the prosecutor's table. The assistant United States attorney,

Thomas Windstalker, a forty-five-year-old Cooke City resident with a sterling reputation—sterling enough to risk angering a judge—knew and trusted Will.

"Your Honor," he said, "may I have a brief consultation with Ranger McCarroll? After all, he was the arresting officer. If he has pertinent information, I should see it."

Annie debated calling a brief recess, or chastising Will and Windstalker for not meeting before the arraignment, but she knew that after taking Archie to the vet in Gardiner, Will had spent the entire night on horseback, searching for her mother. Plus, her physical state was so tenuous that she feared any delay would result in her having to cancel the arraignment, which would no doubt end up with someone else called in to hear it. And nothing—nothing—would force her to do that.

If Agent Richter and Sheriff Holmberg's theory that what happened to her mother and dog was an attempt to pressure her off the bench, she would not allow those responsible the satisfaction of knowing they'd succeeded to any degree.

"Go ahead," she said. "But make it quick."

Windstalker leaned sideways and listened as Will spoke to him in a low, but clearly agitated voice. Then Windstalker took the proffered envelope and stood.

"Your Honor," he said, "I'd like to approach the bench."

Annie felt the room begin to sway. Dry heaves would follow shortly, within minutes.

"Very well," she said testily. "Both parties please approach the bench."

"I'd like for Ranger McCarroll to be included," Windstalker said.

Annie's sigh was audible.

"All right."

Once assembled before her, Windstalker took the photograph out of the envelope Will had given him and slid it across the surface of the desk to Annie. He looked toward Will.

"Will?"

Will stepped forward. He pointed to the faint outline on the ground.

"Gleeson claims he had just arrived at the spot where he shot Twenty-one, but as you can see, there was a tent at that site. It had snowed a little during that night, but it all melted by midmorning. The tent has to have been there between the time it snowed, which I can show to be around midnight, and early that morning. But it had been taken down by the time the hiker who went to investigate the shot he heard arrived on the scene."

"Meaning what, Mr. McCarroll?"

"Meaning Gleeson didn't camp outside the park that night."

"What does it matter where he camped?" Owens said.

"For starters," Will replied, "you need a permit to camp in that country."

Owens's face lit with a grin.

"So charge him with not obtaining a permit. Hell, we'll plead guilty right here and now and be done with all of this."

Will looked up at Annie.

"It also means Gleeson lied, Your Honor. And if he lied about where he camped, what's to say he's not lying about Twenty-one attacking him?"

Annie fell silent, staring at the photograph for a full two minutes.

"Please return to your tables," she said.

As the group settled into their seats, Annie looked out at the courtroom. The reporters watched intently, pens poised. Other onlookers studied her, trying to predict the outcome of the arraignment. Some looked ready to mutiny.

"Mr. Gleeson, please rise," Annie said.

Gleeson slowly straightened, a defiant glare on his sullen face.

"Based on the evidence before the court today, I find that probable cause exists to support both of the government's charges against you. I hereby declare that you shall stand trial, the date of which will be set within twenty-four hours. You are not to leave this jurisdiction during that time, Mr. Gleeson. Do you understand? Bail is set at fifty thousand dollars."

Hands curled into fists, Gleeson took a step toward the bench, shouting, "I shot that fuckin' wolf in self-defense."

Owens sprinted to grab his client. Annie signaled a guard.

"You just upped your bail to a hundred thousand. Take him away."

Gleeson was far from ready to give in. He fought Owens, and had almost broken free of the lawyer's grasp when two guards descended upon him. As they physically pushed him toward the door leading to the back of the building, where a car waited to take him to the jail, he spewed more venomous words Annie's way.

"You're messing with the wrong man," he said. "The wrong people."

Annie didn't miss a beat.

"Two hundred thousand," she said matter of factly. "And a contempt of court citation."

Pounding the gavel once, she stood. Hopefully she'd make it to her chambers before the dry heaves hit.

Justine could read what was happening from the look on Annie's face.

"Court dismissed," she ordered angrily. "Everyone on their feet."

# FIVE

"MIGHT NOT BE SUCH A GOOD IDEA TO GO BACK THERE."

Will McCarroll paused, hand on the knob of the 102-year-old door that led to the back of the jailhouse, and turned to look at Ranger Lynze O'Connor, who was seated at a desk in the building's receiving room. Lynze monitored the building's comings and goings, a duty she hated for the simple reason that it kept her inside, which isn't why she'd come to Yellowstone.

The creases at the corners of Will's eyes signaled that her warning had missed its mark.

Not much made Will McCarroll smile. But pissed-off prisoners were a sure thing. And this morning's arraignment meant Chad Gleeson would, indeed, stand trial for killing 21.

"Which one?" he replied. "The arsonist? Or the East Coast asshole I caught tracking that moose?"

"Both. But it's the New Yorker who worries me. He's really mad, Will. There's something really creepy about him. I heard him telling your arsonist guy that he's got powerful connections and he's going to use them to come after you." Lynze paused, scrunched her pretty features into a look of earnest confusion. "Is there still Mafia in New York?"

Grinning, Will disappeared through the door.

"McCarroll, you son of a bitch."

Will's eyes scanned the holding cells on either side of the room. Large enclosures with wood slat floors, each with a sink, a bench that ran along the back wall, two cots, and on each outside wall, high—nine feet off the ground—a long slit of a window, armed with black iron bars.

This morning, Will counted three occupants, two men on one side, a juvenile male on the other. The two men he recognized. He'd arrested both, in separate incidents, the previous afternoon and evening, before he got the call about Judge Peacock's mom being kidnapped.

The younger of the two had jumped to his feet at the first sight of Will. Now he stood, clutching the bars, looking almost skinny enough to slither through them. He wore the same wire-rimmed glasses, T-shirt, hiking shorts, brown Smartwool socks, and leather sandals Will had arrested him in. In terms of outward appearance, he looked more like a tree hugger than a wildlands arsonist.

Will stopped even with him.

"Mornin', Hank. Thought I'd come by to see if you'd gotten a good night's sleep."

"Son of a bitch," Hank repeated. "This place constitutes cruel and inhumane punishment. I'm gonna report you to my lawyer when I get out."

"I think it's 'cruel and unusual,' Hank," Will replied, smiling, "but you go right ahead and do that. I agree, this place could use some updating. All that's lacking is something called a 'budgetary allotment,' which the current administration doesn't seem inclined to worry much about. But you look to me like a man with considerable influence. Maybe after your stay here you can get things rolling with your friends back in DC."

Hank missed the sarcasm entirely.

"You can't keep me locked up. Not for something as stupid as starting a fire. I told you. I didn't know they were prohibited."

As he toyed with Hank, Will kept an eye on the New Yorker. Despite the fact that the impeccably groomed, Cabela's-clad prisoner appeared entirely absorbed in picking at the dirt under his manicured nails, Will knew he wasn't missing any of the interaction between Will and Hank.

"Far as I can figure," Will said to Hank, "you passed no less than six signs after you left Pebble Creek. Not to mention the talk you got from the backcountry office when you applied for your camping permit. I just came from visiting the ranger there. He remembered you. And the list of rules and regs he gave you."

Like a macaw with a meager vocabulary, Hank repeated, "Son of a bitch," then turned and skulked to the bench at the back wall.

He dropped down on it, keeping his distance from the New Yorker—who was the real reason Will had stopped by this morning, on his way out of Mammoth. Will could never get out of the busy park headquarters and back into the hills fast enough, but his evidence against the suspected poacher was pretty much all circumstantial. It might not stand up in Judge Peacock's court. If that happened to be the case, he wanted to make sure he provided his own form of deterrence.

"What about you, Mr. Biagi?" Will said, as if he'd just noticed the other man. "How'd you sleep?"

"Fuck you," Biagi replied without looking up from his hands, the right one of which sported a gigantic gold ring with an emerald.

He couldn't see the grin this brought to Will's face, but Will sensed he felt it.

"So what're you thinking of those buddies of yours this morning?" Will said. "You sitting up all night on that hard bench, while they're back at camp, drinking coffee and eating sausage and eggs cooked over a fire, bragging about the six pointer they shot yesterday. Right about now, they're just hoping you got yourself lost last night. Hopin' to see you limp into camp soon."

Biagi never stopped his manicure.

"Think they'll show face here when you don't come back? Mammoth isn't exactly one of their favorite places, you know, it being park headquarters and all."

Will could see his baiting was getting to Biagi.

"'Course, they're good businessmen. They'll eventually show up." Will paused. "So who is your outfitter?"

For the first time since the previous evening, Biagi made eye contact.

"You can't question me without my attorney here."

"Maybe if you tell me who it is," Will continued, unfazed, "I can rustle him up for you and we can get you out of here just as soon as you go before the judge this afternoon."

"This afternoon? Last night the guard told me I'd see the judge this morning."

Will would normally have delivered the news that the arraignment was delayed with glee, but armed with the knowledge of what had caused the delay, he delivered it somberly.

"Judge Peacock's a little busy this morning. But don't worry. Rules say we gotta arraign you within twenty-four hours, then if we've got probable cause, we can hold you 'til trial. Unless someone comes in and posts bail. 'Course for someone like you, I imagine posting bail won't be a problem. You sure you don't want to tell me to get ahold of your outfitter?"

"I came here alone."

*Alone and with a hunting rifle and jacket full of ammunition.*

Will flashed a smile.

"Yeah, and I'm the pope."

"Fuck you."

Will was getting nowhere. Stepping so close to the bars that his nose brushed cold steel, he lowered his voice.

"You listen to me, Biagi. When your guide either works up the courage to bail you out of here or you're done seeing Judge Peacock, you tell the son of a bitch something. You tell him that the next time he brings some fat cat in here from the East Coast with promises of bagging something exotic—something for everyone to get their rocks off about—I'm gonna nail not just his client, but him too. I'm gonna' shut him down. And then see that he rots in a federal prison."

Biagi stared at the wall behind Will, but Will could see he was listening.

"And if you're smart you'll get your money back. 'Cause if I ever see you in this park again, with or without that fancy rifle that's waiting out there for you, I'll arrest you on sight. You're not welcome back here, Biagi. You come within ten miles of Yellowstone and I'll know it. I'll *smell* it. And you don't want that. I promise you, you don't want that."

For the first time, Biagi smiled.

"Oh, I'll be back," he said.

That was it.

Will reached for the Taser gun hanging from his belt.

The last time he'd used it was when a prisoner threw feces at him through the bars.

Somehow Biagi's smirk made him just as crazy as the shit had.

"Holy fuck," Hank cried, falling backward until the back of his knees hit the bench. He looked over at his cellmate.

"He's not kidding around."

Just then the door into the holding area opened.

Lynze O'Connor appeared. Her eyes widened when she saw Will's hand on the Taser gun.

Will glared at Biagi.

Lynze took it all in in silence, then said, "Will, Peter Shewmaker's on the phone for you."

Eyes fixed on Biagi, Will said, "Tell him I'll call him back."

Lynze paused just a heartbeat, then replied, "He said it's important. He knows you're here. If I tell him you can't talk to him, you know he'll just head right over here."

Lynze gave Will one last look, then disappeared as the door closed behind her.

Will knew Lynze was right. Shewmaker's office was only a hundred yards away. It infuriated him when Will tried to avoid him.

Will dropped his hand to his side.

Biagi knew better than to grin outright, but before he turned away, Will saw the smug look on his face. It took every ounce of restraint not to pull the Taser gun out again.

As Will strolled to the door, Hank—obviously emboldened by the new turn of events—called out.

"Hey, Grizzly Adams. I saw something last night. Something I think you'd be interested in. Maybe I'd be willing to tell you what it was if you drop the charges against me."

"You're full of shit, Hank," Will replied, his stride never slowing.

"I'm not messin' with you, McCarroll. I saw something going on last night, at that building over there. The one by Liberty Cap. Before all the sirens and shit started."

The only structure by Liberty Cap was Judge Peacock's house.

Will stopped, turned, studied Hank.

He was a skinny thing. Weak as an elk calf born too early. Only way he could've seen anything that the others hadn't seen at the same time—in which case they'd all be pleading with Will right now to cut a deal—would've been if he'd been looking out the window. And that would've required hanging by it with his bare hands.

No way in hell could Hank even pull himself up to the bars, let alone hang there long enough to see anything. Hank must be a little smarter than Will took him for, trying a story like that.

"Yeah right," Will said sarcastically. He was halfway to the door when Hank tried again.

"I couldn't actually see what happened back behind the house, 'cause that's where the vehicle pulled in. But I could hear some shouting. And I saw it when it pulled away."

Will froze, then swirled around to face him.

"What did you see?" he said, striding toward where Hank stood, clutching the bars again.

"If you want to know that, you'll have to cut me a deal."

Will reached through the bars, grabbed Hank by the neck.

"You'd better not be pulling my chain," he said.

Hank's form went limp when Will tightened his grasp.

"I'm telling you the truth. I saw something last night. I'll tell you everything if you let me out of here. If you get the judge to let me off."

Will let him loose, and reached for the keys in his pocket. Keeping an eye on Biagi, he opened the door, turned Hank around, and pulled both skinny arms behind his meatless torso. As he slid a pair of handcuffs on his wrists, he said, "We're going to see the judge right now. You'd better be able to back up what you just said or you're in a whole lot of trouble."

Lynze O'Connor's expression registered almost as much amusement as it did surprise when Will walked back through the door, pushing Hank ahead of him.

"What a morning," she said, shaking her head. "Peter finally hung up. My guess is he's on his way over here right now."

Will looked around, glanced out the window behind where she sat.

"Where's Gleeson? LE should have brought him over here by now."

"They did," Lynze replied. "But Heck Buckley's attorney was waiting here. He'd already posted Gleeson and Buckley's bail. Can you believe it? They took off in Buckley's Hummer right before you got here."

"Son of a bitch," Will said.


Rod Holmberg and the FBI agent Will had met the night before at the stone house—he couldn't remember his name now—were just walking down the courthouse steps when Will pulled up to the Pagoda Building with Hank.

He rolled down his window, and called to them.

"You fellas are gonna want to hear this," he said.

Holmberg made a beeline to Will's SUV. The two men had worked together several years earlier, when Holmberg was first elected, on a case in which a poacher fled to Livingston, where Holmberg arrested him. They'd developed an instant liking and respect for one another.

"What's up, Will?" Holmberg asked.

"Judge Peacock still inside?"

"Yes, we just finished bringing her up-to-date. She was going to leave for the vet, to check on her dog, but I don't think she has yet."

Will nodded toward the passenger seat.

"I arrested this guy yesterday afternoon. He spent last night in jail. He's got something he wants to tell us. I think Judge Peacock should hear too."

Holmberg bent his long frame to get a peek inside at Hank. Agent Richter had caught up and now stood directly behind him, looking on.

"Okay," Holmberg said. "I'll go catch her before she leaves. See you inside."

# SIX

"YOU'RE TELLING US THAT YOU SAW A VEHICLE APPROACH the stone building adjacent to the Liberty Cap last night, sometime after dark?"

Hank didn't like the way this was going. He thought that all he'd have to do was tell that asshole McCarroll what he'd seen, then, in exchange for the information, he'd be let loose to go home. He hadn't expected this—two big, tough-looking motherfuckers, one from the FBI, the other a sheriff, grilling him. Plus Will—*and* the judge. Of course, she pretty much just sat silently, staring at him. But that was almost worse than the third degree these other jerks were giving him.

Hell, he hadn't expected this at all.

Still, he couldn't afford to be found guilty of setting that fire. And considering the fact that he did set it, and that that little weirdo backcountry ranger who issued him his camping permit had, indeed, told him he couldn't set a fire—so it'd be his word against Hank's, and two guesses who'd win that one?—it looked like the odds of his getting convicted were pretty fucking good. In which case, he'd just end up having to go to jail. 'Cause he sure as hell didn't have any money to pay a fine. Or get himself a real attorney.

So he'd better handle this right. It might just be his only chance.

Luckily, the judge looked pretty damn upset. Hank knew that something big and bad had happened the night before—even if he hadn't pulled himself up to look half a dozen times to watch the goings-on, he'd've been able to know that from all the lights and sirens—so he'd figured what he saw before law enforcement showed up would be valuable. But hell, this was like hitting the lotto. After the FBI dude slipped up and called the creepy stone building next to that dildo they call Liberty Cap the judge's "residence," Hank could hardly believe his luck. He hadn't just been a witness to a crime—it had happened at the judge's own fucking house! No wonder she looked like that. He'd heard somebody whisper somethin' about her mother being missing. Hell, if she had that much at stake, she'd jump at the chance to let him walk—if, in exchange, he gave them information that could help them find who did it.

And the information he had could definitely lead them to who did it. All they'd have to do is drive around, and eventually, they'd find it.

Hell, he'd recognized that white Suburban right off the bat. He'd seen it all over Gardiner, and up by Jardine a whole bunch of times too. Didn't know who it belonged to, but even after dark, when it passed under the streetlamp where the driveway met the road, he could see the tan panel they'd used to replace the front right fender. Looked like crap, but then half the vehicles in Gardiner—at least during the winter, it wasn't true once the tourists starting coming through—looked at least as bad. Yep, all he had to do was tell the judge that, and he'd walk. A free man. Lesson learned.

Hell, he hadn't meant any harm by the fire. No way he would've let it get out of control. But it had been cold up there. What were the odds that asshole Will McCarroll would be up that far above Pebble Creek? He'd had an earlier run-in with him, years ago, but luckily McCarroll didn't seem to remember it. 'Cause McCarroll seemed to Hank like a man who held a grudge. An angry man.

Of course, a lot of those backcountry rangers were

oddballs. They had to be to want to spend that much time alone. Hank understood in a way. He was a loner too. But Will McCarroll—Hank had heard McCarroll took being a loner to another level altogether. Yep, there was something not right about that Will McCarroll. The guy liked his job just a little too much.

A voice suddenly jerked Hank out of his musings.

"What else did you see?"

It was the crew cut, commando guy now.

"I told you. I saw the SUV pull in behind the stone house about a half hour after it got dark. I couldn't actually see it after it pulled in 'cause it pulled around back. Then, maybe ten or fifteen minutes later, I heard voices. Kind of like shouting at each other, but still trying to be quiet, if that makes sense."

"Go on. What did the voices sound like?"

"The loudest one was a dude. He was like yelling at someone. There were a couple others, but they weren't as loud. One of 'em sounded like an old lady."

The judge gasped.

Good. He had her. Hank summoned up a sympathetic look her way.

He wouldn't just get let off on the arson thing, he might just end up some kind of hero. He liked the idea of being a hero for Annie Peacock. She might be a little old for him, and a judge, but she was hot.

"Go on," the commando ordered.

"When I heard that—the voices—I pulled myself back up for another look. I had the feeling something bad was happening. I still couldn't see anything 'cause they were still parked behind the building. That's where the voices were coming from—from behind the house."

"What happened next?"

"Well, after a minute or two, the SUV suddenly just shoots out of the driveway, headed this way, toward Mammoth. I mean, something had happened 'cause the gravel was flying and they were definitely in a hurry to get out of there."

The sheriff took over again. They were tag teaming him. He'd seen them do this on *NYPD* reruns.

"How good a glimpse of the vehicle did you get?"

"Good enough to tell you what it was." Both the sheriff and the FBI guy leaned forward at this comment. It gave Hank a sense of power. "Chevy Suburban. White."

"What year?" Holmberg asked.

"Don't know. It's older. I've seen it—"

Suddenly the judge's hand shot out, like she was a cop directing traffic or something. She'd been sitting there, just staring at him, almost like she wasn't processing any of what was going on in front of her—which had begun to worry Hank. He was almost glad to see her come alive.

But when he heard her voice, how pissed off she sounded, Hank got scared. Real scared.

"If you thought something bad was going on," the judge said, her voice measured, her eyes so intense and angry that Hank just wanted to look away, but he knew that would make it look like he was lying, so he didn't dare, "why didn't you call the jail's guard and report it?"

"Report it?" Hank echoed, thrown off as much by the question as the crazy look on her face.

"Yes. Report it," she echoed back, her voice no longer measured. "Didn't it occur to you that you could have made a difference? That you might have been able to stop them . . . ?"

All it took was a gesture from the sheriff—his reaching out, touching her forearm—and a single word—"Judge . . ."—and Annie Peacock seemed to shrink, right before Hank's eyes.

"I'm sorry," she said. "I know better."

Holmberg gave her a reassuring look, then turned back to Hank.

"Let's get back to the Suburban. You said you'd seen it before. Up here, in Mammoth? Or in Gardiner?"

Hank's mind raced. He had to think real quick. Things weren't going so well. The judge may have said she was sorry but she didn't look too happy with him.

Maybe he shouldn't blow his whole wad right now. He'd better hold onto some of it, for when she calmed down a little bit. Then he could reason with her. Maybe even still turn out the hero.

Yep, that's what he'd better do. Not give them everything. At least not right now.

If they were gonna play hardball, he could play their game.

"I just meant I've seen white Suburbans like the one I saw last night. They're all over the place."

"You didn't recognize this one in particular? There weren't any distinctive markings on it? A stripe? Maybe a business name?"

Hank's mind flashed on the rusty panel on the front right bumper.

"I didn't see nothin' unusual," he said. "'Course, it was dark. And like I said, it was moving pretty fast when it pulled out of there."

"Anything else you'd like to tell us?"

"No, not really."

The sheriff stared at him for a good thirty seconds. Then he looked at the FBI creep, who shook his head. Holmberg nodded at Will.

"You can take him back now."

"Back?" Hank echoed. "You mean back to jail? Wait a minute. I told you what I saw. I thought we had a deal . . ."

*"Deal?"*

It was the judge again. If she looked pissed off before, right now she looked ready to sentence someone to die. By decapitation. But it was Will McCarroll she was staring at, not Hank.

"You offered this man some kind of deal?"

McCarroll had been standing behind Hank all during the interview, but a few seconds earlier, when Holmberg gave him the nod, he'd moved to Hank's side, and grabbed him by the arm. The man had hands of fucking steel. Still, Hank could feel his grip on his arm clamp down even harder at the judge's words.

McCarroll froze, then real slowlike, let go of Hank's arm, and straightened to full height to face the judge. Hank figured McCarroll stood about six foot one, but at that moment he looked to Hank a little taller than that.

Hank had to give the guy credit—he definitely wasn't intimidated by her.

"Pardon me?" McCarroll said, but the way he said it, it sounded to Hank a lot more like *"What the fuck did you just say?"*

The judge wasn't about to back down. Hank sensed these two had some kind of history.

"Who gave you the authority to strike a deal with this man?"

Annie Peacock said it in a way that clearly meant McCarroll would be in a whole shitload of trouble if that's what had happened.

For a moment, Hank considered the possibilities here: of telling the judge that's just what McCarroll had done—offered him a deal—but when he looked at the man—at the expression on his face, and the electric feeling emanating from his posture—he decided that might be buying more trouble than he'd already bought.

McCarroll took a while to answer.

"The only deal struck with this man," he said, his disdain for the question audible, "was that he'd tell us what he saw last night, from his cell. I never promised him anything in return."

Judge Peacock looked at Hank.

"Is that true, Mr. Vincent?"

For a moment Hank waivered, but then he stole another look at McCarroll and stuttered, "I guess so. Technically anyway. But I just figured . . ."

It was hard to tell what would have made Judge Peacock more angry—if Hank had said McCarroll did, indeed, offer him a deal to talk, or if he denied it. There was no mistaking the fact that she looked mad as hell right now.

"You figured?" she parroted. "I think what you figured, Mr. Vincent, is that you could stand by last night and watch a crime being committed and not even bother to mention it to anyone who might be able to do anything to stop it. But today, when you realized it might help you out of your predicament, you've decided to become a Good Samaritan."

She paused to let her words settle in.

"Take him away."

Will jerked Hank out of his chair by the arm.

They headed for the door, beyond which was parked the law enforcement vehicle that would take Hank back to the jail.

"Ranger McCarroll?"

They were almost through the door when Judge Peacock's voice stopped them in their tracks.

Will turned, slowly again. He looked at her, but didn't say a word.

"I may have been out of line just now," she said. "I should not have accused you of making a deal."

Will did not hesitate. He met her eyes with a stare so cold that even Hank couldn't believe the guy was that heartless.

"You got that right," he said.

And then he ushered Hank out of the room.

# SEVEN

"I LIKE TO SAY THAT YELLOWSTONE IS NOT A PLACE, IT'S a process."

The *click click click* of cameras had become so commonplace to Interpretive Ranger Randy Hannah that he no longer noticed it, nor the video cameras pointed his way.

Twenty-six tourists hung on his every word. Behind him, as if putting on a show for the photographers, Angel Terrace spouted ribbons of steam, its blindingly white surface brilliant and translucent in the morning sun.

Not unlike the heat that radiated in waves off Angel Terrace, Ranger Hannah radiated enthusiasm for his job. While many of the seasonal park rangers hailed from the East—and came to work at Yellowstone without first educating themselves about the West, or the park itself—Randy had grown up in Idaho; rafting its rivers, fly-fishing its streams, snowshoeing in the Sawtooth Mountains. Randy's passion had long been wilderness. The opportunity to live and work in the park, which had come to Randy four years earlier, upon graduation from the University of Montana with a degree in environmental studies, had only fueled that passion. That showed; and visitors, some of whom had come thousands of miles to escape the humdrum of their daily lives, and to be inspired and awed, simply ate it up.

"Let's move on now to Canary Springs," Randy said after

explaining to the crowd that they now stood on top of one of the world's most powerful and deadly sites—a giant caldera that—when it blew, which should take place within the next sixty thousand years—would annihilate not only all of Yellowstone and the neighboring country, but change the climate of the entire world.

"Yellowstone's hot springs represent some of Earth's most extreme conditions. Yet certain organisms not only survive here—they thrive.

"This amazing palette of colors is created by billions of microorganisms called thermophiles that thrive under conditions that would kill a human being—heat and gases. Different species flourish under different conditions—for example, some like cooler temperatures, others hot. Some prosper in the presence of gases, they take nutrition from them, while others may find the gases such as hydrogen sulfide—especially where they're strongest, at the vents— deadly. Each winter a bison or two will die while trying to find warmth near the vents. Another factor is whether the water is calm or swirling. Finally, light—some love shade, the others like bright light. Cyanobacteria use light for energy; however, the hydrogen sulfide is lethal to them. Other gas-loving thermophiles consume the hydrogen sulfide near the vents. It's a perfectly balanced system. Really phenomenal. Absolutely phenomenal."

At times, Hannah seemed almost rhapsodic.

"Do you smell that odor? That's hydrogen sulfide gas. Threadlike filamentous microorganisms love the stuff. They link up in chains and live on the hydrogen sulfide coming up through the vents."

After Randy guided the crowd along the upper terraces— from Canary, to New Blue, to newly active springs on top of Minerva—he thanked them for their attention, bid them all a safe trip and, after answering a few questions, lifted his felt hat from his head and swiped at the sweat on his brow. It was going to be another hot one. He was glad to have the Terrace Walk tour over with early in the day.

He turned to head back to the boardwalk that led to the

Lower Terraces, then on to the Albright Visitor Center where he was set to do desk-duty for the next four hours. It wasn't until then that he noticed two visitors—a fortyish man and his young son—still standing there, looking at him apprehensively, as though they wanted to talk to him but didn't have the nerve. Somehow the boy looked familiar.

Randy flashed his warm smile as he approached them. He directed his question at the boy, as something told him he was the reason the two had lingered.

"Any questions you'd like me to answer before I leave?"

Then the recollection of the cherubic face in front of him now, standing at the front of a recent crowd earlier that summer, eagerly hanging on Randy's every word, kicked in.

"You've been at some of my other talks, haven't you?" he said, his grin growing. Randy took great pleasure in encouraging the interest of young visitors to the park. Like a Mormon youth on a mission, his belief—that his most important responsibility as a ranger was to instill an appreciation and love for Yellowstone and all its wildness in the young people who would one day be responsible for ensuring its protection and survival—energized him each minute of each day on the job. It didn't matter how hot the sun beat down on him as he stood in wool pants and felt hat next to hot springs that generated additional waves of heat, if a kid wanted to learn more about the geothermal features of Yellowstone, or the wolves, or the bears, Randy Hannah would oblige him until he dropped from sheer exhaustion.

The boy looked up, nervously, at his father, who cleared his throat.

"Yes, you did see Zach here earlier. A week ago. We spent several days in Mammoth and Zach spent practically every minute here on the boardwalk."

The lack of enthusiasm in the man's voice made Randy think something was wrong.

"How can I help you?"

Again, the father answered for his son.

"We left Mammoth, kind of in a hurry, and went down to Yellowstone Lake. And then Canyon Village. We hadn't planned to come back this way, but Zach insisted. He's been pretty upset ever since we left." Now the father, who remained nameless, looked down at the boy, grave concern reflected on his newly tanned face. "Zach?"

Zach's chin quivered as he finally raised his eyes to meet Randy's.

"I made some of the springs dry up. I put coins and stuff in them." A tear dropped from one eye. "I knew I wasn't supposed to. You said that in your talk—that no one should touch the water, or put anything in it, 'cause it could change it. That it could ruin what it took hundreds of years to make. I did it anyway."

Randy could hardly bear to see the torment the boy clearly felt.

"Zach," he said. "Listen to me. You're right, I said all that. And it's wrong to put anything in the waters here, even your finger—especially your finger 'cause you could get seriously burned. What you did was wrong, Zach, but I also told you that things here are constantly changing. The springs never stay the same. Remember how I said that years ago Minerva was the biggest attraction here at Mammoth?"

Zach shook his head.

Randy pointed down below them, to a vast, dry expanse of limestone. It cascaded in steps down toward the road below them.

"Look at Minerva now. It's been dry like that for years. But there are brand-new springs on top. I just saw them for the first time last week. What you did was wrong, and I thank you for admitting it to me, but I can see you've learned your lesson. And I don't want you feeling responsible for some little fluctuation in a spring or mudpot here."

Zach's face livened up.

"It's not little. There was water there one day, then it just all went away. Right after I put my stuff in it."

Randy put a hand on Zach's shoulder.

"Where? Can you show me?"

Zach looked up at his dad. It was clear they'd discussed how to handle this.

Kevin Knudtsen nodded solemnly.

"Follow me," Zach said.


"Just a little ways more," Zach Knudtsen said over his shoulder as Randy and Zach's father followed him along Upper Terrace Drive. They'd left the boardwalk and hurried past Cupid's Spring, the New Highland, and White Elephant Terraces. As they approached Orange Spring Mound, Zach pointed to a parched area.

"See," he cried. "It's dried up. All the water's gone."

"But Zach," Randy said, "New Highland Terrace has been dry for a long time."

"Not there," the boy said, his finger—less chubby than it had been two weeks earlier, when the Knudtsen family arrived in Yellowstone—pointed beyond the parched ground in front of them.

Randy squinted.

"You went back there?" he said. "Zach, that's off limits. It could be dangerous back there. A lot of this area is just a thin crust covering springs so hot they'll burn right through your boots."

Zach had already stepped onto the forbidden zone. His father did not react. He seemed to have turned things over to Randy.

Randy grabbed Zach by the arm.

"You can't go back there. And I'm telling you, you didn't do anything to dry this area up."

The boy resisted turning around. When he did, Randy saw that tears ran down his cheeks.

"I did," Zach said. "I know I did."

Randy gently pulled the boy back to safe ground.

"Tell me," he said, bending down, eye to eye with him.

"I walked around there," Zach said, pointing to the outer edge of an area that had clearly once teemed with water. "I saw a little water squirting in the air and I wanted to get closer."

"There are some vents back there," Randy responded. "Sometimes they look like small geysers."

Zach nodded.

"See? Now you can't see them."

Randy straightened, looked in the direction Zach had pointed, squinting.

"You wait here. I'm going back to look. But you have to promise me you won't follow. Do you promise?"

Zach seemed relieved to have Randy take him seriously. He nodded emphatically.

Randy looked toward the nameless father.

"I'll keep him here," he said.

Randy picked his way across the chalky, ash-colored travertine that had formed when water heated by the magma chamber lying under the Yellowstone Caldera combined with gases containing carbon dioxide as they rose through the limestone, dissolving it. The limestone had been left behind when the inland ocean that covered the area during the Paleozoic era receded. When that heated water reached the surface, the carbon dioxide gas it carried was released and the dissolved limestone precipitated out, depositing travertine. It was the travertine that formed the terraces and other features seen at Mammoth.

Travertine was especially delicate, but despite his admonition to Zach, Randy knew he was on safe ground. Each interpretive ranger was assigned certain hot springs to monitor regularly. It had been two years since Randy had been assigned anything from the Upper Terraces, but he knew the ground he walked on could support his weight. As he skirted New Highland, he started getting excited about seeing the springs that he knew Zach was referring to. A lot of the rangers didn't get into the geothermal aspects of the park, but—apparently like young Zach—Randy found the entire process fascinating and exciting beyond compare.

He turned to give Zach a reassuring glance before disappearing around a hill. The boy stood staring at him anxiously.

With a smile and a little wave, Randy continued around the rise.

Then he stopped in his tracks.

The last time he'd been up there, springs bubbled and steamed across the entire area. Small geysers, maybe four of them, shot water and hot gases skyward.

What he faced now was parched travertine. Not a drop of water within sight.

Oddly, however, there had been water. Recently. Geologists were able to tell when an area last had water by the color of the surface. Randy, being the enthusiastic student he was, had learned the science.

Scowling, he lowered himself to a crouching position, eyeing the orange filamentous bacteria that had recently been entombed in a coat of travertine.

Zach was right.

There had been water there. Recently. Perhaps as recently as Zach had said.

Standing again, he picked his way carefully back to where Zach and his father stood.

Upon seeing the look on Randy's face, Zach's expression mirrored both triumph—at being proved right—and grief.

"See?" he said. "It's all my fault."

"No," Randy told him emphatically, although his voice no longer held quite the same tone. "It isn't your fault, Zach. I told you, Yellowstone is constantly changing. You didn't cause it to dry up back there. It's just a coincidence."

Finally the father spoke up again.

With a sigh, he said, "Zach feels that he should turn himself in."

Randy studied the boy.

"Zach," he said, putting his hand on Zach's shoulder. "How about this? You've turned yourself in already. To a ranger in Yellowstone. You did the right thing. You came to me and told me what you'd done."

"That's all?" Zach said, his eyes instantly brightening. "I don't have to go to jail?"

Despite the nagging feeling tugging at him at that moment, it wasn't the least bit difficult for Randy to summon a smile.

"No," he said. He paused, then followed with, "Are you enrolled in the Junior Ranger Program?"

"Yes," Zach replied eagerly.

"Did you get your badge yet?"

Zach's spirits nosedived as quickly as they'd just risen.

"I didn't think I could get one now."

"Well, you can," Randy said. "And you should. 'Cause I can tell you love this park. If you didn't, you wouldn't feel so badly about what you did."

Randy glanced at his watch.

"How about this? I've got to make a quick stop first, but then I'm heading over to the visitor center. Why don't you and your dad meet me there, and I'll see that you get that badge?"

Zach looked up at his dad. It was clear the incident had caused some tension between the two.

"Can I?" he said.

Kevin Knudtsen reached for Zach's hand.

"Of course."

Then he turned to Randy. Randy could almost see the words squeezing past the lump in Knudtsen's throat. Damn if Randy didn't feel one too.

"Thank you," Knudtsen said.

"You bet," Randy answered.

# EIGHT

A BLAST OF LATE AFTERNOON HEAT MET ANNIE AS SHE stepped out the back door of the courthouse. Instinctively, she turned toward the stone house, already practically able to smell the dinner her mother would be fussing over in the kitchen. And then the sight of her Subaru caught her, and Annie's temporary insanity—her brief reprieve from reality—evaporated.

Annie never drove to work. Her house was located not more than a couple football fields away. But after calling Dr. Kennedy when she got to work that morning and hearing she could pick up Archie at the end of the day, she'd run home to get her car. She didn't want anything to delay getting her beloved Lab back, not even by the few minutes it would take to walk over and get the car. She couldn't bear another night alone in that house.

The news Archie would survive the brutal attack—he'd been shot twice, and kicked repeatedly in the head and ribs—and the prospect of getting him back had been the only thing keeping her going the past few days.

Oblivious to the crowds always coming and going just outside the Pagoda Building, Annie made a beeline for her car, which was parked behind the building.

"Judge Peacock?"

Her hand already on the Subaru's door handle, Annie

debated briefly about opening it and just climbing inside without responding. Especially since she thought she recognized the voice.

She closed her eyes, took a deep breath, and turned, with a sense of dread.

She almost didn't recognize Will McCarroll out of uniform.

"Got a minute?" he called, as he crossed the lawn that separated the Chittenden House, which served as headquarters to the Yellowstone Association, from the courthouse.

He was dressed in well-worn jeans and a short-sleeved tan shirt. Annie found herself surprised to see the blond hair on his forearms, which were usually covered by his uniform shirt. At least in court. And no hat covered the unruly blond hair that showed traces of gray.

A pair of sunglasses swung from a lanyard around Will's neck. He squinted into the sun as he strode purposefully her way.

"I'm afraid I don't," Annie announced as soon as he came within earshot. "I'm picking Archie up from the animal hospital this afternoon. I have to get there before it closes."

The message was clear, but even as she issued it, Annie wondered why she'd felt compelled to do so. She had more than enough time to get to Gardiner before Dr. Kennedy locked his doors. And she knew damn well he was expecting her and wouldn't leave before she picked up Archie.

Will had stopped about five feet from her, facing her. Eyeing several tourists who were getting a little too close to an elk that had wandered down from above Mammoth, he remained silent for several seconds, then, without looking at her, said, "This will only take a minute. I think it'd be worth your while."

"Okay," Annie replied. She reached inside her briefcase for her sunglasses and slid them on. Light sensitivity was one of her worst symptoms. Somehow right now she also liked the idea of hiding behind them. "What is it?"

"I don't think Hank Vincent told us everything he knew."

Annie reflexively lifted the glasses off her nose to get a better look at Will.

"What makes you think so?"

"I ran into him earlier today. At the gas station. He owns a towing service and he was moving a pop-up trailer some-one abandoned there."

Eyes still on the tourists, Will went on.

"He asked me where the investigation stands. He was real interested. Then he made a comment, something like, 'Someone who could help solve what happened would be a real hero.' He was baiting me, letting me know he still knows something, but that he's not giving it up without some guarantees."

"Let me guess. That he won't be prosecuted."

"Exactly."

"Why are you telling me this, instead of Sheriff Holm-berg? Or Agent Richter?"

"Because Vincent's not going to work with either of them. In fact, if we get them involved, my guess is he'll shut up for good. There's only one way to find out what he knows and that's by offering him a deal." McCarroll paused. Several of the tourists had pulled out cameras now and were creeping ever closer to the grazing elk. "I can take it to him. But you'd have to sign off on it."

"Offer him a deal?" Annie responded, incredulous.

"Yes."

The glasses came off altogether as she stepped toward him.

"Don't you remember who you're talking to? The same person you dragged over the coals last winter for sticking to the letter of the law?" Her voice rose shrilly.

Will finally turned his eyes on Annie. What she saw in them—an anger, maybe even hatred—made her wish he hadn't.

"Sticking to the letter of the law back then sent over a thousand bison to their deaths for no reason." He said the words with such disdain that Annie automatically drew back. "We're talking about a campfire now, one that didn't do any damage, versus a human life. Your mother's. I just thought you might want to think about it. Maybe there's been enough blood lost because of the letter of the law."

"I can't," Annie replied tersely. She too turned her eyes on the tourists, though she did not actually see them. All she could see was her mother's face, that last evening, as Eleanor pleaded with Annie to be careful on her drive to and from Livingston.

And then she thought about the bison.

Almost as if reading her mind, McCarroll said, "I hear the Reverend paid you a visit."

What was it about this man that made her so crazy? Did he intuitively know the buttons to push? She'd never believed in love at first sight, but the opposite theory seemed to hold true for her and Will McCarroll. They'd despised each other from the first time they'd laid eyes on each other.

"Nothing in this goddamn park stays where it should," Annie said. She opened the car door, flinging it wide so fast that its lower edge scraped the front of her shin bone. The pain was excruciating, but she didn't let it show on her face, didn't utter a sound. She was too angry, and too proud.

"Thank you for your suggestion. I need to go now."

"It's your call," Will said, showing no emotion.


A half sob, half laugh escaped Annie when the door swung open and Dr. Kennedy stepped into the clinic's waiting room, a leash in hand and a mountain of yellow fur limping closely behind.

Despite the two surgeries, and ribs that were still healing, when Archie heard Annie's voice, he broke free of the lead and bounded for her.

Archie had never just wagged his tail. The entire back half of his body went into the process and now, at the sight of Annie, even the severity of his injuries couldn't hold him back as he licked away Annie's tears, the sweep of his tail—and rump—growing wider with each squeal of delight escaping Annie.

His beloved mistress had returned for him.

"Is he really going to be okay?" Annie said from where she kneeled on the ground, trying to wrap her arms around his squirming torso. She could feel that he'd lost weight.

"He's a tough one," Dr. Kennedy replied. "Those two bullets did a fair amount of damage. My biggest concern was getting him through the surgeries, and he came through those with flying colors. It might take him a while, but he'll be okay."

"I don't know how to thank you."

"Seeing you two reunited is thanks enough," Dr. Kennedy replied with a warm smile.

When Annie reached for her bag and began rummaging for her wallet, Dr. Kennedy said, "We can deal with that later. I think your pal just wants to go home."

As he walked them to the car, where he gently lifted Archie into the back of the little station wagon, Dr. Kennedy said, "Your ranger friend did a nice job that night he transported him here."

The description of Will McCarroll as her friend threw Annie off.

She muttered a half-hearted, "That's good to hear."

Dr. Kennedy seemed determined that Will get his just due.

"Archie could've bled to death from that bullet wound to the chest on the ride down the hill, if your friend hadn't held him on his lap like he did, to keep his upper body elevated. Couldn't have been easy driving that road with this big guy on his lap."

"Will McCarroll did that?"

The tone with which she said the name seemed to startle Dr. Kennedy.

"Yes. I told him yesterday he'd probably saved Archie's life."

"Yesterday?"

Annie assumed Dr. Kennedy was confused. Will brought Archie in four days ago, not yesterday.

"Yes. When he stopped by to check on him. He's been in

a couple times," Dr. Kennedy responded, giving Archie one long last appraisal, followed by an affectionate pat on his head.

"Nice guy, that Will McCarroll."


"Nothing?" Annie Peacock cried. "You haven't come up with anything at all?"

Rod Holmberg, who sat opposite her in her office, running his fingers along the brim of the hat that rested on one knee, shook his head in frustration.

"Not a thing. We're following up on every registered Suburban in the area, but there are over three hundred, and so far it's gotten us nowhere. And of course, we could be dealing with someone registered in another county, or state."

"Hank Vincent's your best lead so far?"

"Your Honor," Holmberg replied, then corrected himself with "Annie. So far it's our only lead. No one else has reported seeing anything. And we've had law enforcement combing every inch of the area behind your house, all the way up to the Beaver Ponds and beyond. There's no sign they headed out on foot. We're certain Vincent's right about that—that they were driving when they left, and that your mother was in the vehicle. But aside from what Mr. Vincent had to say—and frankly, his record, and the fact he has charges pending against him, doesn't make him the most credible of witnesses—we have nothing else to go on."

Annie debated telling Holmberg that Will had visited her to say he believed Hank Vincent knew more than he'd shared with them that day. But Will had warned her that getting Holmberg and Richter involved with Vincent again could "shut him up for good." Should she trust Will's instincts on the matter?

Holmberg seemed not to notice her preoccupation.

"None of the prints taken at the scene are unaccounted for," he said. "The note left on the table was printed from a standard Canon printer—it's about the most popular printer out there—and there were no irregularities in the printing, other than the fact it may have been a little low on ink, so tracing that's going to be nearly impossible.

"Agent Richter and I believe we need to shift focus now. We won't stop looking at and for evidence, and most importantly, for your mother—I have two full-time officers on this and as you know, the Park Service has dedicated a full-time law enforcement officer, as well as instructed all law enforcement to make this a priority. But we also need to follow our own logic . . ."

"You mean go with your theory that someone wants to scare me off the bench?"

"Exactly."

"And where do we stand on that?"

"Gleeson. Heck Buckley. At this point, they're our most likely suspects. With the wolf trial pending, and your record of imposing the maximum penalties for poaching and loaded firearms within the park, we have to look at the possibility they could want you off the bench badly enough to do something desperate."

"You haven't found anything from the cases I handled as a prosecutor?"

"Richter has two FBI agents working on that. So far they haven't come up with any red flags, but that doesn't mean they won't when they dig deeper," he replied. His fingers finally stopped working the hat's brim. "Let me ask you something . . . in our investigation so far, it seems that you're not particularly popular with the Church of White Hope."

Annie let out a bitter laugh.

"I wasn't. But apparently all that's changed. I actually had a visit from their leader yesterday afternoon."

Holmberg drew himself up in his chair.

"Jeremiah Dayton?"

Annie nodded.

"He likes to be called 'Reverend.' He stopped by yesterday morning to tell me the church is praying for my mother and me. And to say that their members are out there, actively looking for her. It was interesting because he didn't actually come out and say that the church believes Gleeson and the antiwolf coalition are responsible, but he made it pretty clear that's exactly what they think."

"How?"

Annie scowled, tried to remember Dayton's exact words from the day before. She normally had a mind sharp as a tack for details, but her disdain for the church, and especially its leader, was so great and caused so much turmoil in her when he appeared at her door that it cast something of a fog over yesterday's visit. And of course, he'd arrived just as she was starting to feel light-headed anyway.

She shook her head.

"He said something about the protest the other day. That hadn't Buckley and Gleeson done enough damage the night before, without putting me through a protest too."

This visibly confused Holmberg. "The picture I got was that the church and the anti-wolf coalition usually see things eye to eye."

"That's an accurate picture. I'd have used the same terms to describe their relationship."

"Would you have expected the church at the protest during Gleeson's hearing?"

"Let's put it this way, it surprised me when I saw they weren't there."

"You're pretty sure they weren't? You got a good look at the crowd?"

"Yes. I stood right there, at that window, and watched law enforcement arrest Heck Buckley. That's when I noticed that none of the church members were there. At least no one I recognized."

"Seems kind of odd."

"I thought so too, until Dayton told me the church vowed not to take part in the protest, after what had happened the night before."

"How'd the church even know at that point what had happened the night before?"

Annie let out a caustic laugh.

"Nothing stays secret around here. Word spreads pretty fast."

Holmberg still seemed troubled. He shifted in his chair and Annie thought he was about to get up and leave.

"What is it, Sheriff?"

When he didn't respond right away, she followed with, "You know I'm not your normal victim or victim's family member, don't you? I believe my position, and my experience, make it incumbent upon you to keep me informed. On absolutely everything."

Holmberg still remained silent.

"I'd rather hear what you're struggling with right now than be sheltered from it. In fact, I insist upon it."

Eyes downcast, Holmberg shook his head slowly from side to side.

"Agent Richter has more experience in these matters than I do."

"Yes?"

"Well, in cases like these—if we're correct about our theory that someone wants you off the bench—there are certain patterns."

"Go on."

"Agent Richter thought it'd be a good idea for me to prepare you for the possibility that whoever kidnapped your mother might resort to some pretty ugly pressure tactics."

"Such as?"

It took a long while for Holmberg to bring his eyes back up to meet Annie's. "Sometimes, when they don't get the response they're hoping for, this type of person, or persons, ratchets up the stakes. We wanted you to be aware of that possibility. Especially since you're still here, still hearing cases."

"Do you mean that you believe they may torture my mother? Is that what you're trying to say?"

Holmberg met her gaze and this time, without hesitation, replied, "Yes."

Annie closed her eyes.

"If that's the case, then maybe I should hope she's already dead."

Both sat silently for what seemed a long time, until Holmberg rose to his full six four height. He stood there, clearly angst ridden and wishing to make things better before he left.

"How's your dog doing?" he said finally.

Annie could see how badly Rod Holmberg needed to hear good news. Her heart suddenly went out to him. He was suffering too—and feeling a horrendous weight of responsibility. If indeed Eleanor Malone had survived thus far, the clock was still ticking. Agent Richter's suggestion only emphasized the danger inherent in that fact.

Despite that knowledge, Annie mustered a smile—the first true smile in days. "He'll have a long recovery, but he made it through. I brought him home yesterday."

The news visibly touched Holmberg. Perhaps, Annie thought, knowing Archie survived whatever had happened at her house that night gave Holmberg hope that her mother had too.

He looked at Annie, nodded, then took a few seconds before speaking.

"We'll do everything humanly possible to get your mother back to you too," he said softly.

"I know you will, Sheriff," Annie replied. "And I'm very grateful."


Hank Vincent hated working. He, in fact, did as little of it as possible, subsisting primarily off the elk and deer he hunted throughout the year, and heating his trailer with wood he collected every fall. But summer was the one time he had a chance to actually make money—cash, he never accepted anything else—and so, every summer, as much as he hated it, he activated his cell phone and put up half a dozen posters in town to remind the locals that he was on hand to provide towing services.

WHY WAIT? was his company logo—though he hadn't

actually really formed a company. He thought it a very clever logo and had it put on his old truck and printed in red Magic Marker at the top of each poster. And then, for the mentally challenged, which by Hank's estimation included the majority of the population around Gardiner, he added a second line:

*GO LOCAL. NEXT CLOSEST TOW TRUCK IS 70 MILES AWAY, IN LIVINGSTON.*

Nobody ever called him on the extra ten miles he'd added. Okay, eighteen. He'd been averaging maybe two or three jobs a week this summer, and usually whatever he was towing needed to go all the way to Livingston, where they actually had a car dealership and a couple different repair shops. And since he charged by the mile, and had upped his fees to account for gas prices, plus a little extra, he'd actually been doing pretty well. Until, that is, he got arrested. If he got socked with a big old fine for the fire he'd set the other night, he'd be screwed. Even if he worked all the way through hunting season—which wasn't gonna happen—Hank couldn't come up with the kind of fines Judge Annie Peacock was known to impose for breaking the rules inside the park.

That kind of thinking had prompted Hank to decide that he ought to put some signs up north too—in Emigrant and Chico. Chico Hot Springs Resort, with its five-star restaurant, drew a classier kind of tourist—the kind that tipped well. So long as he was charging for gas, he might as well see if he could drum up some business in Chico. And he liked driving up that way. Hank had always thought he'd been born in the wrong era. That he was a mountain man at heart. Driving through Yankee Jim Canyon and the Tom Miner Basin made Hank feel like he was traveling back in time. His heroes—John Colter, Jed Smith, Jim Bridger— had traveled the canyons of the Yellowstone. Another Jim— "Yankee Jim" George—settled in one and built a toll road to squeeze tolls out of the Northern Pacific when it passed through. Hank could relate to that kind of thinking, that kind of entrepreneurship. It wasn't all that different than the deal he tried to strike with that ice princess of a judge. Hell, he still couldn't believe she didn't take it. But something about the look on Will McCarroll's face the other day, at the gas station, made Hank think there was still room to negotiate.

Hank had spent the afternoon putting up half a dozen hand-printed signs at gas stations between Gardiner and Emigrant, and then sidetracked over to Chico, where he tacked up another three. Now as he pulled back onto Highway 89 to head home, he could see it was going to be one of those drives. With only two lanes, and most of the way, double yellow lines to keep people from passing on its curves and hills—like a couple of teenagers had done the previous summer and ended up in the ground as a result—Highway 89 drove tourists in their fancy cars absolutely crazy. For some reason, even though they were on vacation, they were always in a fucking hurry. They hated getting stuck behind locals' trucks, like Hank's, that maxed out at fifty or sixty, even when he wasn't towing anything. Hank actually took a perverse pleasure in slowing down when he saw them come racing up behind him in his rearview mirror. Next thing you knew, they'd be veering left to get a look around him, at what was coming, but they were usually too chicken to actually pass, since with only one or two sections of the highway as exceptions, you could never see very far before a hill or a curve, and who knew what was coming their way? Hank liked to mess with them. Sometimes he'd even veer left with them, just to block their view.

But now, as he glanced in the rearview mirror at the vehicle barreling his way—a big old SUV—the hair on the back of Hank's neck instinctively bristled. He pushed his foot down on the gas. The road ahead was clear, which would give it a good chance to pass. But this time, Hank didn't want that. Not yet anyway.

He wanted a chance to check it out first. See if his hunch was right.

The SUV drew within ten yards of him, then slowed to match Hank's speed.

Yep. A Suburban. White. Older model.

*With a rusty front right fender.*

Hank had recognized the Suburban that night. He'd seen it around town, and he knew he'd see it again. Eventually. He'd been planning for this, really, ever since the judge refused to cut him a deal.

The sun's glare against the windshield of the Suburban made it difficult for Hank to see inside. He could tell there were two men. The driver wore a cowboy hat.

Hank had been accelerating, to give him time to figure out what to do. Now, he slowed down, gradually, so as not to be obvious about it. The Suburban pulled closer. When it veered left, to get a look at oncoming traffic, Hank couldn't help but smile.

Hank didn't pull his little trick—the one where he veered left at the same time to make it impossible for them to see. They had a clear shot, no one coming and no blind spots for at least two hundred yards.

The Suburban honked once, then pulled into the lane for northbound traffic. Hank didn't look its way as it passed. In fact, he slowed, increasing the distance between the two vehicles to a hundred yards, and then, just past Corwin Springs, he even let two assholes pass him so that once they reached Gardiner, he wouldn't be so visible.

In Gardiner, just before the bridge, the driver of the Suburban put his left turn signal on. Hank watched as the vehicle turned onto the narrow road, barrelling up the hill in low gear.

He hesitated, but only a matter of seconds. Then, sticking his arm out the driver's window, his index finger pointing north and east while the others curled into a semifist, Hank followed suit. His truck was practically invisible in the tornado of dust kicked up by the Suburban.

# NINE

ANNIE KNEW THE MOMENT SHE SAW HOLMBERG AND
Richter drive up, before they even got out of the white jeep
with the green-and-brown lettering that said PARK COUNTY
SHERIFF. Before she even saw their faces—the grimness reflected in their eyes.

She had just come downstairs after a rough night, during
which she got only three or four hours of sleep. Tortured
sleep at that. She was crossing the living room, headed for
the kitchen when she heard the crunch of gravel in her
driveway and turned to see them pull in. Luckily she'd already slipped into the jeans left on the floor beside the bed,
from her short walk with Archie the night before. They
used to walk miles every night after work. They'd only
managed to make it to the mouth of Old Gardiner Road last
night but the bandaged Lab had enjoyed every step, and
seeing his tail wagging as he sniffed elk droppings and
even tried to chase a Uinta ground squirrel—hundreds of
them made the hotel grounds their home—had lifted Annie's spirits. But during the night, lying there torturing herself with thoughts of where her mother was, they'd again
sunk.

She headed for the door. Archie followed a couple steps
behind. He growled now whenever someone dropped by.

"It's okay," Annie said, patting his head. She straightened, took a deep breath, and opened the door just as the two men stepped up onto the front porch.

"Morning, Your Honor," Holmberg said.

Richter worked up a pathetically disingenuous smile and nodded at her.

"Something's happened," Annie said. She wasn't in the mood for pleasantries.

"Yes," Richter said. At the same time, Holmberg declared, "Maybe."

Annie looked from one face to the other. Each looked equally miserable, but right now she didn't give a damn what either man felt. Her heart in her throat, she replied, "Which is it?"

Eyes fixed on Annie, Holmberg silenced Richter with a gesture.

"We don't know for sure yet," he said. "We certainly hope this is a false alarm, but we're concerned enough that it may have something to do with your mother that we decided to notify you now. I pray to God we're wrong."

"You're concerned that *what* has to do with my mother?"

Agent Richter seemed determined to play some role in delivering their message.

"Are you aware of the cemetery, about a mile past the arch?"

"The old Gardiner Cemetery? On the Old Yellowstone Trail Road?"

"Yes."

"I've never seen it, at least not up close. I've seen the fence around it when I biked up to the base of Electric." Suddenly Annie's hand came up to cover her mouth, stifling the sound she made.

Holmberg reached out to steady her.

"Maybe we should have driven up to Livingston and asked Judge Marsano to issue the search warrant."

"Warrant for what?" Annie almost shouted.

As always, Annie could count on Holmberg to be direct; on his gaze not wavering, nor the sense he was there, in part, to support her.

"A fresh grave was dug in the cemetery last night," he said. "There's no indication of who did it, or who—or what—is buried there. But if it results in a criminal charge, we want to make sure we've jumped through all the hoops. We can't exhume it without a search warrant. We came to ask you to issue one."

"Based on this affidavit," Richter added, pulling a neatly folded document out of the inside pocket of his jacket. He unfolded it, and presented it to Annie. "Which I'll swear to, as the case agent."

Without expression Annie skimmed it, then turned and strode purposefully through the living room, into the kitchen. She picked up the phone and punched in a number on its speed dial.

"Justine? I know it's Saturday, but I need you in the office immediately."

She listened to Justine's crisp response—"be right there"—then pivoted.

Holmberg and Richter had followed her into the kitchen. She remembered the last time they had been there and saw that they did too.

Archie hovered at her side, unable to resist an occasional low growl, despite both men's attempts to pet him.

"You'll have your warrant in thirty minutes," Annie said.

"Thank you," Holmberg said. "We're heading back to the cemetery but we'll send an officer to the courthouse to pick it up. And we'll get back to you with word as soon as we've—"

"No," Annie said. Her tone left no room for discussion or argument. "You won't get back to me. We can stop at the courthouse now—Justine lives in Mammoth and should be there by the time we arrive. I'm going with you to the cemetery."


Until the previous night, ground hadn't been broken for over fifty years in the little cemetery that sat on a barren, windswept hill three-quarters of a mile outside the town of

Gardiner. Most of the cemetery's residents had been born in the mid- to late 1800s and died early in the 1900s, although a grave or two sported dates as recent as 1958. Mainly hidden from sight, the graveyard experienced more wild animal traffic than it did human, especially if the last two-legged visitor failed to secure the chain used to latch the rusted gate to the ten-foot-high wire fence intended to keep out the buffalo and pronghorn that frequented the area.

Technically, though it was located west of the Roosevelt Arch and entry gate, the bodies long buried there had the honor and distinction of finding eternal peace within the boundaries of Yellowstone National Park.

The sight as Annie approached, however, was anything but peaceful. She'd opted to drive her own car, following the sheriff's jeep down the hill to Gardiner and under the Roosevelt Arch to the cemetery. She'd brought Archie along.

On the occasions she'd biked or walked the Old Yellowstone Trail Road, she'd rarely passed another vehicle—motorized or non—or person. The scene now was reminiscent of that at her house less than a week earlier.

A wave of dizziness hit her. She'd forgotten to take her medicine that morning.

She steadied herself when she first stepped out of the car. Holmberg, who'd immediately been approached by two park law enforcement officers, neither of whom Annie recognized, excused himself when he saw her and strode her way.

"You don't look very good. Why don't you let one of my men drive you home?"

"No," Annie replied sharply. "I just need a minute. I'll be fine. Please, don't let my presence interfere with what you have to do."

Holmberg seemed to know better than to argue. He turned and headed back to where he'd left the rangers standing. Beyond him, in the background, the activity on the hill reminded Annie of an ant farm. At least a dozen uniformed men and women—some in Park County Sheriff's uniforms, but most in the green-and-gray of the Park Service—scurried about, talking into two-way radios. Several carried shovels and picks. Word spread quickly that Annie had arrived. As she walked slowly up the hill, some of those assembled smiled at her awkwardly; others avoided eye contact.

Not a good sign. Apparently everyone there knew what they expected to find.

As Annie slid through the open gate, a group of six or seven people who stood amidst the crumbling tombstones suddenly grew silent. They'd been standing in a semicircle, hiding it from her view, but when they turned in unison toward Annie, they inadvertently parted, allowing her a view of what had brought all of them there.

Annie gasped.

A large mound of fresh dirt and rocks rose from ground as flat, dry, and hard as a moonscape. On top of it, stabbed into its surface, sat a cross made of dead branches and roped together with baling twine. At its base lay a flat piece of wood—maybe six inches by eight. A word had been carved into it but Annie could not make it out.

She moved toward it, eyes fixed on its surface.

"Annie."

She hadn't noticed Les Bateman among the others. He grabbed her by the arm.

"You shouldn't be here. Let me take you home."

Annie shook him off, and continued forward until the single word carved with a pocketknife registered.

*MOM.*

Her knees threatened to buckle. Les renewed his grasp on her elbow.

"Come on," he said, exerting pressure to turn her back.

Annie's eyes grew wide, and wild. Once again, she shook free of him.

"Will everyone please stop telling me I shouldn't be here?" she said, her voice rising in volume and pitch with each word. "I'm here. And I'm not going anywhere—" She took a deep breath, closing her eyes momentarily, and then opening them again. The sight hadn't disappeared. Hadn't changed at all. "—until you show me what's under there."

Holmberg had approached and now stood at Annie's shoulder. Holding a document high above his head, he called out, "You heard her. The warrant's been issued."

Annie felt relieved at having the attention drawn away from her.

"Let's get to work."

Because of the extreme care being taken, it took over two hours for two Park Service Law Enforcement rangers and one Park County deputy to empty the newly dug grave of its contents. With each scraping of shovel against rock, eyes turned to Annie.

She ignored them, focusing entirely on the hole in the ground that was growing wider and deeper with each thrust of the shovel, trying not to think. Trying not to jump to conclusions. Archie sat quietly by her side.

The wind had picked up, bringing with it a new chill to the air. Les Bateman, who had been taking photographs of the scene, walked up to Annie and placed his jacket over her shoulders. Annie nodded, her eyes never leaving the grave.

Minutes later, she began seeing hard, compacted earth when each shovel lifted. They were reaching the bottom of the hole, so close to undisturbed ground—too close now to hide a body—that Annie began to breathe fully.

It had been some kind of hoax. A cruel joke.

She reached over, put her arm around Archie, and pulled him close.

"I think we're okay," she whispered, stroking his head.

A new sound, a hollow *clink,* caused her to freeze. Suddenly all activity stopped and a dead silence took over.

Annie saw one of the young rangers who'd been digging look up at Peter Shewmaker, eyes wide. The Park County deputy nodded to Rod Holmberg. The two men had been huddled to the side, talking quietly, but now they hurried to the edge of the hole.

Les Bateman crouched over the hole, snapping away, camera aimed into its center.

Annie jumped to her feet.

People had closed in on the site, blocking her view. She put a hand on the shoulder of a young woman in uniform, who turned and literally shrank a size when she saw it was Annie.

Annie stepped to the edge of the hole.

Glancing up, Holmberg saw her and called out, "Keep her away."

Almost simultaneously, she felt a tight grip on her upper arm and turned. Agent Richter.

"Let go."

Angrily, with a strength and force that clearly surprised the FBI agent, she jerked free.

She watched in horror as Peter Shewmaker folded at the waist, instinctively pulling a pair of plastic gloves out of his pocket. He slipped them on and reached for something— from her vantage point, all Annie could see was what looked like plastic—at the end of a shovel. Shewmaker brushed clumps of dirt away from the object with his gloved hands, pausing to let Bateman take a close-up.

When he straightened, he held a coffee can. Brand-new. No rust. Its plastic lid had been sealed shut with duct tape.

He extended his arm, handing it to Rod Holmberg, who had also donned gloves. Richter had given up on Annie and joined Holmberg at the opposite rim of the hole.

By the time Annie worked her way to the two men, Holmberg had already removed the tape and the plastic lid. She saw him wince as he looked inside, then tipped the can toward the agent. Richter showed no emotion.

"Let me see."

Both men were clearly startled to lay eyes on Annie. Holmberg quickly placed the lid back on the can. Annie caught a whiff of its contents and felt her stomach flip.

"You don't want to, Your Honor," Holmberg said. "Believe me."

"Open it," Annie said flatly.

Holmberg closed his eyes briefly, then, apparently convinced of the futility of refusing her, he lifted the can Annie's way.

Without a word, he removed the lid and tilted it to allow the filtered sunlight to fall on its contents.

Annie let out a cry.

Head spinning, she could not catch her breath.

Les Bateman dropped his camera and came to her, placing a long, skinny arm around her shoulder.

Pushing him aside, Annie took one more look. Then she pivoted to the side, bent double, and vomited.

# TEN

ANNIE HALF EXPECTED TO FIND WILL MCCARROLL AT A
bear jam. She knew he spent most of his time in the backcountry, often on horseback, but she also knew that Hells
Angels were traveling through the park in groups, on their
way to a "convention" in Cody, and that all backcountry
rangers had been pulled in to help law enforcement patrol
the roadways and campgrounds in an effort to prevent any
disasters.

She'd also heard there was a mother grizzly and two
cubs who had been frequenting the Swan Lake Flats area,
unusual for this time of year, and so when she left the cemetery, she'd headed directly there.

Her reasoning paid off.

She'd just rounded the bend of West Loop Road, immediately past the Hoodoos—tall columns of petrified stone,
where two technical climbers belayed their way down the
sheer cliffs—when traffic came to a dead stop. Annie pulled
over at a narrow pullout and parked, leaving the windows
down for Archie, and began walking along the shoulder of
the highway, passing dozens of stopped cars and RVs headed
toward the south and east side of the park—Old Faithful,
Norris, and perhaps eventually, Yellowstone Lake.

Up ahead, in the middle of the two-lane road, she saw a
ranger, flagging cars along impatiently. It was sometimes

almost impossible to tell rangers apart, at least from any distance, since they wore the same uniform, and for some reason, most of the men seemed to have similar builds—tall and lean; but even at a distance something about this one's posture, his obvious disdain for the task at hand told Annie it was McCarroll. She wouldn't expect a man like McCarroll to take well to what often amounted to traffic duty; not when his chosen environment was the backcountry and wilds of Yellowstone.

When he first noticed her walking his way, Will took her for a tourist and appeared annoyed to see someone had actually gotten out of their car to get a better glimpse of the bears lumbering their way toward the crest of the hill on the south side of the road. Confused by the fact that he'd never seen her in jeans and a T-shirt, with her hair pulled back in a poor attempt at a ponytail, when he finally recognized her, he continued to flag cars along, yelling, "Keep moving," but all the while, his eyes were pinned on Annie.

She came to a stop in front of him and said, "I need to talk to you."

Will stopped flagging traffic and ushered her to the side of the road.

He turned to face her.

"I heard," he said simply.

Annie replied through a clenched jaw.

"They cut off her ear," she said. She wrapped trembling arms around her torso, which had also begun shaking.

Will placed his hand on her shoulder.

"This means she's still alive. That's a good thing."

"I know," Annie replied. "Of course they have to do DNA testing to confirm it's really my . . ."

Tears began streaming down her face.

"What can I do?" Will said.

A car stopped next to them to see what the crowd was all about. Without taking his eyes off Annie, Will shouted, "Move it!" and the startled driver pressed on.

Annie met Will's gaze.

"I want to talk to Hank Vincent."

Other than a slight lift of an eyebrow, Will's expression didn't say much.

"I'll go now," he said. "I'll bring him to you."

"No," Annie replied. "I want to go with you."

Will reached for the two-way radio clipped to his belt.

"Five-hotel-one-two?" he said into it. "This is five-tango-one-five."

*"Five-hotel-one-two,"* a voice answered almost immediately. *"What's up, Will?"*

"Hey, Wyatt. What's your location?"

*"Heading north from Norris. Had a little altercation down there between bikers."*

"I'm working a bear jam at Swan Lake Flats. I need to leave. How long will it take you to get here?"

*"Five minutes. Tops."*

"Great. I'm leaving now."

There was a moment's hesitation that no doubt reflected a concern for the departure from standard procedure—Will's leaving a bear jam unattended.

But then the voice on the other radio uttered, *"Got it. Five-hotel-one-two."*

While there were some rangers who felt threatened by Will—his brusque and defiant nature, plus the fact that he had been in law enforcement longer than any other ranger in the park—most, like Wyatt Worthington, considered him something akin to a legend. Regardless of which camp someone fell into, nobody questioned Will. It was as simple as that.

"I owe you one," Will replied, then, ignoring the growing line of vehicles, he ushered Annie toward his car, which was parked off the road, already facing north, toward Mammoth.

As they climbed inside, Annie heard him mutter, under his breath.

"Let's just hope that bear doesn't get hungry in the next five minutes."

* * *

"Don't we have to find out where he lives?"

Annie glanced sideways at Will as they headed down the hill from Mammoth.

They'd decided Will would drive the Park Service Law Enforcement vehicle on their visit to Hank Vincent. Will had dropped her off at her car, then held up traffic in both directions to allow her to do a U-turn on the busy road. He followed her Subaru down past the Upper Terraces and the Mammoth Hot Springs to her house, where the plan was to drop off both her car and Archie. Reluctant to part with him, at the last minute Annie asked if they could bring the dog along and Will quickly agreed.

Now the grateful Lab hung his big head over the back-seat, between them, tail wagging. If it weren't for the notebook-sized shaved area on his chest, and the stitches from the surgery to remove the bullet, it might seem his ordeal had never happened.

"He lives up past Corwin Springs," Will replied. "I've already checked it out."

They fell silent as Annie thought about Will's statement—he'd apparently planned to pursue Hank Vincent for more information with or without Annie's cooperation or consent.

As they passed through the entry gate, with a wave from Will sufficing for the rangers manning it, Annie saw a Sheriff's Department vehicle heading toward the cemetery. They must still be working the crime scene.

Will cast a sideways glance at her.

"You sure you're up to this?"

"Yes."

Annie turned away from the sight on the hill and stared out the side window, at the pronghorn that frequented the short grass between the entry gate and the arch. It had turned brown now, with the late summer sun, making it harder to pick out their sleek, tan bodies. Until they turned your way, and then the bold black markings gave them away.

"Maybe it's not worth it," Will said quietly as they drove through Gardiner.

"What do you mean?"

Will braked as an errant mule deer trotted across the street.

"What happened was a warning," he said. "They want you off the bench. If you resign, you might get your mother back."

They'd passed the shops, bank, post office, and restaurants and had just reached the strip of motels at the town's outskirts. Suddenly Annie ordered, "Pull over."

Will pulled into the parking lot of the Motel 8, and stopped the car.

"Do you see that?" Annie said, pointing to the World Energy Resources, Inc. sign that greeted visitors as they arrived and departed the little town.

"When people like me start caving in to forces that have no respect for what places like Yellowstone mean, forces that would use any means to exploit it if it means making a couple extra bucks, then we might as well just turn it all over to companies like the one that just put up that sign."

"That damn sign's there for a reason, that's for sure," Will replied bitterly. "But this doesn't have anything to do with exploration, Your Honor."

"I know it doesn't," Annie replied. "But what's the difference if I back down in order to allow poachers and outfitters to plunder Yellowstone's protected wildlife, or if we open the gates to the energy companies and say, 'Come on in fellas, it's yours for the taking'? Either way, I'm not doing my job. Either way, the inhabitants of one of the last truly wild places on this planet are the ones that pay the price. We do too, but we go on living. They pay with their lives."

Annie turned her eyes from the sign—particularly the image of buffalo in the Lamar Valley—to Will.

Suddenly overcome with remorse and a combined, confused grief, she blurted out, "You blame me, don't you?"

Will did not need her to explain what she was talking about.

"This isn't the time to talk about that," he replied gently.

"Listen, let me go get Vincent. Whatever he knows, I'll get it out of him. I promise. And you won't have to be involved."

"That's not even an option," Annie replied coldly.

When they passed by the bison capture facility moments later, she stared straight ahead.

So did Will.

# ELEVEN

"Excuse me," Ranger Randy Hannah said to the young brunette dressed in a Park Service uniform—basically the same uniform Randy wore, but somehow no one would ever recognize that to be true.

Brian Wise's assistant could stop traffic in that uniform, and despite the seriousness of his mission, Randy felt unnerved standing there, waiting for her to acknowledge his presence.

"Yes?" she said, finally looking up from her computer screen. Randy heard a door open, then realized it came from her computer. He'd interrupted her instant messaging.

He cleared his throat.

"I need to speak to Brian."

She smiled politely, eyes drifting back to the screen.

"He's out of town. He'll be back a week from Wednesday. Can I give him a message?"

Randy hesitated. Brian Wise had held the position of Yellowstone's lead geologist for thirteen years. Some rangers became obsessed with wolves, others with the grizzly, for Randy it was Yellowstone's hot springs and geysers. Its mudpots and fumeroles. Brian recognized that and appreciated Randy's passion. He'd always made the young ranger feel welcome to come to him with questions, or just to discuss the love they shared for the features whose protection were the basis of President Ulysses S. Grant's decision to establish the nation's first national park. Randy would rather deal with Brian than anyone else, but he wasn't sure this could wait.

"Is someone filling in for Brian while he's gone?" he said tentatively.

The young woman laughed.

"Yeh," she said. "Me." She finally turned her full attention to the clean-cut ranger and gave him a look that could not be misinterpreted.

"What can I do for you?"

Randy wasn't used to being propositioned.

"Is Brian available by phone?" he said nervously, venturing a look at the nametag on her shirt. Emilie. "Or e-mail?"

The sound of another door opening emanated from the computer. Emilie's eyes darted back to the screen. Her smile faded.

"I really don't think he'd want to be bothered," she said, clearly eager to get back to what she'd been doing before being interrupted. "He's on his first vacation in three years. Is this some kind of an emergency?"

Randy stood there, silent, for several seconds. He wanted to answer, yes, that it was an emergency but couldn't bring himself to sound so dramatic. Not to Emilie anyway. Then an idea came to him.

"Brian showed me a book he has on the hot springs. Is there any chance I can borrow it?"

Emilie made a sound like air being let out of a balloon.

"Whatever," she said, waving Randy toward the door behind her. "Just be sure to leave Brian a note telling him which one you took."

Half a minute later, Randy walked back through the tiny office, with four volumes cradled in his arms.

"Thanks," he called over his shoulder, after reaching the door.

"No problem," Emilie replied.

She never bothered to look up.

# TWELVE

THREE POINT THREE MILES OUTSIDE GARDINER, WILL turned east on a side road named Papeesh, which immediately angled into the foothills and began climbing. One lane, dirt, the kind of road that can't be traveled in the winter without four-wheel drive, Papeesh cut a scar across barren hills, switchbacking as it gained altitude. Too high and dry to attract the newer, more upscale cabins and lodges that had begun populating the region, Papeesh instead served as home to several long-deserted houses and barns, which is why Annie was surprised to see curtains blowing in an open window and a plastic swimming pool filled with water in the front yard of a small, rundown frame structure that might otherwise have looked abandoned. A dog on the porch jumped up, tail wagging, barking excitedly as they neared, but it was unable to chase them as a thick rope had him bolted firmly to a lawn chair handmade of logs.

A quarter mile past the house, Will turned again, this time onto what looked like an old logging road. There were no markings or street signs of any kind. It looked like it got no use at all, but Annie knew better.

"You've been here already, haven't you?" Annie asked.

"Drove by," Will replied. "I was curious."

Despite her love for the lushness of the Pacific Northwest, it hadn't taken Annie long to adapt to and fall in love

with the terrain surrounding Mammoth—the desert scrub
brush and a sea of hills that rolled, one after another, until
they reached one of the jagged ranges or peaks surrounding the area. But as the jeep worked its way up the hill now,
she found this lifeless terrain harder to appreciate—that is
until she looked over her shoulder and saw the view of the
Yellowstone River, winding its way through the valley like
a brilliant blue ribbon. On the other side, ranchland, and
then the steep climb to a set of dramatic cliffs, dominated
at the far north end by Devil's Slide—a red gash of raw
earth made millions of years earlier when a chunk of gla-
cier broke loose and, like a giant sickle, slashed what
looked like a bloody swath out of the otherwise pristine,
gray rock ridge.

Another view—one every bit as unusual—greeted her
when Will turned the jeep up an incline with two narrow
ruts as a road and a blue trailer came into sight.

Annie's eyes grew wide as Will brought the jeep to a halt
and pulled the emergency brake into play.

"Oh my God," she said.

Will couldn't suppress a grin.

"Imagine coming home drunk."

"Hank Vincent actually lives in that?"

The trailer—old, rusted, with several broken windows,
sat at an angle that made it appear it might slide down the
hill. Several large boulders had, in fact, been rolled to the
downward side of it, indicating that Hank Vincent was also
aware of the possibility.

"Yep." Will had climbed out of the jeep and was walking
around, studying the place. "About four years ago we had a
mudslide up here. My guess is it tried to take Hank and his
trailer down the hill with it."

"And he never got it put back in place?" Annie asked, incredulous.

"Looks stable enough for now," Will said, as if the inconvenience, and absurdity of living at a twenty-degree angle wasn't even a consideration.

Annie joined him as he circled around the back of the

trailer, picking her way through beer cans, discharged shotgun shells, lengths of rope, nails, a coil of barbed wire. Antlers littered the ground everywhere.

"No," Annie cried when she turned to see Archie gnawing on an elk's leg, the hoof still attached.

Looking around, Annie saw several more, all of which appeared to have been worked over by sharp teeth. The chain attached to a post at the back door and two empty bowls explained just whose teeth. Hank apparently owned a dog.

Behind the house was a shed. A large set of elk antlers hung above its door, which stood open, but Annie was not inclined to look inside.

She stepped up onto the wooden platform that served as a porch at the back door. For some reason, it had stayed in place, but had apparently torn loose from the rest of the trailer during the mudslide.

"Do you suppose he's at work?" she said, standing on her tiptoes to get a look inside the plastic window, which had clouded with age.

She looked over at Will, whose eyes were glued to the ground. Annie noticed elk droppings, lots of them. He headed back toward the front.

"I think I'll just sit in the car while we wait," Annie said, the excitement and anticipation of learning something about her mother diminished by the sense of the person she'd be compromising her sworn oath for if she offered Hank Vincent a deal.

"Could be a long wait," Will finally replied to her back.

"What do you mean?"

"Vincent hasn't been here in a while."

"Why do you say that?"

"Look around. No car tracks, no footprints—except ours. Remember that big windstorm we had Thursday night? It was big enough to wipe any prints clean, especially up here, on this hill, without any trees." Annie's heart sank as she looked around, ready to contradict Will, to find a flaw in his thinking. But her desperate need to do something to help find her mother threatened to choke her as she realized Will was right.

"Hank Vincent," Will said, "definitely hasn't been here since then."

"He must not have seen anything," Annie said, the despair in her voice touching a place in Will's heart that he hadn't allowed himself to visit in a very long time. "Otherwise he wouldn't have run. Left town. He would have stayed and used it somehow."

"That's possible," Will said. "But I don't think that's it. I've been asking around. Hank Vincent's lived here his whole life. As destitute as he is, he's not going to leave, become a fugitive, in order to avoid a twenty-five-hundred dollar fine. There's no restitution involved. He's been working this summer. He could set up payments. Hell, jail time would even make more sense than leaving everything he knows. A guy like that just wouldn't do it."

They'd headed back down the hill. Will was driving even more slowly than he had on the way up. They were approaching the house they'd passed, Hank Vincent's closest neighbor. The dog began to bark the moment they rounded the bend and came into sight.

"Then why would he decide to leave?" Annie said.

"Maybe he didn't," Will said, as he jerked the jeep right, onto the sagebrush adjoining the little yard.

The dog jumped up on its hind legs, straining against the rope, yapping excitedly. The front screen door opened and a woman in her early thirties stepped out. She was dressed in cutoff jeans and a tight-fitting tank top that said RIVER OTTER FLY-FISHING OUTFITTERS that did nothing to hide her ample chest, nor the rolls of flesh left from the birth of the two-year-old girl now clutching at the ragged hem of her shorts.

Squinting in the morning sun at the unannounced company, she lifted the child, yelled at the dog to shut up, and headed, barefoot, toward the jeep.

"Can I help you?" she said. Once she stopped shouting at the dog, her voice had a pleasant ring to it.

"We're looking for a neighbor of yours," Will replied as he stepped out of the car. "Hank Vincent."

She made a face that Will couldn't quite interpret as her lips turned up in a smile but her eyes looked concerned.

"Join the club. I'm looking for him too. Son of a bitch just left this poor dog up there without food or water. I been puttin' some out but he just went up there and sat and waited all day every day, and I got tired of walking up the hill to feed him. Finally just tied him to the porch."

"How long's Hank been gone?"

The wind had blown her long brown bangs, streaked with a harsh silver, into her eyes. She pushed them aside with her free hand. Archie's head emerged from the back window and the child shrieked with delight.

"Let's see," she said, twisting her body to let the little girl pet him. "At least since Monday. I went into Livingston that day and brought Hank back some herbs from the health food store up there. I always do that. He can't sleep at night. I'm kind of into that kind of stuff, you know, natural remedies and I got him takin' some valerian root. Anyway, when I got back, and took it up there, Hank wasn't home. And I haven't seen him since."

She'd been directing all her comments to Will, and ignoring Annie altogether, who remained seated in the car. But then Annie spoke up.

"Does he disappear like this very often?"

The woman bent to look inside, her breasts almost toppling out of her tank top. She seemed for several seconds to be taking Annie's measure, then, suddenly, her eyes opened wide and her hand shot up to cover her mouth.

"You're that judge, aren't you?"

Instantly uncomfortable, Annie simply nodded.

"Oh my," the woman said. "We've been praying for your mother. All of us have."

Annie's discomfort quickly turned to curiosity.

"All of you?"

The woman nodded energetically.

"Yep. All of us from the church. Reverend Dayton told us we could bring her back to you with our prayers so I've been praying every day."

"Thank you," Annie said awkwardly.

"Been prayin' for the salvation of that son of a bitch Gleeson too even though he doesn't deserve it. And Heck Buckley."

Will had been standing on the opposite side of the car, talking to her over its hood, but now he circled round to stand next to her.

"Why would you pray for Gleeson and Heck Buckley?"

The breasts slid back into her top when she straightened to face Will.

"'Cause they did such an awful thing. Even sinners need forgiveness. But I tell you, it's hard to forgive anybody'd do something so awful, especially to an old lady."

"But how do you know it was Gleeson, or Buckley, who kidnapped the judge's mother?"

She looked surprised by the question.

"Reverend Dayton told us."

"And how would he know?"

She snorted what sounded like a laugh of incredulity.

"The Lord told him, that's how. The Lord talks to Jeremiah, and then he shares the wisdom he receives with his children."

"You're one of his children?"

It looked like she was going to laugh again, but she didn't.

"Yes," she answered. "You could be too. You both could. All you have to do is believe."

Both Will and Annie fell silent, but it was clear from the look on her face that the young mother was piecing together the puzzle. She bent at the waist and locked eyes with Annie through the open window.

"Does Hank have somethin' to do with what happened to your mother?"

Will answered before Annie could.

"No," he said. "In fact, Hank was in jail the night the judge's mother was kidnapped."

Elbows on the edge of the window, she turned to eye Will, as if taking in his uniform for the first time.

"You put him in there?"

"Yes. All we want to do is talk to him. Ask him a few questions."

After taking a few seconds to digest this information, she directed herself to Annie.

"You asked if Hank disappears like this a lot. No, he doesn't. Especially not this time of year. He's gone a lot during hunting season, but that's because he has to be. I never seen Hank do this kind of thing before. He tries to make a little money during the tourist season. It doesn't make sense that he wouldn't tell me he was gonna leave and ask me to take care of Snoose here, 'cause Hank's crazy 'bout Snoose."

Those words solidified Will's sense that something was wrong, perhaps very wrong. He looked inside the car at Annie. She sensed it too.

He reached for the wallet he kept tucked in the console and removed a business card from it. Extending his arm toward her, he said, "Do me a favor? If Hank shows up, give him this and have him call me. Tell him he'll be glad he did. Or if you hear anything about where he is, I'd be grateful if you'd call yourself."

Straightening, she eyed the card.

"Law enforcement, huh? I hear Hells Angels are coming through the park next weekend."

"They're already there."

"Really?" she said. "Damn. I gotta get down off this hill more often. You'da thought I'd hear them go by, down on Eighty-nine."

"Will you make sure Hank gets that?" Will said, nodding toward the card in her hand.

The baby had grabbed the card and begun sucking on it.

"Hank's not real big on law enforcement," she said. "Especially you, I imagine, if you arrested him. But I'll tell him. And if I hear something, I'll give you a call."

She eyed Annie again, gave her a genuinely sympathetic smile.

"I'll keep on prayin'," she said.

Then she stepped back and Will started back down the dirt road. When he glanced in the rearview mirror, she was still standing, watching.

He knew before glancing her way that Annie was upset.

"What are you thinking?" she said. "What does it mean?"

Will shook his head.

"It could mean any number of things. Or it could mean nothing, that maybe Hank got lucky and is shacked up somewhere."

"That's not what you think."

"No, it's not. But I'm not jumping to any conclusions either."

"You think something's happened to Hank, don't you? And that it has to do with what he saw the night my mother disappeared?"

Will stared straight ahead. They'd come to the highway. He waited for traffic to clear before pulling back onto it.

"Yes," he said. "That's exactly what I'm thinking."

# THIRTEEN

"Jeremiah Dayton is here."

Annie looked up from the brief she was reading to see Justine standing in the doorway, clearly chagrined.

"Tell him . . ." Annie started. She stopped midsentence when Dayton's face appeared over her clerk's shoulder.

"Good morning, Your Honor," Dayton said politely.

Justine looked like she might reach out and slap the smile right off his mug.

"I thought I told you to stay in my office."

"It's okay, Justine," Annie said, dismissing her with a curt wave of the hand. She turned her eyes on Dayton. "I'm afraid I'm very busy, Mr. Dayton"—she refused to call him Reverend—"Is there something I can help you with?"

Taking this as an invitation, Dayton slid by Justine, into Annie's office. As had always been the case when Annie had seen him before, he was wearing a starched, long-sleeved white shirt, tie, and black slacks.

"I promise not to take much of your time," he said.

Once safely inside, he looked back at the door, which stood wide open. Justine had disappeared.

"May I?" he said, reaching for its knob.

Annie hesitated briefly. After their conversation with Hank Vincent's neighbor the day before, she and Will had driven directly to Livingston to tell Rod Holmberg what the woman had said about Heck Buckley and Chad Glee-son being involved in Eleanor Malone's disappearance. Holmberg's first response was to reprimand Will for going to look for Vincent without first informing him. Then he picked up the phone to call FBI Agent Richter and arranged for the two of them to head up to the Church of White Hope that morning to interview Jeremiah Dayton.

Before Will and Annie left, Holmberg ordered Will to stay out of the matter, to leave talking to Dayton to the sheriff's department and the FBI.

*But he hadn't ordered Annie.*

With that thought in mind, she replied, "Yes," now to Dayton.

Dayton shut the door, then lowered himself gracefully into the leather chair facing Annie's desk. He was long-limbed and agile. He crossed one leg over the other, expos-ing expensive snakeskin cowboy boots. Not a speckle or scratch on them.

Annie did not question him, nor offer pleasantries.

"First of all," Dayton started, "words can't express my horror, and sorrow, at what those savages did to your mother."

Either Dayton had heard what happened at the cemetery through the grapevine or he'd already been interviewed by Holmberg and Richter.

"Thank you." Annie said it without emotion.

"As I told you when I visited you last week," Dayton went on, "the entire church is praying for you. We've had members out searching the hills, campsites, riverbanks prac-tically day and night."

"So I hear, Mr. Dayton, and I'm grateful. Please pass that along to your members."

Acknowledging her request with a nod, Dayton went on.

"My people have decided we're not doing enough. And so, last night, in a special meeting we called—after hearing of the heinous cruelty your mother was subjected to—we came up with another idea."

He reached into the front pocket of his shirt and with-drew a checkbook.

With Annie watching him, he began to scribble on it.

"This is reward money," he said. "If anything is going to make someone come forward, it'll be this."

He turned the checkbook her way.

*The Eleanor Malone Search and Rescue Fund. $50,000.*

Stunned, Annie stared at the check.

"I don't know what to say."

"There's no need to say a thing. Some of our members may have had their differences with you over your interference with our rights to provide food for our families, but there are no differences on this matter—not when a woman's life hangs in the balance."

Despite the check displayed in front of her face, his words rankled Annie.

"With all the elk and deer around here, there's ample opportunity, Mr. Dayton, to put food on the table without breaking the law. Your people have been using Yellowstone's protected wildlife as an *income* source. Not a food source."

Dayton lifted a finger to his pursed lips as if to shush her.

"Let's not argue," he said soothingly. "Please. Let us help you find your mother."

Annie wanted to snatch the check from him and rip it to pieces, but for some reason, she could not.

Dayton lowered his hand, placed it across his heart, and continued.

"You may not believe in such things, but my followers can tell you that I have a power. It's right here," he said, tapping his chest. "In my heart. And in my heart, I've always known that your mother is still alive. This money can bring her back to you. Along with our prayers, of course."

Against every instinctive bone in her body, Annie felt the wall she'd put up suddenly crack as the reverend's words inserted just the tiniest seed of hope into it.

As a prosecutor in Seattle, she had seen firsthand how effective substantial rewards could be in solving an investigation.

"It's a lot of money," she said.

Dayton shook his head modestly, then lowered his voice.

"I'm going to ask you to keep what I'm about to tell you between the two of us," he said. "I know I can count on you to do so. The Church of White Hope is comprised primarily of simple people who believe in living off the wonders of this glorious earth the Lord gave us. But we also enjoy the membership of some very wealthy individuals. Very generous individuals. We're blessed that way. We can afford this amount." He ripped the check out of the checkbook and placed it precisely on the desk in front of Annie. "And if this doesn't do the trick, we'll write another one for just as much. Because we can afford that too. So please, let us help you. Let us help your poor mother."

Annie sat, totally silent and still, for several seconds.

"Thank you," she finally said, wishing she could come up with something more heartfelt, but unable to do so.

Dayton rose, pocketing his checkbook as he did so.

"The TV and radio stations will be announcing the reward tonight, and we're posting it in every store, restaurant, and motel from here to Bozeman. We'll find your mother, Judge Peacock."

He turned and started toward the door.

"Reverend Dayton . . . ?"

Pivoting gracefully, as if he already had it choreographed in his mind, Dayton replied, "Yes, Your Honor?"

"Do you know who's responsible for my mother's kidnapping?"

He hesitated just briefly.

"Know?" he replied. "Just as I told Sheriff Holmberg and the FBI agent this morning, I have my suspicions, but I don't *know*. Not with absolute certainty."

"May I ask who you think is responsible?"

"Of course. And I'm sure my answer will come as no surprise. I believe Chad Gleeson and Heck Buckley are behind what happened."

"Why is that?"

Annie waited for Dayton's declaration that the Lord himself had told him.

She wasn't prepared for the reverend to provide the explanation he did.

Standing half a dozen feet from her, he met her gaze.

"I had close ties with both men. That was never a secret. We saw eye to eye on many issues, issues you became involved with as a judge. Surely you were aware . . . ?"

"Yes, I was. Please, go on."

"I may have shared certain beliefs with those two, and their followers, but what they did crossed a line I will never be able to understand, much less forgive."

Annie couldn't resist.

"Didn't you tell your followers they should pray for Gleeson and Buckley's forgiveness?"

Annie's words—or perhaps the hint of sarcasm in her voice—threw Dayton. But only briefly.

"I'll share something with you," he said. "Something I'm not particularly proud of. I may be a man of the cloth, and I do my utmost to live by the Lord's word, and the Lord says we must forgive even the most vile of sinners. But I don't always practice what I preach. You see, sometimes I simply can't. So yes, I did tell my parishioners to pray for their forgiveness, but I have not done so. And I will not."

Annie studied him, digesting his words, trying to read him.

"You haven't answered my question. Why do you think Gleeson and Buckley kidnapped my mother?"

Again, Dayton did not shy away from her gaze.

"Because I know how they felt about you. And I know what they said when they talked about how to get you off the bench. And . . ."

He stopped midsentence.

"And what?"

Now his eyes averted her scrutiny.

"And *what*, Reverend Dayton?"

With a sigh, he locked eyes with her again.

"And . . . I know what they are capable of . . . What happened yesterday—your mother's . . ." He couldn't bring himself to say it. ". . . I've seen them do that before."

A quiet gasp escaped Annie.

"What are you talking about?"

"Two years ago. One of the men who'd poached with them for years turned on them. Snitched to law enforcement in exchange for having charges dropped. I watched Chad Gleeson hold his hand down on his kitchen table while Heck Buckley cut it off."

Annie's cry filled the room.

"Did you tell that to Sheriff Holmberg?"

"Yes, Your Honor," Dayton said. "I did."

Her anguish prompted the reverend to take three long steps toward Annie. He dropped to a bony knee beside her chair.

"Try to stay strong, young lady." He reached up and lifted her chin with a forefinger. "I know that bunch. Someone won't be able to resist the fifty-thousand-dollar reward. Just like the poacher who snitched on them, someone who knows something will come forward."

He hesitated before adding, "We just have to pray it happens in time to save your dear mother."


Will's mood was foul enough without being called in for "road duty," but as far as the Park Service was concerned, the need to ensure the safety of the tens of thousands of visitors driving through Yellowstone each day took precedence over the lower profile backcountry patrols, which meant that when someone who worked the roads called in sick, Will would inevitably be called back to civilization. He'd been lucky today, however, in that he was patrolling the stretch of road between the northeast entrance at Silver Gate and the north entrance in Gardiner. This morning's chagrin at the prospect of spending most of the day in his jeep was compensated for by only one thing—the fact that it gave him a chance to start his day in the Lamar Valley.

His shift didn't officially start for another two hours, but he'd already driven to a point just west of the Pebble Creek campground, parked his car on the side of the road, and climbed the hill behind it. With the sun's glow little more than a faint promise outlining the towering Absarokas to the east, and the pastoral beauty of the Lamar Valley to the south—its fields and gentle hills dotted with grazing bison, its namesake river meandering lazily across the canvas— Will began setting up his spotting scope. The sky held the promise of sun, but the air held a chill. Will took some of it deep into his lungs, stared out across the valley. A car whizzed by, its speed indicating the driver had no awareness—or concern—of the possibility of a bear, bison, or even the occasional wolf, suddenly stepping into the road. Off or on duty, Will would normally have pursued it with a vengeance, but now he zoned it out. He needed some peace of mind, some grounding. Some time to think.

He felt like he was going crazy and he didn't know why.

Even as that thought entered his mind, he realized that he did know. At least in part.

Over the last twenty-five years the only constant for him had been the peace he found in Yellowstone. It was his solace. His sanity. His mission and purpose in life. Will had always known that what had happened would have driven him crazy if he'd had to live anywhere other than Yellowstone. But life in Yellowstone had a tendency to put things in perspective. Here, any one person's life—tragic or otherwise— became almost insignificant. Not unimportant, not without pain, or joy, or passion; but witnessing the cycle of life—the tremendous hardships and struggles to survive—go on season after season, year after year, had given Will a perspective and a strength that made his own hardships diminish in the whole scheme of things. It made them tolerable.

After a winter that threatened the survival of the strongest and most tenacious members of a herd, a winter that inevitably left old or weak animals to slowly freeze to death, every spring bison cows gave birth to gangly piles of orange fur. The grizzly mama would emerge from her den with her cubs, scolding them, teaching them, watching over them with a fierce tenacity. Each night the sun would set over the Gallatins, and rise again the next morning over the

Absarokas. It didn't matter what happened to any one person on this planet. Broken hearts, death, financial woes, despair. Life in Yellowstone—despite its hardships, despite its cruelty—went on. It always returned to the most phenomenal beauty and miracles; on a daily basis, moments that took Will's breath away. And that's what kept Will McCarroll going.

But for the past twenty-five years, whenever that sanctity was threatened—inevitably by poachers—Will had had a proven way to respond. He reacted by pouring his heart and soul into tracking the culprits down, bringing them to justice. If he didn't succeed, he worked the case night and day, lived and breathed it, until the next offender came along to keep him occupied and feeling his time in Yellowstone—his life—made sense. That it was worthwhile.

But what had happened to Annie Peacock's mother not only represented a new level of threat to his world, the world around which his entire life revolved, so far Will hadn't been able to do a single thing to stop it, to fix it, to find Eleanor Malone. He hadn't done a single thing to eliminate the possibility that judges like Annie could be scared off the bench. Will did not believe that Annie would cave in to the kidnappers, but if that were the end result of Eleanor Malone's kidnapping, Will's world would be threatened on a scale that he had never even dreamed possible.

That prospect was enough to make a man like Will McCarroll a little bit crazy.

But Will had to admit to himself that there was more to the unease he felt, the sense his entire world had been rocked.

There were his feelings for Annie.

Will had closed his heart off years ago. He'd turned inward, become someone more in tune with wild, four-legged, and winged species than his own. Not that he'd spent all his nights alone. It had taken several years after Rachel's death, but eventually, he'd allowed himself an occasional fling—preferably a one-night stand. That went on through his thirties and early forties, inevitably with visitors passing through the park. He'd dated a park biologist early on, and that—having to face someone he simply would not allow himself to connect with on any level other than the physical—had been enough of a disaster to ensure he'd never hook up with someone who worked or lived in the park again. Eventually, by his midforties, he decided that even the one-night stands were hardly worth it.

Will knew it wasn't a normal existence, but it was the existence he'd chosen. The existence he felt safe with. No connections, no complications. No feelings of any significance. Just a steady state, one that Will was comfortable with. One that he could count on.

But Annie Peacock had now shaken that world as well. She had evoked emotions Will believed a thing of the past. Protective feelings, concern. Her vulnerability and grief pained Will. He'd sworn he'd never have such feelings for another woman, another human being. But they'd snuck up on him with Annie—with this woman, who, ironically, until recently, he'd despised. How could the cold, confidant woman he'd seen on the bench, the one who'd made a decision that caused Will so much grief and outrage, have such an effect on him?

None of it made sense, and Will now wished he could will it all away and return to the world as he knew it before Eleanor Malone was kidnapped. He knew how to deal with that world. This one was a crapshoot.

Will had been mechanically setting up the scope as he grappled with these thoughts, but now, as he lowered his forehead to the scope's eyepiece, movement in the periphery of the field of vision immediately caught Will's attention. A wolf.

He adjusted the focus and when he did, his heart skipped a beat.

Twenty-two.

The alpha female of the Druid pack. Ever since she'd lost her mate, rumor had it that she'd been restless, wandering the valleys and, during the warmer days, the plateaus high above the Lamar. Will hadn't seen her since #21 had been shot by Gleeson.

She looked ragged. Wolves who left their packs rarely survived, and he could tell that what had happened had already taken a terrible toll on 22.

So absorbed in studying her was he that he lost his customary sixth sense. The voice took him by surprise.

"I thought I'd find you here."

Will lifted his eyes from the scope.

Randy Hannah, wearing his usual smile and the uniform that said he was either on duty, or soon to be, headed Will's way, climbing the steep hill in long, youthful strides. Will noticed the Yellowstone Prius Randy drove—with a picture of Old Faithful painted on its side—parked behind Will's jeep.

Will usually resented any intrusion on his early morning outings, but that never applied to Randy.

"What the hell are you doing out here in the wilds?" he said, grinning. He kept one eye on the dot—Number 22—that he could make out moving slowly across a ridge above and beyond the river. "You lose your way to the mudpots or something?"

Randy stopped and nodded at the scope.

"Who you got out there?" he said.

"Twenty-two." Will stepped sideways to give Randy a look.

Randy bent his five-ten frame over the scope. While Will followed 22's progress with a naked eye, Randy zoomed in on her.

"Fucking Gleeson," he said after getting a good enough look to evaluate her condition.

"You got that right."

"Looks like the rumors are right," Randy said, straightening. He continued to stare out across the Lamar, following the dot moving toward the Thunderer Mountain with his naked eye. "She's left the pack."

"She's been looking for a new mate ever since Gleeson shot Twenty-one," Will replied. "None of the Druid males are up to the task." He paused. "If she doesn't rejoin the Druids, or find a new pack, at her age she'll be lucky to make it through the winter. Of course, if anyone can make it through hard times, it's Twenty-two."

"I hope you're right," Randy replied earnestly.

Below them, on the road, a car had slowed. A green Volvo. Will recognized it. *Wolf watchers*. It pulled off and parked behind Randy's Prius.

The wolf watchers in Yellowstone were a community in and of themselves. A diverse group that, after the reintroduction in 1995, had started coming from all over the country, and the world, to spend hours each day simply hoping to get a glance of a wolf. Thirteen years later, many had actually bought homes nearby, in Cooke City or Silver Gate. Wolves were their passion. And Will was their hero.

Will recognized the couple who got out of the car and were now trudging up the hill. Tom and Edith Wurley, a retired military officer and his wife from Connecticut. They were pretty much a fixture at wolf-watching sites throughout the park. He waved. On the road, another car had stopped. A middle-aged couple and a boy emerged and started up the hill after the Wurleys. Will had never seen them before.

He turned to Randy. Something about his young friend did not seem right today.

"I know you didn't drive out here just to burn up that big salary we're paying you on gas," he said. "What's up, Randy?"

Randy's smile had already evaporated with all the talk about wolves, but his expression grew even more grave. He eyed the approaching visitors, waving at the family.

"Something's wrong, Will. The hot springs . . . they're going crazy. I mean some of the springs in the Upper Terraces have dried up. Like overnight."

Will had never seen Randy like this.

"That's what the geothermal features are all about, Randy. You know that. Change. Nothing stays the same up there in Mammoth. Hell, I only go up there and really walk around maybe once a year, but every time I do, I feel like I'm visiting a new planet, it's changed so much."

"I know that, but this is different. I've been doing some research . . ."

The Wurleys had crested the hill. Will nodded their way, then put a hand on Randy's shoulder. "Why don't you go talk to Brian? He'll tell you there's nothing to worry about."

"Brian's out of town for ten more days," Randy answered. "This can't wait that long."

Will snorted a laugh.

"Nothing's gonna happen in that amount of time, Randy. Hell, nothing's gonna happen while we're still alive. Unless that caldera decides it's time to blow, and then we won't be around to worry about it, will we?"

Randy managed a feeble smile in response. Tom and Edith Worley had called out a hello, then observing the unspoken rule of wolf watchers, set up their scope a respectable distance from Will's. They had apparently already zeroed in on 22.

The family, however, continued on toward where Will and Randy stood. Randy looked troubled by the exchange the two men had just had, but he managed a smile and a wave for the newcomers.

The boy—Will guessed him to be around ten—ran up to Randy.

"Hey, Zach," Randy said, reaching out to pat him on the shoulder. "I thought you guys had gone back to Ohio."

"My dad took a whole month off," the boy replied excitedly. "So we can stay here. We saw your car and I made him stop so I could tell you."

Randy couldn't help but grin.

"Good for you," he said. "And you're in luck. This is my friend, Will McCarroll. Wait 'til you see what he has in his scope."

The boy's parents had finally caught up to him. Will took note of the warm hug they both gave Randy.

"Will, this is Kevin and Amy Knudtsen," Randy said. "Zach and his parents are friends of mine."

Zach beamed at Randy's proclamation of friendship.

Will nodded a hello at the parents.

"Want to take a look?" he said to Zach. He lowered the spotting scope to Zach's height.

Zach pressed his eye to it, then cried out, "Is that a wolf?"

"Not just any wolf," Will replied, "that's a pretty famous wolf. Number Twenty-two. She was the alpha female of the Druids."

"Was?" Kevin Knudtsen asked.

"The alpha male was killed recently. Twenty-two left the pack. She's out on her own right now."

"That's so sad," Amy Knudtsen said.

"How did the male die?" Kevin asked.

"A poacher shot him," Will replied. The tone of his voice, as much as the words, silenced everyone but Zach.

"Someone should shoot the poacher."

"Zachary!" his mother cried.

Will and Randy eyed each other and tried not to smile, then Will reached out and tousled the boy's hair.

"I don't blame you for feeling that way, Zach," he said, "but if I do my job right, the man who shot Twenty-one will pay for it."

"What's your job?"

Randy answered before Will had a chance.

"Will's been one of the park's backcountry rangers for a long time. It's his job to protect the wolves, and the bears, and all the wildlife here in Yellowstone, and he's the best there is at that."

Zach stared at Will, wide-eyed, while Randy turned to his father.

"I hear you're staying in the park for a while."

Kevin's newly tanned face split with a toothy, enthusiastic smile.

"We just don't want to leave," he said. He looked over at Amy. "This has been the best thing that ever happened to us." His eyes then turned to his son. "And to Zach. I called in and took all my vacation for the year, and used up my accrued sick days.

"We can't afford to stay in the hotel that long so we bought camping equipment. We're at the Mammoth campgrounds."

"That's pretty cool," Randy replied.

"We think so," Kevin said proudly. "And one of the things I promised Zach is that he'd see a wolf. Now he has."

Will had been watching the scene on the hill across the river. His bare eye had picked up a new dot, approaching Twenty-two.

"He's about to see one more," he said.

Tom and Edith Wurley had already zeroed in on it.

"Hey, Will," Tom Wurley called out excitedly, "it's that young male from the Swan Lake pack."

"I'll be damned," Will muttered to himself.

Zach moved out of the way and Will bent back over his own scope, a sense of anticipation and wonder filling him.

After all these years, it had not left him. The thrill a sight like this gave rise to in his otherwise blunted soul and heart.

The alpha female of the Druids, out looking for a mate after losing hers, and a healthy young male visitor, from Swan Lake. Most likely he'd already challenged the alpha male of his pack, without success, and then, full of testosterone and lacking the fear he by all rights should have had, he'd headed out to start his own pack.

It was nature at its most primitive. Both animals' very survival might well depend upon the outcome of this meeting.

And Will got to watch it with his own two eyes.

Oblivious to the human beings a mile away, the two creatures performed a dance. This was the beauty, the sacred nature, of Yellowstone. A place where people could still see wild animals acting naturally.

Will didn't know it, but everyone's eyes were also on him, waiting for his pronouncement, but they all knew better than to talk to him at that moment. There were rules—unwritten, but cast in stone just the same—within the wolf-watching circles. A hierarchy, an order. Will despised pecking orders, or elitism or snobbery of any kind, but like it or not, he was at the top of that pyramid.

"My guess is she'll think he's too young," he finally said.

They all watched a while longer while the two wolves circled and sniffed at one another, marking tufts of grass and sagebrush frequently.

"I hate to do it, but I have to get going," Randy announced. "My shift starts in forty-five minutes."

"We'll walk you to your car," Kevin Knudtsen offered.

After their good-byes, the Knudtsens started toward the road with Randy. Fifty feet away, Zach suddenly stopped, turned, and called out to Will.

"You gonna make sure that Twenty-two doesn't get shot too?"

Will had returned to looking at the encounter across the valley, but now he straightened and gave Zach a solemn look.

"I'll make sure," he said. "You have my word."

This seemed to please Zach, or at least ease the anguish he'd apparently been feeling after hearing about Twenty-one.

As they passed the Wurleys, Tom offered to let Zach look through his scope, which was more high-powered than Will's. Will watched as Tom and Edith pointed out another popular site for spotting wolves on a park map to Zach's parents.

Randy stood by.

His exchange with Randy was bothering Will. Despite Randy's good nature, and obvious affection for the Knudtsens, Will could tell he was upset. Will felt he'd let his young friend down.

As the group parted ways with the Wurleys and headed down the hill to their cars, Will debated calling Randy back. But to say what? Yellowstone's geothermal features were defined by change—usually slow and subtle, but sometimes quite radical. When Brian Wise returned he would be able to convince Randy his concerns were needless.

Still, Will didn't feel right.

He'd just lifted a hand, cupped it to his mouth to yell to Randy, when he saw the two dots on the horizon take off at a run. Twenty-two had decided to test the young male's level of interest.

With one more glance his young friend's way, and a nagging sense of guilt, Will turned back to the scope.

# FOURTEEN

ANNIE HAD HIT ROCK BOTTOM.

Ever since the night of her mother's disappearance, everyone around her had cautioned her to "take it easy," "take some time to yourself," but in reality the chaos that had followed the kidnapping, along with Annie's workload, had been her saving grace. If it hadn't been for her work, for her determination to maintain business as usual—and in doing so, send a message to her mother's kidnappers—she would have gone mad.

But even work couldn't erase the image inside that coffee can, nor the thoughts that image gave rise to, and now, as she lay in bed with Saturday morning approaching, and no reason to go into the office, nothing to distract her from the horrible reality that had become her life, she felt herself sinking into despair. Yet she knew that her very survival depended on forcing herself out of bed, forcing herself to go through the motions.

And then a soft snoring beside her—Archie—reminded her of another important reason to try to maintain the normalcy of her life.

She reached over, stroked the Lab's soft, blocky head, reveled in the steady, soft breaths, and the rise and fall of his chest, signs that he was very much alive. That he wasn't going to desert her. Maybe she'd take him for a little longer walk this morning than the others he'd had this week, down the old Gardiner Road. Yes, that's what she'd do. Archie would love that.

If only this dizziness would pass. This morning it—like everything else—seemed harder to deal with.

Sheriff Holmberg had declared new hope for finding Eleanor Malone alive. While DNA testing would not confirm for several days yet that the ear belonged to her, Holmberg told Annie the crime lab had already confirmed that circulation to the ear indicated its owner was still alive. He'd vowed to redouble their efforts.

Lying in the semidark, Annie lifted her hand into the air, into the center of the shaft of first morning's light that filtered through her parted window curtains, and stared at the ring she'd slid onto her hand the night of the kidnapping. Even on her third finger, it threatened to slide off. As a young woman, her mother had a rounder figure than Annie. Later in life, Eleanor had delighted in the pounds melting away, but her arthritic joints insured the ring wouldn't slide off and be forever lost. Now Annie took it off, clutched it to her chest.

She closed her eyes against the approaching morning. Outside, a bull elk bugled. Was it that time of year already? When she opened her eyes again, she held the ring back up to the light.

Just what had transpired—what hell had her mother endured—to lead to her wearing it now?

She mustn't lose hope. Archie needed her. And if her mother were still alive, she needed Annie. Desperately.

Annie glanced at the clock on her bedside table.

Five forty-five A.M.

She threw back the covers—slim protection against the nighttime temperatures that had dropped into the thirties—and padded across the room, to the robe she'd tossed on the dresser. If Eleanor were there, she'd no doubt comment on the fact that Annie's room resembled the chaos she'd lived in throughout grade school and high school. Annie had actually done a major about-face in the years since, even to the point that Eleanor had once—right after moving in and having Annie follow her around, picking up after her—told Annie she'd become a bit "anal." But Annie wasn't anal about housekeeping now. Not this week. Everything lay exactly where she'd thrown it earlier, after coming home from work, or getting up in the morning.

On her way to the bathroom, Annie glanced in the mirror above the dresser. Her thick, dark hair rioted in every direction. Even in the dark, she could make out the black half circles under her eyes.

In the bathroom, she didn't look in the mirror. Deliberately didn't turn the light on.

She did, however, flip the hallway light switch as she started down the stairs, clutching the railing to steady herself against the dizziness.

She felt Archie's warm breath on her bare heels.

Halfway down, he began to growl. A gutteral, primitive sound, one that the old Archie had never been capable of.

Annie froze.

She'd left the porch light on. Through the opaque window that made up the top half of the door, she made out the faint outline of someone standing outside. The only person she might expect a visit from at that hour was Sheriff Holmberg, but this person did not stand that tall.

Annie grasped the railing and eased one foot up, onto the stair behind her. As she began to work her way backward up the stairs to the telephone in her bedroom, her eyes fixed to the door, the figure suddenly stepped forward—directly into the shaft of light from the porch lamp—and in that instant, she felt a flash of recognition.

A sharp rap followed. Then another.

"It's okay, bud," Annie told Archie, her heart racing, even as she realized she needn't be afraid.

She descended to the first floor and crossed the small hallway to the door. When she opened it, Archie let loose a short, high-pitched whelp of enthusiasm, then turned into a groveling, tail-wagging whirl of motion.

Will McCarroll stood in the doorway, dressed in jeans and a fleece jacket.

"Hey there, fella," he said, crouching down to Archie's level, his hand running down the dog's back. "Better not get too worked up."

He looked up and suddenly Annie flashed on the image that had stared back at her moments earlier from the mirror.

If it made any impact on McCarroll, he did not show it.

"Morning, Your Honor," he said.

Behind him a brisk wind stirred up leaves that a storm during the night had stripped, prematurely, from the cottonwood that shaded Annie's front porch.

"How would you like to go for a ride?"


"You must be psychic," Annie said after a long sip from the styrofoam cup cradled between her trembling hands. While Will took Archie outside for a short walk, she'd excused herself to get dressed and run a brush through her hair. Then they'd climbed inside his 4Runner and, as they passed through Gardiner, stopped at the corner convenience store for coffee and bagels.

"Now that's something no one's ever accused me of before," Will replied.

"I woke up feeling like I'd go crazy if I didn't do something constructive today."

"Last thing this park needs is another crazy judge."

Annie glanced Will's way. His coffee cup hid his mouth, but the corner of his eyes held a rare hint of humor. But when Will lowered the cup, his tone was dead serious.

"What are Holmberg and the FBI telling you?"

"There's not much to tell. They still don't have anything tangible. Just theories."

"The theory being that Gleeson and Buckley are working together, and that the kidnapping was intended to intimidate you into letting Gleeson off? Which of course would score a big victory for Buckley and his antiwolf coalition. They get the hysteria level up about wolves, kill off one of the most magnificent animals in the park, and send the world a signal that you can get away with it if you call it self-defense."

"Yes, that's the theory right now," Annie replied. "But that's all it is. A theory." She half turned to study his face. In profile, the deeply etched lines at the crease of his eyes and on his forehead made him look older than he did head-on. "What are you thinking?"

"Gleeson's just one of dozens of outfitters that have been bringing poachers into this park for years now. It's big business. Only money makes people do things as crazy as kidnapping someone. Money and a sense they can get away with it. Still, I'm not totally buying it."

Annie had spent enough years prosecuting criminals to know how their minds worked.

"Unless," she said, "Gleeson's absolutely confident no one can prove he was involved in my mother's kidnapping. If he somehow knows he can't be convicted of anything, he and Buckley might want to use the publicity from what's going on to further the antiwolf coalition's goals."

"I guess that's possible," Will replied, "but it's a bold move. And risky. It all depends on his being successful in scaring you off . . ."

He paused and Annie knew he was waiting for reassurance from her that that wouldn't happen.

But she couldn't give it to him. At least not right now.

When she did not reply, Will continued.

"None of it quite makes sense to me. Which is why it hit me last night. Judge Sherburne. If anybody can figure out what's going on, it'd be him. Nobody understands the forces that impact this park better than he does."

Ever since she took the job as Yellowstone's magistrate judge, the near constant references to her predecessor, and—truth be told—the reverence with which even his name was spoken, had bugged the hell out of Annie. But pride—which she'd always acknowledged to be one of her greatest weaknesses—now seemed like a twisted, self-centered indulgence. From a strictly legal point of view, Annie had looked at some of Sherburne's decisions with skepticism—even, at times, downright disapproval and incredulity. But all that mattered now was finding her mother, and if Judge Sherburne could help shed light on what may have led to her kidnapping, Annie would gladly join the legions of his admirers. But there was one problem.

"I thought his stroke left him unable to speak."

"It did," Will responded.

Annie refrained from voicing the obvious response—how in the hell then would Judge Sherburne be able to help?—and instead said, "Have you visited him before?"

"Couple times," Will replied, lifting his cup of coffee to his lips—a clear signal that was all he wanted to say about it.

Other than the "well, shit," he muttered when they passed under another WERI sign with the rotating globe at the south edge of Livingston, Will didn't say another word the entire forty-five-minute drive.

That was okay with Annie. The dizziness had moved to her stomach now. Maybe it was nerves too, but she felt like the dry heaves might be coming on.

They pulled up in front of a long redbrick structure—"Mormon brick," Annie had learned the non-Mormons in the area called it—that spanned an entire block. Rainbow Living Center. It had white pillars and roofline, a bit Monticello-like, and grand maple trees shading its many porches.

Will strode up the sidewalk with the assurance of familiarity and she suspected he'd been there more than the "couple" of times he'd confessed to, especially when the shapely brunette at the reception desk addressed him by name. Annie could swear she also stifled a grin.

They headed down one wing of the building. When she saw a sign for a restroom, Annie hurried past Will, saying, "What room is he in?"

Will turned, surprised, then recognized where she was headed and said, "I'll wait down the hall for you."

Annie practically ran the last few yards to the bathroom, sweat beading on her forehead. It was a relief to find no one else inside, though it wouldn't have mattered—she had no choice. She stood over the porcelain sink, grasping its cool surface with sweaty hands and waited for the waves to come, waves of her body trying to rid itself of its toxins. Twice, she doubled over retching, but as usual, nothing came out. Just another cruel, useless trick being played on her body.

She stood there, still, for several minutes, then glanced up to look in the mirror. The eye circles had darkened. She stared at herself, at the fear in her eyes, and suddenly she was looking into the eyes of the white wolf on her office wall. Number 22. Annie's eyes were brown, not that gorgeous green. But the instinctive sense of the wolf in that remarkable photograph Les had taken, the sense that she was in the midst of a struggle for survival, stared back at Annie.

She wet a paper towel and wiped her face. Then she waited.

After several minutes, it passed.

She took a deep breath, and stepped back out into the hall.

Will was standing several doors down, looking out a window.

When she approached, she could tell he tried to avoid looking at her, but then he chanced a look and said, "You okay?"

Annie simply nodded.

They turned a corner, passed a dozen doors on either side, and then stopped in front of a partially open door.

Will cocked his head, peeked inside; then, standing in place, pushed the door open enough for the room to come into view.

It was bright and good-sized, with mahogany furniture that completed the Monticello theme. The bed, bearing an ornate, carved headboard, sat center stage.

At first Annie thought the room empty, but then she followed Will inside and once they'd gotten through the door she saw him. He was sitting, back to them, in a wheelchair, looking out the window.

He did not turn to look at them, but something about the change in his posture told Annie he knew he had visitors. Will took several long strides to the wheelchair and laid a hand on the shoulders that were still surprisingly sturdy.

"Morning, Your Honor," he said as he circled around to the window so that Sherburne could see him. "How're they treatin' you today?"

Annie could see the left side of Judge Sherburne's profile. His face looked without expression—until she came fully around beside Will, and saw she was wrong. The right side hosted a twisted grin and a gleam in his eye.

Wild white hair swept over a balding crown. Will reached out and straightened Sherburne's glasses, which had tipped to the left—which is where everything on his body seemed to want to go.

Sherburne's intense gaze went to Annie and would not let go.

Will chuckled.

"Still got an eye for the ladies, huh?" he said. "Judge, this is Annie Peacock. Your successor."

A flicker of surprise flashed across the right side of Sherburne's face.

He made a grunting sound that at first startled, even embarrassed, Annie. Then she realized it had been a greeting.

She reached out to grasp both of his hands, which were sitting on his lap. The right one angled up, from the wrist, and grasped back firmly while the left one did not move.

"It's so nice to finally meet you," Annie said warmly. An acute sense of shame overtook her at having indulged a sense of resentment for this man. "Yours is a tough act to follow, Your Honor."

Tears quickly sprang to Sherburne's eyes. He nodded, grunted again.

Annie's heart went out to him, but, at the same time, it about dropped into her stomach. What had Will been thinking? How could Judge Sherburne—trapped inside a body newly foreign to him—be of any help in finding out what had happened to her mother?

Will must have sensed her thoughts. He pulled a chair over from a breakfast set in the corner of the room, offering it to Annie. When she declined, he placed it directly in front of Sherburne, and while Annie stood watching, Will lowered himself into it.

He wanted eye contact. Close eye contact.

"Judge," he began, "have you heard anything about what happened last week at the stone house?"

The judge closed his eyes.

*The stone house.* Annie wondered if he was envisioning the house he'd lived in for over three decades. The house he'd raised two children in, and walked home to for lunch from his office.

The house with a view of Minerva. And Liberty Cap.

Sherburne took a deep breath, then opened his eyes again. He nodded.

Yes. He had heard.

His eyes moved from Will to Annie. He did not make a sound, nor did any part of his body, other than his eyes, move; but Annie did not mistake the compassion and sympathy he wanted, desperately so, to convey to her.

"Thank you," she said softly, reaching out again to squeeze both his hands. As Will leaned closer, she let go, and backed up to stand against the windowsill.

For the first time, Annie noticed a stack of newspapers. In the otherwise neat-as-a-pin room, a pile of newspapers—weeks of them, and they had been read, their condition made that very clear—was the only thing that jarred the perfect harmony that Rainbow Living obviously strove to achieve for its residents.

That and a weathered backpack propped up on Judge Sherburne's pillow.

Their minds and bodies might have been in a state of chaos, but Rainbow Living made damn sure their residents' rooms were in order.

"There are lots of different theories going around," she heard Will say, "about who would want to kidnap Judge

Peacock's mother. Naturally, the strongest one is that whoever did it wants her off the bench."

Sherburne made a soft clucking sound, and nodded again, almost imperceptibly.

He agreed with this theory.

A sense of foreboding stirred in Annie.

"But the investigators are getting nowhere," Will went on. "And time could be running out." He looked at Annie, clearly concerned about her reaction to what he felt he had to reveal next. "The kidnappers sent Judge Peacock a grisly message the other day . . ."

Sherburne closed his eyes and nodded. He'd heard.

"You know the park better than anyone. You know the players, the pressures, the politics. I thought maybe you'd have some thoughts, some ideas on who might do this kind of thing. That's why we're here. That's why I brought Annie to meet you."

Sherburne's chest rose with a deep breath. He opened his mouth to speak. At first nothing came out. And then a sound that had no meaning. He pressed his eyes closed.

"How about this?" Will said. "You just listen. Annie and I will ask you questions. If your answer is yes, lift your hand. If it's no, don't respond. How about that?"

Like an obedient primary student, the right hand tilted upward.

"Great," Will said. He turned to Annie. "We don't want to tire him out. Why don't you start?"

Annie stepped forward and dropped to one knee beside Will to bring herself eye to eye with Judge Sherburne.

"You nodded your head in agreement when Will told you the theory is that someone wants me off the bench. The FBI and the sheriff are focusing on Heck Buckley and the antiwolf coalition, and Chad Gleeson. Would you agree?"

The eyes never left Annie's face but to Annie's surprise, the hand stayed put. Once again, his lips on the right side of his mouth parted. A series of incomprehensible sounds spilled out, their plaintive quality piercing the hearts of everyone in the room, including Sherburne himself.

"He wants to explain," Will said softly, his tone indicating that he, too, had been taken off guard by Sherburne's failure to endorse the Gleeson and Buckley theory.

But Sherburne had no way of doing so. The pain in his eyes, the depth of the frustration and despair, forced Annie to swallow back tears. It wasn't right to put him through this.

Will, however, leaned toward the elderly magistrate again.

"This isn't a solitary individual. If it's Gleeson, he's not acting alone. Think about it, Judge, think about how many illegal hunters there are out there, locals who bring fat cats in from all over the country for a trophy animal. You've had dozens of them, hundreds in your courtroom. You despised them, held their feet to the fire. But the poaching's just grown. They loved knowing you were out of the picture, then Annie here came along. She's not you, but she's no pushover either and they know it. You were there thirty-two years, wasn't it?" He didn't wait for an answer. "Well, as you can see, Annie's a young woman. Let's just say they decided they're not willing to put up with another thirty years of strict enforcement of the T and E Act, or the Lacey Act.

"I think Gleeson shot that wolf deliberately, to get Buckley involved. So that the antiwolf coalition messes up the picture. Gleeson, his network of hunting buddies, they're under the radar. Gleeson's got an airtight alibi for the night of the kidnapping. Maybe they've got big money funding them from back East, but they're intangible—just a bunch of hunters who've decided poaching is a legitimate way to make a living. And the beauty is, since it was a wolf Gleeson shot, they figured it'd be natural for Buckley and his group to take the blame."

As he continued with his theory, Sherburne began shaking his head back and forth. No. No. No.

He tried again to speak. Tears welled up in his eyes. This time they were tears of anger and frustration.

His eyes moved purposefully across the bed and came to rest on the pile of newspapers.

Annie's concern about straining him kept growing.

"Will," she said, "I think we should go now. Come back another time."

In a burst of anger, Sherburne grunted. His eyes went to Will, then pointedly, back to the newspapers.

"Come on," Annie said, standing. She put her hand on Will's shoulder firmly. "We should let Judge Sherburne rest."

"No," Will replied. "He's trying to tell us something."

Will leaned closer to the judge.

"Is it the newspapers?" he asked. "Do you want me to get them?"

With a sigh, Sherburne's right hand practically leaped off his lap.

Yes.

Will strode over to the bedside table and grabbed the stack of papers.

Returning with them in hand, he crouched in front of Judge Sherburne and said, "Okay, signal when you see what you want."

As Will turned the front page of each section his way, Sherburne's eyes did not stray. About three sections into the *Billings Gazette* from the day before, in the national news section, Sherburne's hand angled up again.

"This one?" Will said, placing the rest of the stack on the empty chair behind him and placing that section of the paper on the judge's lap.

Annie eyed the articles along with Will as he slowly scanned the front page. Judge Sherburne's eyes scanned along with them. Annie had expected to see something about hunting, or poaching, but when Sherburne finally grunted again it was on a column that contained a half dozen newsbriefs—a major airline filing for bankruptcy, the vice president's wife recuperating from a mastectomy, a summary of newly proposed legislation. Nothing relevant. Will turned to the next page.

Sherburne's sigh forced Will to turn back again.

"There's nothing about hunting, or poaching," Annie said.

"He's trying to tell us something . . ." Will replied.

Sherburne looked up with hopeful eyes, but just as he did, a gratingly cheerful voice called out, "Time for physical therapy."

A short, heavyset blonde swept into the room. She wore a disturbingly dark lipstick, almost purple in color, and a nametag that said "Nomie."

Paying little attention to his visitors, Nomie kicked the brake latch to the "off" position on Judge Sherburne's wheelchair with a practiced toe, and began wheeling him backward, away from Will and Annie.

"You folks will have to come back a little later," she said. "You must not have noticed the visiting hours sign. Judge Sherburne has a full schedule this morning."

The enraged, animal-like sound that Sherburne made caused Annie's hair to stand on end.

"Now, now," Nomie said, "let's not get temperamental. I tell you what, how would you like to show your friends the progress we've made?"

She looked up at Annie and Will, as if they were enjoying aperitifs at a lawn party, and said, "He took two steps yesterday. Assisted steps, of course, but two steps! Isn't that wonderful?"

Will's eyes were glued to Sherburne's face, the right side of which was twisted in anger and frustration.

"We're not done talking," Will said. "He's been trying to tell us something, but we couldn't quite understand. We just need a few more minutes. Will you please give us that?"

Just then Nomie noticed the papers on the floor.

"Oh," she said condescendingly. "I see. He's obsessed with the news. We have a young volunteer named Sasha who comes in and holds the paper for him to read every day. Don't share this with the speech therapist, but I swear Sasha understands him better than anyone here. She'll turn the pages for him, then hold them real still 'til he's done with an article. Helps time pass. But it also seems to frustrate the judge. I may recommend that they stop delivering the paper to him . . ."

She'd wheeled him close to the breakfast table, upon which sat a pitcher of water.

Sherburne lifted his right arm and with one sweep of his arm, sent the pitcher flying.

This set the nurse off.

"Why'd you go and do that?" Nomie cried. Then, again, she turned to look at Will and Annie. Actually, mainly Will. She obviously hadn't picked up on how attractive he was when she first stormed into the room. Now, it helped her regain control.

"He's just frustrated," she said in one of the most disingenuous and condescendingly patient voices Annie had ever heard. "His mind works perfectly but he can't communicate what he wants to say. Plus, Judge Sherburne wants out. It's natural. All our residents do at first, but for some reason, Judge Sherburne feels it more strongly than just about anyone we've ever had here. He just stares out that window, day and night. Thank goodness he gets lots of visitors. Rangers and such from the park. In fact, Judge Sherburne had a little adventure a couple weeks ago . . ."

Suddenly her eyes widened. She zeroed in on Will.

"You're the one, aren't you?" She let out a little giggle. Annie had become completely confused. "I thought I recognized you, but you don't have a uniform on today."

"Don't know what you're talking about," Will replied.

"You're the one who snuck Judge Sherburne out of here. Oh my gosh, you'd better watch out. If the floor supervisor sees you . . ."

"Give us five more minutes with him. Alone. Please."

"I'm sorry, no can do. My schedule's back-to-back. I've got the pool reserved for Judge Sherburne right now."

One look at the fury and frustration on his friend's twisted face and Will pointed to the door.

"Out," he yelled.

Nomie's eyes went wide and wild.

"Security! Security!" she screamed.

Will took a long look at Sherburne. A hint of the old gleam had reentered the old man's eye.

"Will . . ." Annie said.

Will bent over, gave Sherburne a hug, and said, "I'll be back. I promise."

Then as Nomie ran into the hallway to see what was taking security so long, he grabbed Annie's arm and steered her toward the door.

"Come on. Take a right, the back door's this way."

They'd just stepped into the hallway when Will pivoted and ran back into the room. Annie watched him grab the newspaper they'd been looking at when the nurse from hell entered the room.

"Hang in there, Judge," Will urged his friend.

And then they were gone.

"So what was that about?"

They'd managed to escape the Rainbow Living Center through the back door without being confronted. A law-abiding citizen all her life and never before on the run, Annie's heart had been in her throat as they sprinted to Will's car, but Will had a shit-eating grin on his face the entire time.

Now they were driving through downtown Livingston, headed toward Highway 89 and home, with Annie sneaking glances into the side-view mirror for pursuers.

"Back there?" Will answered innocently.

"Yes, *of course* I mean back there."

"Nothing really. It's just that from time to time I come up and take Judge Sherburne for a ride."

"How?"

"You mean how do I do it, or how do I get away with it?"

"Both."

"Doing it is easy. I just wheel him out to the car. He's lost so much weight since his stroke he's easy to lift. And

I've made a couple friends there who cover for us." That explained the receptionist, Annie thought. "Usually no one ever knows the difference. Last time they did."

He turned and looked at Annie. The humor drained from his face.

"He has every right to leave, you know. They can't stop him if that's what he wants."

"I imagine it's about safety," Annie said. She regretted it instantly, realizing it made her sound like the bureaucrat she was. And that was apparently just how Will took it.

"It's not about safety," he said, his hands tightening on the 4Runner's steering wheel. "It's about rules. Rules that make it easier for them to fill places like that with people either so drugged up and intimidated, so fucking fearful because they've ended up dependent on people who are paid—paid—to take care of them, that they've allowed themselves to be turned into sheep. But not the judge. He'll never let them do that to him. Wait 'til he can talk again."

Annie fell silent as they pulled onto Highway 89 and Will swung into the left lane, passing a pickup driving too slowly for his liking. Its occupants were a Stetson-wearing cowboy and on the seat beside him, the dog of choice for Montana ranchers—a blue heeler. As they passed, a second heeler's head popped up between the two.

As Annie took in the jagged peaks of the Absarokas, towering over the valley grasslands and the Yellowstone River as it wound its way down toward its confluence with the Gardner, she tried to imagine Will sneaking Judge Sherburne out for a joyride. She knew she would be haunted by their visit to this honorable, dignified man now trapped in a world that clearly bordered on hell for him.

"Where do you take him?" she asked quietly.

"To the park. That's where he wants to go."

"Where in the park?"

"You really want to know?"

"Yes," Annie replied. "I do. Very much."

Will glanced sideways at her.

"Our first stop is always your house," he said. "We pull into the lot across from you. I angle the car so he can look at the house, and at the terraces, and we just sit there."

Annie drew in her breath.

"Where else?"

"It depends. Usually it's at night—that's the safest time to sneak him out of there 'cause most of the Nazi staff has gone home. If it's already dark, we mainly just drive around Mammoth. He tires pretty easily."

She expected Will to fall silent then, as was his habit, but it soon became clear this was a story he wanted to tell. One he had to tell.

"One night," he said, "there was this full moon. He wanted to go out to the Lamar. I kept him out all night, got him back in bed just before the first shift at that hellhole starts."

The idea of these two disparate souls—this loner, rebel of a ranger, and a popular, respected judge felled by a stroke—roaming Yellowstone together at night touched Annie to the depths of her soul.

"What did you do in the Lamar?"

"We mostly sat there, with the windows rolled down. He could see the buffalo, and hear the wolves. And we talked."

"You *talked*?"

"Well, I guess it was mostly me. But it felt like it was both of us, like we used to do all those years. I used to stop by the courthouse and we'd talk about the park's history, and the Old West—Sherburne had a thing about Western history—and how we can't let our guard down. How we have to fight the poachers, and the development that threatens the wildlife that leave the park, and the commercialization of Yellowstone. 'Cause we both know that if we don't fight, we'll lose it. We'll lose what we love about Yellowstone, what makes Yellowstone wild."

Annie turned to study Will's profile. Usually she felt it necessary to steal glances his way, but something was happening, changing, between them, and this time she dared to keep her gaze fixed firmly to the sight.

"What did you talk about that night?"

"About when we die, having our bodies dragged out into the Lamar to be recycled into the food chain. He told me that once, years ago, he used those exact words—that he wanted to be recycled into the food chain. I promised him that night we sat there, looking out at the bison, that I'd make sure that happened."

"How could you do that? Tell him something that's not possible."

"Not possible?" Will echoed, reverting to his trademark sarcasm that Annie had almost forgotten about. "Or not legal? Because I don't give a damn if it's legal or not. I gave him my word, and whether you want to believe me or not, I'll keep it."

They both fell silent. Annie was certain Will had said more than he really intended. Perhaps more than he wanted. She wondered if he'd withdraw from her now, like he always did. But then Will cleared his throat.

"He cries. Every time I bring him to the park. He smiles at first—mostly with his eyes, but sometimes it's that lopsided, goofy grin. For a while he'll look like a little kid in a candy shop. But then, when it's time to go back, he cries. Every time."

Will took a second to compose himself.

"The least I can do for that man," he finally said, "after all he's done for Yellowstone, is see that one day he never has to leave."

He glanced Annie's way then. A tear worked its way down her cheek.

They drove in silence for another twenty miles, passing ranchland blessed with the Yellowstone's water, cattle fat from a summer of grazing, horses energized by the cool turn of weather. All framed by the Absarokas to the east and the Gallatin Range to the west.

Annie had never known such beauty. It had given her untold comfort in the days before her mother disappeared, but now, while she recognized its magnificence, she could only long for those earlier days and the exhilaration this drive had once inspired in her.

A flock of trumpeter swans passed overhead, then honed in on the waters of the Yellowstone, gracefully descending until the cottonwoods on the riverbank blocked them from sight.

"So now it's your turn," Will said.

"What do you mean?"

"I mean I spilled more of my guts to you today than I've ever done in my life. Now, if you don't mind, I'd like to ask you a question."

"That seems fair," Annie replied, curious but clueless about where he was heading, which is why his next words startled her.

"Is it cancer? Chemo?"

"I don't know what you're talking about."

"Is that what's wrong with you? I'm not trying to pry, but it seems to me you're going through enough already, without also trying to hide being sick. If I can help in some way . . ."

Annie had always been such a private person. Aside from her mother, she'd told no one. And that was how she planned to keep it.

"It's that obvious?"

"I watched my sister go through chemo. Is that it?"

Annie took in Will's profile. Somehow she couldn't imagine him having a sister.

"I'm sorry," she said. "Is she okay now?"

"Fifteen years later and she's still running her own company and raising a couple of spirited teenagers. Alone."

Annie was taken off guard when he turned and locked eyes with her, ever so briefly.

"You didn't answer."

Annie closed her eyes, laid her head back against the neck rest.

"I'm terribly grateful that I'm not going through what your sister went through, what so many people do. But in a way it might be easier to say yes, it's cancer. Because then you might understand."

"I know I'm not the sharpest tack in the box," Will

replied, sarcasm creeping back into his voice, "but you might try me."

Annie opened her eyes, turned to see he was looking at her again. His eyes held none of the contempt she used to see there. All they held now was concern.

And in that instant, before Will turned his gaze back to the road, she decided to tell him the truth.


"I came to Yellowstone to start over," Annie began. "I'd gone through a really tough year, and I just didn't feel I could stay in Seattle any longer."

Once she started talking, Will's instincts told him not to look at Annie. That to do so could stop her. He kept his eyes on the road now.

"Want to tell me what made the year so tough?"

"I'm not sure it's relevant," she replied, pausing. "Actually, it *is* relevant because that's when I started taking the SSRI."

"SSRI?"

"It's an antidepressant."

"I'm afraid you've lost me. Antidepressant I understand, but not the rest of it."

"SSRI stands for selective serotonin reuptake inhibitor," Annie answered. "It's a type of antidepressant. It's *the* antidepressant of the day. Or perhaps I should say the decade. Doctors prescribe it now for everything from depression to headaches to having a couple bad days."

"Go on."

"My husband and I hadn't been getting along for years. He wanted to have a baby. I didn't."

She paused again. Will sensed there would be a lot of pauses, that discussion of her personal life was a new and difficult thing for Annie. He debated telling her she should feel free to stop her disclosure, yet, somehow he also sensed that it was important to her to be doing this. And the truth was, Will wanted to know. He wanted to understand this enigmatic woman who'd caused such a firestorm in his life.

"It wasn't that I never want to become a mother," she finally went on. "But I'd known for a long time that Rob and I weren't going to make it. He was unhappy about the energy I put into my job. Funny thing is, the more he complained, the heavier the caseload I took on. What does that tell you? It finally came to a head, and I filed for divorce."

Will slowed for a cowboy on horseback who was herding a cow along the side of the road.

"That's enough to make anyone depressed," he said.

Annie snorted a derisive laugh.

"It gets worse." She took in a deep breath. "About the same time, I learned something. Something that I just couldn't handle without some help. Seven years earlier, my first year as a prosecutor, I'd sent a man to the penitentiary for ten years for a crime he'd insisted throughout the trial that he wasn't guilty of. Two years into his sentence, he committed suicide. He'd been gang-raped, and denied parole. He wrote a suicide note swearing he was innocent, but saying he couldn't take another eight years of what had apparently been living hell for him there in Monroe. He hanged himself in his cell.

"That haunted me, all those years, but I tried to believe I'd done the right thing in prosecuting him. Until the day after my divorce became final . . ."

"What happened then?"

"Another man confessed to the crime."

Will remained silent.

"That put me over the edge. I went into a depression. My doctor prescribed an SSRI and I started feeling better. Six months later, I came to Yellowstone, felt excited about life again, and quit the drug. No problem." Another pause. "At least not that time."

"That time?" Will replied. "There was more than one?"

Annie nodded.

"I started taking it again. Last winter. Actually the doctor prescribed a different SSRI. A brand-new one. He said it worked faster."

Will had been taking all this in, trying to digest it.

"I thought you said you were happy here. What made you start taking an antidepressant again?"

Annie's next words chilled him to the core.

"The slaughter."

The slaughter. That's what everyone in the park called it. The previous winter, over a thousand bison had been hazed, captured, and then sent to slaughter. Wild animals, animals who had known nothing but wide open valleys and plains, crushed, terrified, into transport trucks and shipped to slaughterhouses.

Their crime? Leaving the park to look for food.

Why did that warrant such drastic measures? Because, despite the fact it had never happened, and was virtually impossible due to the circumstances, the cattle industry had succeeded in perpetuating a myth that bison leaving the park presented a genuine risk of transmitting brucellosis to cattle. The cattle "threatened" by the bisons ignoring Yellowstone's invisible boundaries happened to belong to the Church Universal and Triumphant, whose property adjoined the northwest corner of the park. Over a thousand bison marched to their deaths to protect a handful of cows who were never in danger. Who could easily have been moved away from the advancing bison if the threat of brucellosis were real.

It had been Will's worst nightmare. In all his years with the Park Service, nothing had ever impacted him the way the slaughter had. He understood, all too clearly, what Annie was telling him. Her depression. He—and many others—had experienced it too.

And he'd blamed Annie for it.

As if she were reading his mind, she said now, "I know you thought I could stop it."

Will could not lie to her.

"I did." And then he added, perhaps cruelly, perhaps because he believed it so deeply, "Sherburne would have."

He could almost feel her wince at those words.

"There was no legal basis for stopping it. The Interagency Bison Management Plan calls for slaughter when the bison can't be hazed back into the park. I kept praying that CUT would ask that it be stopped, or that one of the suits being filed by all the environmental groups would come up with a new legal ground, something that hadn't already been tested, something I hadn't been able to think of myself, but they didn't. Apparently, they couldn't. And so I had no choice."

She waited, and Will knew she was hoping he'd tell her it was okay. When he didn't, she went on.

"I started taking an SSRI again. Maybe I could have gotten by without one if I hadn't lived right there in the park. If I didn't have to watch those magnificent animals marching down the hill every day to find food, knowing what waited for them on the other side of the arch.

"I needed something to help me function, and the new SSRI did that. But then, when summer came and I felt strong enough to deal with what I had done—or, as you pointed out on several occasions, what I *hadn't* done—I felt I was ready to stop taking it. And that's when my other hell started. Withdrawal."

Will suddenly realized that her handling of the bison situation, the position she'd felt forced to take, had nearly cost Annie her sanity.

"You mean withdrawal from the antidepressant?" he asked.

He felt Annie finally turn to look at him.

"Hard to believe, isn't it? Yes. When I tried to stop taking this new drug, I got deathly ill. Vomiting, dizziness. I couldn't get out of bed. I didn't even make the connection until I saw a lawsuit that had been filed against the pharmaceutical company that manufactures it. That's when I began researching and found out I wasn't the only one who couldn't get off their SSRI."

"Your doctor didn't tell you what was happening?"

"My doctor denied it was even possible. So I went to another doctor. He said the same thing. The night my mother was kidnapped, I'd been to Livingston to try a new doctor—

a psychiatrist—and he basically told me that what I was experiencing couldn't possibly be from the drug."

"But your research tells you it is," Will said.

"Yes. A couple experts are writing about it now. The pharmaceutical companies still don't talk about it, but it's starting to be acknowledged. Some people just can't get off once they start taking it. Literally. No matter how hard they try, they find they can't quit. Others manage to get off, but go through hell in the process. SSRIs work. They helped me, but there's a dangerous downside that no one warned me about."

"What did the doctor in Livingston tell you to do?"

Annie snorted another laugh.

"He said if I'm certain my symptoms are from stopping the drug—which he clearly didn't believe in the first place—I should just stay on it."

"You obviously aren't taking his advice."

"No. Never," Annie replied. "I'm slowly weaning myself from it, but as you can see, the symptoms haven't stopped."

"Are you sure you want to do that . . . I mean right now, after all that's happened?"

Annie's voice took on a heartbreakingly courageous tone. But Will could tell she was close to breaking.

"If I give in now, I'm afraid I'll never beat this. I'll get through it. I've found a support group. Online. At least I no longer feel alone."

The realization of what this woman had endured—the hell her decisions on the bison suits had put her through, was *still* putting her through—and the harshness with which he himself had judged her stunned Will. He had felt so smug, so morally superior to her, when in reality, Annie had shown incredible courage doing what she'd done.

He reached over, found her hand, and squeezed it.

"No," he said. "You're not alone."

It took several seconds for Annie to let go.

# FIFTEEN

"You've gotta be kidding."

Chad Gleeson stared at the picture on the front page of the ten-day-old *USA Today*. Two wolves, both magnificent, and both familiar to Gleeson, stared back.

It was clear from the expression on the face of the well-dressed hunter, who had just carefully placed the newspaper on the table in front of Gleeson, that he was not kidding.

He was serious. Deadly serious.

"You scored Twenty-one. Now I want Twenty-two."

"Are you nuts?" Gleeson cried. "Read this fucking article again. If that judge doesn't buy that it was self-defense, I could end up in prison."

The hunter laughed.

"They're not going to put you in prison. Your daddy's not going to let that happen. They'll fine you. Granted, it'll be one hell of a fine, but all the more reason you should take this job. Charge me whatever you want—it'll help with your legal expenses—just get me this." His finger landed squarely on the white wolf's nose. "The alpha female."

Gleeson shook his head.

"Twenty-two never leaves the park. And until my trial, I'm banned from it. Besides, rumors are she's out on her own now and looking like shit. I can get you a better-looking female outside the park. Something that'll knock the socks off of your buddies back home. Right here, in the Beartooths, or over in Idaho. Hell, in Idaho they wouldn't even fine me."

They'd been sitting at a corner table at the Log Cabin Cafe in Silver Gate. Now as the waitress approached with a pot of hot coffee, both men waited for her to warm up their cups before resuming the conversation.

The hunter was clearly losing patience.

"I bet I'm your best fucking customer, especially with all the people and big bucks I've brought you over the years. And now you're telling me that counts for nothing?"

"Listen," Gleeson replied, sweat beading on his upper lip. "I know all that. And I appreciate the business. You've been great. And I've done my damnedest to give you, and the pals you send my way, whatever they want—trophy animals nobody else back where you come from will ever stand a chance of nailing to their walls." Gleeson looked around. He wanted to be sure none of the other diners heard. "But this is insane. Why Twenty-two? And why now? Jesus, look," he grabbed the newspaper, shook it in the air, "her fucking picture's been plastered all over this country."

Even as the words left his mouth, a look of understanding suddenly passed across his face.

"That's it, isn't it?" Gleeson's face gave away his incredulity. "She'd be the ultimate now, wouldn't she? Just look at her, at what it says right here."

His eyes turned to the photograph's caption.

*The alpha pair of Yellowstone's Druid pack, wolf #21 and 22, considered by many to be two of the most majestic animals on the face of the earth. Twenty-one was shot by a local hunter Friday. He claims it was self-defense.*

Gleeson snorted a half laugh. "What a coup—bringing her home after all the publicity."

"She is magnificent," the hunter said. "And you better believe I'm not the only one thinking about going after her. That's definitely part of it, but only part. I've got a more personal agenda too."

"I bet you do," Gleeson replied.

Both men stared at the photograph. Twenty-two's eyes, unblinking, seemed to hold the mysteries of the world—of life itself.

"I wish I could help you," Gleeson said, a finality entering his voice. "I really do."

The wooden chair scraped the floor as the hunter stood abruptly, tossing several dollars on the table. He reached for his three-hundred-dollar sunglasses, and the BlackBerry he'd been using to conduct business when Gleeson arrived to meet him fifteen minutes earlier.

"Okay," he said now, his voice almost serene. "No problem. Guess I'll have to start making calls."

Gleeson snorted again.

"You're bluffing."

As the multimillion-dollar-salaried CEO of an East Coast consulting firm whose clients included the Pentagon and several major news networks, the hunter was not used to being questioned—or accused of bluffing. Ordinarily he wouldn't waste another second with anyone who had the nerve, or stupidity, to do so. But this was important to him, and Gleeson was the best. He knew that. That's why he'd chosen him in the first place, and passed his name along to his type-A chronies, for whom instant gratification and glory were like a drug. No price was too high to pay for the benefits.

Steel gray eyes fixed upon Gleeson, the hunter laid his BlackBerry back on the table and reached into the back pocket of his Cabela hunting pants to produce a folded sheet of paper.

With measured precision, he unfolded it, then laid it on top of the *USA Today*, which still lay like a place mat on the table in front of Gleeson. Holding the lined paper down with one hand, he ran the other across its surface like a hot iron, flattening it. It struck Gleeson as odd, incongruous somehow, that as well-manicured as the hunter's nails were, each had a line of dirt under it.

Half a dozen names had been scrawled in ink on the paper, one beneath the other. After each name a phone num-

ber appeared—all began with 406, Montana's only area
code. Several entries took up more than one line, with an-
notations like: *Bighorn sheep, $10,000. No license required.*

Or: *trophy elk, $3,000 each; griz, $15,000.*

Gleeson snatched it from the table, his face flushed as he
skimmed over its contents.

He recognized most of the names, knew the hunter was
not bluffing.

"Your prices do seem a little out of line," the hunter said,
his tone taunting. "I guess it's getting more competitive out
there. A lot of your colleagues make—what, fifteen or
twenty grand a year? One day out with someone like me
and they can double or triple that."

"These guys are amateurs," Gleeson said. "Jokes."

"That's not the information I've received."

"If you want to end up arrested and fined twenty thou or
more, go ahead. Call them."

"That's an odd argument for you to make," the hunter
said, a smile finally twisting his thin lips. "Especially right
now."

He studied Gleeson.

"I make fifteen million a year. Do you really think the
threat of a twenty-thousand-dollar fine—or a forty- or fifty-
thousand one for that matter—means dick to me?" Again,
he jabbed a finger at the photo on the front page. "That.
That means something. And if you won't give her to me,
I'll find someone who will."

He snatched the sheet of paper out of Gleeson's hand,
stuffed it in his pocket, and reached for the BlackBerry.

"Wait," Gleeson said. "Hold on."

Having regained the upper hand, the hunter lowered
himself back into his chair.

Gleeson looked agitated, almost ill.

"All right." He kept his voice low, his eyes sweeping the
room. "I'll do it. But here are the rules. I'll lead you to her,
but then I'm gone. I can't be anywhere near there when
you kill her. But I'll set you up. I'll do everything but pull
the fucking trigger."

"I think I can accept that."

"And you don't carry my card, you wipe my phone number out of your cell phone, computer—whatever the hell that thing is." He pointed to the BlackBerry. "And if you get caught, if anyone starts asking questions, my name never comes up. Got it?"

"Getting a little paranoid, aren't you? We've always had that arrangement."

"That's my deal. Take it or leave it."

The hunter studied Gleeson, thinking. Both men knew he was going to take it, but he wasn't the CEO of a successful company for nothing. He was adept, expert actually, at the close.

"How much?" he asked.

Gleeson grew silent.

He was already facing the charges for killing 21. He'd worked with this guy enough to believe he could trust him to keep his word and not bring Gleeson into it, but if he got caught, and didn't keep his word, under the Lacey Act and the Endangered Species Act he could be looking at up to five years in prison and a $250,000 fine for setting this up.

The alternative, he knew, was losing one of his most valuable clients. Someone who had brought in hundreds of thousands of dollars to Gleeson over the years.

"A guaranteed fifty grand," he said, "even if you miss her. A hundred if you don't."

The hunter eyed Gleeson, unblinking. Gleeson reigned in Yellowstone country. Killing 21 attested to that—and to his familiarity with the Druids. The hunter would not rest, not be content, until he claimed 22.

"None of those other assholes can even get you close to Twenty-two," Gleeson added, as if reading his mind.

The hunter's expression finally softened, but just a bit. "I'd hope the taxidermist will be included in that price," he said testily.

Gleeson exhaled a troubled sigh.

"I'll throw that in, free of charge."

They reached across the table and shook hands.

"Same guy who mounted my antelope?" the hunter asked. "And the mountain lion? He does good work."

"Same guy," Gleeson replied.

# SIXTEEN

WILL COULDN'T BELIEVE HE'D OVERSLEPT. THE LAST TWO nights, he'd lain awake, thinking about Annie and what she'd told him. It had stayed with him, haunted him, especially the role he'd played in her misery. But that didn't excuse his oversleeping. Twenty-five years on the job and he'd never been late. He was, in fact, known for being perpetually early, despite the fact that out in the backcountry there were no time clocks to punch.

But there was a horse outside waiting to be fed. And an expansive territory to patrol.

He jumped up, splashed cold water from the basin over his face and hair, then threw on his uniform and headed for the door.

Just before stepping outside, he paused next to the dresser they'd issued him his first year in the backcountry. The picture on it had been new then. Its age had begun to show in the past several years and he'd been tempted to take it into one of those places in Bozeman that said they could restore just about anything. But he was afraid to take the chance it might instead be destroyed.

Before grabbing the felt hat that hung from a peg beside the front door, he looked at the picture and said, as he did each morning, "See you tonight."

Donning the hat and the duty belt hanging next to it, he headed out the door.

He heard Kola nicker at the sound of the cabin's door opening, then again—more loudly—when Will actually came into view. The paint mare belonged to the National Park Service but she had been Will's mount for so many years that everyone referred to her as "McCarroll's mare."

"Mornin' girl," Will said as he strode past where she stood in her round pen to the small shed that housed her feed. "Sorry I'm late."

He didn't notice her lameness until she loped over to the gate to meet him. She was favoring her right front leg, nothing dramatic, but the way Will's gut responded to the sight, it might as well have been a compound fracture.

He dropped the two flakes of alfalfa on the ground and climbed between railings.

"Let me see, girl," he said, bending to lift her hoof.

Doubling it behind her, he saw the problem right away. "Damn."

He was brushing away the dirt compacted in her shoe with his bare fingers, when the two-way radio he'd stuffed into his pants pocket came to life.

*"Five-tango-one-five?"*

He recognized the voice right away. Betty Stanmeyer, the campground host down at Pebble Creek.

Within the wolf watching circles, being given a two-way radio was somewhat akin to a visiting dignitary receiving the "key" to a city—the ultimate for those dream-inspired souls who spent countless hours each day with eyes glued to a hill a mile away. A two-way radio amounted to nothing less than a status symbol, a sign of perseverance, longevity, and proper respect for the unwritten rules of wolf watching in Yellowstone country.

Still, Betty wasn't supposed to access the frequency used by law enforcement, nor use it to contact rangers directly. But shortly after the wolves had been reintroduced to Yellowstone in '95, several wolf watchers, including

Betty and her husband, had received threats and Will had given Betty his frequency—for emergency purposes only.

She was a good lady, a little too eager at times to do things like call him on the radio, but she meant well and Will liked her.

He straightened now, eyes still on Kola's hoof, and lifted the radio.

"Morning, Betty," he said. "What's up?"

*"Will, you've got a visitor down here at the campground. Tavner Marek. He was about to unload his horse and head up to find you, but I told him not to bother. That you'd probably be riding by any time now."*

"I should be," Will replied. "But Kola took a nail. Looks like it won't be easy to pull out. She'll need the farrier. Did they ever pick up the trailer I left there?"

*"Just yesterday. They weren't too happy about having to come all the way out here to get it. Said you'd promised to bring it back."*

"Yeah, well, I'm gonna have to walk her down and call for someone to pick her up and take her to Mammoth."

His pronouncement was followed by muffled conversation over a host of static, then Betty's voice returned.

*"Tavner says you don' t need to call anybody. He'll haul her in for you."*

"That's the first good news I've had all morning."

After another noisy interlude, Betty added, *"He'll meet you at the trailhead."*

"Great. Tell him to give me an hour. Maybe more. She looks pretty tender."

*"He's shakin' his head okay,"* Betty said. *"Give Kola a big hug for me. Don't know what you'd do if somethin happened to that horse of yours."*

She finished with a crisp, *"Ten-four and out."* Will heard her conversing with Tavner Marek for at least thirty seconds more, until she realized she was still holding the button down.

Will strode over to the hay he'd dropped on the ground and tossed it to Kola. While she munched contentedly on it, he hauled a couple buckets of freshwater from the hundred-gallon tank mounted alongside the shed. This— the ability to draw water from the tank—was a short-lived luxury each year, lasting only during the months nighttime temperatures didn't freeze it, which amounted to no more than three. The rest of the time he and Kola hauled water from the year-round creek that fed Trout Lake.

As he stood watching Kola eat, Will quickly revamped his plans for the day. He had intended to patrol the north border, from above Pebble Creek to Hellroaring Mountain. With hunting season just around the corner, locals were getting antsy. He'd found a caped-out elk carcass the other day and hoped he'd run into whoever did it. Will had learned one thing in all his years of rangering: if poachers succeeded once, they always came back. He wanted to catch the son of a bitch at it again. Nail him. Now he'd have to spend half the day hauling Kola to Mammoth. There were two horse facilities in the park—one just south of Mammoth, the other in Tower, but the farrier spent most his time at Mammoth. Will hoped he could tend to her right away. If Kola would be out of commission for a while, he'd have to pick out another horse and beg a ride back to Slough Creek for the two of them.

Hell, half a day was starting to look optimistic. His whole day would have been shot if Tavner hadn't shown up.

As he led Kola down the hill, Will wondered why Tavner would be looking for him. Will liked Tavner. A respected and avid outdoorsman from Livingston, he had been elected president of the Paradise Valley Wildlife Association, a group that blended a love of and desire to protect wildlife with another great love: that of hunting it. Because of that bent, in a state like Montana the PVWA was often more successful at accomplishing conservation-friendly goals than the more radical environmental groups.

Tavner had been outspokenly critical of a proposal for an annual bison hunt, insisting that PVWA would only con-sider supporting such a hunt when bison were officially categorized as wildlife, with their management taken from the Montana Department of Livestock and handed over to the Department of Fish, Wildlife, and Parks, where it should have been all along. It was a balanced and reasonable position to take and Will, who'd long and vehemently opposed the hypocrisy of the DOL managing wild bison, appreciated it. Like Will, Tavner had made an enemy of the Department of Livestock, which did not want to give up control of the bison under any circumstances; but also like Will, Tavner was a man of principle, who had the courage to take a position and hold it—popular or not.

Now as Will led Kola gingerly down the last fifty yards of the rock-strewn trail, Will could see his friend backing his pickup and trailer up to the trailhead.

When he got out of his truck and spotted Will and Kola, Tavner yanked his cowboy hat off his head and used it to wave. The fiery red hair had dulled in recent years, but his beard, though tinged with gray, still looked like a small bush someone had set on fire. Long and lean, Tavner climbed up into the trailer, checked the lead securing his chestnut gelding to the front compartment, and swung the gate behind her in place to make room for Kola.

By the time he'd finished, Will had drawn within earshot.

"You're a sight for sore eyes," he called out. "Especially that trailer of yours."

Tavner took several long-legged strides Will's way, hand extended. Will grasped it warmly.

"Took a nail, huh?" Tavner said, nodding toward Kola.

"Looks like a carpentry nail. How the hell do you suppose something like that happens out here?"

"Got me," Tavner replied.

With a light tap on her rump and a clucking noise from Tavner, Kola stepped gingerly up into the trailer. Will followed, tying her head the opposite direction of the gelding.

Horse loaded, the two men climbed into the cab of the truck.

As they pulled away from the trailhead and onto the highway, Will radioed Mammoth to report what had happened, and that he and Kola were on their way to the horse corrals. He asked to have the farrier meet them there right away.

When he finished, he flipped the two-way to the off position and looked over at Tavner.

"I don't expect this is some kind of social call."

Tavner pushed his hat back on his head.

"Wish it were, Will. Wish it were." He paused as he braked for a line of cars slowed to appreciate the bison grazing alongside the Lamar River.

A cloud of dust rose from the group. Neither Will nor Tavner needed to wait for it to clear to know that two males were already practicing for the rutting season.

"I heard a rumor," Tavner said, eyes dead ahead, "and thought I'd better pass it along to you. Just in case there's somethin' to it."

"I'm all ears."

Tavner shook his head slowly.

"It's not good, Will," he said. "It's not good."

Shooting Tavner a sideways glance, Will remained silent.

"One of our members," Tavner went on, "a good friend of mine, pulled me over in Livingston last night. Told me some Eastern fella has been asking around, trying to find someone who'll help him."

"Help him with what?"

Tavner paused briefly, then finished with, "Shoot a wolf. In the park."

Now that he'd started, the words came out in a rush.

"And it's not just any wolf, Will. It's Number Twenty-two. He saw her picture in the paper and now he wants her. He's offering big money for someone to take him in and get her."

Hands instinctively clenching into tight fists, Will listened, unblinking. The anger was instinctive but he'd learned to put it aside until later. He couldn't let it get in the way.

"Those damn trophy hunters," Tavner went on. "I mean, we've gotta stop them. Used to be a man poached 'cause he was down on his luck. Shooting a deer off-season was the only way to put food on the table. Even I've turned my head at that in the past.

"But this is different. This is out-of-staters coming into Montana and saying to hell with the rules, to hell with the license, to hell with the fact that these are protected animals. They want the biggest and the best—a trophy to take home and mount on their wall along with the others they paid a fortune for. They have no respect for us, or for the wildlife they're taking. Hell, what they want is to rob us of the best DNA in the herd. 'Cause that's the only thing good enough for them.

"And the thing that galls me, the thing that makes me almost crazy, is it's our own people—locals—who make it possible. All for a buck." He drew in a deep breath and lifted his shoulders high again. "Know what else it does?"

Will glanced at Tavner again.

"It gives a bad name to all of us who hunt, those of us who follow the rules and care about wildlife. That's what it does. And I tell ya, that's what really burns me."

Will waited a few seconds—both to process the information and to allow Tavner a chance to calm down. Then he voiced the question foremost on his mind.

"Who'd he get?"

Tavner knew the effect his answer would have on Will.

"Rumor has it it's Gleeson," he said.

As conditioned as Will had become over the years to put aside emotion in these circumstances, hearing Gleeson's name was like not just learning your wife had had an affair, but that it had been with your best friend.

"Apparently this guy called around first," Tavner explained, "to see what his options were, and probably to drum up a little leverage with Chad. These guys, they like to think they're clever, smarter than anyone who'd choose to live here. But my guy says it's Gleeson."

"When?" Will said.

"That I can't tell you. At least not for sure. But my guess

is soon. The guy was already in town. You know these assholes—they want instant gratification. They come in, get what they want, leave. Don't waste any time."

Will fell silent again, as did Tavner.

As they arrived in Mammoth, then turned south to climb the final hill before the horse corrals, they passed the stone house. Tavner apparently noticed Will's eyes fixed upon it.

"Any word yet on the judge's mother?"

"No," Will replied. "It's like she just vanished into thin air."

"That's too bad. Judge Peacock's a good woman, and a good judge. Think they did it to scare her off the bench?"

"That's one of the theories."

"Be a damn shame if that happened," Tavner replied. "Sometimes she's a little too by-the-rules for my liking. But I think that's because she's trying to prove herself." He paused. "She's not Sherburne, but I have the feeling that with a little time, she might just get there."

Will allowed thoughts of Annie to momentarily distract him from what Tavner had told him.

When Tavner turned the pickup and trailer off the asphalt two-lane and onto the gravel road leading to the stables, Will jumped out to open the metal gate at the start of the drive, then, after shutting it, followed on foot the remaining two hundred yards. By the time he reached the trailer, Tavner had already unloaded Kola.

Tavner handed Will her lead.

"I appreciate your coming all the way down here from Livingston to tell me what you heard," Will said. "It took courage."

Still, despite the danger inherent in what he'd just done, Tavner seemed reluctant to hurry off, his conscience unburdened. He kicked at a grasshopper that landed in the dust in front of his boot. The motion sent several of the colorless insects springing into the air.

"I hate putting you in the middle of something like this," Tavner said. "Could be dangerous, what with Gleeson, and the others who're doin' the same thing, having so much at stake. And it doesn't help having Gleeson's old man be mayor of Cooke City." He paused. "Shit, Will."

"Don't worry about it, Tav. Really. And don't tell another soul. I don't want you getting yourself in trouble."

"Thing is, I just knew that if anybody can do somethin' about it, it's you. And I know how you feel about the Druids."

Will turned his gaze east, toward the country he'd started the day out in. The wilderness that had been his home for over two decades. "The Druids have been my neighbors ever since the reintroduction," he said. "The goddamn best neighbors someone like me could ask for."

"I figured that's how you felt," Tavner said.

Such talk bordered on being cloyingly maudlin for two men like Will McCarroll and Tavner Marik, which is why the shout that interrupted it almost came as a relief.

"McCarroll."

Will and Tavner turned toward the gate behind them. They hadn't noticed the Park Ranger car pull over.

Too lazy to climb over the gate or open it, Curt Hardy, one of Will's least favorite rangers, stood, arms resting on the top railing, hands cupped around his stingy mouth.

"Where the hell's your radio?" Hardy wanted to know.

"In the truck," Will yelled back, nodding toward Tavner's pickup. He didn't add that he'd turned it off.

"Shewmaker wants you at HQ. Stat."

Hardy was one of those guys who liked talking in code.

"I've got to see to her first," Will replied, laying a hand on Kola's rump.

Hardy and Will had some history together. They'd been hired as interpretive rangers the same year. Aside from that fact, they had only one thing in common, and that was that they both immediately realized they didn't have the patience for the visitor contact required of interps. As a result, when a backcountry ranger position opened up their second year, both had jumped at it. Their relationship had never recovered from the fact that Will got the job, and twenty-six years later, still held it, while Hardy continued to put up with visitors.

Making life miserable for Will was one of Hardy's greatest pleasures. Something he felt he had coming.

"Pete told me to bring you back with me."

"I'm not leaving 'til I see the farrier," Will replied, turning away, in effect dismissing the other ranger.

As far as Will was concerned, Hardy would have lasted about one winter in the backcountry.

The wheels of Hardy's car spit gravel as he did a three-point turn and shot back to the headquarters to report Will's disobedience.

In a nervous gesture, Tavner grabbed hold of his jeans at the waist, hiking them up.

"I can wait and give you a ride, Will."

"No need, Tav. It could be a while."

With a resolve that looked especially hard-earned, Tavner stuck out a bony hand.

"Okay then. You let me know if I can do anything to help." He curled his fingers around the hand Will extended his way. "Anything. You hear?"

"I'll do that, Tavner," Will said. "I'll do that."


"I thought Curt told you to get over here right away."

Will had ducked into the second-floor employee bathroom before heading up to his boss's office, only to find Shewmaker emerging from a stall, pulling up the zipper on his pants. The room was otherwise empty.

"He told me," Will replied. "But I told him I wasn't going to leave my horse 'til I heard what the shoer had to say."

Shewmaker finished buckling the black, government-issue leather belt and stepped to the wash basin. Will headed for the urinal.

"What's so important that it couldn't wait?" Will asked, face to the wall.

"Something's come up," Shewmaker replied, tilting the dome of his head forward, toward the mirror, to search for gray hair. "You're going to Red Lodge. Tomorrow."

Will turned, looked over his shoulder. His eyes met Shewmaker's in the mirror.

"I'm working tomorrow. Why would I go to Red Lodge?"

"They've called a roundtable there. About Twenty-one, and all the publicity the shooting's generated. It's getting out of hand. They want to bring all the parties to the table, invite the press. Let the world know we're all addressing the issue in a rational manner, and not letting fiery rhetoric like Heck Buckley's take over. The Park Service needs to be represented. I'm sending you."

"Why not send Tom?"

As the park's wolf biologist, Tom Ansley had earned legendary status when he spearheaded the reintroduction in 1995. No one served as Yellowstone's voice of the wolves more effectively than Tom. Or was more widely respected.

"Tom's back in the hospital," Shewmaker replied.

Ansley had been diagnosed with esophageal cancer earlier in the summer and although he'd returned to work, he had been having a rough go again recently.

"Sorry to hear that," Will replied. "But this makes no sense, Pete. We both know I'm a rotten spokesperson for the park. How many times have I been reprimanded? Now you're actually sending me as a spokesperson?"

The door suddenly opened in a rush of cool air from the hallway. A darkly handsome and ponytailed man, also in uniform, stuck his head through. Paul Olbermann—Shewmaker's deputy supervisor and second in command in law enforcement. He nodded at Will without expression, then zeroed in on Shewmaker.

"Here you are," he said. "We need you. Right away."

Shewmaker turned off the water and shook his hands over the sink, eyes straying one last time to his hair.

"What's going on?"

"A researcher over in Canyon just discovered his car was broken into last night. They got his telemetry equipment."

This grabbed Shewmaker's attention. Sticking his hand in front of the motion detector on the paper towel dispenser, he groused, "When are those guys gonna learn not to leave thousands of dollars' worth of equipment in their cars overnight?"

He grabbed the brown sheet that dropped down from the dispenser, did a half-assed job of drying his hands, then balled it up and tossed it angrily into the wastebasket.

Will had stopped urinating midstream, eyes fixed on Olbermann.

"What about the codes?"

The "codes" were radio frequencies assigned for individual collars attached to animals in the park. Through the use of telemetry, and knowing the radio frequency of the collar each animal wore, researchers could keep track of their movements in and, even more importantly, outside the park.

"His book's gone too," Olbermann replied.

Will yanked his zipper up.

"Which researcher was it?"

"Patrick Jackson."

Will kicked at the exposed pipe below the sink.

"Damn!"

Jackson worked exclusively with grizzlies and wolves. That meant his book would contain the frequencies for all collared animals.

*There were two collared members of the Druid pack. One was the alpha female.*

Shewmaker dismissed Olbermann with a nod in the direction of the hallway and a curt, "I'll be right there."

Olbermann disappeared in another rush of cool air.

Turning to Will, who still stood in the middle of the bathroom, eyes successfully blanketing the thoughts racing through his mind, Shewmaker said, "Let's get something straight right off."

He recognized the expression on Will's face. Knew what it meant. Trouble.

"You're going to this roundtable. But you're not there as

a spokesperson for the Park Service. You're there to answer questions, listen, and report back to us. Just this once I'm counting on you not to say anything that I'll have to defend you for later."

"You expect me to toe the line now? After that asshole came in here and killed the alpha male?"

"You know the Park Service's position. Chad Gleeson was carrying a loaded weapon inside the park. He shot and killed a protected animal. Regardless of whether he gets off for killing Twenty-one with his self-defense strategy, the loaded weapon's illegal. Plain and simple. That's our position."

"Well, I can't do it, Pete. Not tomorrow."

Shewmaker backed up to lean against the metal door to the stalls directly across from the sinks and watched Will wash his hands.

"What do you mean you can't?"

Will avoided Shewmaker's gaze in the mirror.

Should he disclose what Tav Marek had just told him?

He and Shewmaker had butted heads many times, but when the chips were down, Will had always been able to count on Peter to back him.

And now the theft of the telemetry equipment and codes.

Even Peter couldn't deny the coincidence.

This situation, however, was different than others they'd been through, others when Shewmaker had ultimately—albeit reluctantly—stood behind Will.

Peter played everything by the book, which meant he would feel compelled to take Tavner Marek's rumor up the chain of command. In that event, Will, who'd long ago fallen into disfavor with the higher-ups for his no-compromise attitude, would be taken off the case. No way they were going to allow Will McCarroll to handle a situation this explosive, not with the entire country keeping a close eye on Yellowstone and its wolves.

"Something you're not telling me, Will?" Peter said, studying Will in the mirror.

Will took his time washing his hands.

"Why so little notice?" he said. "Whose harebrained idea is this anyway?"

Peter made a sudden move for the door.

"I've got to tend to this telemetry business," he said briskly, reaching for the handle.

Will beat him there. Back to the door, he stared down his boss.

"Pete?"

Everyone who worked for him joked about Shewmaker's telltale eyes. If he had bad news to deliver, his law enforcement rangers usually could read it in a single look at his face.

Now, to Shewmaker's credit, he didn't avoid Will's gaze.

"Otto Gleeson," he replied. "He contacted Public Affairs, and they referred him to me."

Will's expression remained neutral, despite the fact that at that instant, he instinctively knew his life would never be the same.

"He asked specifically for you, Will," Peter said, clearly trying to justify his actions. "And this park has to have a presence there."

Now what Shewmaker's eyes revealed was his dread for the reaction he expected from Will.

But Will did not react. He did not, in fact, say another word. Instead, he stepped back from the door, opening it politely for Shewmaker.

"Tomorrow," Shewmaker said sternly. "Starts at eleven. The town hall in Red Lodge."

He slid through the door, not looking back. Not making eye contact again.

"Be there."

# SEVENTEEN

ANNIE SAW HIM JUST AFTER SHE AND ARCHIE MADE THE turn for home—a lone figure, maybe a quarter mile ahead on the Old Gardiner Road. It was impossible to really recognize anyone from that distance, but still, she knew intuitively who it was striding purposefully her way. Will McCarroll.

Archie apparently recognized him too, for he began whining, pulling against the lead.

The figure disappeared with the road as it dipped below a hill. When Will came back into sight, Annie reached down and unfastened Archie's lead.

"Okay."

Archie made a beeline for his pal.

When Annie and Will came face-to-face several minutes later, she could tell something was wrong. Still, Will tried for a half smile.

"You know," he said, "I could cite you for that."

"For . . . ?"

"Dog off-leash in the park."

"I'd have to plead guilty," Annie replied, grinning broadly. "To avoid the embarrassment of a trial if nothing else."

This time the smile actually reached Will's eyes.

"You might get by with just a verbal warning this time."

A breeze blew Annie's hair across her face. She pushed

it aside, holding it away from her eyes, to look at him. She liked looking at him. Not because he was attractive, which he was; but because when with him, she constantly found herself wondering what was going through that mind of his.

It was rare for her to have a clue. Especially today.

Something had definitely brought him there. Although she was pleased to see him, she had a sense of foreboding about just what that something was.

"Aside from hoping to bust me, what brings you up here?" she asked. "Shouldn't you be out in the backcountry? Or working some kind of jam?"

"My horse took a nail and I had to hitch a ride in to the stables to get her taken care of."

They'd turned toward the Mammoth end of the road—a road used by horse-drawn carriages traveling between the park headquarters and Gardiner during the 1890s and early 1900s. Now the bumpy, overgrown double ruts were mostly used by bicyclists, and locals who cherished an environment free of tourists.

Annie picked up her pace to keep up with Will.

"Will she be okay?" she asked.

"Yes. But she won't be able to take any weight for a few days."

The wind from the north, where clusters of cumulous clouds hugged the top of Mount Evert, had suddenly picked up, bringing with it a chill.

"What happens now? Will you take another horse back with you?"

She'd clearly hit a nerve.

"I was just told I have to go to Red Lodge tomorrow. No point in hauling another horse up to Slough Creek."

"Red Lodge?" At first, Annie thought Will hadn't heard her. But when she glanced sideways at him, the look on his face made it clear he had.

"What is it?" she said.

Will shook his head, scowling.

"There's a roundtable tomorrow, to discuss Twenty-one's killing. They're sending me as the park's representative."

"That sounds like something you'd be interested in doing."

Will's short, humorless laugh took her by surprise.

"My boss wants me there, but believe me, I don't dare say anything. This is all about PR, the media." He paused, then added, "At least, that's what Peter thinks it's about . . ."

"What do you mean?" Annie asked.

"Never mind," Will said curtly.

"What is it?" she said.

Abruptly, Will stopped walking. He turned to face Annie, his demeanor all business.

An acute feeling of unease overtook Annie.

"I can't find that newspaper I took from Sherburne's room," he said. "I think I lost it."

"I have it," Annie replied, vastly relieved to think the missing newspaper might be to blame for Will's mood. "I must have gathered it up with my bag."

"Great," Will replied. He took a step closer to her, locked eyes with her.

"I want you to read it. Go over it carefully, every article, every word."

They'd stopped on the crest of the hill just above and behind the Mammoth Hotel and the Chittenden House. The wind had become so strong that Annie had to raise her voice to respond.

"What is it?" she asked. "Why are you acting like this?"

"If anyone has a feel for who might be behind your mother's kidnapping, it's Sherburne. Remember that. And promise me you'll take the newspaper he gave us the other day seriously. It means something."

Alarmed, Annie replied, "Why don't we go back to my house now and take a look at it together?"

"I don't have time now. I'm waiting for a ride back to Pebble Creek."

"I'll drive you."

"There's no need for that," Will replied. "The next shift starts in—" he glanced at his watch "—about fifteen minutes. Someone from law enforcement will be heading that way, but I need to get over to the visitor center to catch a ride."

They'd started down the final hill. Annie reached out, touched Will's arm.

"I want to do it," she said. "The truth is that sometimes I almost can't bear to go back to that house ..."

Will slowed, turned to look at her.

Annie waited, sure he would decline her offer.

"Okay," he said. "I'll call and cancel my request for a ride."

Annie had just flipped the right turn signal on to turn onto the Grand Loop Road, when Will said, "Wait. Can we stop by the stables?"

She pushed the signal off.

"No problem."

Will felt relieved that Annie hadn't demanded an explanation for his behavior—the unexpected appearance, and his comments about the roundtable in Red Lodge, which he'd regretted the moment they left his mouth.

He could tell she knew something was up and that she would like to know *what*. They'd stopped by her house to get her car, and confirm that she had the newspaper Judge Sherburne had given them. Annie tried to give it to Will, but he refused.

He couldn't tell her that he might not have the chance to return it to her.

After tomorrow, Will might not be able to help Annie find her mother. And Will did not trust the authorities to solve the mystery of Eleanor Malone's disappearance. The trail had grown cold. The leads originally followed had been logical enough—he did not fault the sheriff or FBI for pursuing them—but now it was time for more innovative thinking. And that—the ability to think outside the box— was a talent Will knew to be in short supply with local law enforcement.

He harbored hope that the plan he'd laid out for himself

could have a positive outcome on two fronts—both in solving the mystery of Eleanor Malone's disappearance, and in making a bold statement about poaching in the park.

But Will had served in the Park Service long enough to know that once he put his plan into action tomorrow, anything could happen to him. Anything. It might not just be his job he was putting on the line. And if the worst case scenario proved true, he didn't want Annie to be left alone, relying solely upon the authorities to get her mother back.

But he couldn't tell Annie that.

Nor could he tell her the real reason the roundtable had been called.

He glanced over at her. As she stopped to let tourists—an entire busload of them—cross in front of her Subaru to the hotel, Will went back over his logic, trying to find holes in it.

Will was the last person the Park Service would choose to send to a meeting like that being held tomorrow—a meeting which would be heavily covered by the media. Will had a record of speaking his mind, regardless of how that reflected on Yellowstone and its policies. His being asked to attend a roundtable like the one in Red Lodge made zero sense—at least until Will heard who had called the meeting—*and* asked specifically that Will represent Yellowstone.

Otto Gleeson.

Chad Gleeson's old man. The mayor of Cooke City.

Why would Otto Gleeson, who despised Will, request his presence at the wolf roundtable? And tomorrow, of all days—only one day after Tavner Marek advised Will that someone had hired Chad Gleeson to help him shoot #22?

And just one day after telemetry equipment that would enable its thief to lock in to 22's location was stolen?

If Chad Gleeson were behind that theft, he'd know that only one thing now stood between him and fulfillment of his client's wish.

Will McCarroll.

How big a coincidence was it that Gleeson's father called

a last-minute roundtable, in Red Lodge of all places—
which required at least one overnight stay—and that he re-
quested Will's presence, which ensured Will would be out
of the park?

The tourists had finally cleared the road. Annie acceler-
ated.

When she pulled up to the stables, Will jumped out of
the car.

"Be right back."

The double doors to the barn stood partially open, the
right one swinging and creaking in the wind. Will stepped
through, into the barn.

At the far end, a tack room served double duty as an office for John Miklovic, the stable manager. That door stood
open as well.

Will crossed the long, high-roofed barn, stopping at the
stall in which he'd left Kola several hours earlier.

"Feelin' better, girl?" he asked, reaching through the
bars to straighten her jet black forelock, which had splayed
over her eyes.

Munching contentedly on alfalfa, she nickered a greeting back.

"Don't get too spoiled," Will said before moving on.

He stuck his head inside the tack room. Other than a radio blaring Willie Nelson from the top of a desk cluttered
with horse magazines and empty cigarette packs, Miklovic's
office was void of life. Movement outside, through the barn's
back door, caught Will's eye. He headed for it.

Almost a dozen horses stood in various stages of being
untacked, tails whipping at flies, lead ropes knotted loosely
around the top rail of a three-rail fence, noses uniformly
hidden in grain buckets hanging from nails pounded into
the rails.

Will strode toward the corral, watching as Miklovic
lifted a saddle off a bay mare and deposited it on an empty
stretch of fence. Though Mik walked with a pronounced
limp, the cause of which he'd never chosen to share with
Will, his skinny physique seemed uniquely suited to the

various, almost yogalike positions required in moving about his charges—ducking under this one's rope, switching bridle for halter on another, wiping down an older gelding that looked especially hard ridden. He'd been doing this job for as long as Will had been in the park, and took extraordinary pride in it.

The prick of the horses' ears indicated the tune Miklovic whistled was not lost on them. It stopped when he saw Will.

"Howdy, stranger," Miklovic called. His long gray hair, knotted in a ratty ponytail, hung out from under a misshapen straw hat whose outer rim had unraveled a good inch or so.

"Hey, Mik," Will answered, stopping to run a hand down the back of a broad-chested Rocky Mountain gelding. "Looks like someone rode these guys hard."

"Fucking wannabe cowboys," Miklovic answered, his Austrian accent still strong four decades after arriving in Yellowstone—never again to leave. "I spotted them right off. Shoulda told them the only way they'd see this park is on one of them yellow buses."

He doubled over, lifted the horse's rear foot with no resistance from its owner, and used a pick that seemingly had materialized out of nowhere to pry free a grape-sized rock wedged in its frog.

He straightened, then clasped his hands behind his lower back, which obviously was giving him trouble.

"From now on," he said, "I see some Easterner or Southerner wearin' cowboy boots fresh from the box and I'm turnin' 'em away. Tellin' 'em to go down to Jackson Hole and sit on one of those saddles they got for seats down there at the Cowboy Bar. Hell, they'd probably fall off. Sons of bitches . . ."

Will couldn't help but smile.

"Hey, Mik," he said, striving for nonchalance. "Is Riley still up at Tower? I'm heading into the backcountry in the morning. Kola's in no shape for that."

"He's up here now, stall right next to Kola. But Riley's already spoken for tomorrow. Too bad, 'cause next to Kola, he's the best damn backcountry horse I got."

"You got that right," Will said, trying to hide his disappointment.

Before Miklovic bought Kola six years earlier, Will's favorite mount for patrolling the dangerous north border had been Riley.

The danger was attributable not only to the rough terrain that separated the northwest corner of Yellowstone from neighboring Montana, but also to the activity that took place there on a regular basis.

Poaching.

Over the past decade, elk antlers had come to be a hugely profitable commodity, especially in Asia, where they were considered to have aphrodisiacal properties. An ounce of antler could bring in up to $1,400. A typical mature six-point bull elk delivered forty-five to fifty pounds of antler. Over the past decade, traffic had grown accordingly, and industrious poachers had found that they could disappear into the vast backcountry of Yellowstone's Lamar and Hayden valleys, score hundreds of antlers, then haul them up steep trails into the Jardine area, where someone would be waiting to haul them away and off to market. While law enforcement rangers knew of the activity, with only twenty-two backcountry rangers patrolling over 2.2 million acres of territory, the odds of actually catching the criminals in action became slim to nonexistent. Still, Will patrolled the northwest border of the park with a vengeance.

The most dangerous encounters Will had ever had in his twenty-six years as a ranger had taken place in that region. The bigger the money at stake, the more ruthless and dangerous the poachers. It was customary for each ring to have one heavily armed member on horseback, circling back time and time again, making sure they weren't being followed by law enforcement—a goal Will had thwarted repeatedly. But having a good mount was imperative.

Riley had tracked poachers with Will and other law enforcement officers for over a decade. He knew the backcountry as well as any ranger. Better than most.

"Who signed Riley out?" Will asked now.

Miklovic's mouth twisted into a sideways pucker as he tried to remember.

"Damn. It was one of them young upstart rangers, but I can't keep their names straight anymore."

He lifted his hat off and scratched his head.

There was a theory within the park that, after a number of years on the job, biologists—like the bison biologist, who'd grown a long, brown goatee, and the grizzly biologist, who'd packed on fifty pounds and now walked with a hunched back—tended to take on the appearance of the focus of their expertise. With his hat off, Will was struck by the resemblance of Mik's coarse-haired ponytail to that of the Appaloosa mare now swishing around her head.

"I can give you Torch. He's already up at Tower, and he's damn near as sure-footed as Riley."

"Great," Will replied.

"What time you need 'im?"

"Early. Maybe four thirty, five A.M."

Mik returned the hat to its nest and chuckled.

"Well I'm sure as hell not gonna be there at that hour. Gettin' too old to roll out of the sack any before six," he said. "But that's okay. You don't need me anyway. Hell, my job would be a lot simpler if everybody knew horses good as you."

"Your job would be obsolete, old man," Will joked.

"Hey, don't be thinkin' you're some spring chicken," Mik replied with a laugh. " 'Cause you ain't."

"We've been around the block some together, haven't we?" Will said. The sudden, plaintive note in his voice caused a look of puzzlement in Miklovic's eyes.

"You're not plannin' on dyin' or somethin', are you?" he said.

"Not anytime soon," Will replied. "Okay, gotta run. Thanks for taking care of Kola."

"Okey dokey," Miklovic called out, already turned back to the last horse still wearing a saddle, a black paint named Moxie, who was a favorite with all the rangers for her steady disposition and smooth gait.

Will heard Moxie let out a contented sigh at being given freedom from the saddle.

He started back toward Annie's car, cutting through the barn for one more quick look at Kola. As he emerged from the other side, the late afternoon sun blinded him until he saw Archie's big head hanging out the back window.

Will was just opening the car's front passenger door when Miklovic came running up behind him.

"Forgot to ask you," he said, huffing from the exertion. "The form. Damn things. Used to be we did everything on a man's word. Now they're hell bent on making all of us miserable with paperwork."

*The form.* Will hadn't thought about that. Shewmaker thought he was heading to Red Lodge in the morning. No way he could get him to sign off on Will checking out a new horse.

"I'll bring it in the morning," Will replied, regretting having to lie to Miklovic.

"Okey dokey. Just tack it to Torch's stall door. I'll be at Tower later in the day."

The old man gave a half wave, glanced curiously at Annie, then turned back toward the barn. But just as Annie put the car in reverse and began backing out of her parking spot, he reappeared in the barn's doorway.

"If you're gonna stay out in the backcountry for more than a couple days," he called to Will, "you'd better take some extra grain along. Torch burns calories faster than any horse I've got."

Will glanced Annie's way. He knew Mik's words had not been lost on her.

"Will do," he called back.

Another quick wave, and Miklovic disappeared back into the barn.

Silent, Annie pulled the Subaru back onto the two-lane.

It wasn't until she'd turned east and passed over the Gardner River on the Grand Loop Road that she voiced what was on her mind.

"I thought you said you were going to Red Lodge tomorrow."

Will hesitated, then said, "I'm supposed to."

"But you're obviously not going to. Not if you're checking another horse out in the morning."

Will did not respond.

"It may be none of my business," Annie said, eyes pinned on the narrow road that had begun winding its way up onto the Blacktail Deer Plateau. Her speed and attention to the view outside her windshield reflected a keen awareness that only experienced visitors to the park, and its residents, fully appreciated—that at any moment any manner of wildlife—elk, deer, bear, wolves, coyotes—could step out of the brush and trees lining the road and directly into the path of their car. "But I'm concerned. I know there will be repercussions if you don't go to Red Lodge tomorrow. You're obviously planning something . . ."

Will held his silence.

"Okay," Annie said. Her voice had suddenly taken on a quality Will did not recognize. "Call it selfish," she paused, clearly nervous about finishing the sentence, "but you've become my ally.

"I don't know why, but you've gone out of your way to help find my mother. Looking for Hank, the visit to Judge Sherburne . . ."

She took a deep breath. Will sensed she was fighting tears.

"You've given me hope, Will. Hope I desperately need. I figure if someone like you keeps caring, keeps thinking about her, we may just find her . . ."

Will looked over at her. When she first arrived in Yellowstone, he remembered thinking her appearance to be harsh. Now, in profile at least, she appeared soft, almost childlike, like she was about to start crying.

He hadn't had to comfort a crying woman in over twenty years.

Will muttered a soft, "Shit."

Annie stared straight ahead.

They fell back into silence as they passed over the bridge at Tower Junction. A young mother had fallen to her death from that same bridge earlier in the summer, leaning too far over the railing for a family photo. Will had had nightmares about it for weeks.

Will knew instinctively that Annie had said her piece. She wasn't one of those women who would want to talk this subject—or any other—to death. She wouldn't push any harder. But he also knew that she deserved better than to have him leave things where they now stood.

"I can't get you involved," he said, eyes scanning the red-rocked canyon walls below the road, to the spot where he'd rappelled down to help bring the body up. The process had been made all the more trying by the fact that the grieving children and husband—accompanied by a phalanx of law enforcement personnel—had stood on that bridge, watching.

Annie's knuckles were white from her grip on the steering wheel.

"This doesn't have something to do with my mother, does it?"

It hadn't occurred to him that Annie might have connected his plans with her mother's disappearance.

To not confide in her now would be nothing short of cruel. He had to trust her not to betray his confidence.

"It has to do with the wolves, Annie. With Number Twenty-two."

Annie reacted almost as visibly as she might have had Will told her it did have to do with her mother.

"The alpha female?" she replied, her voice high.

"Yes."

"Please. Tell me."

Will drew in a slow, deep breath, hesitating only briefly before replying.

"I received a warning earlier today. Someone's planning to kill her."

These words so startled Annie that at first she failed to notice the coyote making a dash across the road, Uinta ground squirrel—dug up from its hibernation—dangling from its mouth. She swerved, narrowly missing him.

"That's crazy," she said. "Especially now. The entire nation is focused on those wolves."

Will stared out the window as the landscape gave way from the deeply etched Black Canyon of the Yellowstone, with its steep, rocky walls, to the wide open expanses preceding the Lamar Valley, and continued.

"Exactly. But these guys—I guess he's a successful businessman from the East Coast—think they're invincible. The publicity, that picture of Twenty-two in *USA Today,* it just made her all the more desirable. She'd be the ultimate prize now for a trophy hunter. They love thinking they're bigger than the system, that they can get away with anything. This guy's been asking around for a guide . . ."

"And someone's agreed to do it?" Annie cried, incredulous.

Gleeson's name balanced on the tip of Will's tongue, but he knew better than to voice it. Annie was already hearing the case, and under unparalleled pressure because of it, a fact that Will could not displace from his mind. He couldn't facilitate Gleeson's legal defense by offering the presiding magistrate information that could later be used in a charge that she was biased against this defendant.

"Yes," he said simply. "According to my source, who's reliable, someone's agreed to do it."

Negotiating an especially sharp curve in the road, Annie's expression suddenly reflected her epiphany. And disbelief.

"You're heading into the backcountry to stop them!"

"If I *can* stop them," Will replied.

They'd just crested the rise branching off to Specimen Ridge when Annie abruptly swung her car into a pullout and angrily shoved the gear lever into park.

She turned to Will.

"You can't do it. You have to tell Peter Shewmaker. Don't do this alone."

Will met her gaze with steely eyes.

"This is my territory, Annie. My life. It's not a *judiciary* matter." The disdain with which he said the word was not lost on Annie. "At least not yet."

Annie looked away.

Realizing he'd wounded her, Will reached out, touched her shoulder.

"I'm sorry." He paused, searching for words to undo the damage. "You're new here. You don't understand how these things work."

Annie turned back to him. This time the warm, dark eyes that were usually so veiled, so guarded—against the world, and especially Will McCarroll—were without defense.

"Then make me understand."

Will knew he owed her that much. And now, he had a more practical motive for making her understand. He had to convince her not to intervene.

"If I tell anyone," he said, "and I should not have told you, this thing will become a circus. There'll be so much politics and chaos, with people jockeying for position. Twenty-two's safety will be lost in the shuffle—it will become all about publicity, how to manage it."

"But that," Annie said, "publicity, attention—would scare them away, wouldn't it? The poachers? Isn't that what you want?"

Will's hands balled into tight fists.

"What I want," he replied, "is to *get* the sons of bitches. Even if they got scared away this time, they'd be back. The only way to stop them for good is to catch them. If I can do that, they'll never come back, and the others like them will know they can't get away with this. Not here. Not in Yellowstone."

"You'd be pulled off this, wouldn't you?" Annie said. "If you told your supervisor . . ."

Her insight surprised Will.

"Yes. And I'm the best man for this job. I'm the only man for this job."

Eyes fixed ahead, on the roadway that had been overtaken now by evening's shadows, Annie said, "You could lose your job over this."

Will had thought of little else since making his decision.

"If I *can* stop them, if I can save Twenty-two, it will be worth it."

With a sigh, Annie pulled back onto the roadway. Behind them, in the rearview mirror, Annie saw the sun's final fiery moments as it melted into Electric Peak and Sepulcher Mountain. They drove on in silence. By the time they reached Pebble Creek, it had grown cool. Still, as they sat there, a full moon just beginning to show itself over the Thunderer, to the south and slightly east, Will rolled down his window. He needed more air. At that moment, he felt he could not get enough.

They sat, still not talking, until Annie shifted against the seat to face Will.

"I've heard rumors. About why you're so passionate about poaching."

Will refused to turn her way, staring instead out the side window.

"You mean about my wife. And my son?"

"Yes," Annie replied softly. She waited. When he didn't answer, she said, "It's true?"

The moon had emerged from behind Thunderer in full now. Will's eyes never left its perfectly shaped globe as he told Annie the story.

"My wife and baby were killed by a hunter's bullet. When they were out hiking. Inside the park. Above Soda Butte. It was my second season here."

He paused, his gaze following a wisp of cloud dancing its way across the lunar light.

"We thought we were living a dream. Rachel was twenty-three. Carter had just turned one."

"They never found who did it?"

"No. They never did."

They fell into silence again until an eerily, hauntingly beautiful sound filled the night. It came from behind them, in the hills above and north of Pebble Creek.

A call. For her lost mate.

Annie drew her breath in.

"That's her," Will said when the last of its melancholy echoes had ended. "That's Twenty-two."

He finally turned to Annie.

His eyes reached for hers, as surely as a desperate hand, during a crisis, reaches for the comfort of another.

"Listen to her," he said. "Don't you understand?"

Annie could only nod at first.

"I do," she replied. "Finally, I do."

Will opened the car door, but remained seated, reluctant to leave. He twisted, reaching over the backseat to pat Archie's head. The *thump, thump* of his tail against the seat somehow comforted Will.

Annie's presence comforted Will.

He had been alone for so long. For the first time, it felt he had been alone too long.

He looked at Annie.

"Would you consider coming to my cabin? Would you spend the night with me?"

# EIGHTEEN

WILL'S CABIN WAS EXACTLY WHAT ANNIE HAD IMAGINED. Made with rough-hewn logs that had withstood Yellowstone's harsh winters for over eighty years, it consisted of a single room. A bed stood against one wall with the cabin's only window above it, and a dresser next to it. A woodstove filled one corner. A makeshift kitchen consisted of a sink whose water source was a twenty-five-gallon plastic drum hanging from the ceiling, and floor-to-ceiling shelves filled with dry goods, pots and pans, books—several John Muir, Annie noted, and all wilderness and wildlife oriented—and half a dozen bottles of Johnnie Walker.

A rocking chair sat in front of the stove.

"Outhouse is in the back," Will said as he hung the kerosene lamp he'd lit on the porch on the wall next to the door.

He watched Annie taking everything in.

When he saw her eyes go to the framed photograph on the chest of drawers, Will walked slowly over to it, picked it up and handed it to Annie without saying a word.

A lovely young woman sat on the stairs Annie had just climbed, with a baby boy on her lap. Her smile, and that of the child, literally lit up the photograph.

Annie felt a pang—she could not tell whether it was at the thought that the lives of the two had been cut short so violently and prematurely, or the realization that she had never in her life experienced the kind of happiness—the love—that radiated in those young, hopeful eyes.

She walked back to the dresser, carefully placed the photograph where she'd first seen it.

When she turned, Will stood directly behind her.

He reached for her face, cupping it with both hands, and pulled her lips to his.

They did not speak as they undressed each other, standing in the cabin lit only by the kerosene lamp.

They didn't speak as Will lifted Annie and carried her to his bed. Each saw in the other's eyes what they wanted to see. Each felt in the other's body and touch what they needed to feel.

In that small backcountry cabin, surrounded by elk, and wolves, and bears, they explored each other slowly and silently, as if they had all the time in the world.

But when Will finally parted Annie's legs and braced himself over her—when he entered her for the first time— he said softly, "Open your eyes."

And before long, both their voices mingled with those filtering in the window from the wild.


"I'm scared."

Will had just fallen asleep and started "the dream"—a dream he'd had over and over again in the years after meeting Rachel, and before she and Carter died—a dream in which he was flying, soaring over mountains and rivers and valleys, when Annie's soft voice awakened him.

He rolled over, pulled her naked body close to his. It felt as though they'd done this—lain together, spoonlike, after exhausting themselves making love—many times before.

"About your mother?" he said softly back.

"No," she replied quietly. "I'm afraid that something will happen to you. Please, Will, don't go out there."

Will rolled onto his back.

"I have to, Annie."

"Your life is more important than Twenty-two's."

Rolling back onto his side, Will rose on one elbow, searched for Annie's face in the soft moonlight filtering in through the cabin's window. His voice hardened, but only slightly.

"What makes you think we, as humans, matter more than that wolf? Or any wolf? We humans are the ones who've practically destroyed this planet. Twenty-two has helped restore it—she's brought balance back to Yellowstone's ecosystem. That's more than I could ever hope to achieve."

Annie reached for his face, held it so that she could look into his eyes.

"I respect you for believing that. But right now you're more important to me than Twenty-two. I've lost my mother. I don't want to lose you too. I don't want to be left alone."

Will bent over her, kissed her cheek gently.

"Ah, Annie, you'd never be alone. Not here. You know that."

Resigned, Annie nestled her head between his shoulder and neck and fell silent for several minutes, while Will's mind turned to plans for the fast-approaching dawn.

"You never answered my question earlier," Annie finally said.

"Which question?"

"When I asked you if any of this has to do with my mother."

Will closed his eyes, drew in his breath. When he opened them again, he looked at Annie.

"You're asking me if I think these same poachers are behind your mother's kidnapping?"

"Yes, that's what I'm asking."

"My gut instinct is they are."

The tears that welled up in Annie's eyes caught a glimmer of the moonlight.

"Then go get the bastards," Judge Annie Peacock whispered.

# NINETEEN

WILL DROPPED LIKE A ROCK BEHIND THE GELDING.

The groan of the rusty-hinged door signaled that some-one had just entered the barn.

Seconds later, it groaned again. They'd closed it behind them.

Crouched behind Torch, Will reached up, slid off the halter he'd just put on the gelding, grateful he hadn't yet buckled it.

Torch's breathing drowned out the first few steps, but then Will heard the quiet crunch of boots on the barn's cedar chip–strewn floor. He rose, just enough to peek over the horse's sturdy back, grateful he'd decided not to turn the light on in the stall.

Will had entered the barn in complete darkness, but now a faint shaft of early morning light played across the floor that separated the row of stalls lining one wall from those on the opposite wall.

*Damn.*

Who'd be there at this hour? Mik had said he wasn't planning to come in until later. Must be another ranger. If so, Will could bluff his way out of the situation. Unless it was that asshole Curt Hardy, who'd give just about any-thing to nail Will doing something unauthorized. But it couldn't be Hardy. He hadn't gotten on top of a horse in a dozen years, ever since he'd resigned himself to the interp desk.

Will's pulse slowed. He could handle this.

The footsteps came closer. He'd let them pass, take a peek after they did.

But instead of walking by, they stopped in front of Torch's stall.

"Mornin', Will."

Will recognized the voice. Slowly, he straightened to his full height.

"Morning, Mik," he replied.

John Miklovic looked tired. Not happy to be out of bed.

"I was just checkin' Torch's feet," Will said. "About the form—"

Miklovic moved his hand across the air in a short, choppy wave, cutting Will off.

"It's too early in the morning to be bullshitting each other. You don't have the form. I hear you're supposed to be in Red Lodge."

Will did not avoid Mik's gaze.

"That's right," he said. "Listen, Mik, I hated like hell lying to you yesterday, but—"

Another chop of the air from Mik and Will shut up.

"I didn't come here to confront you," Miklovic said. "About the form or anything else." He paused. "You and me've been working together for over two decades. You're sure not some ass kisser who never breaks a rule, but I never known you to do somethin' like this. Something we both know could get you fired.

"I figure if whatever you're up to is that important to you, it'd probably be important to me too. To this park. So I didn't come here to make trouble for you, Will. I came here to give you this."

It was the first Will had noticed of Miklovic's oversized canvas jacket. He'd never seen him wear anything like it.

Mik twisted to slip out of the jacket and Will saw a large hump protruding from under it, on his back. Within seconds, the jacket dropped to the ground and Will saw the cause of the disfigurement.

Mik had strapped a black case over his right shoulder, under the jacket.

Intrigued, Will slid the heavy door open and stepped out of the stall.

Free now of the jacket, Mik slid his arm out of the strap attached to each end of the case.

"Here," he said, offering it to Will.

Will recognized it immediately. Still, incredulous, he lowered the case to the ground, kneeled beside it, and flipped it open to see its contents.

A telemetry set.

Will looked up at Miklovic.

"Figured you might need it," Mik said.

"But how? How could you know?"

"Hell, Will, I knew somethin' was up by the way you was acting yesterday. Then after work, I stopped by the Blue Goose. Couple of your coworkers were in there. They were talking about you going to Red Lodge tomorrow—to the wolf talk. About how nutty it was to send you."

He scratched his head, as though reliving the previous evening.

"But you'd told me you needed a horse for the back-country today. None of it made sense. So I bought them a drink, got them talking. One of 'em mentioned how one of them science fellas had had his telemetry equipment stolen, and bingo—it all just kind of became clear to me. Like some kind of . . . what the hell's that word? You know, that means you suddenly figure out something really important? I mean something that could change your whole life?"

"Epiphany?" Will replied.

"Yea. Epiphany. That's it. It was like I had an epiphany, but all I knew at that point was that you was up to something, something big. Something risky. And then Tavner Marek just happened to be comin' in the bar when I was leaving. I'd seen him and you talking yesterday. I could tell it was somethin' pretty serious, so I twisted his arm, and he came clean. Once I finally had it figured out, I decided to stop by Janet's house . . ."

Will didn't even attempt to hide his surprise.

"Janet Nakoa?"

Janet Nakoa ran the Park Service warehouse. While she wasn't hard to look at, her disposition was such that everyone pretty much steered clear of her unless they absolutely had no choice in the matter.

"Yeah," Mik answered. "She and I, well, sometimes we . . . you know, her husband died a couple years back. And I've been livin' here alone all this time. Once in a while, we both need a little company."

Will was hard put to know which news to be more surprised about—that Mik and Janet had something going or that she had given him the telemetry set.

"Janet Nakoa gave you this equipment?"

"Let's just say I called in a little favor," Mik replied with a toothy grin. "Don't worry. She got the better end of the deal."

Maybe it was the hour. Or the fact he'd gotten no sleep.

Or the prospect of never seeing Mik's homely face again, but Will found it hard to say anything for a few seconds.

"I don't know how to thank you."

Mik pretended not to notice Will's emotional state.

"Just one way," he said.

"What's that?"

"You and Torch take care of each other."

"We'll do that, Mik," Will replied. "I give you my word."

"One more thing," Mik added. "Last I heard, day before yesterday, somebody'd spotted Twenty-two up near Druid Peak. But you probably already knew that."

"I did. And that's the way I'm starting out, but ever since Twenty-one died, Twenty-two's been on the move. All over the place. That's why the telemetry will make such a difference. Especially if Patrick Jackson's equipment fell into the wrong hands."

Mik seemed to be thinking about what Will had just said.

"You got the code for her?" he asked.

"Got it right up here," Will answered, tapping a finger to his temple.

Mik set his jaw. He looked wide awake now, but still terribly out of sorts at the events—and hour—at hand. Will knew Mik to be a man who liked the simplicity of his life, the predictability of each day. Both of which were facilitated by obeying the rules he'd had handed down to him.

Will had, in one fell swoop, managed to compromise all of that, and that fact clearly grieved him.

As the old Austrian stood there in an agonized state, Will half expected him to change his mind, take back the telemetry case. Or to launch into a tirade.

But instead Mik reached out, put a hand on Will's shoulder.

"Go get them bastards," he said, steel gray eyes drilling into Will's.

Then he turned and limped out of the barn, pulling the door closed behind him.

# TWENTY

ANNIE LITERALLY COULD NOT READ THE PLEADINGS sitting on the desk in front of her. It wasn't that she hadn't slept more than an hour or two the night before, or that, by the time she arrived at the Pagoda Building for work, she had already hiked several miles in the dark, down to where they'd left her car at Pebble Creek.

It was the sight of Will disappearing into the trees after she'd dropped him off half a mile from the stable at Tower. One moment he was there, with her, his presence giving her strength and hope, and the next he'd been swallowed by the wilderness.

A dozen questions raced through her mind, blurring the words and the legalese she was supposed to be concentrating on for a hearing the next day.

What would happen when Peter Shewmaker found out that Will had disobeyed his orders to go to Red Lodge?

As disturbing as the prospect of Will being fired was, it frightened Annie far less than the next question. Was Chad Gleeson really planning on killing 22, and if so, what might he do if Will McCarroll got in the way?

And finally, was it possible, as Will suspected, that all of this played into her mother's disappearance?

Just when Annie felt she might drive herself mad with

these questions—questions she had no ability whatsoever to answer—another came to mind.

*What about the newspaper Judge Sherburne gave them?*
Will believed his old friend knew something.

Finally, Annie had come upon a question she could at least *try* to answer.

She pushed back from her chair, grabbed her fleece jacket, and called out the door to Justine, "I have to run home."

Archie greeted her at the door with a wagging tail.

Patting his head distractedly, she headed for the living room, where she'd left the newspaper on the coffee table. Now she grabbed it greedily.

The day she and Will had visited Judge Sherburne, she had skimmed over it after Will dropped her off. This time she would read every word of every article.

Annie dropped onto the couch. Settling back against the cushions, she unfolded the paper and began reading.


With a soft nudge to his belly, Will urged Torch into a smooth-gaited canter.

The day's first light had begun creeping across the landscape and he wanted to make it across the open sage flats that led out of the Tower Junction area before he became visible to cars traveling the Mammoth-Tower road.

Half a mile later, horse and rider reached a junction. Without guidance, Torch took the left hand fork, continuing north.

They followed along Elk Creek for two miles, spotting numerous mule deer grazing, and then half a mile farther, they crossed the suspension bridge over the Yellowstone River. Now they were in open sage land and able to make good time.

At the junction with Hellroaring Trail, Will dismounted, giving Torch free rein to graze as Will loosened the bungee cord holding the telemetry case to the pack he'd tied behind his saddle.

The wind had picked up, and with it came a bank of ominous clouds, rolling in from the west.

Removing the telemetry receiver, Will set the frequency to 1057.96—the frequency assigned Twenty-two's collar. Then, he held the antenna high in the air, facing east.

Twenty-two had last been seen up above Pebble Creek, which was far enough away that he had no real expectation that the antenna would actually pick up anything, but Will knew she was on the move, which meant it was at least a theoretical possibility that she'd be within range. Still, he considered this first test more practice than anything else.

Will had mapped his route to his planned destination—the area around Druid Peak—with the goal of keeping him mostly in the backcountry and out of sight. It would require him to travel the Buffalo Plateau Trail north, where he would connect with the Poacher's Trail and actually leave the park before dropping back into Yellowstone on the Buffalo Fork Trail, which bisected with the Slough Creek Trail. It wasn't until that point—the intersection of Buffalo Fork and Slough Creek trails—that he actually expected to pick up any signals from 22.

Which is why, after a long period of anticipated silence, Will practically dropped the receiver when it went off. While lowering it to put it away, he had unintentionally turned ever so slightly toward the west.

*Beep.*

It was faint, but real. Coming from somewhere west of Hellroaring Mountain.

Torch startled when Will leaped back into the saddle, but the gelding stood solid when Will raised the antenna high, toward the northwest.

*Beep . . . beep.*

Two beeps this time. Several seconds apart.

It couldn't be. *Could it?*

Had 22 managed to travel that far—a distance of over fifteen miles—since last night, when Will felt certain he'd recognized her call from high above Pebble Creek?

He tried it again, this time starting the sweep due east, toward Gardiner.

No sound.

But as he continued in a half circle and rotated toward the north, that changed.

*Beep . . . beep . . . beep.*

There was no question.

Twenty-two was on the move again.

Hellroaring Mountain and the vast area west of it was home to one of the park's most successful packs. She'd apparently decided to go mate shopping there.

His heart racing, Will pulled Torch's head up.

"Change of plans, old boy."

When Will turned Torch's head ever so slightly, the rest of the powerful animal followed, executing a U-turn on the narrow trail that could easily cause inexperienced riders, or flighty horses, to plummet down the steep hillside to the raging waters below.

They would remain on the Yellowstone River Trail and head north and west toward the home range of the Hellroaring wolf pack.

Rain had begun falling.

Just short of a half mile up the trail, they reached the confluence where the cold, clear water of Hellroaring Creek met with the deep, surging waters of the mighty Yellowstone. A beach of fine sand led up to sheer walls that lined the Black Canyon of the Yellowstone.

Overhead, an osprey watched from her nest.

Will knew the area well.

Reaching Hellroaring Mountain required crossing the creek. Will worked Torch off the well-traveled trail, down toward the water.

As a ranger, he'd warned many a hiker not to try fording the creek. Two years earlier a twenty-seven-year-old from Vermont died when he lost his footing among the boulders and rocks and was swallowed by the water, which was deceptively big and fast.

Up ahead, Will had told that hiker—as it turned out, in vain—a mere 1.8 miles, a stock bridge crossed the creek.

But that was 1.8 miles in a direction Will no longer wanted to go.

He dismounted, surveyed the situation.

He looked at Torch. Remembered his promise to Mik.

While a hiker risked drowning in the rushing waters, one wrong step and a horse's pencil-thin leg could easily snap.

With fall approaching, the water levels were lower, low enough to afford more visibility than the last time Will had been up this way.

Will studied the water, the rocks. He walked up and down the bank, fifty yards in both directions. He was satisfied he could make the crossing safely, but he couldn't be sure about Torch. Mik's words echoed in Will's mind.

*You and Torch take care of each other.*

As he returned to Torch's side, the gelding nickered a greeting, and in that instant, Will made his decision.

"Okay, big guy," he said as the rain turned suddenly from soft to pelting. "Let's head to the stock bridge."

# TWENTY-ONE

"He *what*?"

The desk chair's springs shrieked like a puppy whose tail had just been stepped on as Peter Shewmaker lurched forward to reach for the phone's handset.

Peter knew instinctively that he did not want to take the rest of this call on the speakerphone. Park Service employees loved to linger outside in the hallways whenever something out of the ordinary was happening inside any of the supervisors' offices. Peter long ago learned they seemed to have a built-in radar for such things—the moment anything started up, people began making trips to the bathroom, or to the copier down the hallway. Both of which took them past Peter's door.

He stood now and pushed it shut.

The room went silent, but not the voice on the other end.

Peter could hear Otto Gleeson swearing up a storm even before the receiver touched his ear.

"I said the goddamn son of a bitch isn't here," Otto shouted.

Voices in the background—what sounded like a heated exchange—told Peter that the wolf roundtable had already begun. Gleeson had to be calling him from his cell phone—no doubt after managing to stir up everyone present with some inflammatory statements.

Peter glanced quickly at the clock on his wall.

"It's only twelve thirty," he said. "I bet he had car trouble."

But even as the words left his mouth Peter knew otherwise—knew that trouble—the real kind, the kind only Will McCarroll was capable of stirring up—was brewing.

Peter should have trusted his gut on this one. The moment he'd agreed to Gleeson's request to send McCarroll to the wolf roundtable something had told him the decision would backfire on him.

He just didn't expect it to happen this soon.

"What kind of a representative of the Park Service did you send me?" Gleeson fumed. In the background, a voice on a loudspeaker pleaded for order.

Peter knew it was useless to remind Gleeson he had been the one to choose McCarroll, not Shewmaker. Gleeson was on a rampage, and Peter would be lucky to get a word in edgewise.

"We went out of our way to include you assholes in this thing," Gleeson went on. "We decided to put together a table of representatives from every sector in these parts and we had the class, the dignity, to include the Park Service— even though you arrogant sons of bitches have done nothing but try to put us out of business."

"Us?" Peter finally broke in defiantly.

"You know what I mean," Gleeson replied, for once flustered by his slipup.

"I think I do," Peter said. "I think you mean the outfitters, and hunters. Like your son, Chad. But—to the best of my recollection, anyway—you're no longer in that business, Otto. You're the mayor of Cooke City now. A man charged with looking out for the good of his citizenry. Not just his son's rap sheet. Or pocketbook."

If it weren't for the noise in the background, Shewmaker might have assumed that Otto had hung up on him.

"Listen, you son of a bitch," Otto finally replied, his voice almost a growl. "You don't want to cross me. You may be Park Service, but that doesn't mean I can't get you fired. You get that fucking McCarroll here—now—or I'll hold you personally responsible."

One didn't rise to the position Peter Shewmaker held within the Park Service by being a maverick. Quite the opposite usually proved true. In order to last an entire career within the Park Service, in order to thrive and end up in a position of authority, it was imperative that one learn to compromise, to subjugate personal biases and opinions to the greater good, as determined—and defined—by the Park Service.

Part of that greater good was being good neighbors to the communities serving as entryways to Yellowstone. In particular, Gardiner, Cooke City, and West Yellowstone. Even if doing so required compromise and—quite often undeserved—diplomacy.

Still, at that moment all the years of playing by the Park Service book, of making nice to assholes like Otto Gleeson, came to a head for Peter.

"Mayor Gleeson," he replied. "I'm going to pretend you never said that. I'm going to pretend that some two-bit politician with a wolf killer for a son never threatened me."

He could hear—and practically see—Gleeson's apoplexy.

"I'll have your ass on a platter, you fucking piece of shit," Gleeson hissed back at him. "Whether Will McCarroll shows or not, you're *history*. Do you hear?"

Without saying another word, Peter Shewmaker slammed down the phone.

He sat, staring at it. Then in a fit of frustration, he kicked at the corner of his desk.

A group photo that had been taken at the most recent law enforcement training session had been propped up against the wall at the back corner of his desk. Now it toppled forward, facedown on a pile of loose papers.

Peter picked it up, staring at it, his eyes automatically drawn to a face in the back row.

The Mammoth law enforcement division had run the

four-mile obstacle course that day, a test designed to prepare rangers for the pursuit of fugitives—possibly armed fugitives—into the backcountry.

Two straps could be seen over one person's shoulders— Will McCarroll's. He stood, ramrod straight, in the back row. The straps represented the fifty-pound backpack Will had insisted on wearing during the trials. After all, he'd explained, that's at least the weight law enforcement would carry during the real thing.

The fact that a young, new, testosterone-filled ranger had called Will a "hot dog" and "showboater" that morning hadn't caused Will to so much as flinch.

Fifty pounds on his back, Will had won the trial that day. He even beat Peter, who came in second.

Peter had watched as the young ranger, who came in a distant fifth or sixth, tipped his hat to Will that night at the barbeque that always followed a training session.

But as he stared at the picture now, Peter saw that the face in the back row showed no sense of victory.

No gloating. No pleasure.

Will McCarroll's expression registered what it had for over two decades now. An expression that was pretty much impossible to pinpoint.

A combination of . . . just what was it?

Peter studied it.

Resentment? Determination? *Fatalism?*

It was that—that last emotion—that most disturbed Shewmaker now.

Will had always had an air of fatalism about him. Most folks who knew and worked with him attributed it to what had happened that second year he was a ranger.

Now, it occurred to Peter it was more than that.

"What the hell are you up to, Will?" he asked, staring intently at this man he'd worked with for over seven years, yet sometimes felt he hardly knew.

Then he dropped the picture—frame and all—into the steel gray wastebasket beneath his desk. And picked the phone back up.

He sighed, waited, phone in hand. Almost put it back down.

But then he punched a number.

"Dispatch? Put a call out to all law enforcement on duty. If anyone sees a sign of Will McCarroll, I want them to call me, and me alone, stat. Got that?"

He stopped to listen to the reply.

"No, I have no goddamn idea where he is, or what he's driving. Or riding. I just want him found."

# TWENTY-TWO

WILL AND TORCH CROSSED THE STOCK BRIDGE WITHOUT incident, but by the time they'd retraced the 1.8 miles back down the other side of the creek to rejoin the Yellowstone River Trail, Will's frustration had kicked in. The day was dwindling. If 22 were moving as determinedly as she apparently had been since the night before, she might now be out of range.

Without dismounting this time, he reached behind the saddle and unhooked the telemetry case.

He held the antenna as high as his arms allowed.

Silence.

Twisting, he scanned at least 270 degrees.

"Damn."

Will looked at the settings he'd entered earlier, checked the frequency, then tried again, this time rotating full circle.

Had the first reading been some kind of error? Was 22 back above Pebble Creek, with Chad Gleeson closing in on her, aided by the use of the stolen equipment? That's where Will had been headed—until he'd heard those faint beeps telling him 22 had moved. Now, with so much at stake, he began to question his decision to head toward Hellroaring Mountain.

He took a deep breath. Reasoned through the situation.

Twenty-two had been showing clear signs of unrest. She was looking for a mate. A companion to spend the winter with. Will had known of other wolves who had traveled the kind of distance she'd have to have traveled to now be near Hellroaring.

And telemetry was a science. Though Will did not have occasion to use it himself, he'd been around plenty of biologists who relied upon it.

Should he turn back, stick to his original plan? Or should he trust the faint but certain beeping from the receiver he'd heard earlier?

"Shit," he muttered to himself. He shielded his eyes from the rain, closed them momentarily as he continued thinking his predicament through.

Twenty-two had maintained her status as the alpha female of the Druids for seven years. She accomplished that in large part on heart. And passion.

The same heart and passion that would explain her heading to Hellroaring to find a replacement for 21.

Vowing not to second-guess himself again, Will nudged Torch in the ribs with his boots.

"Let's make up for that lost time."

Torch eagerly obliged. Surefooted, the gelding seemed to understand precisely what Will wanted of him.

They'd just reached the spot directly across from where Will had paused an hour and a half earlier, wrestling with the question of whether or not to ford the river, when he spotted them.

Two sets of prints.

One belonging to a horse. The other, leading, made by man.

A sense of dread gripped Will.

*Did Gleeson already have the jump on him?*

Will dismounted, bending to examine the tracks. They were recent, made after the rain had softened the parched earth enough to leave impressions—which had now begun filling with rain.

If the rain kept up, soon they would be washed away.

Back astride Torch, Will kept his eyes on the ground, watching for the prints to branch off of the main trail, especially when they approached the area where the telemetry had indicated 22's presence.

But instead of turning north, toward Hellroaring, horse and rider had forged ahead.

Confused, Will got out the receiver again.

Nothing.

Maybe that explained why the prints continued west. Perhaps Gleeson had also pinpointed 22, recognized she was heading west and now, like Will, having lost a signal, he'd made the reasonable assumption that she'd continued in that direction. After all, the Hellroaring pack's range was vast, extending all the way up to Jardine, north of the park's boundary. Maybe 22 had picked up the Hellroaring pack's scent and was now hot on its trail.

With Gleeson in close pursuit.

But to Will's way of thinking, there was one thing glaringly wrong with that picture.

Gleeson was a pro. No way he would risk leaving tracks on the main trail.

And then a plausible explanation came to Will.

*Unless he believed that Will now sat at a roundtable in Red Lodge.*

Gleeson had every reason to believe that the ploy he'd hatched with his father to get Will out of the way had worked. And Will knew him to be bold enough to do just about anything—so long as he didn't have Will McCarroll to contend with.

With a click of the tongue, Will urged Torch to pick up speed again. At a slow gallop now—anything faster would be disastrous—they climbed the steep trail to a ridge almost two hundred feet above the Black Canyon. Then they descended again, to Little Cottonwood Creek, and after that, its parent, Cottonwood Creek.

Finally, the trail began following the Yellowstone closely again. Eyes still fixed upon the ground, Will saw that the rider had climbed back on his horse. The single set of tracks disappeared from time to time, when the trail became mostly rock, but always reappeared.

What he perceived to be Gleeson's boldness pushed Will to the limits of his vow to Mik to take good care of Torch, who, oblivious to the promise, had escalated the pace into a full gallop.

"Whoa, boy," Will called against the wind, reining him in.

Three miles from Cottonwood Creek, at the Blacktail Creek junction, they turned west, just as the rain became vicious, torrential, adept at washing out most fresh tracks within minutes. Someone with lesser experience would have trouble picking out the faint traces that remained of some, but Will saw just enough to know he hadn't lost the other rider's trail.

The tracks continued well beyond Hellroaring, where Will had originally intended to turn off. After passing Crevice Lake, just as Crevice Creek came into sight, Will brought the telemetry receiver out again.

Silence.

The tracks had become so few and so hard to pick out that Will was about to turn back when he came upon proof positive he was still on the right trail—a pile of fresh manure in the middle of the wooden bridge over Crevice Creek.

Will's excitement proved short lived, for on the other side of the bridge—at the point where the Yellowstone River Trail began climbing steeply again—all signs of the horse and rider abruptly ended.

Will slid off Torch, his boots splattering mud as they thudded to earth, and walked ahead a quarter mile. Then he retraced the gelding's prints several hundred yards in the opposite direction. Nothing.

Just as the UPS driver knows the peculiarities, the little ins and outs, of the route he's serviced for decades, Will knew this trail and all its possibilities.

There was only one explanation for the abrupt disappearance of tracks—only one other turnoff available to someone traveling it.

As reckless as Gleeson had been in the past, Will still could not imagine him choosing this option.

A short distance off the Yellowstone River Trail, the Crevice Creek patrol cabin provided much needed shelter to back-country rangers. More than once over the years, it had saved a life when a sudden and violent blizzard blew over the Ab-sarokas to descend upon Yellowstone's highest reaches. The cabin was only accessible by rangers and Park Service main-tenance workers with the combination to the padlock on its front door—which meant Gleeson would have to break in to take shelter there. Doing so would not only risk calling at-tention to his presence in the event someone passed by, it would also add another felony offense to the list of crimes for which he'd be nailed if he were, indeed, caught.

Will found it hard to believe Gleeson would put that much at risk—before he granted his client's wish anyway.

Still, Will knew this backcountry like nobody else, and there was no other explanation for the sudden disappear-ance of tracks.

Will turned Torch around cautiously—the narrow trail dropped off to raging waters a hundred feet below—then steered him off the trail and up the steep hillside.

Once on top of the ridge, hidden by stands of white bark pine—seventy-five percent of which had been killed by the pine beetle, depriving the grizzly population of some of its prime nutrition—Will got as close to the cabin as he dared before dismounting and tying Torch to a tree. He would travel the rest of the way on foot.

Will worked his way around to the cabin's backside, which, as he recalled, had just one small window.

Drawing his gun, crouched low, Will moved from tree to tree until the rustic cabin came into view. When it did, what he saw threw him completely off guard.

A chestnut gelding, tied to the porch railing.

Will recognized it immediately.

# TWENTY-THREE

ANNIE RECOGNIZED THE VOICE FIRST. IT CAME FROM UP ahead, one of several hallways she had to cross to get to Judge Sherburne's room.

"No, no, *no.*"

It was the forced cheerfulness that registered with her.

"No time to dillydally."

Before Annie could turn back, the nurse who had blown the whistle during Will and Annie's visit to Judge Sherburne four days earlier rounded the corner.

She'd chosen a cherry red lipstick this day. It matched the red leather belt she'd cinched tightly around the white blouse at her ample waist.

Annie glanced at the nametag. "Nomie."

Annie dropped her eyes and began digging in her brief-case, fearful Rainbow Living's version of Nurse Ratched from *One Flew Over the Cuckoo's Nest* would recognize her and set the alarms off again. But she needn't have worried. Nomie maintained a hawklike focus on her current charge—a frail woman in her eighties pushing a walker at a speed that seemed to frighten her.

"But I need to use the restroom," the woman said as they passed Annie, with Nomie steering her by the elbow.

Nomie would have none of it.

"I gave you the chance to go before we left your room. We can't be late for group therapy, can we?"

"No," the octogenarian replied weakly. "I guess not."

"Besides," Nomie went on, "I've got a full plate this afternoon and a hot date tonight. And I can't be late."

Annie continued to busy herself with her briefcase until they'd turned down the next hallway. When they did, she hightailed it to Judge Sherburne's room.

The moment she walked through his doorway, a strong sense of déjà vu—or perhaps just the same gut-wrenching sense of tragedy—hit her.

The room was immaculate. Bed made. Nothing out of place. It smelled of disinfectant.

Something did not seem right to Annie.

Judge Sherburne sat in the same position he'd been in the last time Annie had walked through that door. Even with the back of his wheelchair to her as he stared out the window at the courtyard, Annie could tell that Sherburne was not faring well at Rainbow Living.

Quietly, Annie pulled the door shut behind her and crossed the room.

Sherburne seemed to sense that this visitor wasn't staff. He twisted as far as his impaired body allowed for a look.

"Hi again," Annie said softly as she placed a hand on his bony shoulder.

When Sherburne saw it was Annie, the bittersweet smile on his face signaled such a sense of both joy and grief that a lump formed instantly in Annie's throat.

Still, Annie swore that his smile was less lopsided this time. The left side of his mouth had lifted, ever so slightly, along with the right side.

"Look at you," she said spontaneously, her voice filled with affection.

Sherburne did not try to respond. Instead, he took Annie in with those warm, sad eyes. They were the eyes of a man who, despite having seen and heard—and now experienced—life's bleakest, most grim realities, still held tremendous dignity and grace.

Annie settled on the windowsill, facing him.

"You're losing weight," she said.

Sherburne grunted dismissively. *Don't worry*.

He nodded at her, as if to say, *Talk. Tell me why you're here.*

Annie smiled at his impatience.

"I'm here for two reasons," she said in response.

Sherburne's eyes did not stray from her face. An atomic bomb would not have dislodged them at that moment.

"First," she said, "because Will believes you know something about what happened to my mother. He thinks there's something in the newspaper you gave us that day."

Sherburne's eyes livened with hope as he nodded.

*Yes.*

"I read every word on every page," Annie said, almost apologetically, "and I don't see it."

Sherburne took in a deep breath and Annie knew he was about to speak. But the sounds came out in monosyllables that made no sense either alone or when strung together.

The tone with which they ended was unmistakable. Frustration.

"I'm sorry," Annie said. "I wish I understood. You have no idea how much I wish that."

Sherburne raised his right hand, holding two fingers up.

Annie stared at it, brow furrowed.

"What . . . ?"

With no small effort, he lifted his hand higher, halfway to his chest, and folded the index finger, leaving the other one pointing toward the ceiling.

A knot formed in Annie's stomach. She did not understand. It pained her to see how frustrated her visit was making Sherburne.

Sherburne opened his mouth again. Painstakingly, he pursed his lips. Closed his eyes. As focused as a child tying his first shoelace, Annie could practically see him striving to remember the speech therapist's instructions.

Annie bent low, straining to hear.

"Www . . . www . . ."

Bursts of soft air brushed the skin on Annie's cheek.

Had she not looked into his eyes at point-blank range, Annie might still not have understood.

But she did look into them, she searched them, desperate to help him, desperate for him to help her, and when she did, a single word came to mind.

"Will?"

Sherburne's chest collapsed with relief. He nodded.

"I get it," Annie said. "I told you there are two reasons I'm here. You think Will is the other reason, don't you?"

Sherburne nodded. He'd exhausted himself.

"Yes," Annie replied. It was impossible not to be excited at this first real conversation between them. "Will *is* the other reason. He's in trouble, and I'm worried he's also in danger . . ."

Sherburne's expression went dark at the suggestion, but before Annie could say more the door opened and it suddenly felt as though someone had sucked all the air out of the room.

Annie looked up. Sherburne, it appeared, didn't have to in order to know who'd just entered.

Nomie, hands on hips, fresh coat of lipstick applied.

"Well, well," she said, "look who has a visitor."

Even with no control over more than half his body, Sherburne's entire bearing changed instantaneously.

"Time for our evening walk," she said, approaching the wheelchair.

The moment she came within his view and reached for the handles on the back of his chair, Sherburne stiffened and glared at her. Then, as she kicked the lever locking his wheels in place, in a gesture of defiance, he lowered his good foot—the right one—to the floor. When Nomie tried to back the chair up, it spun in a half circle.

Nomie's face reddened.

"Now you cut that out," she said, bending down and lifting Sherburne's foot. She flipped the footrest in place, then literally dropped his foot on the silver plate. "You're acting like a child."

Straightening, she glanced at Annie and said, as though she had no doubt Annie would sympathize, "He's becoming more difficult by the day."

Annie pushed away from the window, rising to her full height, which gave her a good six inches on the nurse.

"Why do you think that is?" she said angrily.

Nomie was nonplussed. Or oblivious. Or, most likely, thinking about her hot date.

"Who knows? He's getting fewer visitors these days. It always happens. When a patient first moves in, everyone comes to visit, then they start dropping off . . ."

Suddenly Nomie's heavily made-up eyes—her eyelashes looked like Tammy Faye's—narrowed.

"Didn't we meet before?"

"No," Annie replied. "This is the first time I've been here."

"Oh," Nomie said. "Well, you remind me of someone. Can't put my finger on it."

She looked down at the judge, who'd descended into a deep depression.

"I've got to take him for a little walk. He has to get out of his room at least once a day." She glanced at her watch. "And visiting hours will be over before I get him back here. You'll have to come back another time."

Annie placed a hand on the back of Judge Sherburne's wheelchair.

"It's important that I talk to him."

The gesture wasn't lost on Nomie. She pushed Annie's hand away and grabbed a firm hold on both handles, turning the judge toward the door.

"Talk to him?" she said with a laugh. "Honey, in case you haven't noticed, Judge Sherburne isn't doing much talking these days."

She trained her Tammy Faye eyes on Sherburne now, and while in theory she continued to talk to Annie, it was clear it was the judge she was addressing.

"That's because he's not working hard enough. He's been too distracted. Thinks he's still presiding in the courtroom or something. That he doesn't have to work hard at getting well, like the other people in here do. But we've decided to change that, haven't we, *Your Honor*?"

She'd already begun rolling him toward the hallway.

"Say good-bye to your friend," she said merrily before the two of them disappeared into the hallway.


An hour later, Annie burst through the door.

Judge Sherburne sat on the side of his bed, in his pajamas. Head down. Annie wondered at first if he'd fallen asleep sitting up.

She'd gone as far as Highway 89 before doing a fast U-turn during which she'd almost collided with a police car.

After pulling into the Rainbow Living parking lot, she'd waited in the Subaru, eyes glued to both the front and the side exits of the building. Her heart quickened when a cowboy in a beatup pickup pulled up and sat near the curb, the motor running. The truck had an NRA and Bush/Cheney sticker on it. The mud flaps bore a naked woman, back arched, in profile.

Within seconds the front door of Rainbow Living flew open and out pranced Nomie. She'd changed into tight jeans and a short jacket. A little bulge of flesh showed between them. Annie waited until the two had lip-locked, then pulled out of the lot, before she entered the building.

The reception desk sat empty. Annie hurried by.

Judge Sherburne's closed door caused her a moment's pause. But then she heard footsteps coming her way, down the hall, and she threw it open, slipping inside.

*"Where are your newspapers?"* she said.

Startled, Judge Sherburne's head jerked up.

"She took them from you, didn't she? She threatened to do it last time, when Will and I were here. She won't let you have them, will she? It's her way of punishing you."

Had he shouted "YES!" Sherburne's grunt of affirmation could not have been more clear.

Annie crossed the room, lowered herself to the bed beside him.

"She has no right," she said, the anger roiling inside her like a storm brewing over the horizon. "What about the nurse's aide who used to read to you?"

She turned to Sherburne.

A tear had gathered in his eye.

"She's stopped her, hasn't she?"

This time, Annie didn't wait for an answer. A woman possessed now, she got up, strode to the closet, and threw open the French double doors.

An assortment of shirts and pants—organized by color—hung in parallel rows, shirts on top, pants below. Annie riffled through them, stopping to yank a khaki shirt off its hanger, then a pair of neatly pressed blue jeans.

"Here," she said, turning back to Sherburne. "These will do."

She returned to the bed, threw his clothing beside him.

Sherburne simply stared at her, confused, perhaps even concerned by this change in the usually sedate Annie Peacock.

"I'm getting you out of here," Annie declared. "That is, if you want to go? Would you like to come back to the stone house with me?"

So abruptly and unexpectedly did Sherburne react—by pushing himself to his feet—that he lost his balance and, before Annie could anticipate it, crumpled to the floor.

Annie dropped down beside him.

"Are you okay?"

Sherburne nodded, his eyes gleaming as he grabbed the railing on the side of the bed with his good hand.

"Let me help you," Annie said.

Once she got him standing, Annie slipped the shirt and pants on over his pajamas.

But after she'd helped Judge Sherburne into his wheelchair, he began to fuss and Annie felt certain he'd changed his mind.

Her heart sank.

Maybe, though, it was for the best. She'd never acted so impulsively. She hadn't thought any of this through.

Still the thought of leaving him there turned her inside out.

Sherburne had lowered himself into the wheelchair without resistance, but now he pointed with great angst at his bed.

"Do you want to get back in bed?" Annie said. She didn't attempt to hide her disappointment.

Sherburne snorted derisively. Still, he continued to point at the bed.

Confused, Annie pushed him closer.

When he could reach out and touch it, he clumsily dug at the covers.

Annie helped him, lifting the hand-quilted bedcover, then the top sheet. She had no idea what he was trying to do.

"You want to make it look like you're asleep in bed?"

*No, no.* Sherburne shook his head.

Annie was growing nervous about someone finding her there, seeing Judge Sherburne dressed in street clothes at that hour.

When Sherburne tried to slide his hand under the mattress, Annie lifted the mattress up off the box springs—only a matter of inches, but enough for Judge Sherburne to smile, and for Annie to see what he was after.

A stack of folded newspapers.

Annie let out a laugh. He'd been hiding them.

"These are important, aren't they?"

Relieved, Judge Sherburne sighed, nodding, as Annie grabbed them and stuffed them into her briefcase.

The next second it became apparent that Judge Sherburne was still not ready to leave. His eyes had swept to the backpack that Annie had noticed sitting upright on the bed the first time she and Will had visited. Tonight it was on the dresser. He nodded at it emphatically.

"Shall I grab that too?" Annie said.

Sherburne nodded.

Annie took two long, hurried strides to the dresser, and reached for the pack with one hand, hoping this was the last of Sherburne's surprises. She kept glancing at the door, expecting someone to charge through it at any time and set off alarms.

She'd assumed the pack was empty, but when she grabbed one of its straps, its weight was so great it almost fell to the floor. Sherburne practically jumped out of the wheelchair to catch it.

"I got it," Annie said, cradling it against her body with her other arm.

When she began to slide it onto her back so that she'd have both hands free to push the wheelchair, Sherburne reached for it, adamant.

He finally relaxed when Annie placed it on his lap.

*"What the hell are you doing here?"*

Minutes earlier, after stealing up to the cabin to sneak a look inside through the back window, Will observed Randy Hannah kneeling in front of the potbellied stove, feeding it wood.

He'd realized the moment he'd seen Riley, the sorrel gelding tied outside—the horse that Will had hoped to take into the backcountry for his mission—that he hadn't been following Chad Gleeson after all, but instead he'd been on the trail of the "young upstart" Mik had referred to.

But until he looked in the window he hadn't realized it was Randy Hannah who'd beaten Will to checking Riley out.

The realization that he'd made such a costly mistake was a tremendous blow. It had taken him past the area where the receiver had last signaled 22's presence—past where he would have turned off had he not caught sight of the tracks—and had cost him hours.

Hours that might ultimately cost 22 her life.

If it weren't for the absolutely grim expression on his young friend's face as he stoked the fire, Will would not have announced his presence. He would have gotten right back on Torch and retraced his tracks. But as he watched Randy from the back window, something about him alarmed Will.

He circled around front and entered the cabin.

Randy's head jerked up from the fire. A grin transformed his face.

"Will!"

"What are you up to?" Will replied.

Randy's grin faded so fast Will almost wondered if he'd imagined it in the first place. Despite being bronzed by a summer spent walking the hot springs and boardwalks, Randy looked pale. He glanced over Will's shoulder.

"You alone?"

Scowling, Will pulled the cabin door closed behind him.

"What's up?"

Will took in the clothing drying in front of the fire— camouflage pants, a black T-shirt, hiking boots.

"And where the hell are you going dressed in that?"

Randy's words came in a rush. "Remember when I told you I thought something was wrong?"

Their earlier conversation came back to Will.

"The geothermal features?"

The fire crackled, shooting sparks on to the floor. Randy automatically closed the door.

"Well, I don't just *think* now," he said, looking up at Will triumphantly. "I *know*. I'm on my way to find out if my theory is right."

"What the hell are you talking about, Randy? *What* theory?"

Randy's eyes darted back to the door.

"Someone's drilling near the park," he said. "It's affecting everything."

Will sighed.

"I thought we'd agreed that you were gonna talk to Brian Wise about this."

"Brian's father died, just before his vacation ended. It'll be another week before he gets back now. This can't wait."

*Just what I need,* Will thought. Still, Randy's appearance and behavior worried him.

"Okay," he said. "What's happening? The geothermal features are constantly changing. Why are you so sure this is different?"

*"Why?"* Randy asked, his voice cracking. "I'll tell you why. I was hiking Norris Geyser Basin two days ago. Steamboat blew."

Will couldn't hide his impatience.

"Steamboat blew twenty-three times in one year, back in the eighties."

"Yeah, and then it went dormant."

"Randy, I'm telling you, wait and talk to Brian."

Randy became agitated.

"Pearl Geyser's waters just turned muddy," he said. "Practically overnight. Ledge Geyser erupted twice—in the past week."

He'd begun counting on his fingers as he recited his list.

"Minerva's coming back to life. Orange Spring Mound's dry. Completely dry. Have you seen it in the past couple days?"

Will laid a steadying hand on his shoulder.

"Okay, okay. I see. But we've had thermal disturbances before. There must be a hundred scientists and universities and agencies monitoring them. If something's happening, they'd know. Once Brian's back, if there's something to be concerned about, he'll be all over it. You know Brian . . ."

Nothing he said was going to convince his young friend.

"These aren't natural shifts in activity," Randy replied. "I've been studying, Will. Believe me. The only thing that can cause this great a shift in such a short time is outside forces."

"Like . . . ?"

"Drilling."

"Drilling's illegal."

Will should have expected the look Randy shot him.

"Since when do *you* believe that something being illegal means it's not going to happen in this park?"

Will could not hide his need to get out of there before he lost any chance of finding 22. It could be heard in his voice.

"Well, just what exactly do you think you can do about it? This park sits on two-point-two million acres. If someone's out there doing something that's messing with the geothermal activity in Yellowstone, how the hell do you think you can find them? You planning to ride the entire park?"

Randy shrank at the rebuke.

"I don't have to," he said quietly. "I think I know who it is."

Dejected, and clearly disappointed by Will's response, he turned back to the fire.

Will reached out again and rested a hand on Randy's shoulder.

"I'm sorry, buddy. I don't mean to blow your concerns off. Tell me. Who do you think it is? Who's drilling?"

Randy stopped poking at the fire and turned to face Will again. His expression was so pained, and so earnest, that his next words hit Will with the force of a small truck.

"The Church of White Hope."

Will stared at his young friend, trying to determine if he was joking.

"You don't mean it."

"Think about it, Will. Who else has enough private property, close to the park, to get away with something like drilling? To pull it off without anyone knowing?"

"I don't know. That's pretty wild."

"Ever try visiting that place?"

"I'm not exactly the churchgoing type."

"That's not my point. They've got guards posted at the gate. I tried to go in there yesterday, just to ask a couple questions. These two armed goons called their PR person—tell me why a church needs a PR person—and he told them to turn me away." Reliving the incident clearly agitated Randy. "And what kind of church feels the need to have armed guards patrolling its property anyway?"

"You won't get any argument from me," Will said.

"They're a bunch of nutcases. I've arrested half a dozen of them for poaching. That area's always been a haven for poachers. They pack their kill out of the park and have someone waiting right there, just over the border, to shuttle them away. The church members don't even have to arrange a shuttle."

He paused, thinking.

"But drilling makes no sense. They'd eventually *have* to get caught, and then what?"

Randy shook his head.

"I don't know," he said. "But I've got to find out if I'm right."

He dropped to one knee, reached for a camouflage jacket spread on the floor, methodically turning it inside out to let the flannel lining dry.

Will stood there, literally counting seconds in his mind while he tried to assess the likelihood of Randy's theory. With no small amount of dread, he said, "So what are you planning?"

Randy made a valiant, but vain, attempt to appear nonchalant.

"Just to ride up there and check things out."

Exactly what Will had feared.

"Can't it wait?" he said. "I'll go with you if you can be patient. Just give me a day or two."

Randy looked up from where he still kneeled on the floor. A warm smile washed over his face, returning it to its normal youthfulness. But the usual gleam—idealism—was absent.

"Don't worry, Will. I'll be fine."

Then, after a pause, his brow furrowed and he said, "Wait a minute, what are *you* doing here?"

Will mustered an embarrassed smile.

"As it turns out, I've been following your tracks. I thought I was on to a poacher."

He could practically see the wheels turning inside Randy's head as the younger ranger turned his focus to Will and away from his own mission.

"Weren't you supposed to be in Red Lodge today?"

"Goddamn," Will replied. "Do you suppose there's anybody within a hundred miles of here that doesn't know my business?"

"Well, that's what I heard," Randy replied somewhat sheepishly. "Maybe I wasn't listening very well . . ."

Will turned to glance over his shoulder, through the front window.

"You heard right," he said quietly.

Now he had Randy's full attention.

"If you're supposed to be in Red Lodge, what're you doing up here, following a poacher who doesn't exist?"

"Oh, he exists," Will muttered, still averting eye contact.

Unwilling to give up in his pursuit of the truth, Randy waved a hand in front of Will's face like a flag at the start of a drag race.

"Fair's fair. I told you what I'm up to. Now it's your turn."

Reluctantly, Will met Randy's scrutiny.

"Believe me, you don't want to know. You don't need to know."

"It's Twenty-two, isn't it?"

"What do you know about Twenty-two?"

"Hell, Will, I don't know anything about her. I just know *you,* and the only time I've seen you look like this is when it concerned Twenty-one or Twenty-two. I'm right, aren't I? Come on. Tell me."

Will hesitated.

Both he and Randy had embarked on a course that would put their jobs on the line. While he harbored serious doubts about Randy's theory, and worried about this mission he'd embarked upon alone, he admired the young ranger for doing something about it. But that was no reason for involving him in what Will was up to.

Hopefully Randy still had a long career with the Park Service ahead of him. By now, word of Will's no-show had no doubt gotten back to Shewmaker. Will's career may already have ended.

"Listen, Randy," he said, "if you see Twenty-two while you're out, or any fresh scat or tracks, do me a favor? Radio me."

He hadn't really answered Randy's question, but Randy knew intuitively that he'd gotten all he could out of this man, this mentor he'd so looked up to for the past couple years.

And Will's plea for help appeased him somewhat.

"You think she's headed this way?" Randy asked.

"I don't know what to think. I picked up her signal down at Hellroaring junction, then lost it. Then I got sidetracked following your tracks. I better get back out there now, while I've still got a couple hours of daylight to make some time."

Randy's face fell.

"Sure you don't wanna stay and keep me company? I'm gonna wait out the rain here. I'll cook up some spaghetti. Be nice to have some company."

Will couldn't help but smile.

"I'm tempted," he said, "but no. I have to retrace my steps, find that signal again. You spending the night here?"

"If it keeps raining. But we're supposed to have a full moon tonight so if the rain stops, I'm outta here. Full moon would be perfect for me to snoop around the church's property."

Will paused, quickly running over the route Randy would be taking in his mind. He had most of the more dangerous trails behind him already. And Riley could travel them all blindfolded. What troubled him was the idea of Randy prowling around the heavily guarded property of the Church of White Hope. Especially at night.

"You sure I can't talk you into waiting for me to go on this wild-goose chase with you?"

Randy waved him away with a hand in the air.

"Go," he said. "I'll be fine. We'll have a beer and tell each other our stories when we both get back to Mammoth."

Despite his keen sense of urgency, something made Will reluctant to go.

But at the same time, he knew that with every second

that passed, 22 could be widening the distance between them—and perhaps, at the same time, narrowing the separation between her and Gleeson.

"Good luck, kid," Will finally said.

The wistful smile Randy returned would stay with Will a very long time.

"You too, Will."


In most ways Will McCarroll was a maddeningly pragmatic and practical man. But he had a superstitious, spiritual side. He believed that certain animals offered strength and protection. In particular, the bison. When patrolling, he sometimes picked up a tuft of bison fur, stuffing it in his pocket for protection and the instinctive wisdom wild creatures possess, a wisdom not blunted by the "rational" world.

Now, as he stepped down off the porch, he paused at Riley's side, pulled a tuft of the soft, kinky fur out of an inside pocket of his jacket, and stuck it under the rope tying Randy's sleeping bag to his saddle.

# TWENTY-FOUR

ANNIE'S ANXIETY ALTERNATED WITH A STRANGE AND foreign elation, and seemed to coincide with each new landmark they passed as they raced back to Mammoth.

The sight of a sheriff's patrol car; the thought of alarms going off at Rainbow Living when someone checked on Judge Sherburne during the night; as she passed Livingston Drug, Annie's hope that the travel bag she'd grabbed held any medications Judge Sherburne might need—those things brought on the anxiety. But then she'd steal a glance sideways and see the expression on Sherburne's face, and the anxiety not only eased, it gave way to an unbridled joy. A sense—no doubt vicarious—of release and purpose.

Sherburne, entirely oblivious to Annie, sat in the passenger seat, dead silent. Even in the dark, the car's interior lit only by the dashboard and a full moon, Annie could see his eyes, enormous, devouring the night landscape. As they drove down Highway 89, they fixed upon the jagged peaks of the Absarokas, backlit by the bright night sky, and seemed loathe to let go.

Annie did not try to make conversation.

Twice she had to brake suddenly for mule deer—once just before Yankee Jim Canyon, and again between Corwin Springs and Gardiner. The second time a lone doe stood in the middle of the road, frozen in Annie's headlights.

Annie came to a full stop. After several seconds of indecision, the doe continued across the highway. Two babies hurried along behind her, and then a cautious young buck.

Annie snuck another look at Sherburne.

If ever eyes could smile, his were grinning now.

After passing through Gardiner, Annie had the choice of taking a shortcut to the entry gate, or detouring a quarter mile west to drive under the Roosevelt Arch.

Employees and residents—their daily routine having taken on a sense of the mundane—universally took the shortcut, but now Annie turned right and headed for the arch.

She thought she heard Sherburne sigh when they passed under it.

As they neared the entry gate, Annie swerved into the employee lane, barely slowing to wave at Jim, the ranger on duty. She'd been hoping he'd be occupied with visitors' cars, but the lane next to the little log building stood empty.

Nighttime duty could be lonely.

As usual, Jim had recognized Annie's vehicle as it approached. He opened his window in anticipation, leaning out to wave. Normally Annie stopped and visited until the next park visitor pulled up. It was customary for this community of people who lived and worked together to exchange pleasantries and news—part of the culture of Yellowstone. Its human inhabitants may have come from all over the country, but once they were there, once they'd decided to make Yellowstone their home, they were united by a bond—a passion—stronger than that found in the smallest of towns. They became family.

*I heard you climbed Electric. How was it?*

*Sara told me Mickey's back in the hospital. He gonna be okay?*

*Did you hear that number eight charged someone up at the VC? They're talking about dehorning him again.*

Annie had thrilled when, after several months, she'd finally been flagged down at the gate for such a visit. She looked forward to the camaraderie with Jim and the other rangers her trips in and out of the park afforded her.

But now she simply waved back and kept going.

Jim could see she had a passenger. Did he recognize Judge Sherburne?

After she'd passed, Annie glanced in the rearview mirror. The ranger still leaned out the window, staring at her taillights, bewildered.

The road beyond the gate started out in open terrain but soon began following the Gardner River, which percolated and rushed along its south side, road and river winding their way through a small rocky canyon.

Sherburne's gaze turned skyward, toward the high rocky cliffs. Annie knew what he was looking for. Bighorn sheep. She slowed, glad for the moon and hoping he'd get his wish.

At the 45th parallel, a sign declared that they'd crossed from Montana into Wyoming. At the Boiling River, where visitors liked to soak in the hot springs that bubbled and warmed the Gardner's cold waters, a law-enforcement vehicle, coming from the opposite direction, had stopped and waited now for Annie to pass so that it could pull into the parking area from which bathers hiked a mile to the thermal waters.

"Must be ten o'clock," Annie observed.

Her Subaru's lights caught the ranger's face. Vic Gladner.

None of the rangers minded the job of closing down Boiling River at night—a sign at the trailhead warned that bathers must be out by ten o'clock—but Vic was one of the few unmarried law-enforcement officers and it was rumored that he particularly enjoyed the chance to shoo violators out of the water. Especially if they happened to be female. And especially if they happened to be naked.

Upon seeing who had the duty tonight, Sherburne let loose with an unmistakable giggle.

Annie found herself grinning all the way up the hill to Mammoth, a grin that widened when the car's lights took in a bison and two pronghorn.

As they rounded the last hairpin curve and began the final ascent to the park's headquarters, Annie had already begun anticipating what they would see, and how it would affect her passenger.

The Subaru forged up the narrow road, shoulderless to the north, and skirted by a hill on the south.

At the top of the incline, the hill suddenly dropped away, allowing the entire Mammoth complex to come into sight.

So, too, did a herd of over thirty elk that had spent the summer months up high, in the hills and valleys of the Hayden and the Lamar, but a week earlier—to the pleasure of park visitors, but often the dismay of law enforcement— had migrated to lower country that included the grassy lawns surrounding the visitor center and hotel.

As Annie slowed to let Sherburne take in the sight, three bull elk, bearing six-point antlers—one with a span the size of a Humvee—crossed the beams of the Subaru's head-lights. Regally, leisurely, their glorious crowns borne with amazing ease and grace, it was as if they drifted aimlessly. However, both the Subaru's occupants knew that nothing could have been further from the truth.

Cows grazed in groups of three and four on the hotel lawn, seemingly oblivious to their power over these majes-tic males—until a lone elk's bugle filled the air, raising more than a few female heads from the grass.

It was for Annie such a powerful moment—one that brought her to the brink of tears—that she dared not look over at Sherburne.

Still, nothing had prepared Annie for her new friend's re-action a minute or two later, when she pulled into the drive-way of the stone house.

"Does this look familiar?" she said, her voice overly cheerful as the headlights swept across Liberty Cap and came to rest on the two-story stone structure that had served as home to Sherburne and his wife Rosemarie for more than three decades.

Annie did not know the old Judge Sherburne. She'd heard plenty about the renowned, crusty, but respected park magistrate, but she'd only come to know this man whose life had taken such a tragic and lonely turn.

And while she'd gotten a sense of his wife as a strong and kind woman, she'd only met Rosemarie once, the day she offered Annie the piano. Less than a week later, the judge's wife died of a heart attack.

But all Annie needed to know about Judge and Rose-marie Sherburne—about the life they had led together, and the joy it had given him—could be read in her passenger's face at that instant.

Sherburne stared at the house, eyes filled with tears. Annie could not tell if they were tears of joy or pain.

She suspected both.

"Let's go inside," she finally said softly.

# TWENTY-FIVE

"Put him on," Chad Gleeson yelled into the phone.

Despite an angry wind channeled into a rage by the Black Canyon of the Yellowstone, and rain pelting down on them, Gleeson had steered his trustworthy buckskin off the steep trail onto a rocky outcropping perched high above the river. They now stood poised perilously over the Yellowstone, only feet away from the sheer drop-off into its walled canyon. One false move and they risked tumbling hundreds of feet to the rock- and boulder-laden riverbank below—or, perhaps worse yet, the raging river itself.

But Gleeson knew it to be the one place he could make a phone call.

He turned his head inside the hood of his parka and away from the elements howling down on him and pressed his cell phone to his ear to hear the voice on the other end.

"Gleeson, is that you?"

The voice's curt, eastern clip made the question sound more like an accusation.

Gleeson didn't waste time on pleasantries.

"This is the last place I'll have cell phone coverage, so from here on out, we'll have to rely on two-ways, and in this terrain, we're lucky if they're good for a couple miles. And don't forget they can be intercepted—by anyone. So listen carefully 'cause I won't repeat any of this over the radio. I've already told JB the plan, but I want you to hear it too. From me."

The buckskin had caught sight of a single line of grass peeking its way out of a crack in the closet-sized rock upon which they stood. Anticipating his move for it, Gleeson jerked its head back. The horse froze.

"One of my men picked up Twenty-two's signal," Gleeson continued, "up near Hellroaring. I'm on my way there now."

"Hellroaring?" the voice on the other end echoed. "We're set up here, above Slough Creek. That's where you said I should be, what I was supposed to do. I've been camped out in this goddamn rain, just waiting to hear from you. How the hell am I going to get over to Hellroaring?"

Gleeson was not in the mood for this.

"Calm the fuck down," he said. "How the hell could I know she was gonna travel twenty miles in one day? You should be thanking me for having the foresight to send someone out ahead of us with telemetry. Otherwise, you might've been camping out for a week while we looked for her. This actually isn't such a bad thing . . ."

"Not a bad thing? Are you losing your fucking mind?"

"No," Gleeson said. "Listen. I'll have one of my guys pick you up on an ATV. He'll drive you down to Cooke City, through the park to the north entrance, then up past Jardine. There's a network of Forest Service roads up there and he'll get you as close as he can to where we last located her. When my man picked up on her it looked like she was about three miles south of the border, still in the park. I'll find her, get a GPS on her. Meanwhile, you'll set up a camp and wait to hear from me. When I pinpoint her, I'll call with the reading. You sure you know how to use GPS?"

"Of course I do," the voice replied, before breaking up with static. Gleeson twisted the phone toward the east which allowed him to hear again. ". . . a goddamn GPS unit's not going to get me where I need to go. I told you, I don't ride. And I'm not in shape to hike all over the goddamn park."

Gleeson's mind raced.

This new scenario had complicated things. Maybe he should pull out . . . but now they knew where 22 was. And the money at stake . . . he'd earn more on this one job than he had the entire year.

Plus he couldn't forget his reputation. He'd become known as the outfitter who delivered.

"You've got no choice," he finally replied. "I'll come get you, bring you within half a mile of her. But that means you've got to get on a horse." He paused. "And once I get you close to her, it's up to you."

Gleeson thought he heard some swearing, but the static returned. He shifted the horse's head toward the north and it cleared.

"You're going to leave me there? On a fucking *horse*? And how do I get the wolf out? I sure as hell can't pack her."

"I'll give you a camouflage net to put over her. Then, once you get back to where I dropped you, I'll have my men go in and bring her out."

What Gleeson hadn't mentioned was the fact that by that time, he planned to be down in Gardiner, making himself visible at the local bar. Or if it were too early in the day, the local Subway.

The weather and the disgust he felt for this client frustrated Gleeson, but discussing the details—the reality of what they were about to achieve—began to have an exhilarating effect on him. The old high, the thrill of the hunt, was kicking in, like it always did. Bagging Yellowstone's most renowned alpha female—22—would be a crowning achievement, even for someone like Gleeson. And anyone who knew anything about the business would know damn well that Gleeson had all but pulled the trigger.

A new enthusiasm lifted his voice.

"The beauty of this new situation," he said, "is that that fucking wolf couldn't have picked a better place to be killed. It's almost like she wants to help us get her out. There are so many back roads up there—the Park Service can't even begin to patrol a fraction of them—and we know them all. Once we get her across the border near Jardine, you're home free. So just think of this new development as a minor inconvenience."

His client, however, didn't seem to share his enthusiasm.

"With what I'm paying you, that fucking wolf ought to be served up on a silver platter. Instead I'm mucking around in the rain and mud."

Gleeson felt himself losing his patience. This asshole wasn't only an ingrate, he was a coward, gutless—yet, once Gleeson got him what he wanted, he would go back East full of tales about his grueling and dangerous hunting trip into the wilderness.

Gleeson's horse suddenly shifted weight. He was growing impatient too.

From his outlook, high above the river and clear of the trees, Gleeson had a panoramic view of the northwest corner of Yellowstone. Indeed, he could see well into Montana. That's where he trained his eyes now.

A heavy black sky extended all the way to Electric Peak. But several miles beyond, as if someone had taken a piece of charcoal and drawn an almost perfectly straight line across it—north to south—then smudged everything east of that line, Gleeson saw the eggshell blue of a Western sky.

He turned his horse back toward the trail, pressing the phone to his lips.

"Put JB back on."

Muffled voices could be heard during the handoff.

"What's up, bossman?" Gleeson's head guide asked.

Gleeson cringed. It was only midafternoon and JB's tongue had already thickened with alcohol.

"Break camp right away," Gleeson said, "and get him up to Jardine. This storm's gonna pass. That means we'll have a full moon tonight, and that I can keep moving 'til I get a fix on Twenty-two. I want you in place and ready to go when I call. Got it?"

"Got it," JB replied through a sea of static. "Listen, boss," he said, "your dad's been trying to—"

The phone went silent.

"What about my dad?" Gleeson yelled back, twisting first in one direction, then another, trying to get reception.

"JB? What about my dad?"

No response. Still, Gleeson held the phone to his ear as he nudged the buckskin into a soft trot.

Then, just in case JB could still hear him, he added, "And lay off the fucking whiskey. I want this to go off without a hitch."

# TWENTY-SIX

NEVER BEFORE HAD THAT SOUND HAD ANY EFFECT ON Will other than to thrill him, but now it sent a chill of another kind down his spine.

A sense of dread, and imminent danger.

"Damn," he muttered, mentally willing the voice to fall silent.

But a full moon and the answering cry from a nearby ridge apparently proved too much to resist.

The voice waltzed along the cool night air again.

Soulful, passionate, achingly beautiful.

And again, the reply.

Equally soulful. Eager—more welcoming than threatening, though Will knew that 22 had put her life at risk in entering another pack's territory.

Twelve years of observing 22, hearing her, had etched her voice indelibly into Will's consciousness. But even if he hadn't recognized it now as belonging to the alpha female of the Druid pack, the readings he'd been taking over the past hour with the telemetry would have convinced him it was her.

Did anyone else hear? And if they did, did they know who the voice belonged to?

The sky had mostly cleared hours earlier, as Will worked his way up Hellroaring Mountain, but clusters of thick, dark clouds—reminders of the afternoon's downpour—still remained. They now marched determinedly across the sky, chased by an invisible force, obscuring the moon, then—in a dramatic burst of light—allowing it full, glorious display. Will never understood how the moon might one night look almost inconsequential in size, and then, on a night like this, seem to take up half the sky. Tonight a halo also encircled it, a band of terrestrial mist, shedding enough light for Will and Torch to travel off-trail, following the signal Will had picked up after turning off the Yellowstone River trail and heading north, on to Hellroaring.

But high atmospheric winds had picked up in the past half hour, and now as Will sat on Torch, taking measure and listening, the moon again became obscured—at first, just a thin layer blotting its wattage, leaving still enough light to make out the rocks and trees he negotiated around. Then, in an instant, the night turned black, completely moonless, and Will signaled Torch to stop.

Like some time-lapse video set on high speed, this went on, with Will using the voice and the telemetry to narrow the distance separating him from 22. Twice, when the clouds cleared, giving way to the full orb, her cry could be heard again.

He was getting closer.

The sky darkened. Will waited, eyes turned heavenward.

But this time the clouds stayed. After ten minutes, with no hint of light, Will dismounted. To continue on the rocky hillside would be too dangerous.

He untied his sleeping bag, pack, and rifle, sliding them off Torch's back.

The gelding exhaled contentedly, dropping its head to graze the sparse but resilient grass that thrived in the dry, rocky alpine soil.

Comforted by the fact that the moon's disappearance had silenced 22, Will stretched out on top of his down bag, rifle propped against a rock next to him.

He stared at the sky, thinking. Planning.

Listening.

Will knew the night sounds of Yellowstone's backcountry like the New Yorker knows the horns and sirens twenty stories below, like the sailor knows the lapping of water against a hull. And like the city dweller and the sailor, the sounds comforted Will, lulled him to the very brink of sleep.

Exhausted, he closed his eyes.

But almost immediately, the heavens erupted in brilliant light.

Like waves on the ocean, the clouds continued their sweep eastward, clearing the way for a moon even bigger and brighter than the last.

Will's eyes opened and instantly, he sensed it. Her presence.

Her voice rang out.

And then he saw her. Standing on a ridge, perhaps two hundred yards away, silhouetted against the moon. Head turned to the heavens, heart leaping skyward. Announcing her presence, and her intentions.

*Twenty-two.*

On the other side of the ridge, due north of where Will lay, another pair of eyes were fixed upon the same sight.

Chad Gleeson's teeth flashed in the moonlight.

He'd already slipped the cartridge in. Now he lifted the rifle. Couldn't help it.

Twenty-two just stood there, in his fucking crosshairs, pouring her heart out to the sky.

"Horndog," Gleeson whispered in delight.

He eased his finger through the trigger. Tightened it.

The instinct was just so fucking strong, so primal. How could he pass up the chance of a lifetime? He drew in his breath, held it in his lungs, as he always did before that last pull on the trigger—the one that inevitably meant a hard-on for Gleeson. And death for the bullet's recipient.

But even as he held his breath, somewhere, deep in the recesses of his primal mind, a voice of reason called out to him, and Gleeson paused.

Two months from now he faced trial for killing 21. He could end up in jail, and paying fines of over $250,000. Worse yet, he stood to lose his hunting and guiding privileges.

And what did he have to show for it? No head to mount on the living room wall. No life-sized wild wolf—mouth open, fangs gleaming—to greet his hunting guests in the entrance to the lodge. Not even a fucking photograph of the park's most renowned alpha male.

And now that he'd found its mate, he stood to become—in an instant—$100,000 richer. Almost zero risk was involved. He even had a nice insurance policy in place: he'd be down in Gardiner, at the Blue Goose, when it all came down.

Lots of witnesses. No chance of his own hands being dirtied.

The howl echoed between ridges again.

One of the reasons Chad Gleeson had achieved as much success as he had in the outfitting world was that he not only had the balls it took to deliver what he promised, but he was also smart.

Gleeson took one last, longing look through the crosshairs, then he lowered the rifle. He strode over to where he'd shackled the buckskin and shoved the firearm roughly into its slot on the back of the saddle.

He bent low, loosened the binds on the horse's legs.

Before mounting, he took another GPS reading.

This time, he would leave nothing to chance.

# TWENTY-SEVEN

WILL BOLTED UPRIGHT INTO A SITTING POSITION AND reached instinctively for the telemetry receiver.

*How long had he slept?*

Instead of the black ceiling he'd last stared up at, streaks of light to the east, over the Absarokas, made it possible to make out the ridgeline where he'd seen 22.

He could see Torch, some twenty-five feet away, head half dropped, motionless.

Daybreak, however, was still at least a half hour away.

He'd last checked his watch at 2:45 A.M. Two and a half hours had passed since then. Twenty-two could move miles in that time. What if he'd lost her again?

Climbing the nearest rock, he held the antenna high and began the slow circle that had become his ritual. The beeps started at 45 degrees north by northeast—*beep . . . beep . . . beep*—growing stronger as he faced due north, then easing off as he continued his clockwise arc.

Even at their loudest—due north—the beeps were weaker now than they had been at his last reading.

After he'd sighted her the night before, 22 had disappeared from sight and remained quiet, but on each of the subsequent readings he'd taken, the strength of the signal gave Will comfort. Something—no doubt the wolf that had returned her call—was keeping 22 around. Reassured, he'd unintentionally allowed himself to doze off.

But while Will slept, 22 had started moving again—heading north it appeared, toward high, rocky country. Barren ground, where she would be more visible. More vulnerable.

Will had knotted Torch's lead loosely around a limb the night before. The horse grazed peacefully as Will strode to him. He lifted his head, his breath mushrooming in the cool morning air, and nickered when Will lowered the grain bag from the line he'd strung between two lodgepole pines.

Torch's breath, and his soft, warm nose brushed Will's hand as he dipped his head inside the bag.

"Eat up, big guy," Will said, holding it for him. "I have the feeling it's gonna be one hell of a day."

Standing there, Will surveyed the sky.

From beyond the tall, craggy Absarokas to the east the sun's rays had reached out for the last straggling clouds from the evening before, turning their undersides a pale candy orange and pink against a fast lightening sky.

To the north, the direction 22 was headed, high-elevation peaks still shadowed the slopes and contours of the park.

After Torch had filled his belly, they started out.

Trails had become barely perceptible and impossibly narrow, traveled only by bighorn sheep, mountain goats, and the occasional mule deer. Soon, when the first hint of snow arrived like an unwanted in-law, grizzlies would cover the same ground, heading for dens hidden in the high rocky crevices and cracks.

Ninety-five percent of Yellowstone qualified as no-man's land. This was the no-man's land of no-man's land, explored only by a handful of adventurous humans thirsty to know all that the earth and its wildness can teach—or, as Will knew only too well, by poachers, who knew that they stood little chance of detection here.

Will had tracked those poachers up these same hills

countless times over his two and a half decades as law enforcement, usually with little luck.

They tended to come down on horseback from north of the park. They'd perfected an almost flawless routine, never working alone, always posting a lookout who was assigned to circle back time and again to make certain they weren't being followed. Emboldened by the sheer vastness of the region, their weapons, and the promise of more wealth than any of their neighbors who lived within the law would ever see, so many had traversed these parts over the years that a trail just north of the park border had long ago been nicknamed the Old Poacher's Trail. The name became official when it started appearing on Yellowstone maps.

Working Torch cautiously up one craggy rise after another, Will stopped frequently to let the horse rest and to take readings. It was hard to tell if they were gaining ground on 22, but at least they didn't appear to be losing any.

But then, after traveling several miles, their progress came to a dead stop. A black, talus slope spread like a dark, shiny sea in front of them—flat, jagged pieces of rocks deposited when glaciers receded centuries ago, breaking into fragments the mountains they'd carved, littering them precariously along high-elevation slopes.

Many of the smaller rocks had been overturned recently—evidence of bears digging for the tiny cutworm moth who, in the mysterious chain of life, had migrated all the way from Iowa cornfields to end up providing nourishment to the park's largest predator, a creature five thousand times its size.

In Yellowstone, sections of talus rock were often the size of a football field, but this one went on in precisely the direction Will needed to travel for well over a hundred yards, almost as far as Will could see. Because of how they were formed—the rocks deposited at the steepest angle—talus slopes were extremely dangerous. A misstep could easily trigger a slide.

Will would either have to detour around the talus on horseback or leave Torch behind and climb the rock field on foot.

Will knew the terrain beyond the talus field, due north of it, well. While a few miles farther north it could be traveled by horse, for the next couple miles, it was not horse country. With great reluctance, he realized he would have to part with his loyal companion and proceed on foot.

But he could not leave Torch here.

Will pivoted the gelding in a slow circle, eyeing the options surrounding them, none of which pleased him. Then he turned the horse's big head back in the direction they'd just come and nudged him back along the path they'd just taken.

A mile or so earlier, as they'd climbed, Will had seen a small alpine meadow to the east. He would leave Torch there.

As Torch carefully picked his way back down the rock-strewn hillside, Will struggled with what could turn out to be a critical decision—for Torch as well as for Will.

Prudence dictated that Will tie the horse, making certain he would be there when Will returned. If he were not, the consequences to Will could be considerable, even disastrous, especially if he were in pursuit of poachers—or they in pursuit of him.

But if something were to happen to Will and he'd left Torch tied to a tree, the gelding would not last a single night. While it was warm enough that most of the grizzlies were still hanging out at lower elevations—fattening themselves for their upcoming hibernation—the recently overturned talus rocks, fresh scat he'd passed dozens of times in the past hours, and areas of ground that appeared to have been rototilled by bears digging for biscuit root made clear the fact that the big bear was definitely present.

And 22's travels had convinced Will that the Hellroaring pack was also nearby.

If a bear didn't get Torch, the wolves would.

While Will's mission was to save 22, was it right to risk Torch's life in doing so?

Stepping down off the slope, eyeing the meadow, Torch picked up into a soft trot, stopping on his own when he reached the fall grass, still somewhat green due to the cooler temperatures at the high elevation.

Will dismounted and removed his backpack, then the saddle. It took several minutes to string the pack between two trees, high enough to avoid attracting *Ursus arctos horribilis*.

Torch grazed contentedly, happy to rest, free of his load.

Will stood, looking at him, lead rope in hand. He studied the trail they'd just retraced. Memorized vistas and rocks. Most likely when he returned, he'd need to find his way back quickly. He could not afford to search for the meadow. And Torch. But neither could he leave the horse tied and defenseless.

Finally, he walked to the big gelding, removed his halter, and patted him on the rear end.

"It'd be nice if you waited for me, pal," he said.

"But if I don't come back, or something happens here, you head for home. You hear?"

Torch lifted his big head, tilted it, bumping Will in the shoulder as if to say they'd reached an agreement.

"Good," Will said, turning to walk away. "Now stay safe."

# TWENTY-EIGHT

SWEAT DRIPPED FROM WILL'S CHIN AS HE MOVED SI-lently up the wooded mountainside. The climb up the talus slope had been frustratingly slow, with Will twisting his ankle twice when rocks dislodged underfoot. Once he'd crossed the rock field however, even though still climbing, he'd adopted a fast pace, which he'd maintained most of the afternoon.

It had paid off—Will had practically shouted his joy at the last telemetry reading.

He'd regained the ground he'd lost on 22.

In fact, the beeps now were stronger than he'd ever heard them. So strong, in fact, that Will decided he'd best not get any closer.

His lack of experience with telemetry frustrated him. Any of the park's biologists would have been able to trans-late the signal strength into a distance. But all Will knew was that 22 was close at hand, and not moving. He should let her rest.

Will felt a keen thirst. He'd already drank half his water supply. The late afternoon sun beat down on his backpack.

He'd come across a small, hidden waterfall up this way several summers ago. He could refill his pouch there. He might even strip down for a shower. Yes, a quick shower under the waterfall would do him good.

Stashing his pack, the wand, and his rifle beneath a downed white bark pine, he headed for the short game trail that led to the waterfall.

In minutes, he stood beneath the alpine water cascading out of a fissure in the rocky cliff. Will reached out, cupped some of the icy liquid in his hand, and gulped it greedily.

The urge to cool his entire body, to wash off the sweat and grime that now coated him, was too great to resist. Will eyed a flat, dry rock where he could leave his gun—and the rest of his weapon-heavy law-enforcement belt—and began unfastening its buckle.

But just as he did so, something caught his eye. A glint of light. It blinded Will momentarily.

He lifted his hand to shield his eyes. When that didn't work, he stepped sideways to move out of the glare.

Still Will couldn't see him at first. The camouflage clothing was that effective.

But then the rifle moved, redirecting the late afternoon sunlight reflecting off it, and with a sense of horror, Will realized what he was looking at.

A hunter.

Unaware of Will's presence, he held the rifle tight against his shoulder, directed slightly upward.

Will's eyes moved to where he had it pointed—the ridgeline, directly above the waterfall.

He let out a gasp.

There on the ridge, surveying the unfamiliar surroundings—no doubt waiting for her new friend to reveal himself—stood 22.

Will stepped forward, hand moving reflexively to his firearm, and shouted, "Stop."

The waterfall drowned his voice out.

In one swift motion, he unlatched his gun, slid it from the holster, and pointed it toward the sky.

But the bullet he fired—intended to warn 22, to scare her away—rang out a millisecond after another shot, one that sent terror throughout Will's being.

Horrified, Will's eyes darted back to the ridgeline.

He saw her. Just for an instant. Even at that distance he could see the terror in her eyes. And then, in a flurry of dust and thick white fur, she simply disappeared.

Had she been hit?

On fire with maniacal rage mixed with adrenaline, Will began running toward the hunter.

When the hunter realized another shot had been fired, immediately after the one he'd aimed at 22, slowly, deliberately—like an armored tank under fire but undaunted—he pivoted Will's way, rifle still pressed to his shoulder.

Will dove to the ground. Overhead, a bullet carved its memory through the bark of a quaking aspen.

The hunter did not waver. Ironically, it seemed almost as if shooting the wolf had been a lark, child's play. Almost as if *this*—training his rifle on Will—had been his goal all along.

Will rose to his knees and leveled his gun at him.

Most of the hunter's face was hidden by the rifle as he stared through the sight at his target, but Will saw enough to actually realize he was smiling.

"Stop," Will shouted again.

He saw the subtle movements—at the wrist and shoulder—that signaled another shot on its way, and for the first time in his twenty-six-year career, Will McCarroll pulled the trigger on a gun trained on another human being.

Two bullets crossed in midair.

One man collapsed to the ground.

Will ran to where the hunter lay on his right side, in the fetal position. The bullet had hit him just below the bony fulcrum of his right shoulder blade.

He did not appear to be breathing.

Will checked for his pulse but could not find one.

Carefully, he rolled him onto his back and began CPR.

Hunched over the inert form, alternating mouth-to-mouth

with rapid chest compressions, he shouted, "Come on, damn it. Breathe."

So intent was he on undoing the toll of his bullet that Will did not recognize his victim until finally, after five minutes of resuscitation efforts with no response—no hopeful twitch of a finger or an eye, no shuddering back to life with a frantic gasp for air—Will fell back, onto his haunches.

Despite the fact that he'd literally been eye to eye with the man dozens of times in the past few minutes, it was a glance at the lifeless hand that raised the hairs on the back of Will's neck.

A large gold ring, with an emerald in it. Perfectly manicured nails.

With a sense of dread, enveloped in a new fog of disbelief, Will forced his gaze up to the face.

The feigned indifference was no longer there. The malice in the eyes now replaced by an eerie vacancy. But Will recognized him just the same.

And truth be told, for a fleeting instant, he felt grateful that he had not done so earlier, before beginning CPR.

He'd promised Will, that day sitting in the jail alongside Hank, that he'd be back.

And now he'd kept that promise.

*Biagi.*

# TWENTY-NINE

"CAN ANYONE HEAR ME?"

Will stood, staring at Biagi's lifeless form. He held the two-way radio to his mouth. He'd set the dial to an open frequency so anyone within range could pick up his call.

"Come in. This is Ranger Will McCarroll."

He let go of the transmission button and waited for a response.

Nothing.

"I repeat. This is Ranger Will McCarroll. I have shot and killed a man. On Hellroaring, about three miles from the north border. He shot Number twenty-two and then turned his gun on me."

Will waited for a response.

He doubted one would come. In that terrain, the odds of a backcountry ranger or hiker being close enough to pick up his call were slim.

Still, before picking up Biagi and throwing him over his back, Will climbed a nearby ridge, pressed the button, and again sent out his SOS.

Letting go of the button after the final attempt, he began to lower the radio, eyes on the corpse befouling his beloved Yellowstone.

The anger—and gut-wrenching reality that he'd killed a man—had hit him full force.

Twenty-six years he'd doggedly worked his job, putting himself in danger time and time again without having to resort to hurting another human being. He'd been chided more than once for using the Taser gun when a gun would have been the safer option. Now a man lay dead because of him. It didn't really matter how awful a son of a bitch he was. Will had killed another human being.

The anger welled up, filling his gut and his chest, threatening to make him crazy. He jerked the radio back up to his mouth.

"Gleeson, you son of a bitch," he yelled. "If you're out there and you can hear me, come and get me."

# THIRTY

TWO THINGS OCCUPIED WILL'S MIND THE ENTIRE TIME HE lugged Biagi's lifeless form down the rocky mountainside.

The first was 22.

After it became clear he could not resuscitate Biagi, Will had climbed to the ridge above the waterfall. Heart in throat, he prepared himself for finding 22's lifeless form at the top.

At first Will rejoiced at the fact that she was nowhere to be seen.

But then he saw it—a trail of blood. Biagi had hit her. There was enough blood to believe she may have been badly wounded. Had she gone off to die? Will made several ever enlarging circles looking for more blood—or any other sign of 22—but once the packed dirt on the ridge turned to ground cover, it became impossible to track her.

The second thing occupying his thoughts was whether Torch would be waiting for him when he got back to the meadow. The couple miles Will had already traveled carrying his load would be nothing compared to the choice he'd have to make if the horse had fled during Will's absence: leave Biagi behind—where his body stood a good chance of being introduced into Yellowstone's food chain—while he went for help; or keep walking with Biagi's lifeless weight on his back.

When he got to the meadow, Will scanned the open area, then the tree line. No sign of Torch.

Stiff now, his shoulders feeling ready to give out on him, Will bent at the waist. Biagi's body rolled off, hitting the earth with a dull thud.

Straightening, Will eyed the tree line again, then inserted a thumb and forefinger between his pursed lips. His whistle sailed across the alpine field and reverberated back to him, just as he heard—actually felt—the pounding of hooves.

The last rays of direct sun highlighted the grove of yellowing quaking aspen at the far side of the meadow. As desperate as the situation felt to him, when Torch emerged from the stand at a gallop, Will thrilled at the sight.

Torch tossed his head as he ran toward Will, clearly as happy to see his human companion as Will was to see him.

As he drew close, the gelding saw Biagi on the ground and stopped on a dime ten yards away. Rearing back, he pawed the air, snorted.

When he came back to all fours, eyes wide and nostrils flared, Torch stared at the body, waiting for it to play out its intentions.

"It's okay, fella," Will said, walking to him and laying a calming hand on his neck. "He's not gonna hurt you."

Will stroked the massive neck, then turned his back and stepped toward Biagi. He could feel Torch at his shoulder.

"You check him out," he said, "while I get our stuff."

As Will headed for the saddle he'd stowed, and the bag he'd left hanging from the line he'd strung between two trees, he glanced back over his shoulder to see Torch pawing the ground and nosing Biagi.

By the time he returned, Torch had made his peace with the body. Will had dumped Biagi on an especially lush patch of grass and the horse plucked away at what stuck up between Biagi's hunting boots.

Will saddled him while he grazed.

Before loading Biagi onto Torch's back, Will tried radioing for help again.

"This is Will McCarroll. Does anyone read me?" he said. "I'm transporting the body of a hunter who shot Number twenty-two to Tower. I'll be on the Yellowstone River Trail. If anyone hears me, I want EMTs waiting at the trailhead."

Pulling Torch's head up, Will roped Biagi behind the saddle and climbed on himself. Will had never hunted, but he'd hauled many a carcass in from the backcountry— usually to be tested or examined—on horseback. It occurred to him that Biagi had been easier to tie down than a bighorn, but harder than a mule deer.

He directed Torch back down the trail they'd originally traveled.

With any luck, they'd be back in Tower before dark.


They'd traveled less than two miles when Will heard the sound of metal striking rock. He recognized it instantly—a horse and rider approaching from behind.

With a surge of relief, he steered Torch to the side of the narrow trail, then turned to wait for the rider to appear over the ridge they'd just descended.

But the fast clip the horse traveled concerned him. The trails were steep, with deadly drop-offs.

In his day-to-day job as backcountry ranger, Will would now be preparing to give the rider a stern talking-to.

Now he just wanted to avert another disaster.

When the horse finally charged over the ridge, Will recognized it immediately.

Riley. The horse Randy Hannah had been riding.

He wore a saddle and full pack. But no rider.

Will leaped off Torch and stepped in the middle of the trail, planting both feet and waving his arms as Riley ran his way, showing no signs of stopping.

Will could see reins trailing along either side of the chestnut gelding. He had to stop him. If he didn't, those reins would either get caught up on something or break one of the horse's legs.

"Whoa boy," Will yelled.

In his terror—something had clearly spooked him—Riley hadn't seemed to register Will and Torch's presence at first, but Will's voice clearly connected. He slowed, pulling up just short of Will, nervous and jumpy, eyes wide.

The frothy lather on his coat told Will Riley had been running for miles, which meant he hadn't just thrown Randy, or run off when Randy was on foot.

Will would have been hard-pressed to believe either of those scenarios anyway.

Riley was the best, most bombproof horse in the barn. Not a bolter.

One spring day on a narrow trail, like the one they now stood on, Will had eased his way past a grizz with two new cubs on Riley. He'd come upon a coiled rattler with him another day, and had even been shot at once while he was riding Riley.

Never had the horse bolted or lost his steadfast disposition. It was what made him the most sought-after horse for the backcountry. So sought after that Will had decided to look for another horse, one that he would call his own. Luckily, in terms of temper, steadiness, and smooth gaiting, in Kola, he'd found a match for Riley.

When he looked at Riley's saddle, a terrible sense of foreboding overcame Will.

The tuft of buffalo fur he'd stuck under the rope tying Randy's sleeping bag to his saddle had not moved. It was still there—right where Will had placed it.

Randy's bag hadn't been unrolled since Will ran into him at the Crevice Creek cabin.

Something had happened to Randy. Before Will left the cabin, Randy had told Will that if the storm abated he would take off to investigate his theory that night. The rain *had* stopped, which meant Randy had probably headed out that first evening to the Church of White Hope's property. Even if he'd changed his mind and decided to stay put in the cabin that night, he would have taken off the next morning and used his sleeping bag and supplies the previous night. But the bag had never been unrolled.

The inevitable conclusion voiced itself in Will's mind again. He could not suppress it.

Something had happened to Randy.

And it had most likely happened at the Church of White Hope.

# THIRTY-ONE

ASIDE FROM THE FACT HE WAS IN THE SAME PLACE SHE'D left him that morning—the recliner—nothing about Annie's house resembled what it looked like when she'd left for work eight hours earlier.

Judge Sherburne sat amidst a tornado of newspapers, his recliner still facing the way Annie had turned it the night before—toward the window looking out at Liberty Cap, Minerva, and beyond, Bunsen Peak. When she skirted Sherburne away from Rainbow Living the night before, she hadn't stopped to think there was no way she'd be able to get him up the stairs to a bedroom.

The recliner had been the only answer. Exhausted, she'd helped him into it, then stepped over the backpack he didn't want out of his sight to the window to close the blinds.

Sherburne couldn't talk, but he and Annie had already developed a form of communication, and the throaty note of disapproval in his voice when she reached for the cord told her he did not want the blinds lowered. In a flash of brilliance, Annie had hurried back to the recliner and turned it to face the window.

She'd left Sherburne with a smile on his face, staring out at Bunsen Peak.

And that's how she'd found him that morning. Eyes still glued to the window.

As Annie had hurried to prepare him breakfast before leaving for work, she'd worried about how he'd passed the day. Then she'd remembered the growing stack of newspapers in the back entry that she hadn't yet taken to the little food market in Gardiner for recycling.

"Want these?" she'd asked.

She might have regretted the offer, seeing the state her house was in now—but the expression on Sherburne's face when she walked in from the kitchen that morning with the stack of papers in hand had stayed with her all day, and she was actually relieved now to see the old guy looking bright, if maybe a bit agitated.

He and Archie had apparently bonded, as the dog's big head rested on Sherburne's stockinged foot.

Annie startled, however, at the sight of a pair of scissors balancing on the arm of the recliner.

Sherburne had apparently gotten up and into the kitchen to find them. That explained the overturned TV tray, teacup, and cereal bowl on the floor.

The reason he wanted the scissors became quickly apparent. While the floor around the recliner was littered with mangled, mutilated newspapers, a haphazard stack—actually "stack" implied order and there was no order whatsoever to them—of newspaper clippings had collected on Sherburne's lap and the once bare sections of the recliner's seat.

"I see you found something interesting," Annie said cheerfully, eyeing the chaos.

Sherburne looked up from the single unfolded newspaper on his lap. His hair stood on end. He'd changed into one of the shirts Annie had thrown into his bag for him, but had missed several buttons. Remnants of the tuna salad she'd made for him that morning stuck to his chin.

Still, when his eyes met Annie's, he looked downright exuberant. Almost healthy.

He grunted his affirmation, then nodded toward the clippings.

"What's this?" she said, reaching for one.

Sherburne remained silent.

It was difficult at first to know which article Sherburne had intended the scissors for, for while one side of the clipping was filled by a grocery ad, the other contained two brief articles. Neither had been salvaged in its entirety. One title read, "NRA Still Disclaiming Responsibility for Mall Shooting Spree."

The other: "President Douglas's Proposed Drilling Legislation."

Feeling Sherburne's eyes fixed upon her, she reached for another.

Neither she nor Sherburne noticed when one article slipped between the seat cushion and the arm of the chair.

Sherburne had routinely captured more than one article, but by the third or fourth clipping, a pattern began to emerge. Words and themes jumped out at Annie.

"National Parks May Provide Much-Needed Energy."

"Senator Conroy, Senate Energy Exploration Commission Chair, Calls Directional Drilling Wave of the Future."

"President's Directional Drilling Plan Gaining Momentum."

Annie skimmed through the articles, and suddenly remembered that the newspaper Sherburne had given Will and her the first night she'd met him had contained an article about the same subject.

That article had called it a "strong but substantiated rumor" that President Douglas and his cabinet—several of whom were ex–energy company executives Douglas had worked with prior to going into politics—were planning to propose legislation that would allow directional drilling into public lands, some of which included the national park system.

Annie had noted the news then with some concern, but in light of the fact that her mother's safety was all-consuming for her at that point, and the fact that Will believed Sherburne was trying to direct them to a clue about Eleanor Malone's whereabouts, she hadn't lingered over it.

Now she realized that that article had, indeed, been what Sherburne wanted to bring to her and Will's attention.

Her heart fell.

It hadn't been about her mother after all.

Perhaps Will—and more recently, Annie—had been wrong. Perhaps Sherburne didn't completely understand what was going on—what Annie and Will had asked him that day.

Instead of providing his thoughts on the subject of who might want to get Annie off the bench, Sherburne had been focused upon what mattered most to him—his beloved Yellowstone.

The fact that the legislation was still only being talked about, and if passed, would not go into effect for at least a year, and the urgency in Sherburne's eyes now, as she stared at her, waiting for a reaction, only added to Annie's concern about Sherburne's mental facilities—and dashed any hope that he might provide clues about her mother's disappearance.

The disappointment Annie felt at this realization was crushing.

Still, she had developed such a fondness for this man. A man who had done great things in his thirty-year tenure at Yellowstone. A man who had literally transformed in front of her eyes since she'd brought him back to her house.

No, Annie realized.

*His* house.

This house, this park, was Judge Sherburne's, well before it ever became Annie's, and that would always be the case.

With a sigh, she mustered a smile.

She tried to hide her disappointment, to focus upon the grief her predecessor obviously felt about a place he'd spent his life cherishing and protecting.

A place Annie now cherished too.

"I understand now," she said with an aching heart. "I'm upset about this proposed legislation too."

If she'd hoped her finally "getting" what he was trying to tell her, accompanied by her expression of empathy, would appease the judge, she was vastly disappointed.

Sherburne let out an agitated sigh and violently shook his head.

"You know," Annie said, not ready to give up, "letting them drill in the national parks is just in the talking stage. It's not a sure thing. And if it does pass, it's at least a year away."

Sherburne reached for the articles clasped in her hand.

Puzzled, Annie handed them back.

Wild eyed now, he began leafing through them, his good right hand doing all the work while his left hand clasped the pile doggedly. He dropped the clippings one by one onto his lap as if he were searching for one in particular.

Annie could see his frustration mounting.

Maybe it hadn't been such a good idea to bring him here after all. Maybe she'd overestimated her ability to judge his mental state—and underestimated the abilities of the staff at Rainbow Living. Even Nomie.

She started to get a sinking feeling. She had to calm him, not let him get too worked up.

"Would you like to go for a ride?" she offered, remembering what Will had told her about the times he'd brought Sherburne back to Yellowstone. "We could drive up to Swan Lake Flats, or to Tower. We could sit on the deck at Roosevelt Lodge."

Sherburne shook his head defiantly again and continued pushing the clippings around on his lap, making noises that Annie knew to be his version of swearing.

Annie sat down on the couch, watching. Trying to find a way to distract him.

"I heard something at work today," she said out of desperation. "Do you know Randy Hannah, the boardwalk ranger?"

Sherburne glanced up, nodded, but then quickly went back to task.

"Apparently he checked a horse out of the stables two days ago. He was supposed to bring him back yesterday, but he hasn't been seen since the day he left."

Sherburne stopped, looked up again, brow furrowed.

He wanted to hear more.

Annie went on.

"He filed for a camping permit in the Lamar, for one night." As she started to say more, she realized that while she wanted to get Sherburne off the subject of the drilling legislation, alarming him would not be a good thing either. "They say he's experienced in the backcountry, so everyone's sure he'll be fine. But I guess it made for some excitement today at headquarters."

Judge Sherburne turned and stared out the window.

Annie thought she could read his mind.

"I watch Randy do his talks out that window," she said. "I'm sure you did too when you lived here. Sometimes, when I see it's Randy on the boardwalk, I'll hurry to the Upper Terraces just to hear him give his talk. That boy has such a passion for the hot springs and geysers."

Sherburne nodded. He seemed to relax, as if her words—and the memories the view from the window stirred—comforted him.

Finally he let his eyes drop back to his lap.

It seemed she'd been so successful in getting Sherburne to relax that Annie wanted to prolong it.

She chattered on.

"I guess Randy's been kind of obsessed recently with the idea that the geothermal features are changing too much. One theory I heard today is that *that's* what he's doing out there. Trying to figure out why."

Annie had let her eyes drift to the window too. A trickle of tourists, determined to make the most of the fast-fading daylight, moved along the boardwalk leading past Minerva. If Randy Hannah were out there right now, Annie found herself thinking, he'd no doubt have a cluster of them surrounding him as he patiently answered their questions. All the rangers drew crowds, but Randy's were always largest, and lingered longest.

Annie suddenly felt this inexplicable pang—almost reminiscent of what she'd felt when she'd stepped into the house that night her mother disappeared.

"He seems like such a sensible kid," she mused, still staring outside. "I can't imagine Randy actually thinking there's something going on, or that if there is, he can discover what it is. The features are changing constantly . . ."

Her eyes drifted back to the judge. Just seconds earlier he'd appeared calm, now he was probing clumsily at the space between the chair's cushion and its arm.

Annie stood and padded over to him, feeling worn out.

Then she saw what he was digging for. Another clipping.

So much for thinking the Randy Hannah story had distracted Sherburne from his obsession with the legislation.

"Here," she said, trying not to let her frustration be heard in her voice, "let me help you."

Less than half an inch of paper protruded from the crack. She grabbed it by the edge and pulled it out, not bothering to look at it before she laid it on Sherburne's crowded lap. She no longer wanted to perpetuate this "discussion." It was time to cut it short.

"Come on," she said. "You need to get out. Let's go for a ride."

She watched as Sherburne contemplated the idea. At first Annie felt certain he was going to resist, then, as if he'd had some kind of epiphany—maybe thoughts of his beloved bison out in the Lamar—his eyes widened. He looked up at her, and nodded eagerly.

*Thank God,* Annie thought. There really wasn't time to get him to the Lamar before dark, but just getting him out of the house and off this kick about the drilling would be good. For both of them.

"I just need to change out of these clothes," Annie said. "Wait here one minute while I put some jeans on."

Will had made this same trip up the trail leading to the Crevice Creek cabin less than forty-eight hours earlier.

But that time he hadn't been hauling a body, or ponying a second horse.

Two days earlier his mission had been to save 22—a

mission Will had failed. More and more, as he'd thought about it, the blood trail he'd seen on the ridgeline led him to conclude that the wound inflicted by the bullet had been deadly.

Now Will was on another mission—to find his friend Randy Hannah.

He couldn't fail this time.

They'd been moving at a fast clip—as fast as the steep, rocky trail would allow—but now Will reined Torch in, and for the second time, pulled out his two-way.

"Can anyone read me?" he called into it, urgency lacing his words. "This is Will McCarroll. This is an emergency."

Will wanted to let law enforcement know that he was headed to the Crevice Creek cabin, where he'd leave Biagi's body while he went looking for Randy.

The decision to abandon Biagi's body, even temporarily, had been the most difficult his job had ever forced Will to make, but as he assessed his options, he'd decided it was the only one available to him.

If his fears about Randy were grounded in fact, he had to go looking for the young ranger without delay. The Crevice Creek cabin was on the way to the Church of White Hope.

It was too late to do anything for Biagi, and his body would be safe at the cabin. Hopefully it was not too late for Randy.

For the most part, Will had never been the type who put stock in premonitions. For Will, life was fact-based. He reasoned his way through situations, a mentality that had served him especially well in law enforcement.

But it was the facts, indisputable facts, that now told him something had happened to his young friend.

Randy had taken off, alone, against Will's advice, to investigate his suspicion that the Church of White Hope was conducting secret drilling on its property. As unlikely as that scenario sounded then, it now seemed much more real a possibility.

The facts pointed to trouble.

And then there was the horrible knot in Will's gut—the one not based on fact—which he could not ignore.

"Can anyone hear me?" he yelled, one more time.

When no response came, he nudged Torch back into a trot.

Behind them, Riley matched Torch step for step, unfazed by the leaden cargo on his back.

# THIRTY-TWO

ANNIE WAS DRIVING, BUT JUDGE SHERBURNE WAS clearly in charge of where they were heading.

If Annie missed a turn, or went in the wrong direction, Sherburne let her know.

It hadn't been the Lamar he wanted to visit. When they left the stone house, and Annie had turned on the North Loop Road to head that way, he'd about had a fit. She'd quickly turned around and began letting him navigate.

He'd gotten them headed toward Gardiner, and for a moment Annie actually believed he was having her return him to Livingston, to Rainbow Living. But shortly after they'd passed through the entry gate, entered Gardiner, and crossed the bridge over the Yellowstone, Sherburne began jerking his head violently to the right.

"Here?" Annie asked.

The tiny road that curved up the hill led to just one place. Jardine.

Annie couldn't imagine that's what the judge really wanted but he appeared so doggedly focused on the road that she decided to go along with him.

It had been a partly cloudy day, cooler than usual, and rain began to fall as they drove up the narrow, bumpy road. Unpaved, it was made up mostly of the moistureless clay typical of the area. Annie's Subaru could pass another car its size heading down the hill as she drove up, but most of the vehicles coming up and down the road between Gardiner and Jardine were oversized pickups. Gun racks and the occasional set of elk antlers as a hood ornament were the norm. For them, Annie pulled to the side, not only to let them pass safely but also to give her car at least some measure of distance from the clay and dirt they kicked up. Her windshield had a film of red clay that returned as fast as the wipers swiped it away.

The judge had grown silent, his eyes fixed like that of a hawk on the landscape, searching for something Annie could not begin to identify.

Her eyes grew wide and unblinking as they took in the sights as well. She'd heard a lot about the area in and around Jardine but had never explored it. It was known to be home to a well-armed hunting community and because of rumored poaching activities, not an overly friendly place for newcomers—although the ATV enthusiasts drawn by its hills and mud seemed not to fit that category and traversed its network of trails and backroads freely.

At the turnoff to a narrow road leading south, they came upon what Annie at first thought—from the size and shape—to be a totem pole. As she drew near, she saw she was wrong.

Wood carvings, mostly of bears, adorned many Western homes and businesses—porches, driveways, even barns. Generally they stood two or three feet high, and often carried a cheery WELCOME sign or DO NOT FEED THE BEAR.

But even before she could fully make it out, something about the carving the Subaru now approached sent shivers down Annie's spine—and not just because of its size, which competed with the two- and three-year-old cottonwoods in the stand behind it. As the car rolled its way, a mountain man, armed, and in full regalia—beaver hat, fringed jacket—stood waiting. Fifteen feet high, the stern-faced pioneer pointed south, toward the canyon of the Yellowstone, with one ramrod straight, fringed arm and a creepily long finger. The other hand, arm bent at a 45-degree angle, clasped the barrel of a rifle, the butt of which rested on the ground. Someone had placed the road sign securely between the rifle's barrel and the pioneer's chest—so securely it almost looked like the man had been carved around the sign.

The road sign read: ABOVE THE REST.

As she drew nearer, Annie could see something else— a book—tucked into the crook of the bent arm, held tight against the mountain man's body.

She slowed, pulled over to read the two words inscribed on it.

HOLY BIBLE.

The combination—gun and bible-toting man pointing sternly off into space, with a sign that said ABOVE THE REST nestled snuggly against his chest—caused Annie to press down on the accelerator.

She felt Judge Sherburne's eyes on her.

They continued working their way up the switchbacks, toward the town of Jardine, passing roads with names like Bald Mountain and Palmer Creek, passing a train of mules loaded with gear just before they entered Jardine proper.

Once a mining camp with the name Bear Gulch, Jardine had been a promising gold mining town in the late 1800s. Many of the buildings that had housed thousands during the boom years—including 1946, when ten thousand ounces of gold were taken out of the hills—still stood, boarded up and abandoned. Today, the fifty or so town inhabitants dwelled in modest, sometimes innovative structures lining both sides of the narrow road.

Even though she'd heard of the school bus that had been turned into a home by an eccentric, but supposedly brilliant hermit, Annie stared in disbelief when she actually saw it.

It wasn't the fact that a second, and then third wing had been built onto it, the newest of which apparently housed a wood stove. Nor was it the shaded windows, some of which were broken and covered with cardboard. Nor the trash littering the ground around and under the structure.

What elicited a "My God" from Annie were the "ornaments" chosen to adorn the front hood of the bus. Items clearly placed there for effect: an old radio, a buffalo skull.

The item that most disturbed Annie, however, was the life-size head of what looked like a Barbie doll. It sat staring out at passersby, a creepily idyllic smile on her perfect lips and a gleam in her sky blue eyes. A crown held her blond hair in place, and a pearl necklace adorned her neck.

Annie looked over at Sherburne, whose own eyes were fixed on the eerie sight.

Two doors down, outside a small, solid log cabin, a man impervious to the rain chainsawed his way through a twenty-foot length of lodgepole pine.

Still trying to digest the Barbie doll on the bus's hood, and wondering what type of neighborhood tolerated such bizarre displays, Annie slowed, glancing at the man through beats of her windshield wipers.

Despite the ear-splitting roar of his saw, and the fact that his back was to them, the hunched-over woodsman apparently sensed their presence. He straightened, and turned to glare at them.

Beside her, Sherburne's grunt clearly told her to keep moving.

There was no need. Annie had already pressed the accelerator to the floor.

At the next fork, Sherburne nodded left, and they began to climb another switchback, one so narrow, and the drop-off so dramatic, that Annie didn't want to look down. Across the Yellowstone River a mile or so to the south, she could see the highway leading from Gardiner up to Mammoth.

As treacherous as she'd always considered driving that stretch, it now seemed like child's play to her.

They passed several secluded "ranches" where horses foraged in cramped dirt corrals. At first it surprised Annie to see large wooden structures that looked a child's playground set—minus the swings and teeter-totters. But then she passed one that had a dead deer hanging from it and realized they had nothing to do with children, or play.

Hunting season was still two weeks away. Annie couldn't believe how brazen the poacher who shot the deer was. She made a mental note of where they were—which wasn't easy since the roads were no longer marked—so that she could report it the next day.

She glanced sideways to see if Sherburne had noticed it. If he had, he clearly was not interested. He turned and met her gaze, then nodded forward. *Let's keep going.*

The road was becoming impossible. Still, from time to time a pickup would come roaring up from behind her and after a few seconds' hesitation, pull to her left and roar by. Some didn't hesitate.

"Where the hell are they going?" Annie wondered out loud.

More and more, the slick clay of the road caused the car to slide sideways. Annie sensed a loss of energy, as if the Subaru had taken on deadweight.

She stopped, got out, and looked at her tires. They were coated with clay. Her wheel well was so caked that the tires had begun brushing against the growing accumulation.

This was no longer fun.

Without saying a word Annie got back in the car. She rolled forward to a wide spot in the road, and began a three-point turn. Time to head home.

Sherburne immediately grew frantic.

*No, no,* he shook his head, motioning forward by leaning his body toward the dashboard, as if his weight alone could propel them.

"I'm turning around," Annie replied curtly. "I don't feel safe up here. And it isn't just the road."

Sherburne was adamant. They had to proceed.

"My tires are coated with clay," Annie argued, her voice rising.

Sherburne glared at her, nodding up the road. Resolute.

They'd come to a standoff.

When Annie did not start back up, Sherburne began fumbling inside his coat jacket. When his hand emerged, it held an article. He pushed it toward her.

This caused Annie to lose it.

"The drilling? That's what this is about?"

He nodded toward the article, clearly wanting her to read it.

"No," she said simply. And then she looked at Sherburne, at his wounded expression, his incredible frustration, and the tears began.

"I thought you could help me find my mother," she said, stifling sobs. "Will was sure you knew something. I thought you might be able to help save her."

She dropped her head, buried it in her hands as her shoulders shook.

She sat hunched over the steering wheel, mired in misery and grief, for several minutes, until she felt a gentle hand on her knee.

Annie took in a deep breath, wiped her eyes, unable for a moment to look at Sherburne; feeling ashamed for letting him see her disappointment; wanting—needing—time to compose herself.

Obviously the poor old soul couldn't help himself. He grunted, and Annie finally turned to him.

He pushed the article at her again.

Resigned, she took it.

She recognized it right away. It was the article she'd just retrieved from the chair's cushion. She had been too frustrated earlier to bother reading even the headline.

"Senator Conroy Denies Membership in Church of White Hope."

Annie read the short, two-paragraph article that described the church as extremely controversial, its membership highly guarded. A reporter, however, had uncovered a court-ordered deposition in which the Montana senator had been named as a key member of the CWH's finance committee. Conroy had immediately issued a strongly worded statement denying any connection to the group.

Annie turned to Sherburne.

"Why did you cut this one out? It has nothing to do with the drilling . . ."

Even as she said it, she realized she was wrong. She remembered that another article Sherburne cut out that day had said something that tied Conroy to the drilling proposal.

Annie stopped, thought. Looked at Sherburne again, then up the road in the direction they'd been heading.

"Is this the way to the Church of White Hope?"

The sigh he let out was answer enough, but in addition, he nodded his head heartily. *Yes.*

It took Annie several seconds to digest this.

"You think the Church of White Hope is involved somehow in the drilling proposal?"

Again, *yes.*

"Do you think this could have something to do with Randy Hannah?"

The nod was almost violent in its affirmation.

Annie drew in a sharp breath.

"Then it's more important than ever that we turn back and get help."

She started the car up again, but Sherburne reached over and grabbed her arm.

Annie ignored him.

She wasn't going to play games, not with what Sherburne was implying.

She could hear him taking in breaths, trying to make a sound, but she would not look at him. She knew that to do so might lessen her resolve, and she'd had enough of his calling the shots. She had to go report Sherburne's suspicions.

But halfway through her three-point turn, the judge made a sound that stopped Annie cold.

She braked abruptly, shoved the gearshift roughly into park, leaving the car angled across the middle of the road.

"What did you say?" she said, turning to him, almost angrily.

Sherburne met her gaze. He drew in his breath.

With every ounce of focus remaining in his aged and crippled body, he concentrated. Then, as he let the air out of his lungs, he said it again.

"Ma . . . aah . . . aah . . . ther."

Annie began shaking.

*It couldn't be.*

She grabbed his hand, searched his eyes.

"You think this has something to do with my mother? Is that what you've been trying to tell us all along?"

Sherburne's eyes misted.

Encouraged by his success, maybe even giddy with it, he tried again.

"Eeee . . . eee . . . ssss."

Nobody but Annie would have recognized it, and perhaps under any other circumstances even she would have thought it gibberish, but now she knew, with absolute certainty, what the judge had said.

Yes.

All of this, all of the clippings, and Sherburne's frustration, had to do with her mother's disappearance.

At least in Sherburne's mind.

And instinct told Annie that that mind, despite its outward manifestations, was as keen as it had ever been. Instincts told her that Will had been right about Sherburne all along.

She squeezed her passenger's frail hand, looked ahead, up the road, and shoved the gear shift back in to drive.

"This way?" she asked, the urgency in her eyes now mirroring that in Sherburne's.

He nodded.

# THIRTY-THREE

WILL UNLOCKED THE DOOR TO THE CREVICE CREEK CABIN and threw it open.

When he stepped inside, the image of Randy Hannah drying his clothes next to the fire practically assaulted him, making what he had to do now just a little easier.

He hurried back outside.

Once he'd gotten Riley to calm down, Will had tied Biagi to his own saddle and left him draped across Torch's back, while Will switched to Riley, to lighten Torch's load as they climbed back up to the cabin. Both horses had a long trek ahead of them tonight.

Now he untied Biagi. A quick pull on one of his arms and 210 pounds slid off the saddle like quicksilver, landing in Will's arms. He carried him, cradlelike, inside and dumped him on the bed.

Law enforcement officers carry every tool or weapon that might possibly come in handy, but now what Will most wanted he could not find. Paper and pen. He looked around the cabin.

The branch Randy had been using to poke at the fire still lay, charred, under the cast-iron stove. Will grabbed it and returned to the bed.

On the floor beside it, in awkward letters, he scrawled law enforcement's phone number, then:

DO NOT TOUCH BODY

He gave Biagi a final glance, turned away to leave, but then pivoted back around, picked the stick back up, and signed his note:

RANGER W. McCARROLL

A light, cool drizzle met Will as he stepped back onto the porch. He looked north, toward the park's border, toward the property of the Church of White Hope.

A dark cloud had opened. He would head right into it.

Locking the door behind him, Will tested it twice.

Against his own instincts, before stepping away, he glanced in the window at Biagi. Regretted not covering him.

He hesitated, then looked at the sky again. Just as he did, a bolt of lightning connected the approaching storm clouds to the ground.

Both horses' ears twitched nervously but the animals stood solid.

Will glanced once more through the window, then, conflicted but determined, he climbed on Riley, Torch's lead in hand.

"Okay, fella," he said. "Show me what happened to Randy."

Bowing their heads against the wind, the trio set off into the rain.

Normally Will would have avoided using the network of Forest Service roads that began at Yellowstone's north border and meandered their way between Buffalo Mountain, Crevice Mountain, and Bald Mountain as they worked north, toward Jardine. But the daylight was fading fast, and if he forged his own trail, it could be morning before he got to the Church of White Hope's property. And Will's gut told him that another night without help could be fatal to Randy.

The timing turned out to be perfect. The rain had slowed to an occasional light drizzle by the time he saw the first six-string barbed-wire fencing. He turned west, traveling alongside it until he saw the sign that confirmed what he already knew.

PRIVATE PROPERTY: ALL VIOLATORS WILL BE PROSECUTED.

He'd reached the lower border of the Church of White Hope's property.

He'd been told the church had video cameras placed all the way along the border. He was close enough now that he couldn't risk continuing on the gravel Forest Service road. He would have to enter the property.

Dismounting, and guided by a haze of light that he could not quite figure out, Will could see well enough to cut a middle strand. He walked ten feet, made another cut, then stood back, studying that section of fence. The missing strand was almost impossible to detect. Most of the brush immediately under and on either side of the fencing had been cleared, for security purposes, but Will found one post that had a particularly old and sturdy lodgepole growing just off its center. That's where he cut all the remaining lengths. He quickly guided Torch and Riley inside, then returned, and using the single length he'd cut as a mending piece, he wired the rest of the cut strands back together. Standing back to examine his work, he felt confident the breach would not be detected in anything less than full daylight, and even then, only by a trained eye.

As he cut north, through the heavily wooded property, Will again noticed a soft glow brightening the night sky above the tree line of the next ridge.

He'd entered the church's property from the southeast corner. Will knew that this section of the vast church holdings had once been part of the Crevice Mining District, which abutted the Jardine Mining District—both of which got their start in 1863 with placer mining.

Will had traveled the same ground in pursuit of elk antler poachers the year before the Church of White Hope moved into the area and vacuumed up every free acre of contiguous land in the Jardine and Crevice Mountain area. He remembered coming across an abandoned mill at what had once been the First Chance Mine, on the Crevice Gulch

side, on that journey and then, farther north that same day—
at the old Snowshoe Mine site—the remnants of a thirty-
five-ton, gas-powered, amalgamation-flotation mill.

Will had never been a person who possessed a burning
curiosity about history, but that day, looking at the mills,
and the ruins of what had once been offices and modest
homes for the mines' workers, he'd found himself fasci-
nated. What had returned to a near state of wilderness had
once been a thriving boom camp, its inhabitants long gone,
acknowledged now only by the dilapidated structures in
which they'd once worked and slept. Standing there, Will
had been able to picture the camp's hustle, the excitement,
the grittiness of the miners' lives.

He hadn't been back since, but he'd thought about that
sight from time to time over the years, and now, if his bear-
ings held true, he expected to break into the meadow that
housed the abandoned First Chance Mine within the next
hour or so.

At first the sound was so soft and muffled that he thought
he'd imagined it. But as he moved closer to the strange
glow, Will began to hear an unfamiliar sound. A muffled
*whooshing*. Had he not spent decades in the wilderness, so
many nights sleeping on the ground that he could identify
the sound of an elk's footstep versus that of a moose, the
call of a coyote versus a cry of a wolf, the cry of a sandhill crane versus that of a black-bellied plover, he might
have questioned himself, attributed the noise to the wind.

And then, still some distance away, he saw the lights. Either he was disoriented from having approached from this
direction or the church must have built homes for some of
its members deep in the hills beyond its main encampment,
which was miles farther north, close to the gated entry just
outside Jardine.

The rhythmical sound grew stronger. So did the lights.

Will tied the horses to a stand of lodgepoles and approached on foot.

When he crested the ridge, he stopped short, staring in
disbelief.

He'd been right.

Before him stood the mill he'd come across years earlier. It looked exactly as it had then. But then it had obviously been abandoned for years, decades, and now there were lights, and activity. And that sound.

Suddenly Will realized that the mill did *not* actually look exactly as it had earlier. It was taller. But that was crazy. It made absolutely no sense. No one added on to a building like that abandoned mill, and even more puzzling was the fact that what he saw, what he imagined to be another twenty feet in the mill's height, looked identical to the rest of the building—weathered and worn, as if ready to fall down.

As he stood watching, twice the door to the mill opened. Each time the sound from inside grew louder. Each time a man emerged, hurriedly walked to one of half a dozen other dilapidated structures nearby—this time, what appeared to be an abandoned house—and disappeared through its door.

Will felt as though he were watching a scene out of the *Twilight Zone.*

If the mines had been activated, why would he not know? Why would the buildings appear exactly as they had since the 1940s? Why would . . .

The answer came to him before he could even completely form the last question.

Of course.

*The Church of White Hope is conducting secret drilling.*

Randy Hannah had stood there in the Crevice Creek cabin, eyes wide with fear and determination, and told Will his theory to explain the recent geothermal changes at Mammoth Hot Springs.

Will had trouble believing what he was seeing.

Bent low, staying within the cover of the trees, he used a grid system to examine the ground for signs that Randy Hannah had been there. Staying hidden by the trees, he circled the entire mining camp, but never saw anything that would suggest Randy had witnessed what Will had come upon.

Randy had seen something, however, Will now had no doubt about that fact—and the fact that his young friend was in trouble.

Hurriedly, Will returned to the horses, untied them, and mounted Riley. He urged them on, toward the main compound of the Church of White Hope.

On the way to the main compound, Will decided to detour toward the other abandoned mine site he'd come across six years earlier. The Snowshoe.

Even before he started to hear the same muffled sounds he'd heard at First Chance, Will's sixth sense told him what he would find.

A similar glow lit the night sky ahead. Will headed directly for it, working his way up and down gulleys and drainages, pausing often to listen. Years of backcountry experience had given him the ability to detect a human presence anywhere near him. He felt confident he wasn't being followed.

As Will remembered it, the Snowshoe mill was considerably larger than First Chance's. While First Chance had once consisted of five patented claims, and a mineral zone a hundred feet wide, in its heyday the Snowshoe boasted eleven claims, and underground networks of almost a thousand feet.

Will's memory served him well.

Just as the First Chance looked identical to how it had appeared when he'd seen it years earlier, the Snowshoe also looked like a snapshot frozen in time—if it weren't for the hustle and bustle of workers coming and going, and the muffled sound of drilling. The activity at Snowshoe was easily twice what he'd witnessed at First Chance.

Will stood for several minutes on the final ridgeline before the Snowshoe—still a quarter mile away—watching the scene through his binoculars. Just as with First Chance, the level of activity was more consistent with daytime than the dead of night. But standing there watching in disbelief, Will realized why that would be the case. Wolf biologists routinely flew over any areas inhabited by wolves. *During the day*. While there was no pack actually living just outside the park's north border, the Hellroaring pack made the area just south of the border, inside Yellowstone, its home, and the flight paths taken by biologists tracking the pack no doubt occasionally took them over the Church of White Hope's property. Will felt certain that the drilling activity was only conducted at night for that reason.

Another epiphany hit Will as he stood there, mind racing.

Was that the reason none of the buildings' exteriors had changed? During the day, if no workers moved about and no vehicles came and went, the scene at both the First Chance and Snowshoe mines, from the air, would not have changed from how they had appeared for decades.

Suddenly a comment made by Brian Wise, the park geologist, during a lecture several years earlier came back to Will. It was during one of the annual employee meetings, the idea of which was to update everyone on the status of everything from the carrying capacity for bison, to roadwork, to the geothermal studies being conducted. For two days, different factions of the park were brought together every year. Most saw the occasion more as a chance to network and visit with old friends than to learn anything, especially the veterans. The new rangers, however, tended to take the occasion more seriously.

It was during the Q&A after Brian's presentation about Yellowstone's ever-changing hot springs and geysers, and the fragility—vulnerability, really—of those features to outside pressures, that one such young ranger—as Will relived it now, he realized it must have been Randy Hannah— asked if something as simple as drilling for a well outside the park could inadvertently have an impact inside of it.

As was his tendency, Brian got off track. He used the question as an opportunity to decry the then-current Bush Administration's attempts to open up the Arctic National Wildlife Refuge for oil exploration and drilling. Wise went into a diatribe about drilling in general, which ended in his mocking the recent THUMS operation in California. Texaco, Humble, Unocal, Mobil, and Shell had actually constructed four islands located offshore in Long Beach Harbor where they drilled over twelve hundred wells. *Drilling rigs and equipment had been disguised as resort apartments and buildings.* From a distance, with its waterfalls, abstract sculpture, and the seven hundred palm trees supported by THUMS' elaborate irrigation system, the uninformed observer believed he was looking at a luxury resort. While THUMS had won dozens of design and environmental awards for this feat—what was called "blending oil and gas production with visual appeal and environmental safety"— Wise made a mockery of the whole concept that day, and never did get back to answering the inquisitive ranger's question.

The concept of twelve hundred wells disguised as a resort had stayed with Will.

Now he could not help but wonder—if an oil field operation could be camouflaged as a luxury vacation destination, who's to say the remnants of an abandoned mine couldn't be used for the same purpose? Who was to say that the same concept couldn't be successfully applied to these long-abandoned mines, especially when the scrutiny was minimal—occasional flights overhead by biologists looking for wolves?

The drilling could be taking place secretly, without anyone ever detecting it. Anyone, that is, except a young, inquisitive ranger named Randy Hannah.

Shaken by the enormity of the idea, Will tied the horses inside a copse of quaking aspen and continued toward the Snowshoe on foot.

Trees gave Will good cover until he got within a hundred yards of that portion of the property that had long ago been cleared for roads, buildings, and mining equipment.

This time, when Will began inspecting the ground, he found what he was looking for almost immediately.

Two sets of prints. One left by hooves, the other by man.

Will was certain who made them. Randy may or may

not have discovered what was going on at the First Chance Mine, but he had stood—no doubt wide-eyed—staring at the bizarre sight below him, just as Will was now doing.

Will tried following the prints but quickly lost them in the layer of pine needles and leaves the storm two nights earlier had blown down.

Will dropped back into the woods and lifted the binoculars hanging from his neck to survey the scene below him again.

A uniformed guard wearing military boots walked purposefully across an open area that separated most of the structures from an isolated shed that sat back, nestled against a rocky hillside. Even from that distance, Will estimated the man to be at least six five. At the door to the shed, he reached for a ring of keys dangling from his belt, unlocked the front door, and disappeared inside.

Will had one thing on his mind, and one thing only.

*Was Randy Hannah down there somewhere?*

He swept the scene below again, and it was then that the truck entered his binocular's field of vision. On the opposite side of the camp.

At first Will wasn't exactly sure of what he was looking at. A green tarp had been placed over it, and branches and shrubbery piled on top of the tarp. Only part of the driver's side door peeked out from under it.

A beat-up pickup.

Will could see a faded logo on the door. He adjusted his glass's focus. When he did, the hair on the back of his neck stood on edge.

It read:

WHY WAIT? GO LOCAL.

And underneath: HANK'S TOWING.

# THIRTY-FOUR

STAYING INSIDE THE COVER OF THE TREES, WILL WORKED his way around to the other side of the camp, not stopping until he found himself directly above and behind the pickup.

The comings and goings of workers seemed to have a pattern to it, but the guard was now nowhere in sight. Will waited for several minutes, eyes constantly scanning, and finally decided that the timing would not get better. With a final sweeping glance, he crept down the rocky incline. It provided no cover, but on the other hand, because of where it was situated, very little light from the camp reached it and Will had less than ten yards of ground to cover to get to the truck.

He was almost there when the door to the shed he'd watched the guard enter swung open.

Will dove for the truck, rolling underneath it. He had no idea whether he'd been seen. From under the truck he watched the booted feet of a man—military boots—pause on the front stoop of the shed. Their size convinced Will it was the same guard he'd seen disappear inside.

The guard stepped down to the ground and headed toward the truck, stopping at the driver's side, less than two feet from where Will now lay. Will drew his gun. He could splinter one of his ankles before making a run for it, but just as he lifted it, he heard the driver's side door groan open above him.

"I knew it," he heard the guard say. "Wake the fuck up."

The truck swayed as he reached inside and prodded its occupant.

This elicited a groggy, belligerent reply.

"What the hell you doin, Beau?"

"Wake up, I said," the guard, apparently named Beau, repeated. "Are you out of your mind, sleeping on duty after what happened the other night? Jeremiah's been looking for you."

*Jeremiah.* Jeremiah Dayton—the head of the Church of White Hope?

"What time is it?"

"Three twenty. You been drinkin'? You have, haven't you? Goddammit Cougar, I oughta' turn you in. If we didn't go back to Baghdad, I would."

The truck creaked again as Cougar shifted to a sitting position, ignoring most of what his friend had just said, including the reference to serving together during the war.

"You gotta be shittin me," Cougar replied. "It's that late?"

"I've been *covering* for your sorry ass. Jeremiah had a fit when he heard no one could find you. What'd you do—turn your radio off? I told him you were probably underground and couldn't pick up the call. I said I'd check on the old lady and then find you."

*The old lady.*

Cougar had finally awakened.

"You went down there?" he asked, a serious note entering his voice.

"Yeah," Beau replied. "I can't believe how creepy it is . . ."

"Creepy's not the word for it. Last night I stepped on a fucking snake."

"She doesn't look very good."

"What'd you expect?" Cougar replied angrily. "A blow job? How the fuck would *you* look if you'd had your ear cut off? And been living down there for three weeks?"

Will drew in a sharp breath. *Annie's mother was here!*

"I'd go insane," Beau replied. "That's how I'd feel. But that's not my problem."

"That's right," Cougar said. "You would. Why do you think I've been drinking? Between her and that kid . . ." He paused, the distress audible in his voice, "I'm not handling things well, Beau."

"That kid came looking for trouble."

"Yeah. Well, he got it."

They both fell silent, but only briefly. Beau turned all business again.

"Well, you better wake up and get your ass out of here. Jeremiah wants to see you."

"Shit," Cougar replied.

The first pair of boots stepped back from the truck to make room for another set—identical, but noticeably smaller—which dropped to the ground.

As the two men strode away, Will heard the big man say, "You didn't take those magazines outta there, did you? That crazy guy had some raunchy stuff. What kind of a pervert keeps that much shit in his truck?"

Cougar's conscience didn't seem to extend to Hank.

"We probably did everybody a service getting rid of that one."

Will slid forward several inches to get a look at both men. He was right. The one with the big feet had to be six foot five. The other barely topped out at five six or seven.

"Don't worry," Cougar added. "I left them there for you."

# THIRTY-FIVE

WILL WATCHED AS THE TWO MEN PARTED WAYS. COUGAR headed purposefully toward the building closest to the mill, which appeared to function as the office—no doubt on his way to deal with Jeremiah Dayton.

Beau headed for the mill.

As he lay there waiting for Beau to disappear through the mill's door, Will went back over the conversation he'd just overheard.

*Eleanor Malone was alive and being held prisoner by the Church of White Hope.*

Adrenaline coursed through Will at that realization, but at the same time, an enormous sense of dread descended upon him. Randy Hannah had definitely been caught snooping around the church's property. While he couldn't be certain of Randy's fate, the conversation Will just overheard hinted that something terrible had happened to his young friend.

When both men had disappeared, Will rolled out from under the far side of the truck, the side nearest the hill. He crouched at the back bumper, watching and listening.

The camp appeared quiet. Will lifted the tarp covering the passenger's side door and pulled on the door handle, expecting it to be locked. It wasn't. Ever so slowly, remem-

bering the noise the driver's side door had made, he opened
it just enough to slide inside.

The passenger seat was littered with porn. Will pushed it
to the floor. Guided by the half light from the camp, he began searching for the truck's keys. He rummaged through
the glove box, slid his hand into both side pockets on the
door in search of Hank's keys. Finally, he lay down, lowered
his head under the steering wheel, and felt for the wires
feeding the ignition. By the light of a match, he pulled
them out of the cylinder and slit both wires with his knife.

Leaving them dangling from the steering wheel, Will slid
back out of the passenger door and quietly pushed it shut.

Crouching behind the truck, he waited as two men, deep
in conversation, exited a building at the far end of the row
of structures that ended with the shed and crossed to the
mill. Once they disappeared inside, Will stepped onto the
shed's stoop.

Jimmying the lock open was child's play for Will, but
what he saw when he walked through the door was not.

Totally windowless, the building once served as a powder
house, a storage place for the explosives used to blast away
earth hiding coveted minerals. Over all those years, it still
hadn't lost its smell—a penetrating, musty scent of destruction. Will quickly closed the door behind him and found
himself in absolute and abject darkness. He reached for his
flashlight. When he flipped it on, a single lightbulb dangled
from a cord in the middle of the room. He dared not use it.

Instead, he swept the flashlight's beam around the room,
pausing at a door at the opposite end, which stood partially
open. The darkness the light pierced beyond the door told
Will it was not just another room on the other side.

He crossed to it, remembering the conversation between
the guards he'd overheard.

With that in mind, Will pointed the flashlight down, toward his feet, before stepping across the threshold.

Had he not done so, he would have fallen into a black
hole.

The top of a ladder, old and rickety, rose up, as if eager to meet any form of light.

Holding the flashlight tucked under his chin, Will descended into what felt like an endless abyss. In reality, it was a long-abandoned mine shaft—one which had, back in 1946, been touted as the deepest ever drilled.

Dampness enveloped Will. His foot slipped several times and the ladder's wet rungs made it difficult to get a good grip.

Reaching for a better hold, he lifted his head and the flashlight plummeted down the shaft, bouncing off its walls. Will never heard it hit ground.

Swallowed by darkness now, he focused on the image of Eleanor Malone—and, holding out hope that Randy Hannah was still alive, the young ranger—waiting somewhere below. But after descending nearly twenty feet without any sound or sight of human occupancy, Will began to wonder. And then he heard it.

Almost a whimper.

He recognized it as human, and an expression of fear.

"Mrs. Malone?" he called out.

A gasp greeted him.

It was followed in short order by, "Yes. I'm Eleanor Malone."

# THIRTY-SIX

"YOU'RE ALMOST HERE," SHE SAID.

Will looked down and, a dozen rungs below him, saw a frail hand reaching out to touch the ladder.

When he'd revealed his identity to her, Eleanor Malone had quickly switched on the fluorescent camp light her captors had given her, which allowed Will to descend faster. As he drew near, he felt the hand reach out again and touch his ankle.

Seconds later, when Will finally came even with the cell holding her—a cave cut into the wall—he tried to hide his horror at the sight of Eleanor Malone. Frail and gaunt, blood crusting the left side of her face, her clothes bore a camouflage-like pattern of blood and mud stains. Still, when she saw Will, her hand went automatically to her hair, brushing it back self-consciously.

"You're going to be just fine," Will told her. "I'm a friend of your daughter's. I'm going to get you out of here."

"Annie?" Eleanor Malone said, brightening immediately. "You know my Annie?"

"Yes," Will replied, taking in the chain that led from her ankle to a metal ring fixed to the stone wall.

"Is she all right?" Eleanor asked.

Choking back the anger the sight of her had given rise to, Will replied, "She will be when she sees you."

He stepped from the ladder to the ledge that had been her home now for three weeks. An area perhaps four feet by six in floor space, and not high enough even for Eleanor, at just five feet, to stand straight. Furnished only with a battery-operated fluorescent camp light, a metal bowl that Will suspected served as her latrine, and a sleeping bag and pillow.

Eleanor did not try to rise to greet him. Tears ran down her cheek as Will crouched beside her and wrapped his arms around her.

"You're going to be okay," he said again, more determined than ever.

When he released her, he drew back and locked eyes with her.

"Do you know anything about Randy Hannah?"

A single silent sob shook Eleanor's shoulders, but she maintained eye contact—it seemed, in fact, as if she dared not look away for fear Will might prove a hallucination.

"Was he the ranger?"

Will's fists clenched at her use of the past tense. He nodded.

"They killed the poor boy."

He said nothing, but Eleanor clearly saw the impact this had on Will.

"I'm sorry," she said, reaching out and laying a gentle hand on his arm.

Will took a deep breath. He'd learned to suppress any emotion on the job—to "delay" it if it had to be dealt with at all—but nothing had prepared him for this.

He placed a hand on top of Eleanor's. Her life depended on his being coolheaded.

He nodded at her ankle.

"I imagine you've tried to get that thing off."

A gleam of mischief actually snuck into Eleanor's eye. She lifted her hands to the light for him to see. Her fingertips sported ugly scratches and bruises; the nails had been worn to the quick.

"You've been trying to pry the lock open with your bare hands?" Will asked, incredulous.

"At first," she replied. "But then I realized that was hopeless. So I came up with a new plan . . ."

Eager to demonstrate, in what had obviously become a routine for her, she slid on her rear end to the back wall, to the farthest reach of the chain, carrying the lantern with her. As Will looked on, she reached up to a spot halfway up the wall and began digging with her fingers, flinging loose dirt to the floor.

Will moved closer, watching over her shoulder all the while keeping an ear trained toward the ladder.

Finally, Eleanor stopped and pointed. She lifted the light. Its rays bounced off the smooth surface of a rock that appeared to be eight to ten inches in diameter.

"I've been trying to dig this out. I thought I could use it to break the lock open. Or maybe break the chain free from that." She pointed to the ring on the wall.

"No one's noticed?" Will asked. The image of this eighty-year-old woman using her bare hands to dig into the wall greatly impacted him.

"I can only work for an hour or so at a time." Eleanor's voice held a note of pride. "I tire easily. I pack the dirt back when I'm done."

Will found himself unable to speak. He removed his knife from his belt, and bent over Eleanor's ankle to try to trip the lock open, but quickly realized the knife would not do the job.

He looked up at Eleanor, at her soulful, hopeful eyes.

"I think you had the right idea," he said, joining her at the wall. With his knife and bare hands, he set about finishing the job Eleanor had begun.

She sat back watching.

"How about Archie?" he heard her say quietly from behind him. "Did he make it?"

Will turned to look at her, and for the first time since coming upon the bone-chilling reality that had been her life since she'd been kidnapped, the smile he gave Eleanor was genuine.

"Yes," he said. "He did. He's doing great."

"That's wonderful," Eleanor replied, clearly overcome with emotion. "Just wonderful."

Will went back to work. Within minutes, he could wiggle the rock back and forth in the cradle that had held it firmly in place over thousands of years.

"It's about ready," he said.

He turned to Eleanor again.

"There's a chance—and it might be a good one—that my pulling this out will cause the whole wall to collapse. Or even trigger something bigger. Are you willing to risk that?"

Eleanor had already thought of that possibility.

She nodded. "Just don't leave me. Please."

"You've got my word," Will replied. "I'm not leaving here without you."

"Then yank it out of there."

With his fingers wedged behind the rock on either side, Will positioned both feet against the wall and, with a loud grunt, did just as Eleanor instructed.

As he fell back with the rock on his chest, the wall above the hole began to crumble, slowly at first, then with a *whoosh* several yards of earth collapsed, much of it fanning out over Will.

He pushed Eleanor away, telling her, "Get on the ladder if it doesn't stop."

Eleanor did not budge.

"I'm not leaving you behind either."

The worst appeared to be over. Still, Will feared some kind of delayed chain reaction. He rose, brushing the dirt off his shirt and pants. With just two blows to the chain, it snapped in two.

"Okay," he said to Annie's newly freed mother. "Let's go."


"This isn't good," Annie said, turning to Judge Sherburne. "I don't like the idea of someone we don't want coming along."

With the Subaru's lights turned off, they'd paused at the mouth of the long driveway to the Church of White Hope's compound and debated whether to approach the gate—which Annie could see over a hundred yards ahead. One of two guards crossed in front of the gate, under its light, but did not appear to notice them.

"I'll ask to speak to Reverend Dayton," Annie told Sherburne as they sat there. "I'll just come right out and confront him. Ask him if he had anything to do with my mother's kidnaping."

Sherburne had grunted his disapproval of this approach, and urged her on with his gestures. Still uncertain about the best course of action, Annie reluctantly proceeded down the road to continue their "discussion."

The earlier rain had turned the clay road to slick, sticky mush. Several miles past the compound, a cow elk and calf darted out of the woods and into her headlights, and Annie jerked the steering wheel right to avoid them. The front end of the car slid off the road and into a small runoff channel formed alongside it. Annie tried rocking the car back and forth, switching from drive to reverse to dislodge it, but only managed to dig her way in so deep that it soon became obvious the only way the Subaru would get free would be by being pushed or pulled out.

They'd sat there for two hours now, hoping for someone to come along, yet nervous about just who that might be, and what reason they'd give—if asked—for being there at that time of night. Annie had begun debating walking into Jardine to call for help. If her cell phone worked somewhere along the way, or she found a phone booth—which seemed unlikely in light of what she'd seen on the way up—she could call Sheriff Holmberg. If that weren't possible, she could at least choose whom to ask for help—rather than sit there waiting for someone, perhaps even one of the guards they'd seen outside the compound gates, to come along.

But she couldn't leave Judge Sherburne.

All evening, the same eyes that had previously looked so

frustrated and dead had come alive. But now her friend appeared to be tiring, and nervous.

Annie could not get what Sherburne had shown and told her on their way up to Jardine out of her mind. The Church of White Hope might have something to do with her mother's disappearance.

That possibility made sitting there passively enough to make her crazy. To top it off, she needed to go to the bathroom. Which made her realize the judge might have a similar need.

"Are you doing okay?" she said, turning to him. "Do you want me to help you outside to . . . relieve yourself?"

The right side of Sherburne's mouth lifted at Annie's prudishness.

He shook his head. He lifted his hand and formed an "O" with his thumb and forefinger. *I'm okay.*

"Well, I'm not," Annie replied. "I'm going to sneak into the woods. Be right back."

Annie stepped out into night air that still held the scent of the earlier rain. It was accompanied now by the chill that came with October nights in high country.

She moved toward the trees and immediately came up against a barbed-wire fence. She was about to move down the fenceline, farther away from the car—she could still see Judge Sherburne's silhouette, which meant he could probably see her—when she stopped cold.

A sound—completely foreign to anything she'd heard since moving to Yellowstone—muted, but powerful. Rhythmical. Coming from somewhere within the Church of White Hope's property.

Forgetting now the need to relieve herself, Annie sprinted back to the car, slid inside, and breathless, turned to Judge Sherburne.

"I heard it," she said. "Drilling."

Sherburne's eyes went wide. He jerked his head toward her.

*Tell me more.*

"It's this soft, whooshing sound. It's definitely a machine of some sort. What type of machinery would they have operating out here in the middle of nowhere—in the middle of the night?"

Sherburne shook his head.

They both sat, thinking, for a minute or two.

"I want to go in there and see what I find," Annie said hesitantly. "But that would mean leaving you alone."

"Go."

It was perfectly formed, undeniable.

"I can't leave you," Annie protested.

Sherburne shot her what she might once have taken to be an angry look, but now she knew better.

"Maaahh . . . aahhh . . . ther," he said.

He knew the one thing he could say to convince Annie to leave him there alone to go explore.

"Are you sure you'll be okay?"

He nodded.

"Go."

Her captivity and abuse had so weakened Eleanor that they ascended the ladder with Eleanor hugging the rungs while Will, never more than a rung or two below, cradled her with his arms and body.

Once he got her up to the shed, Will held her, steadying her, as she straightened slowly to her full height.

Will closed the door to what had been her home and placed her hand on the doorknob to steady her before he crossed the room to the front door, eased it open an inch, and snuck a look outside.

As he watched, a black Humvee pulled up to the mill.

The tall guard, Beau, emerged from the mill and walked purposefully toward it. He disappeared on the side opposite Will and closest to the mill. When he opened the car door, the light inside revealed two men—both dressed in dark suits. Will watched as they quickly climbed out. With

Beau between them, the men hurried to the mill and disappeared inside. Even from that distance, and in the dark, one looked familiar to Will.

"Something's going on," he said, turning to check Eleanor out. "We need to hurry. Are you strong enough to walk a short distance?"

Eleanor nodded.

"Let's go," she replied gamely, but when she let go of the doorknob, she immediately stumbled sideways. Will swept her into his arms.

"I can walk," Eleanor protested in a whisper. "Really."

"You may have to if the truck doesn't start, but for now, just go along with me."

With Eleanor cradled in his arms, Will stepped outside. Suddenly another car appeared. Will stepped off the stoop and bolted for the back of the shed narrowly avoiding being caught in its headlights as they swept over the shed, and then Hank's truck.

Perhaps the truck was no longer an option.

From behind the shed, Will surveyed the situation. Several buildings down, he could see lights. The newest car had pulled up to the mill. A guard emerged and quickly disappeared inside the door that Beau and the two newcomers had entered.

"I'm going to leave you here," he said to Eleanor. "But only for a minute or two while I check things out. Is that okay with you?"

Eleanor took a deep breath, closed her eyes. When she opened them again, she said, "Yes. Do what you have to do."

Staying in the shadows, Will moved from one building to another—most of which still appeared to be abandoned—until he came to the one that was lit.

A window on a side wall stood open. Will smelled cigar smoke as he crept under it.

He could hear men's voices. A heated conversation was taking place inside.

"I think they should," said a voice left raspy by decades of smoking. "We had everyone believing it was Gleeson and

Heck Buckley's group who kidnaped the old lady, but now, with what they did to that ranger kid who came snooping around, the game's changed. We can't take any chances."

Will recognized the voice that responded as belonging to Cougar, the smaller of the two guards he'd overheard only half an hour earlier.

"You're all being paranoid. There's nothing to connect us with that kid. I checked with my friend who mucks out the stalls at the stable in Mammoth. He said the kid told everyone he was going into the Lamar. We've already had a couple church members call the Park Service and say they saw him out there. No one's going to be looking for him here."

A third male voice—with a distinctly Southern accent—entered the conversation.

"Yeah, well I got a friend up there too. He's in road construction and he said that ranger had been going around telling everyone he thought there was something unusual going on with the geothermal features."

"It's a big jump from that to the church," Cougar replied. "Believe me, none of them are smart enough to make that connection."

"The kid was."

"Well," the Southerner replied, "I say we don't take any chances."

This didn't sit right with Cougar.

"Killing the old lady doesn't solve anything."

"That kid going missing could eventually bring people snooping around up here. Or what the hell—maybe someone will even come looking for that loser who tried to blackmail the reverend. The one who saw the Suburban leaving the judge's house that night." It was the smoker again. "If that happens, we can't afford to let them find the old lady. And the drilling's gotta stop. Now. Until we know no one else will be snooping around."

"That's what they're in there talking about," Cougar replied. "After Jeremiah got done bustin' my butt, he told me to get all you guys together and stay right here until

Beau came for us. Then I heard him on the phone. He thought I'd left, but I didn't close the door behind me all the way. I was listening. I heard him call Beau and tell him someone important was coming in and that it was Beau's job to make sure nobody ran into this guy while he's here. He doesn't want to be seen."

"Guess they don't trust us," the smoker said.

"Trust us?" the Southerner replied. "Hell, we'll be the ones doin' all the dirty work if they shut this place down."

"You're right about that," Cougar replied. "But what about after we get it all done? What then?"

"What're you saying?"

"I'm just sayin we've all seen a lot go down here. The less we act like we know and the more we act like we don't have big mouths, the better it'll be for us."

"You're probably right," the raspy voice said. "Hey, maybe the reason they had us all come in here is so that they could kill the old lady. Maybe that's what they're doing right now . . ."

"You stupid shit," a new, surly voice replied. "They're not gonna bring in some big shot and kill the old lady in front of him. They're in there making decisions. Killing the old lady is probably one of them."

A chair suddenly grated against the wood floor. The next voice Will heard came from directly above him.

"Hey there's a fucking Humvee parked outside the mill."

The last thing Will heard was Cougar's voice.

"You shithead. I'm not supposed to let you look over there."

Will hurried back to where he had left Eleanor. Once again he scooped Eleanor into his arms and after another pause to look and listen, made the dash for Hank's truck.

Reaching it, he opened the passenger side door and slid Eleanor inside. Not wanting to risk going around to the driver's side, he had to climb over her lap to get to the driver's seat.

Nothing mattered now but getting Eleanor out of there.

It appeared that if he didn't succeed her nightmare was about to turn deadly.

Once situated behind the wheel, he doubled over to find the wires he'd cut earlier. He had just grasped both wires and was about to touch them to one another when Eleanor's gasp stopped him.

Will shot upright, certain he would come face-to-face with a guard.

It hadn't occurred to him that another sight might just as easily cause Eleanor Malone to react so gut wrenchingly.

Annie Peacock.

Standing directly in front of the truck, tears streaming down her face, eyes wide.

*"Mom?"* she mouthed in disbelief.

# THIRTY-SEVEN

ANNIE SLID INTO THE TRUCK ON THE OTHER SIDE OF Eleanor, cupped her mother's face with trembling hands, and sobbed, "You're alive."

Tears streaming down her face, Eleanor Malone simply nodded as she reached for Annie, who collapsed in her arms. Eleanor hugged her tightly to her chest.

Even though he'd kept one eye fixed on the camp, Will had seen enough to make it hard to talk over the lump in his throat.

"Okay," he said firmly, determined to relay the urgency of the situation without having to tell the women what he'd just overheard. "We have to stay focused. We could be found out any second. Even if this old beater starts, we're up against steep odds."

He looked directly at Annie and said, "And desperate opposition."

Annie locked eyes with him briefly and he knew she understood.

Almost as if on cue, the newly arrived guard emerged from the mill and headed determinedly toward the explosives shed.

"Get down," Will cried as the three doubled over in the front seat.

Will saw Eleanor clasp Annie's hand. He lifted his head

just enough to see the guard disappear into the shed's door.

"Okay," he said, rising. "We've got four minutes, tops, before he climbs down that ladder, finds you missing, climbs back up, and sounds the alarm. Listen closely. Here's what we're going to do."

As he spoke, Will lifted his Glock to the light streaming in from outside and checked the bullet chamber.

"If this truck starts, you'll wait here while I distract them . . ."

Eleanor already did not like this plan.

"You're leaving us?"

"That's the only way. If I can divert everyone's attention, you'll have the best chance of driving this thing out of here." He looked at Annie. "Here's what I want you to do. Head right up that embankment. Lights out. Hopefully I'll create enough commotion for you to do that. Once you're over the embankment, swing that direction."

Will pointed north.

"There's only one road leading out of here, and it takes you right by the church's headquarters. Whatever you do, don't stop. Even if they're out there and they try to stop you. Especially if they try to stop you. Don't stop until you get to Gardiner."

Annie had been listening intently, but now she balked.

"I have to get the judge."

Will's eyebrows drew up in surprise.

"The judge?"

"Judge Sherburne. He and I came up here together. He knew what was going on all along. He just had trouble telling us. We got stuck in the mud. He's in my car now . . ."

The news that Judge Sherburne was involved clearly disturbed Will but his response came without hesitation.

"Forget the judge. Even if I'm able to distract them long enough for you to get out of here, they'll start looking for your mother right away. Once they notice this truck is missing, they'll be after you. You can't stop. Drive right through the gate if it's closed. At full speed I think this thing can do it. When you get to Gardiner, call Sheriff Holmberg and let him know where Judge Sherburne is.

"And take this," Will said, handing Annie the gun. "If you need to, use it. Do you hear?"

He turned to Eleanor and reached for something on the back of his belt. His Taser gun.

Handing it to her, he said, "This is how this works." He quickly demonstrated.

Throughout explaining the plan to Eleanor and Annie, Will kept an eye on the door to the shed. Now it flew open.

The guard emerged at a run, headed back to the mill.

"This is it, ladies," Will pronounced.

As soon as the guard disappeared into the mill, Will bent over, touched the two wires to each other.

No response.

"Come on," he urged.

He tried again.

The motor kicked in. Will gave it a little gas, and the truck rumbled to life.

He turned to both women, hand on the door handle.

"Good luck."

"Will?" Annie said anxiously.

He bent toward her, brushed her cheek with a quick kiss.

"Don't waste a second," he said. "As soon as they catch sight of me, all hell will break loose. That's when you take off."

He opened the door and slid outside.

"You'll have a couple minutes at most before they start looking for your mom."


Will's words proved prophetic.

Annie sat, heart in throat, as she watched him disappear into the shadows behind the row of buildings.

Two uniformed guards—the newly arrived guard and Beau—burst through the door of the mill and sprinted to the building where Cougar and the others were holed up.

Within seconds, half a dozen armed men emerged from its front door at a run. In the center of the compound, they hesitated, looked confused and disorganized, as if they didn't quite know what to do or where to go.

Suddenly Annie heard a shout. "Look!"

One of the men pointed toward the hill at the opposite end of the camp.

Will was running up its incline. He paused, turned back to look.

"Go, go," both Eleanor and Annie cried.

Annie heaved a sigh of relief when Will finally sprinted into the trees, the men in pursuit.

She waited for Will's pursuers to disappear into the trees and was just about to shift the truck into first gear when the door to the mill opened again. This time three men emerged: two dressed in suits, and Jeremiah Dayton.

They strode hurriedly toward the Humvee, climbed inside, and sped away with Dayton at the wheel.

Once their dust cleared, the camp appeared deserted.

Annie eased the truck up the embankment as Will had instructed. When she reached flat ground, she worked her way to the road headed north, the same one the Humvee had taken.

Tarp flapping across the windshield and debris flying, Judge Annie Peacock sped away from the Snowshoe Mine site.

Minutes later, they approached the church's main compound. Lights blazed everywhere—in the church, several outbuildings, and the mansion-sized Colonial-style home recently built for the Dayton family, which looked south, over the park. The Humvee sat empty at the bottom of the stairs to the back entry.

"Lay down on the seat, Mom," Annie ordered, pressing the gas pedal to the floor.

Regardless of what happened, she had no intention of stopping, not with Eleanor in the car.

To Annie's relief, they raced past the house and through the gate without seeing a soul.

A look in the sideview mirror as they roared down the driveway explained why.

Behind the house stood a huge warehouse. Its doors stood wide open, lights blazing. Annie could see at least half a dozen figures moving about inside; but from that distance, and with both Annie and the mirror bouncing so violently it blurred the image, she could not make out what they were up to.

When Annie reached the road, she finally slowed.

Gardiner was to the left. Judge Sherburne to the right.

Annie jerked the steering wheel right.


Annie's sense of relief didn't last long.

As she was formulating a mental plan to use Hank's pickup to push the Subaru out of the mud, she saw that was not an option.

Rounding the curve where the elk had darted out, the truck's headlights swept a scene that crystallized her worst fears.

Parked alongside the Subaru, a white jeep with flashing security lights idled, the driver's side door wide open.

A uniformed guard stood on the passenger side of the Subaru, his gun directed through the window—at the judge.

Sherburne apparently had refused his order to open the door.

The gun now swiveled their way.

"Oh dear," Eleanor cried.

"Lay down, Mom!" Annie yelled.

Stuffing the gun Will had given her into her jacket pocket, Annie pulled to an abrupt stop—she wanted to keep the truck, with Eleanor inside, as far away from the guard as possible.

She jumped out, arms in the air.

"I'm Judge Peacock," she yelled. "Thank you for stopping to help us."

She walked slowly toward the Subaru. The guard stared at her, silent, his gun never wavering.

"No need for that," Annie said, smiling benignly. "We got stuck while we were out for a drive. I went for help . . ."

Still no response, but now the guard's eyes moved to the truck. Annie had left the lights on to blind him. Holding a hand up against their glare, squinting, he walked forward. Annie moved behind him.

"What the fuck?" he said as he tried to see the logo on the side of the truck.

"Stop right there," Annie said.

When the guard turned around, the sight of Annie holding the gun, pointed directly at him, caused him to do a double take.

His loud guffaw, however, was not what Annie had hoped for.

He stepped toward her, grinning, one hand holding his gun—which he'd trained on Annie again—while he stretched the other out, palm up.

"Give me that," he said.

Annie lifted the Glock higher, to a direct line with his chest.

"Don't make me use it," she said.

His grin grew broader.

"Even if you knew how to shoot that thing, you wouldn't."

In the next instant, however, the expression on his face changed from amused to threatening.

"I'll give you thirty seconds," he said. "If you so much as smell like you're going to use that, you're dead. Both you and your pal in the car."

A rush of relief surged through Annie. He didn't know about Eleanor.

She closed her eyes. Was there any talking her way out of this? She doubted it.

She'd never shot a weapon before. She felt her finger on the trigger.

If she handed the gun over to him, he would find Eleanor.

There was no doubt in Annie's mind about what she must do.

She opened her eyes, drew in a deep breath.

The guard saw it coming.

But just as his finger, too, tightened around the trigger, he let out a guttural moan and crumpled to the ground.

"Grab his gun," Annie heard her mother yell from where she hung out the window of Hank's truck.

Confused, Annie lunged for the guard's gun. He'd loosened his grip, and now lay writhing on the ground.

When he rolled onto his side, Annie saw the dart, practically dead center in his back.

*Her mother had shot him with the Taser gun.*

Stumbling out of the truck, Eleanor looked as startled by her success as Annie did.

"Bitch," the guard screamed as he reached for the two-way on his belt.

Annie stood over him now, holding his own gun on him.

"Give me that," she said.

When he hesitated, she yelled, "Now!"

At the same moment, Eleanor pressed the trigger on the Taser gun and for the next five seconds, another fifty thousand volts seered through the guard's body.

He buckled into a fetal position, moaning, his pants soiled.

Annie ripped the radio out of his hand, glancing Eleanor's way at the same time. Eleanor leaned up against the truck, holding her free hand to her heart, the Taser gun drooping in the other. She looked disoriented and ready to collapse.

"Mother, are you okay?"

"I think so," Eleanor replied weakly, still clearly stunned by her own behavior.

"Don't move," Annie cried. "I'll be there in a minute."

Bending over the downed guard, who'd stopped struggling, Annie removed his handcuffs from his duty belt and cuffed his hands behind him, palms pointing out.

She hurried over to the car. Judge Sherburne had just emerged and now stood shakily, holding its door.

Still, his eyes danced with delight.

Reaching for the belt holding his baggy khakis up, Annie said, "Sorry, Judge."

She returned to the guard, belted his ankles together, then helped Judge Sherburne make the short trek to the truck, where Eleanor had begun to look better.

"Mom," Annie said, "this is Judge Sherburne. Judge Sherburne, my mom."

"Pleased to meet you," Eleanor said graciously.

Sherburne's grunted response seemed not to throw her.

When she'd gotten her mom and the judge in the truck, Annie climbed in and shifted into gear.

"Hold on," she called, just before she rammed the guard's car.

The blow tossed everyone around a bit. Sherburne seemed to enjoy it, but Eleanor cried out, "What are you doing, dear?"

When she didn't get the result she wanted, Annie backed up and rammed the car again. This time, with a vaccum-like *whoosh*, the other vehicle's air bags inflated.

"He's not going anywhere now," Annie said.

She swore she heard Sherburne chuckle.

Shortly after Annie did a U-turn and took off for Gardiner, the two-way she'd tossed on the dashboard came alive.

*"All guards. Mayday. Mayday. The judge's mother is missing. Close down all exits to the property and maintain constant communication."*

When Annie raced past the driveway leading to the Church of White Hope compound, she glanced beyond the house, at the warehouse. A group of men were pushing a helicopter out into the open.

She pressed the gas pedal down to the floor and did not look back again.

# THIRTY-EIGHT

NO ONE KNEW HOW TO MOVE MORE QUICKLY AND QUI-
etly through the backcountry than Will McCarroll.

As he headed for where he'd left the horses, he heard
shouting a hundred yards or so behind him, saw the occasional flash of a light.

He hadn't seen any horses at the mining camp, nor
ATVs. If that proved true, he could easily reach Torch and
Riley and take off without any chance of his pursuers
catching up with him—until he hit the network of roads.
There were probably vehicles headed that way already. He
would have to cross at least two roads without being seen.
But once he did, he would again have the advantage—
wilderness.

All he needed to do now was keep them occupied and
away from camp long enough for Annie and her mother to
get away.

He slowed, climbed a knoll, and waited until the flashlight beams reached within fifteen yards of him. Then he
bolted in a direction perpendicular to the path that led to
the horses, along the top of the ridge.

"There he is," someone shouted. "We've got him."

Will made sure they saw him one more time, then he
changed course again, heading back in the direction of the
horses, sprinting now.

When Will emerged from the trees at a run, Torch nickered a greeting. Riley startled, then quickly went back to grazing the meager offerings at his feet.

Untying them both, Will jumped on Torch's back and headed south. Riley followed close behind.

Will was just beginning to wonder if maybe he'd rushed his escape and not given Annie and Eleanor the time they needed, when he heard the unmistakable chopping of air.

"Shit," he said to the horses. "Shit!"

He should have known the church would have a helicopter. No doubt they'd used it in flyovers, to plan their operations and ensure that from the air they'd go undetected.

Shattering the stillness of the night, the 'copter's approach felt warlike.

Will soon saw that the swath it cut through the sky was mirrored by a path of light playing across the ground—a wide swath, maybe twenty yards in diameter, coming directly Will's way. He turned Torch's head sharply right.

"Go, boy, go."

Torch responded instantly. Riley was only seconds behind, but that was enough for him to get caught in the searchlight.

As soon as the light picked up the young sorrel changing directions, the helicopter followed suit.

"We've got him in the light," Eli Peters yelled jubilantly into the radio.

A voice of authority, a voice used to being obeyed, responded crisply.

*"Don't lose him. Do you hear? We've got to contain this.* Now."

Eli pushed the radio back to his lips, eyes never straying from the sight of Will McCarroll on horseback below, racing through a draw between wooded areas, jumping downed trees and boulders at reckless speed.

"I read you, Senator Conroy," Eli replied. "Don't worry. We won't lose him."

# THIRTY-NINE

JEREMIAH DAYTON TURNED FROM THE WINDOW, WHERE he'd stood and watched the helicopter take off, and addressed his visitor.

"We can still control this situation," he said, his voice strained but confident.

Senator Stanley Conroy had been pacing ever since they'd rushed back from the mill to Dayton's house. He stopped now and turned to look at the reverend.

"If we don't, my political career is over. And you can kiss that lease—and your pulpit—good-bye. Hell, we can both kiss *Montana* good-bye 'cause we'd be looking at spending the rest of our lives in a fucking prison. And not here in Montana. You know where they send people like me to prison for murder? And what gets done to people like us?" His sudden, high-pitched laugh surprised Dayton. "And ministers. They *love* ministers."

"Calm down," Dayton said, his brow furrowed with the plot hatching at that very moment in his mind. "All we have to do is find McCarroll and shut him up."

This wiped the smile off Conroy's face.

"More blood on our hands?" Conroy cried. "Is that always your solution? I thought you said no one would get hurt. Maybe the old lady—that was a risk we agreed to take—but that was it. That was our agreement."

Dayton ignored him as his thoughts spilled out.

"Listen. We succeeded in making them think the anti-wolf forces were responsible for the kidnapping. It worked beautifully. Think about it. We'd been trying to find a way to get Judge Peacock off the bench before the drilling legislation passes, and those idiots played right into our hands. When Gleeson killed that wolf and Buckley's group shot off their mouths to the whole world, we knew it was the perfect time to go ahead with the kidnapping—because everyone would think it was *them*. And it worked. Didn't it?"

Conroy's thick black eyebrows shot up.

"Worked? We've got two dead people, an old lady on the loose—and Peacock's still on the bench. You call that 'working'?"

"Don't be a smart ass. We couldn't know that ranger would figure out something was wrong with the hot springs," Dayton replied, barely fazed by the truth of Conroy's words. "The part about making them believe it was Gleeson and Buckley *did* work. And this is going to work too. Think about what's just happened. Will McCarroll killed a man—and who was it? *One of Gleeson's clients.* Thank the Lord for that. Who would have the strongest motive to kill McCarroll now—after he just gunned down one of his clients?"

"You sure your information on the hunter being killed is correct?"

"One of our church members infiltrated the wolf group. He called last night and said he was with a group of wolf watchers who were up above Pebble Creek yesterday when they intercepted a radio transmission from McCarroll saying a hunter shot the alpha female and that in trying to stop him, McCarroll killed the hunter."

"So you're saying if we get to McCarroll now, we somehow frame Gleeson for his death?"

"Not necessarily Gleeson. One of his men would work too. It's a natural. These people are going to want revenge for McCarroll killing a hunter. We've already got everyone believing they're willing to kidnap an old lady and cut her ear off. It'll be a piece of cake to make them believe they'd kill McCarroll. Especially over a wolf. These people hate those fucking wolves, and better yet, they take the Bible literally. An eye for an eye, Senator. And 'man was made to dominate the beasts.' Take your choice. They'll see this as a religious war. We just might need to help the authorities along a little . . ."

"I was waiting to hear how you planned to do that," Conroy replied.

The sarcasm didn't daunt Dayton.

"We track down McCarroll and leave him in a shallow grave over near their Cooke City camp. Hands bound, and Gleeson's bullets riddling his body. I've got someone headed over there right now to snatch one of his guns. They're always lying around."

Dayton paused. A thin cloud of doubt passed over his normally piercing green eyes and Conroy, in his paranoia, saw it.

"What's that look for?"

"What look?" Dayton replied, annoyed that Conroy had picked up on it.

"I know that look. Something's bothering you."

Dayton turned back to the window and stared at the night sky.

"It's just those damn wolf watchers. My guy tells me that ever since they heard Twenty-two was shot, they've been out there looking for her. Why can't those people just get a life?"

Conroy snorted a laugh.

"For once I think you're the one being irrational. Wolf watchers are one thing we don't have to worry about. Haven't you seen them—they're a bunch of rich old farts who get off on thinking they're into the wilderness when all they do is stand along the road acting like they're jack shit. None of them actually could handle the backcountry."

"You're probably right. I shouldn't even have mentioned it."

"So what?" Conroy said, anxious to get back to his concerns. "We just let McCarroll loose out there in that back-country until your man comes back with a gun? *If* he comes back with a gun."

"Oh, he'll get a gun," Dayton replied. "Don't worry about that. Those idiots get shitfaced every night. He'll be in and out of their camp before they wake up."

He continued to stare outside. The sky was already a shade lighter to the east. Daybreak was only an hour away.

"No," he said thoughtfully. "We have to take McCarroll out first chance we get, and then we'll just add half a dozen bullets from Gleeson's gun."

Clearly unconvinced, Conroy returned to his pacing.

"Even if that works, killing McCarroll won't solve our problems if we don't find the old lady and shut her up."

Dayton's eyes caught a sweep of light in the sky to the south. The helicopter.

"She can't have gone far," he said. "McCarroll hid her somewhere. Now he's playing the decoy. That's why I had the men split up—half of them going after McCarroll and the rest looking for the old lady. They'll find her any minute now. Then the only loose cannon is McCarroll."

He turned back to face the room, propping his narrow buttocks against the windowsill, long arms crossed against his sunken chest, and waited for Conroy to glance his way.

When he did, Jeremiah Dayton locked eyes with the senator's. At times like this, when he was silhouetted against the window and the coming light of day, his hair actually looked like a halo. It was why he had insisted on a stained-glass window behind the church altar, and that the altar be positioned at the east side of the church—for the morning services.

"If my plan works," he said convincingly, "there's no reason for anyone to suspect us of anything. We've already moved the ranger's body out to the Lamar. They're going to take a look at the trauma to his head and decide his horse threw him."

The more he gave voice to his evolving plan, the more comfortable he grew with it.

"Yes, this should work. Gleeson's men will take the blame for McCarroll too. And no one will ever question us about the old lady. Not after the reward we've offered. That Hank character was the only one who could tie us to the kidnapping. Thank the Lord he decided to try blackmailing us."

Conroy's pace slowed, his eagerness to hear Dayton's reassurance almost palpable.

"All we have to do is sit tight and let things blow over," Dayton went on. "Then we go right back to the plan. To win that mineral lease under the new directional drilling legislation. The only thing you have to do is keep your promise. And as chair of the Energy Exploration Commission, you should be able to do that."

They'd finally hit on a topic Conroy felt he exercised some control over.

"World Energy Resources will technically get the award," he said, "but as its majority stockholder, the church decides where the drilling gets done. It's a double win for you. You get paid to have the drilling done on your property, and money pours in from the lease."

"We'll both do well," Dayton replied, before adding: "As long as we continue to work together."

Conroy didn't respond. He wasn't ready to let go of his concerns.

"You forgot one minor detail. Annie Peacock is still on the bench."

The transformation on Dayton's face indicated Conroy had hit a nerve.

"Damn that woman," he said. "She's like one of those wild creatures out there that doesn't know its place in the universe."

A breeze had begun to lift the sheer curtains that covered the open window behind the desk. Almost as if on cue, a mournful cry drifted in from outside.

The sound of a lone female wolf.

Dayton's eyes filled with a hatred so intense he appeared almost satanic.

"Just like the evil represented by that wolf out there, Annie Peacock needs to be dominated, silenced."

It took several seconds for him to regain his assured, businesslike expression and tone and put Conroy's concerns to rest.

"When they find her mother's corpse, and she sees what Gleeson did to McCarroll, Annie Peacock will go. There'll be no reason for her to stay."

Conroy still looked skeptical.

The bickering was getting them nowhere, and Dayton knew it. He walked to Conroy, placed reassuring hands on the senator's shoulders, and gave him the same earnest, knowing look he donned for his parishioners every Saturday and Sunday at services—the one that caused them to give their worldly goods to the church and follow Dayton to a new and better life.

"It can all still work," he said. "All we have to do is stay calm. And think this through." He paused, glanced purposefully at the two-way radio lying on his massive mahogany desk. "But we can't wait. You have to give the order. Now."

Conroy dropped his face in his hands. Sweat dripped like burger grease from his chin.

Both men knew the risks. Knew it would take a miracle to get them out of this situation.

But Jeremiah Dayton was a man who made miracles happen.

After several seconds, Conroy lifted his head, straightened to his full height.

Slowly, he turned and walked to the desk.

He picked up the two-way. It had been silent a little too long.

"Eli?" he said into it. "You hear me?"

His assistant's voice brought the radio back to life.

*"Yes, Senator,"* Eli Peters yelled over the roar of the helicopter. *"I read you."*

"You still have McCarroll in sight?"

There was a pause. Both Conroy and Dayton stared at the radio, waiting for the reply.

*"We lost sight of him about five minutes ago, sir,"* Peters responded. *"He took cover in some dense forest. We're circling the area. Don't worry. He has to come out sometime."*

Conroy looked up at Dayton, who nodded curtly at him. Conroy drew a long breath in.

"When he does," he said, "take the son of a bitch out."

Zach Knudtsen hadn't slept a wink all night. He could hear his dad and the wolf watcher guy talking outside the tent. It wasn't light out yet, but it wasn't completely black either, like it had been. He could tell they had built a fire. He was glad, 'cause he'd been cold all night.

It was a good thing his mom had stayed behind, at the hotel in Mammoth. She wouldn't have liked this. Not at all. Zach had been surprised when she agreed to let Zach and his dad go to help look for the wolf that got shot. One of the wolf watchers had heard about it when he intercepted a call Will McCarroll made over the two-way radio. But this would've sent his mom up the wall. Especially the stuff Zach overheard about Will being in trouble.

One of the wolf watchers had come into the tent in the middle of the night. He'd shaken Zach's dad awake.

"Listen to this," he'd said. He was holding a two-way radio.

Kevin Knudtsen had glanced at Zach, but Zach knew he should keep his eyes closed, pretend he didn't hear anything. His dad had slipped out of the tent.

Zach could hear several voices talking excitedly, telling Kevin about another call they'd just intercepted on the radio.

"Some guy in a helicopter reported that they were following Will McCarroll. There was a lot of static. We just weren't sure what was going on," a voice explained to Kevin excitedly.

Zach recognized the next voice as belonging to Tom Wurley, the man they'd met when they were with Randy Hannah. Tom and Zach's dad had become friends.

"We kept listening, trying to figure it all out, and then we heard another transmission."

"What did it say?" Kevin Knudtsen, wide awake at that point, asked.

"Someone—apparently on the ground," Wurley replied, "told the guy in the air to 'take McCarroll out.'"

"You've gotta be kidding."

"No, we're not. And listen to this. Maybe we all had too much Irish cream last night, but two of the three of us swear we heard the same thing."

"What?" Knudtsen asked.

"We swear the guy in the air called the one giving the orders 'Senator.'"

The group had moved away from the tent then, leaving Zach to lie there alone, worrying.

He couldn't stop thinking about Will McCarroll telling him he'd be sure to protect 22. He gave Zach his word. Maybe that's why he put himself in danger to protect her. Maybe it was Zach's fault.

Zach's mom would've freaked out about all of this. For sure she would have made them pack up and go home; forget about looking for the wolf that got shot.

But while Zach was worried about 22, and now, about Ranger McCarroll, in a way, he had never felt so happy. He knew now what he wanted to do with his life. He wanted to be a ranger. Like his friend Randy Hannah. And Will McCarroll.

He shimmied out of his sleeping bag and pushed through the tent's flap.

Kevin Knudtsen, coffee cup in hand, sat on a stump, talking in a low voice to Tom Wurley. He stopped midsentence upon seeing Zach.

"What are you doing up?"

"I want to hear what you guys are talking about."

"This is grown-up conversation, Zach."

"About someone trying to kill Ranger McCarroll?"

Kevin and Tom exchanged glances.

"You've been listening."

"I couldn't sleep," Zach replied. "We can't let them, Dad."

Kevin Knudtsen shook his head wearily.

"We're not the police, Zach. And we're not even sure what's going on. This could all be some kind of hoax."

"What if it's not?" Zach cried. "Ranger Randy told us Will McCarroll's spent his whole life taking care of the wolves. We've got to help him."

Edith Wurley had been standing at the mouth of their tent, listening. Wrapped in a Pendleton blanket over flannel pajamas, she padded over to the log he was sitting on and stood in front of her husband.

"He's right, Tom."

Wurley looked up at Edith and replied, "I know. A group of us are heading out in a few minutes. And we've radioed for reinforcements. I want you to stay here and wait for me." He turned to Kevin. "You and Zach should stay too. It could be dangerous."

Zach's eyes teared up as they locked with his father's.

"I'm not staying, Dad. I'm going with you."

Kevin Knudtsen studied his boy in silence. When they'd first gone to bed the night before, they'd laid there talking about Zach becoming a ranger. He'd never heard his boy sound so happy or excited.

Finally, Kevin said, "Okay, son. We'll go too."

Zach ran to his dad and without saying a word, wrapped his arms around him, then he turned and headed to his tent to get dressed.

Edith Wurley had turned too.

"Where are you going?" Tom called after her.

"To get dressed," she replied. "You're not leaving here without me."

# FORTY

TORCH SEEMED TO HAVE GOTTEN USED TO THE DEAFEN-
ing *chop chop chop* of the air overhead. This time he
continued forward through the dense stand of lodgepole
without missing a step.

The 'copter had returned.

Will reined him in.

Rattled by the noise, and the events of the past twenty-
four hours, Riley, however, who had been running side by
side with Torch, matching him step for step, looked ready
to bolt. The last thing Will needed was for the sorrel to give
his location away again.

Grasping the big roan's body between his thighs, Will
shifted his torso sideways, finding himself almost perpendicular to the ground before he grabbed the riderless Riley's halter.

"Easy, boy," he said. "Easy."

He maneuvered both horses up against two close-growing
lodgepoles as the chopper's beam of light once again swept
the ground, coming within several feet of where they stood.

"Whoa," he said as Riley danced sideways.

Will held the halter tight, watching until the light finally
moved on.

Riding off-trail and in a darkness penetrated only from
time to time by the searchlight of the helicopter that had

been sweeping Crevice Mountain overhead, grid by grid, ever since he made his break from the mining camp, Will had managed to maintain a decent speed, navigating mostly by instinct, and the occasional glimpse of the stars, and the great luring hulk of Electric Peak to the south and west.

But now he had a decision to make. When he'd jumped on Torch, he'd heard his two-way radio drop to the ground—at the same time that he heard the footsteps of one of the guards, who had almost closed the distance between them. Will couldn't afford to dismount to look for the radio. If he had, the two-way might have enabled him to stay in the backcountry, hidden by trees, where he'd be provided the safety of canyons and ridges only he knew well enough to traverse in the dark. He could eventually have found a place to call for help on his two-way. But without the radio, he needed to reach law enforcement. Fast. He had no way of knowing if his attempt to divert attention away from Eleanor and Annie's escape had worked. And if Judge Sherburne was still stuck in the car, he too was in danger. As far as Will knew, the three could have been captured. If so, Will needed to get word to law enforcement. But the Yellowstone River separated him from where he had to go, and there were only two places to cross it. The first, and most direct route, would have him follow Crevice Creek to the Blacktail suspension bridge. The other would be to stay north of the park, heading across Hellroaring Mountain, and cross at the Hellroaring–Yellowstone River suspension bridge.

Each route had its advantages and disadvantages. The Blacktail Bridge was the shortest and most direct route to Mammoth, where Will could alert law enforcement to head up to the Church of White Hope.

But Will suspected that that was precisely what his pursuers would expect him to do. Still, he could count on forest cover most of the way—until just before the sturdy suspension bridge. If the Church of White Hope's posse were thinking ahead and waiting for him, he would be a goner—completely exposed for hundreds of yards as he first descended to the bridge and then crossed it. But if they had misjudged Will's actions and weren't there, he could make a quick dash across the bridge, and once on Mount Everts, ride full speed across its mostly barren, grassy hills toward Mammoth. He could flag down a car on the Tower-Roosevelt road and get word to LE.

The longer, more circuitous route would take him across Hellroaring Mountain. That route, too, offered cover for much of the way, but the last two miles were open sageland. And once on the other side of the Yellowstone, the closest support would be at Tower, which housed only a fraction of the law enforcement personnel at the park headquarters in Mammoth. Still, the necessary calls could be made there.

Assuming he would succeed on either route, it would take him longer to reach Tower. If Annie, Eleanor, and Sherburne had been found and captured, every second could make the difference in the outcome.

As soon as the helicopter's roar and its light had faded into the distance, Will nudged Torch.

And headed for the Blacktail Bridge.

# FORTY-ONE

"What do you mean, you can't find him?"

Jeremiah Dayton had snatched the two-way radio out of Senator Conroy's hands when he overheard Eli Peters report the alarming news.

*"We've scoured Crevice Mountain,"* the senator's aide repeated. *"We've conducted a grid search of the entire forested area. No sign of him."*

Beau locked eyes with Dayton. The reverend had called the head guard back to supervise the searches for Will Mc-Carroll and Eleanor Malone from the mansion.

"He has to come out from the cover," Beau said. "He knows we've got men on the ground after him."

"Where?" Dayton asked. "Where's he going? And where will he come out?"

"We know where he's going. Anywhere he can get in touch with law enforcement. We found his radio on the ground. Without it, that means either Tower or Mammoth."

Dayton quickly processed this information.

"So he'll cross the Blacktail suspension bridge."

"Not necessarily," Beau replied. "He could cross over to Hellroaring and use the Yellowstone suspension bridge."

"What would you do?"

Beau measured his response—he didn't want to overplay it, but this was his fifteen minutes of fame and he intended to put it to good use.

"I learned in Iraq never to second-guess the enemy. Ideally, we'd cover both bridges. But we don't have the manpower for that. At least not in the time frame we're looking at."

Conroy didn't like being left out of the conversation. He stepped forward, asserting his presence.

"So what would you suggest?"

"I'd send our men on the ground to Blacktail, and have the chopper move back and forth between the Blacktail and Yellowstone bridges. It's almost daylight. If he's going to the Yellowstone, he's gotta cross a couple miles of open land first."

"You're certain he's headed back into the park?"

"That park is all that Will McCarroll knows. That's where he's headed."

He nodded at Dayton, clearly pleased with the powerful role this new crisis had bestowed upon him. The fucking head of his church and a United States senator, both turning to him for advice!

"That's where we'll get him," he said confidently.


When Annie reached the last sharp curve in the road before entering the town of Gardiner, she pushed the palm of her hand down hard on the horn of the truck's steering wheel, and didn't let up until she'd pulled into the parking lot of the Town Café, where she knew the sheriff's deputies started each day with coffee.

To her surprise, the uniformed figure that burst through the door was not a deputy. It was Rod Holmberg himself.

He strode toward the truck with the walk and look of a police officer ready to crack down on his first offender of the day, but then he recognized Annie.

The next second his eyes moved to the person seated

next to her, in the middle of the front seat, and his jaw literally dropped.

He had never met Eleanor Malone, but he'd spent the past few weeks with the image of her photograph in his head.

For once, the Park County sheriff was speechless as he approached the driver's side of the truck.

Annie rolled the window down.

"Thank God you're here," she blurted out. "It was the Church of White Hope all along! They had my mother. And now they're after Will McCarroll. You've got to get your men up there, and get a helicopter . . ."

Holmberg reached inside the window and put a calming hand on Annie's shoulder.

"Slow down," he said, looking past her, at Eleanor. It was as if he could not believe his eyes. "You mean to tell me that's where you've been?"

"Yes," Eleanor answered simply.

Holmberg was already reaching for his radio.

"This is a ten–ninety-nine. I repeat, a ten–ninety-nine. I want all officers to meet me at the bottom of Jardine Hill. Stat. I will provide more information momentarily, but get your asses on the road. Now."

He lowered the radio, but kept it grasped tightly in his hand as his eyes returned to Annie.

"Now, tell me about Will McCarroll."

Annie took a deep breath.

"Somehow Will found my mother and rescued her. They had her locked up there in a mine shaft." She paused. She couldn't let the emotions the statement itself brought rise to to get the best of her. Not yet anyway. "Judge Sherburne and I had gone up there to look around. We got stuck in the mud, I took off into the compound and ran into Will, who'd just rescued Mom. Will took off on horseback, to divert their attention. They went after him, on foot and with a helicopter."

"Is McCarroll on foot?" Holmberg asked.

"He was the last I saw him, but he was headed for his horse. He'd left it tied away from the mine."

"What was the plan? Where is he heading?"

"We didn't have time to make a plan. They had discovered my mom was missing. All we agreed was that Mom and I would get out of there once they took off after Will."

As she spoke, Holmberg had lifted his radio again.

"Park Service Law Enforcement?" he said crisply into it. "This is Sheriff Holmberg. Put me through to Supervisor Shewmaker."

Peter Shewmaker's voice came over the radio.

*"What's up, Rod?"*

"I have Annie Peacock here, with her mother. Will McCarroll rescued Mrs. Malone last night from the Church of White Hope's property. An abandoned mine."

A brief, stunned silence followed.

*"Will McCarroll?"*

"Yes. And according to Judge Peacock, McCarroll's now being pursued, by air. Probably that old military chopper we've seen them using recently. You need to send the park helicopter up. Stat. And get all your forces headed on the ground toward the church's property. My men and I will approach from the north."

*"Our 'copter's on its way to Salt Lake,"* Shewmaker replied. *"We had a head-on down near Canyon around two A.M. A fatality and two seriously injured. They're being airlifted as we speak. I'll call the chief field biologist and see if one of the wolf project planes is available."*

Annie reached for the two-way. Holmberg did not resist. In fact, when she fumbled for the button, he pressed it for her, holding the radio while she spoke.

"Peter," she said. "This is Annie. There's no time to waste. These people are out to kill Will. They were preparing to kill my mother and they've already killed Randy Hannah."

*"Son of a bitch,"* Shewmaker cried in anguish.

Holmberg took the radio back.

"McCarroll's on horseback, Pete. What's your best guess?"

*"That he's headed for the Blacktail Bridge."*

"That's what I figured."

*"You can bet his pursuers have too,"* Shewmaker said. *"Which means that we'd better get some men there before they do. If we don't, and that's where McCarroll's headed, he'll be a sitting duck when he crosses."*

"I don't see how we can beat them to the bridge," Holmberg replied. "Not if they're already headed there."

*"You're right. But hopefully Will can beat them. If he's on horseback, he's got a good chance."*

"I don't know how good his chances are with a chopper in the air."

There was a short pause, then Shewmaker said, *"Damn, we need aerial support."*

"I'll call for a chopper from Livingston."

*"Listen, Rod,"* Shewmaker replied. *"Have the chopper pick me up on the other side of Rescue Creek. I want to be on it."*

"You got it," Holmberg said.

"And Sheriff," Annie added, "please send an ambulance to the stone house. I want my mother checked out at the hospital in Livingston."

"Of course," Holmberg replied, barking the order into the two-way.

Without another word or glance Annie's way, he disappeared into the jeep, flipped on the red-and-blue emergency lights and siren, and, rocks flying, sped out of the parking lot toward Jardine Hill.

Annie turned toward the sound of sirens entering Gardiner from the north. The morning sun had just reached Electric in a stunning display of its grandeur, power, and beauty. A display that somehow gave Annie hope.

Minutes later, Annie wheeled Hank's truck into the driveway of the stone house, just as the ambulance screeched to a stop at the back entry.

As the attendants helped Eleanor onto a stretcher, Annie told them, "Wait for me. It will just take me a minute to get Judge Sherburne settled inside the house."

Eleanor pushed aside the EMTs' busy hands to reach for Annie.

"You don't need to go with me," she said weakly. "I'll be fine."

"Of course I'm going," Annie replied.

Losing her patience, Eleanor swatted a stethoscope away and tried to rise to a sitting position. Annie gently forced her back on the stretcher.

"Mom, you need to get checked out. *Please.*"

"I will," Eleanor promised, using what remained of her strength to grasp Annie's hand. "But only if you agree to go to that creek . . . I know that's where you want to be. I'm fine."

"Rescue Creek?" Annie said.

"Yes," Eleanor replied. "I insist, Annie."

Annie saw the unmistakable determination in her mother's eyes.

"I can't bear the thought of being separated from you again."

Eleanor Malone managed a heartfelt smile.

"I'll be back here before you know it. I promise."

Fighting back tears, Annie bent to kiss her.

"You behave, you hear?"

"I love you too," Eleanor replied. "Now *hurry.*"

# FORTY-TWO

WILL SAT ATOP TORCH, EYES SLOWLY SCANNING THE landscape splayed out in front of him. A hundred or more feet below, the raging waters of the Yellowstone River, spanned by a steel suspension bridge some forty meters long—imposing and bold and out of place in this pristine wilderness. And a short distance beyond the bridge a most welcome sight—a Douglas fir forest. Shelter—if he could make it along the two hundred yards of Blacktail Creek Trail, which waited just below, to take him to the bridge. And then the bridge itself.

Its steel girdings gleamed cold, damp, and gray in the coming day's light.

The helicopter had not appeared for at least forty-five minutes, as Will skirted first Crevice Creek Trail and then rode above the Yellowstone River to its juncture with Blacktail Creek, staying high above, where trees offered cover. But he couldn't stay hidden forever. And now, as Will assessed the situation from within the last stand of lodgepoles on the north side of the river and contemplated dropping down to the short section of Blacktail Creek Trail that connected the Yellowstone River Trail to the bridge, it was the predawn silence that bothered him.

The dawn felt too silent. Too still.

Will knew that once he ventured forward, it was an all-

or-nothing gamble. And knowing that—what was at stake—he dismounted and walked to where Riley stood, several yards behind Torch.

"We've gotta split up for a little bit, boy," he said, clipping a lead to the sorrel's halter, then tying it chest-high to a lodgepole. "I'll be back for you. Don't worry."

Even as he said it, he knew it could be a lie.

Riley sidestepped nervously. They'd been on the move for hours, and while the unmounted horse had been free to stop and eat what little green grass had survived the summer months in the desertlike climate of the northwest corner of Yellowstone, the horse hadn't wanted to let Torch out of his sight. Even now, instead of dropping his head, he kept his eyes fixed on Will.

Will let out a sigh.

"Damn," he said, untying the lead. It didn't take any effort to get Riley to follow along as he strode back to Torch.

Before mounting, Will stood, silent. Listening, looking.

The helicopter might be on the other side of Hellroaring Mountain, waiting for Will to emerge from the forests; or perhaps it had returned to the church compound to refuel.

Either way, despite his unsettled feeling, Will realized that if ever he were to risk crossing the bridge, now was the time.

He tied Riley's lead rope loosely to his saddle horn.

"Okay, boys," he said, "let's go."

Emerging from the trees at a trot, Will worked his way down the hillside to the trail, eyeing the bridge's surface. He'd crossed it on horseback many times.

Fifteen yards before the bridge, the trail dropped off steeply. Once when it had been wet—as it appeared to be now, from the morning dew—Kola had built up speed on the approach, lost her footing, and ended up in a slide on the bridge's slick surface. The only thing that saved them from going over the side and somersaulting to the rocks and whitewater below had been the placement of one vertical post in the railing, which had caught the mare's right shoulder.

Now, despite their exposure—the three were out in the open, with day about to break over the Absarokas—Will held Torch back as they descended to the bridge.

Once on its surface, he nudged the gelding back into a fast walk.

Halfway across, he actually began to feel home free.

All he could think about was Annie and her mother. Judge Sherburne. After the stand of Douglas firs, he would have to cross rolling, grassy hills. And then he'd reach the highway—with luck, within an hour.

Just as that thought caused him to urge Torch back into a trot, the sky erupted.

# FORTY-THREE

*"WE'VE GOT HIM, SENATOR!"*

Both Conroy and Dayton jumped up from their respective seats. They'd been sitting, mostly in silence, literally watching the two-way radio lie silent on the desk, as the guard, Beau, stood quietly in a corner of the grandiose library.

Conroy grabbed the radio.

"Where?" he said. "Where did you find him?"

*"Blacktail Bridge,"* Peters yelled. *"He's smack dab in the middle of it right now, and we've got him in our crosshairs. All I need is a go from you, Senator."*

Dayton grabbed the two-way from Conroy.

"No!" he yelled. "You idiot. We can't risk losing him in the river. We need a body. Wait until he's on the other side."

Dayton didn't realize that Beau had approached the desk, but now he touched Dayton's arm.

"Sir, I'd suggest they turn him around. There's more cover for McCarroll on the south side of the bridge. And if they lose him on that side, he's got a good chance of getting where he wants to go. Nobody knows that country better than that son of a bitch."

Dayton had been holding the transmission button down for Eli Peters to hear the guard speak.

"Do you read that? Don't let McCarroll get to the other side of that goddamn bridge."


Eli Peters turned to the pilot and yelled.

"Can you turn him around? Force him back to the other side?"

The helicopter had been hovering just yards above the bridge, facing south, toward Mt. Everts. Without a word, the pilot lifted it twenty feet, turning it 180 degrees as he did so, then dropped it down so close to the south end of the bridge that it kicked up a dust storm on that side.

Eli watched the chaos this caused below in fascination. McCarroll's horse reared, then on two hind legs, pirouetted, almost colliding with the horse being ponied as the lead horse changed course. For several seconds, Eli thought they might have caused just the result his boss did not want—McCarroll being catapulted into the river. But McCarroll managed to get both horses under control and now was headed back from where he'd come.

"Let's let the son of a bitch see what we have in store for him," Peters yelled, grinning.

With smooth precision, the pilot brought the helicopter alongside the bridge, even with McCarroll.

Peters turned to a man in quasimilitary uniform sitting behind the pilot and watched as he slid the barrel of his gun out his open window.

"Got him in your sights?" Peters yelled.

Without taking his eye away from the sight, the marksman nodded.

"Once he's on the other side, take him out."

The shooter merely lifted a finger of his free hand in acknowledgment.


Will saw the rifle pointed at him, and wondered at first what kept it from going off. Then it occurred to him.

*Of course, they must have plans for disposing my body.*

He slowed Torch, unwinding the lead rope at the same time to release Riley. With luck, the horses would escape injury.

Since he was unarmed, Will's only hope was to somehow make it back across the two hundred yards of Blacktail Creek Trail without being hit. Then he would have to make a dash to the cliffs above the Yellowstone. Of course, even if he reached the shelter of the trees up on the ridgeline, an entire army of men would be coming along soon. But he'd gladly take his chances in the woods. It was the next few minutes that didn't look good.

The helicopter seemed to sense the assessment going on in Will's mind, staying even with him, shadowing his movements. He could actually see inside. Hunkered down close to the gelding's back, Will watched as the gunner prepared to pull the trigger.

*He's waiting until I'm off the bridge.*

The gun was directed right where it needed to be, anticipating Torch's speed. Will briefly debated jumping off—but he knew he'd be dead within seconds if he did so. Far better to take his chances on horseback.

The north end of the bridge drew near. He kept the gelding moving at a slow, steady pace, and prepared himself for the burst of speed he'd demand from Torch in a few seconds, when the bullets started flying.

The moment Torch's first foot stepped off the bridge and onto hard-packed earth, Will reached back and slapped his rear end.

"Go, boy. Go for it!"

The first shot ripped through the air almost simultaneously with Torch's hoof hitting dirt, whizzing within inches of Will's head.

Torch sensed what Will knew. They were running for their lives.

With Riley nudging them on from behind, they raced across Blacktail Creek Trail toward its junction with the Yellowstone River Trail.

Will heard the second shot a microsecond before the

bullet threw him violently down, onto Torch's sturdy top-side. He'd been hit in the back, six inches below his right shoulder blade.

"Go, boy," he yelled, as pain ripped through his chest. He knew instantly that the bullet had penetrated a lung. The second "Go," came out as air, no sound.

Bleeding, blinded by pain, Will had the strength and presence of mind to hold tight to the saddle's horn, trusting his fate to Torch's instincts while he waited for the bullets he knew would follow.

At the Yellowstone River Trail, the gelding veered west, back toward Crevice Creek. The steep hillside that hugged the trail forced the helicopter to move sideways, into the canyon created by the river. Now it hovered a hundred feet above the water, keeping even with the trail—keeping even with Will, as if they knew they had him and were going to take time to enjoy their deadly game.

Angry, defiant, Will could not get enough air. He was losing consciousness, but before he did, he looked over at the helicopter and lifted the middle finger of his left hand high in the air.

That was when he saw it. Something was happening inside the helicopter.

As another shot rang out, missing its mark, the man in the front seat leaped to his feet and grabbed at the rifle poking out the window.

With his other hand, he pointed behind the chopper, to the bridge.

For Will, it was all happening in a fog. He could see the man screaming agitatedly into a headset he wore. The gunman was yelling back, pushing him away, and then lowering his eye back to the rifle's sight, not willing to give up the kill.

Woozy and lacking a sense of balance now, Will looked back over his injured shoulder, in the direction the man had pointed.

*A young boy was running on to the far side of the bridge, arms waving wildly in the air.*

Behind him, a man in his forties.

They were running right into the line of fire.

Calling upon every ounce of strength he had left, Will took hold of the reins again and turned Torch around.

*He had to get them out of there.*

Waving, he cupped his hand around his mouth to shout, "Go back."

But even if his lungs had allowed it, the helicopter would have drowned him out. Out of the corner of his eye, as the helicopter moved with him, matching the gelding's pace as they raced back toward the bridge, Will saw the gunman zeroing in on him again.

And then, suddenly, the glint of sun off the cold barrel of the rifle literally zipped closed, shrinking to little more than a bright dot—and then disappeared altogether. The marksman had pulled the rifle inside.

The helicopter hovered.

Teetering on the edge of consciousness, when Torch balked at reentering the bridge, Will lost his balance and fell to the earth. The gelding sidestepped nervously beside him, unwilling to leave his master.

Completely exposed and unarmed, Will could not flee. But neither would he cower. He rose to one elbow. He would die looking his killers in the eye.

He could see all the helicopter's occupants standing now, but oddly, they were not looking at Will, nor at the two figures now running across the bridge. No, all eyes in the helicopter were trained beyond, at the tree line on the other side. Will's gaze followed.

What he saw brought him up to his knees, in disbelief.

One person after another—men, women, young and old—emerged from out of the Douglas firs, moving forward determinedly. And angrily. At least a dozen of them. Perhaps more.

As the helicopter lingered overhead, and Will struggled to his feet, figures began popping up above now too, all along on the ridgeline.

Will wondered if he was hallucinating. Was this akin to

the white light people saw before they died—a backcountry ranger's version of angels showing up to accompany
him to heaven?

But then he noticed something. Like those on the bridge,
the people on the ridge carried cameras and camcorders—
which some pointed defiantly at the helicopter. And almost
to a person, they carried something else. Spotting scopes.

Will suddenly realized who they were.

Wolf watchers.

As the group on the bridge continued its march toward
Will, the helicopter's blades churned the air, blowing shirts
open and sending hats flying into the waters below.

Suddenly, just when Will felt certain it would now re-
treat, the chopper dropped even with the bridge again.

The barrel of the gun reappeared.

It was pointed at the wolf watchers.

"Go back," Will shouted with one last gasp.

One by one, the wolf watchers saw it too, but not one of
them so much as flinched. Not even the boy. Especially not
the boy. They all continued marching doggedly forward,
across the bridge that spanned the rushing waters of the
Yellowstone toward Will, as if daring the helicopter, taunting it.

Other than their cameras and spotting scopes, not a soul
among them was armed.

The helicopter lingered menacingly several seconds
longer. And then, just before Will lost consciousness, he saw
it swoop, ospreylike, into the sky and disappear north, toward the Church of White Hope.


"Oh my god," Senator Conroy said. Sweat had begun drip-
ping from his face, snaking its way down his neck, damp-
ening his shirt, which he unbuttoned with shaking hands.

He put the two-way down on the desk and turned to Jeremiah Dayton, who, for once, stood silent. The guard, Beau,
looked ashen.

"What now?" Conroy began screaming at Dayton.

" 'Everything's going to be fine, just fine,' " he yelled, parroting the reverend's words earlier. "What the fuck are we going to do now?"

Dayton would not make eye contact with him. Instead, he fell to his knees and began reciting, "The Lord is my shepherd, I shall not want. Yea though I walk through the valley of death, it shall not harm me."

"Oh my god," Conroy moaned again, looking at him wild-eyed.

He turned to the guard.

"Give me the keys to the fucking Humvee."

# FORTY-FOUR

WILL AWOKE TO FIND PETER SHEWMAKER AND AN EMT hovering over him. He felt the pinprick of a needle on the inside of his elbow.

"Blood pressure's eighty-three over forty-one and dropping," the EMT yelled over the roar of another helicopter as it geared up for takeoff. "He needs fluids, stat."

"Cath's already in," Shewmaker yelled back.

"We need to replace that makeshift flutter valve that guy put on him too," the EMT announced. Even as he spoke, his hands had already begun taping a new three-sided patch to the bullet wound over Will's chest. "He's one lucky guy—who'd've thought one of those wolf people would be a doctor?"

"That may be a first," Shewmaker remarked quietly, hopefully, as he slid the bag of fluids onto the metal hook protruding over the stretcher where Will lay.

The EMT looked over at him, puzzled. "What?"

"Someone calling Will McCarroll lucky," Shewmaker answered.

Just as he felt the chopper lift into the air, Will heard another voice. He recognized it immediately.

*"Will he be okay?"*

The EMTs, equipment, and that god-awful oxygen mask

over his mouth made it impossible to actually see Annie. But there was no mistaking her voice.

Blindly, feeling himself about to drift off again, Will reached his left hand out.

When he felt her grasp it, he allowed himself to go.

# EPILOGUE

"They're back," Will said, a sense of satisfaction softening his voice. He glanced sideways, not wanting to miss the reaction of his front seat passenger.

Judge Sherburne followed Will's gaze, then uttered a contented *"mmm."*

The sandhill cranes had returned. They moved slowly, measuredly, on fragile, sticklike legs, foraging the south-facing hills of the Lamar Valley. The morning sun glistened off dew that would fast evaporate, now that its rays had crested the Absarokas.

As Will negotiated the Park Service pickup and horse trailer around the next curve, he began braking. When he pulled over and came to a stop, there was dead silence inside the truck's cab.

Finally, from the backseat, Eleanor Malone said, "Is this it?"

It took several seconds for Will to be able to answer. "Yes."

He turned to Judge Sherburne. "Do you want to get out?"

Sherburne's hand was already groping for the door.

Will jumped down to the ground and hurried around to the other side of the truck to help Sherburne; while, in the backseat, Annie put Archie—who had been comfortably ensconced on the seat between Eleanor and her—on a leash before opening the door and helping her mother out.

Together, the group approached a newly erected viewing platform. Climbing up its three steps, they headed directly for the plaque displayed at the center of the top rail that encircled the wooden structure.

No one said a word as they read it.

IN HONOR OF RANGER RANDY HANNAH, FRIEND AND PROTECTOR OF YELLOWSTONE NATIONAL PARK.

A carving on the plaque showed Randy standing alongside Minerva Terrace, animatedly talking to a park visitor.

This time Judge Sherburne broke the silence.

With a *hrrmph* he nodded toward something tacked to the post below the plaque.

Angry that someone had defaced the new memorial, Will reached for it. But when he saw what it was, his hand froze.

A laminated photo. Randy Hannah and Zach Knudtsen, standing side by side, Randy's arm around the young boy's shoulders. Both beaming with joy at their shared passion for the hot springs—and their newfound friendship.

With the others looking on, Will removed the tack, and turned the picture over. On the back, in an unpracticed scrawl, were the words: *To my best friend. Forever. Zach Knudtsen.*

Will felt Annie's arm slide around his waist.

At the sound of a quiet sob, Judge Sherburne—his own eyes flowing—reached out to pat Eleanor Malone clumsily on the arm.

With extraordinary care, his own vision blurred, Will retacked the photo to the post.

"Look, Mom," Annie said softy, "bison calves."

Nestled low, in the grassy meadow framed by the viewing platform, a herd of bison grazed. They'd made it through an especially harsh winter—months of sweeping heaps of snow with their massive heads only to be rewarded with meager, lifeless vegetation. Now they feasted contentedly on lush spring grass.

"Some of them were just born," Will observed.

At least a dozen babies—leggy, sunset-orange in color and jerky in motion—hovered close to their mothers, poking their mouths peskily at the cows' undersides, in search of their own nourishment.

All four visitors to the Randy Hannah Viewing Platform—five, including Archie—watched in silent wonder.

Despite the raw emotion stirred by seeing the tribute to their young friend for the first time, the scene playing out below them still managed to mirror the anticipation each felt, an exhilaration at having survived his or her own drama over the past few months: Will's recovery from surgery to repair his punctured lung; Annie's weaning herself from her SSRI while presiding over Chad Gleeson's highly publicized and political trial; Eleanor Malone's, Judge Sherburne's, and Archie's individual struggles back to health.

Just as the bison calves renewed the cycle of life in Yellowstone, this early spring jaunt through the park signaled a new day for this unlikely assemblage of characters.

Judge Sherburne was the first to see the coyote crossing the meadow. The bison had already taken note. When the winter-thinned, thick-coated canine reached the herd, he stepped boldly into it, weaving his way through the mass of fifty or sixty animals. Each time his path brought him close to a calf, half a dozen adults would stop grazing and, in a clumsily choreographed dance, form a spokelike circle—heads turned out—around the newborn. The coyote seemed to be paying them no mind, taking his time as he headed in the direction of the road.

"Oh my," Eleanor Malone cried. "I hope he doesn't get one of those babies. That's what I hate about this place. I know, I know. It's nature, it's all part of the process, but it's cruel. *Nature* can be cruel."

Eyes fixed to the coyote, Will replied, "I'd say he's just passing through. He's got smaller prey on his mind right now."

Almost as if to prove Will's point, the coyote suddenly stopped, eyes riveted to the ground ahead of him. He crouched low, and after a moment of absolute stillness, sprung effortlessly into the air, paws readied, landing in the tall grass. When his head popped up again, a vole dangled from his clenched teeth.

"Oh, my," Eleanor sighed.

When another car pulled up, the foursome returned to the truck. They continued on, mostly in silence, passing an occasional car or RV, and several spots along the road where early morning visitors to the park had pulled off to gawk at or photograph a moose or a bear. A long-tailed weasel—its camouflage coat still snow white—appeared at the side of the road but disappeared again so quickly that only Judge Sherburne, who literally sat with his face pressed to the glass of the window, delighted at the sight.

Throughout the drive, Sherburne's left hand rested atop the backpack that occupied the front seat between Will and him.

As he worked their way across the Lamar Valley, Will slowed at each pullout large enough to accommodate the truck and horse trailer.

"This one?" he'd ask, turning to Sherburne.

Sherburne would either shake his head or grunt his disapproval; but as they approached the oversized pullout for the "hitching post"—used to tie horses for trail rides and backcountry expeditions into the Lamar—he uttered a new sound, this one short and eager.

"I figured this is where you'd want to go," Will replied, a grin splitting his face.

He pulled off, shifted into park, then turned to look at Annie, who sat behind Sherburne.

"Ready?" he said eagerly.

Annie smiled back.

"Ready."

A couple thousand miles east, Senator Conroy pushed back in the overstuffed black leather chair with the tan rawhide stitching, watching the sun rise over the Potomac.

While his wife, Patty, had insisted their Georgetown town

house have a sophisticated, urban feel to it, everything about Conroy's favorite room, the library, reflected his home state of Montana—from the six-point trophy elk head above the double-door entry, to the log mantelpiece above the fireplace, to the furniture—all homegrown Montana leather.

He'd been nursing scotch from the tinted Chevis Regal bottle ever since Patty stormed off to bed sometime around 2 A.M. Now he couldn't even remember what started their fight. Something about the investigation—they'd been fighting about it practically nonstop, but he couldn't remember exactly what had triggered last night's tirade. He stared, blurry eyed, out the floor-to-ceiling-paned window, his view of the water framed on either side by pink blossoms. It was his favorite time of year in D.C. He did remember promising Patty they'd visit the Vietnam Veterans Memorial— where Patty liked to be photographed next to her brother's name—sometime over the weekend.

He'd heard the newspaper hit the front stoop of his town house thirty minutes earlier. You could set a fucking clock by the newspaper boy.

Now the paper lay beside him, still unopened. Beside it lay the commemorative military Colt .45 semiautomatic pistol that had been presented to Conroy several years earlier by the Montana Trappers Association for his "unfailing support." The previous year, however, when a group of grassroots activists succeeded in passing an initiative to ban trapping in Montana, the MTA blamed Conroy for the loss. One of them had even written to demand the pistol back.

Conroy had taken it out of its glass case a couple hours earlier.

He hadn't even had to open the paper to read the full article. It all fit on the front page.

> "Search Warrant Expected to be Served on
> Montana Senator."

The article went on to say that an investigation was underway to see if Conroy had abused his power as head of

the Senate Energy Exploration Commission and that the
feds were looking for additional records pertaining to Conroy's association with the Church of White Hope's illegal
drilling activities. It cited the arrest a month earlier of the
Reverend Jeremiah Dayton for a litany of offenses, including ordering the kidnapping of a judge's mother and the
murders of a park ranger and a drifter. Conroy had skimmed
uneasily over that part, thanking his lucky stars that there
was no way—at least as he'd reconstructed it, time after
time, in his own head—he could be brought into those
charges. But he couldn't resist reading the speculation that
additional charges against Dayton would follow shortly as
several young women in the church had stepped forward in
the past few weeks to say the nondenominational minister
had sexually abused them. An expert quoted in the article
predicted the demise of the church, since its entire existence
was based on its charismatic leader.

The article explained that it had been the execution of a
search warrant on the CWH residence that first uncovered
evidence that Conroy was a member of the church, as well
as e-mails in which Conroy had "guaranteed" Dayton that
World Energy Resources, Inc., whose majority shareholder
happened to be the Church of White Hope, would be
awarded the first mineral/natural gas rights once the administration's National Parks Directional Drilling Legislation
passed. A passing reference in that e-mail to the "deal" between Conroy and Dayton had the press—and all of D.C.—
speculating that Dayton would get a significant cut of the
profits—expected to be considerable—from the lease.

The discovery of the secret exploratory drilling into and
beneath Yellowstone and resultant uproar by environmental groups had pretty much killed the legislation.

Once Conroy's connection with the church became public, America's wrath had turned on the senator, calling for
his resignation. Over the past few months, Conroy had
called in every favor he'd garnered over his thirty years of
service to make sure repercussions for his involvement
would go no further than possible public censure—and,

worst case scenario—his having to resign for the promise of the lease.

That prospect, leaving office in disgrace, had left him deeply depressed.

So Conroy had pretty much been expecting to be served with a search warrant.

What he hadn't expected was the knock on his door so early on a Saturday morning. Still, as he crossed the foyer, he knew who would be standing on the other side.

And what he *really* hadn't expected was what he heard after peering through the peephole, and finally deciding that nothing was to be accomplished by not answering. Besides, Patty had been pretty tanked when she went to bed. Better to have the search warrant served now, with her dead asleep upstairs, than later in the day, when the scene she'd make would serve as fodder for a story of an entirely different kind in the Sunday paper.

The agents looked classic FBI. Couldn't the agency recruit someone who actually dressed in something other than the khakis and windbreaker the guy with the buzz cut wore, or the god-awful blue suit on the black agent with the shaved head? They looked like something out of a bad movie.

Conroy opened wide the door. Last thing he wanted was a photographer capturing the moment.

"Senator Conroy?" the buzz cut said, stepping forward. "My name is Agent Richter. This is Agent Sharp. We're from the FBI."

"Come in," Conroy said pleasantly, not recognizing that he'd slurred the two words.

Once inside the hallway, he turned to face the enemy.

"How may I help you?"

The guy with hair seemed to be in charge. He pulled a folded sheet of paper out of the pocket of his black Cleveland Colts windbreaker.

"We have a warrant for your arrest, Senator."

Conroy literally fell back a step.

"Arrest?" he replied. "You mean search warrant."

"No, sir. It's a warrant for your arrest."

"On what charges? Let me see that goddamn thing," Conroy said, snatching it away from the agent. But even as he did so, he realized he didn't have his glasses to read it.

The bald agent removed a copy of what was obviously the same document from his blue suit and began reading:

"One charge of first-degree murder of an officer of the United States; one charge of attempted murder of an officer of the United States; two charges of conspiracy to commit murder; one charge of solicitation to commit a crime of violence; one charge of maiming within territorial jurisdiction; and one charge of influencing, impeding, or retaliating against a federal official by threatening or injuring a family member, which is a violation of section eighteen . . ."

Conroy's head had begun to spin.

He cut him short with a wave of the hand.

"I need to get my glasses," he said, turning away, toward his library. "And, apparently, call my attorney."

The black agent—even in his state of panic, Conroy was sure he recognized him as a former Redskins defensive end—kept step with him.

Conroy stopped abruptly and turned to face him.

"Allow me the dignity of a few minutes to break the news to my wife. I think I've earned that right after serving this country for over thirty years. Don't you?"

The two men looked at one another.

"Five minutes," the bald one said.

"I doubt I'll be that long," Conroy replied as he shuffled, heavy footed, back to his library.

The agents stood, ramrod straight, staring at the door after it closed behind them. Two minutes passed.

*"Who are you?"*

Their eyes darted up, to the top of the stairs, where a disheveled, partially clad Patty Conroy stood.

Simultaneously, both men sprinted for the library door.

The bald agent reached it first. The shot rang out as he reached for its handle.

Throwing it open, he rushed toward the black leather chair, where Senator Conroy sat slumped in a pool of blood rapidly spreading in all directions, which the agent promptly stepped in, lost his footing, and slid to one knee.

As he was getting up, he heard Patty Conroy's voice behind him.

"Oh my God."

Standing in the doorway, she watched in horror as the other agent searched for her husband's pulse. It was an exercise in futility really, as the back of the senator's head had pretty much been blown off.

"Why aren't you giving him CPR?" she screamed. "Or calling an ambulance?"

Oddly, after eyeing the blood on the floor, she did not attempt to enter the room.

"I'm sorry, ma'am," the agent said, "but I'm afraid it's too late for that."


Annie and Will rode on either side of Riley, with Will holding the sorrel's lead rope loosely. Annie hadn't been on a horse since she was a teenager but when she'd looked Torch in the eye, she knew she'd be fine. Will sat atop Kola, who, long recovered from her lameness, showed the same excitement her master did at finally being out in the wilds again after a winter of restricted activity.

Riley had been Will's idea. Judge Sherburne's eyes lit up when he suggested it. With Sherburne looking on, Will had taken great care in strapping Riley's load to his saddle.

The trail they followed to the crossing of the Lamar River was well worn, but once on the other side, Will steered the horses due south, toward the hills that faced the highway and away from the park trail that continued on along the river, traversing the rich riparian lands.

They passed a sign forbidding off-trail travel.

"You're not worried about being caught breaking the rules again?" Annie asked.

"Isn't that what today's all about?" Will replied.

"Yeah, but you're a hero now," Annie said. "Thanks to you, Gleeson's behind bars and no one in their right mind is going to think they can get away with shooting a wolf inside this park. Sure you want to risk squandering all that good-will by being busted for breaking every rule in the Park Service's book?"

Will shot her a good-natured glance.

"You're the one who put Gleeson where he belongs. That took guts. Especially with the threats you received during the trial. I'm grateful to you, Judge Peacock."

Annie actually blushed at being addressed so formally.

"Maybe it's a victory we should both share."

Will drew back softly on Kola's reins, pausing to look out across the Lamar—its rolling hills bisected by the life-sustaining river bearing its name.

A hint of gloom entered his voice.

"Kind of a shallow victory," he said, "since in the end, it looks like Biagi succeeded in killing Twenty-two."

"Still no sightings?" Annie asked.

Will shook his head.

"Every wolf watcher and ranger in this park has had their eye out for her for the past five months, but other than her collar, there's been no sign of her."

"Her collar?" Annie said, her voice climbing an octave. "You never mentioned that to me."

She'd caught Will off guard.

"I didn't want to upset you," he replied almost sheepishly. "One of the wolf biologists found it. It's possible she was able to shed it—that happens sometimes. But it's far more likely that Twenty-two died from her injuries, and that once she became part of the food chain, the collar was all that was left of her."

When he saw the stricken look on Annie's face, Will stretched his arm out, across Riley, and lifted her chin with his forefinger.

"Hey," he said softly, "today's a day to celebrate."

This declaration caused him to glance back, at the truck. The rising sun, mirrored in its windows, made it impossible to see inside, but Will knew what he'd see if he could. Judge Sherburne staring back at him through the binoculars Will had hung around his neck just before he and Annie took off on horseback.

Will tipped his ranger hat in salute to the old man.

"You two have a real bond, don't you?" Annie asked, looking on.

Will's snort of laughter startled Annie.

"Us?" he said, turning to her. "How about you two? And better yet, your mom and the old man?"

Annie's laugh, the way it mingled with the western meadowlark's and the mountain bluebird's songs—equally pure and unrehearsed—delighted Will.

"When I asked him to move in," she said, still grinning, "that was my biggest concern—that the two of them might drive each other crazy. You know what I found them doing when I came home for lunch yesterday?"

Will's eyes searched Annie's face. He loved looking at her, especially when she was animated and not self-conscious.

"He and Mom were sitting side by side on the piano bench. Archie was at their feet. Mom was playing 'Red River Valley.'"

The words visibly touched Will.

"That's his favorite song. Rosemarie used to play it for him at parties. He'd sit there and get tears in his eyes."

"He must have asked my mother to play it," Annie replied with a sigh. "Isn't that the sweetest thing?" Then it hit her. "Wait a minute? How could he do that? How could he tell Mom what song he wanted her to play?

With another glance back, toward the truck, Will shook his head.

"I imagine he figured out some way." In the next instant, he grew somber. He looked at Annie. "I think he would be dead now if you'd left him in that awful place."

Suddenly uncomfortable with the strength of his emotions, and eager to accomplish their mission, Will nudged the horses back into action.

Like sand dunes in a desert, the hills rolled on, seemingly forever, building in size as the trio of horses moved south.

Just as they neared the top of the next crest—while he was still certain Sherburne's binoculars could pick them up—Will reined Kola to a stop. He leaned sideways, toward Riley, and loosened the strap holding his load to his saddle.

Judge Sherburne's backpack.

A breeze had picked up. It came from the southeast.

*That's good,* thought Will. *With luck, we'll cover the entire Lamar.*

Placing the backpack between his thighs, Will unbuckled its top and reached inside. Carefully, as if he were an artist carrying newly blown glass, he removed the contents.

A heart-shaped, brass urn.

Engraved on its surface were the words: ROSEMARIE ELIZABETH SHERBURNE, and the dates: 1933–2007.

Before he unfastened the hook-styled latch to the urn's lid, Will looked over at Annie. Tears streamed down her cheeks.

"You okay?" he asked.

She nodded.

"This is what he wants," Will said. "Neither of them to ever leave Yellowstone again. You made that possible for the judge. Now we're making it possible for Rosemarie." He lifted the urn's lid, exposing its contents. "And when his time comes, we'll make sure they're together out here again."

Raising the container high into the air and tilting it slightly, Will let the wind take over.

He and Annie watched as the ashes lifted skyward. They appeared to be suspended above them, dancing, lingering briefly.

"Will, look!" Annie cried.

Urn still raised skyward, when Will followed Annie's gaze he let out a gasp.

She was sitting on the next rise, not more than two hundred yards away. Watching them.

*Twenty-two.*

"Hello girl," Will said, his own cheeks wet now.

She sat there, her fierce, fiery eyes connecting with Will's. Then she stood, looked over her shoulder, raised her mouth to the sky, and made a short sound before disappearing over the ridge.

She walked with a slight limp, but otherwise had lost none of her magnificence.

Will watched her go, and then, emotions running wild, he turned the urn sideways, giving all its contents up to a gust of wind.

With 22 gone now, both Will and Annie turned their eyes to the sight of Rosemarie Sherburne's ashes drifting out over her beloved Lamar Valley.

"Promise me something," Will said, unable to look Annie in the eye. "Promise me that if we still know each other then, you'll make sure I end up here too."

Annie swallowed against the lump that had been lodged in her throat ever since she saw the urn.

"I promise," she said, unable to look at Will.

So emotionally immersed were they in the moment, that neither of them saw the pups.

Two of them. Following behind 22.

"Today's a good day," Will finally said. "A day to celebrate."

Back in the pickup truck, binoculars pressed against his eyes, Judge Sherburne watched the pups trot over the hill, after their mother, and grunted his approval.